VALERIE W̶I̶L̶S̶O̶N̶ ̶W̶E̶S̶L̶E̶Y̶ S0-AJB-756

# Ain't Nobody's
# Business If I Do

"An entertaining read...Wesley's fans are likely to find
just as much enjoyment in this novel."
• *Newark Star-Ledger* •

"Valerie Wilson Wesley writes, with delightful insight, the
story of a marriage—the highs, the lows, and the often
dreaded in-betweens. Once again, Wesley gives us an
intriguing cast of characters who are all learning that true
fulfillment comes from when one is true to one's self."
• Benile Little, author of *The Itch* •

"A story of social pressures, family inteference,
interpersonal differences, and the losing and finding
of love. It isn't necessary to be black to understand
and enjoy the prolific Ms. Wesley's latest...
*Ain't Nobody's Business* speaks to universals."
• *Dallas Morning News* •

"A heartwarming tale."
• *Booklist* •

"Valerie Wilson Wesley has tapped into the strengths and
frailties of men, women, family, friends—and marriage—
and explores the price to be paid and the joys to be gained
when we finally grow up. A very enjoyable read."
• Sandra Kitt, author of *Family Affairs* •

## ALA BLACK CAUCUS AWARD WINNER

*Other Books by*
**Valerie Wilson Wesley**

**ATTENTION: ORGANIZATIONS AND CORPORATIONS**
Most Avon Books paperbacks are available at special quantity discounts for bulk purchases for sales promotions, premiums, or fund-raising. For information, please call or write:

**Special Markets Department, HarperCollins Publishers, Inc.,**
10 East 53rd Street, New York, N.Y. 10022-5299.
Telephone: (212) 207-7528. Fax: (212) 207-7222.

# VALERIE WILSON WESLEY

## Ain't Nobody's Business if i Do

AVON BOOKS
*An Imprint* of HarperCollins*Publishers*

Excerpts from "When Sue Wears Red" are taken from COLLECTED POEMS by Langston Hughes, copyright © 1994 by the Estate of Langston Hughes. Reprinted by permission of Alfred A. Knopf, Inc.

AVON BOOKS
*An Imprint of* HarperCollins*Publishers*
10 East 53rd Street
New York, New York 10022-5299

Copyright © 1999 by Valerie Wilson Wesley
ISBN: 0-380-80304-6
**www.avonbooks.com**

First Avon Books paperback printing: November 2000
First Avon Books hardcover printing: October 1999

Avon Trademark Reg. U.S. Pat. Off. and in Other Countries, Marca Registrada, Hecho en U.S.A.
HarperCollins ® is a trademark of HarperCollins Publishers Inc.

Printed in the U.S.A.

10  9  8  7  6  5  4  3  2  1

*For my mother, Mary Spurlock Wilson,*
*and my grandmother,*
*Carmen G. Wilson,*
*who loved to spin a good tale*

## ACKNOWLEDGMENTS

I'd like to thank the visual artists and musicians who so generously shared their thoughts about their creative processes—Iqua and Ade Colson, Janet Taylor Pickett, Roy Crosse, Chris White, Kaaren Patterson, and Oliver Lake. I'd also like to thank Iqua Colson, Cheo Hodari Coker, Samantha Pickett, Charlotte Wiggers, Mary Jackson Scroggins, Rosemarie Robotham, Regina Joseph, Cathy Carlozzi, and Frankie Bailey for their insightful "first-reads" and wise suggestions. I'd like to thank my agent Faith Hampton Childs for her support and friendship and my editor Carrie Feron for her belief in me as a writer and for her fine editing skills. And as always, my thanks to my daughters, Nandi and Thembi, and to my husband Richard for staying in my corner.

Nobody but a fool crossed Aunt Delia, so Eva never did. When Eva was a girl before they moved up North, she had to fight her way through the smell of Vicks VapoRub and greens that lingered in her great-aunt's small, damp house to take her slices of her grandmother's bourbon-laced pecan pie. She would always dutifully dispose of her aunt's nail clippings as the old woman instructed but kept one eye glued to the door when she kissed her wrinkled cheek.

Aunt Delia was a hoo-doo woman; she knew how to work some roots. She could make a person lie, scream or pine six weeks for a man she saw once in the A&P. She could make a snake dance, a cat bark, and when she was young, she'd made six of John Dixon's hens lay double-yolked eggs because he'd talked to her in sweet whispers out of both sides of his mouth.

She had something to do with Hannah Jones' bad

luck too. *Hannah, who walked with a switch that stopped grown men dead, stole Aunt Delia's best beau and wed him before he knew he was gone. She later had the first of three sets of twins six days after she turned thirty-six. Everybody knew it was Aunt Delia's doing because it involved the number six. Her spells always had to do with love, loss, lust and a combination of the number six.*

*Her death at ninety-six didn't surprise Eva; what did was the arrival of the small black box with the words, To Eva Lilton Hutchinson and her sweet man Hutch with all my love and devotion, Your Great Aunt D, printed neatly in red across the top. When Eva opened it, all she found were a few dried twigs and the lingering smell of Vicks VapoRub. She shoved it to the back of a shelf and didn't think about it again until everything had settled into its place.*

*Aunt Delia always did like to have the last word.*

# Hutch and Eva

**FRIDAY, JUNE 13**

The bad luck started late on a Friday night in June, a week after the Hutchinsons' tenth anniversary. The day had been hot, and the night was hotter. It was going on eleven and as usual Eva and Hutch were getting on each other's nerves. After about fifteen minutes of silent rage, Hutch said aloud the words he'd been thinking for weeks.

"I've got to get out."

"And go where? To the bathroom? To the store?" Eva asked. She was lying across their king-size bed, reading the newspaper and glancing occasionally at ESPN.

"Out of here." Hutch swept his hand dramatically to signify everything around him, including Eva, and then slumped down on the edge of the bed like the breath had been knocked out of him.

"Out of where?" Eva asked again.

"Out of here."

"Out of where? The bed? The room? The country?"

"Here."

"What the hell are you talking about, Hutch?"

"Why are we lying to each other, Eva? Why after all these years can't we just tell each other the truth?"

Eva tossed him a dirty look, and with a loud, exaggerated flourish fanned the newspaper in front of her face and spoke through it.

"Get over it." She lit a cigarette, and the smoke curled around the paper in a hazy, smelly wreath.

"Dammit." Hutch narrowed his eyes as it settled around his face.

"I'm not giving it up, if that's what you're bitching about," Eva said. "You have your dirty little habits, which I know you don't want me going into at this point, and I have mine. So get off my ass about it. Besides eating, it's the only physical pleasure I have left," she added with a pointed, nasty edge.

Hutch glared at her for a moment. "I can't think of any 'dirty little habits' I have that are as nasty as that cigarette, and don't blame me. You're the one who never wants to do it."

She hadn't said anything about sex, but Hutch knew that was what she was talking about.

"There's nothing wrong with me. I just get tired of taking the initiative," Eva said.

"What did you say?"

"You heard me."

Hutch got up from the bed, walked to the blue-tiled bathroom that adjoined their white and blue bedroom, peed loudly in the toilet, flushed it and then, leaving the toilet seat up, lumbered into his walk-in closet.

Suddenly, like a man gone mad, he went through his clothes: the smart, expensive suits he wore to lure big clients, his everyday workingman's denims, the tux he'd bought at the insistence of his best friend Donald Mason, who swore that every man should own at least two before he turned fifty (Hutch had six years to go), and the various shirts, sweaters, pants, sweat suits, jeans and jackets that marked his ten years with Eva, his second wife.

Silently, Eva watched him pack, then said after a few moments, "Have you lost your mind?"

"No."

"Then what are you doing?"

"I told you."

"What's going on?"

"I'm just tired, Eva."

"Tired?" Eva folded the newspaper down in front of her and watched Hutch grab the oversize gray suitcase she'd bought him last year for his birthday. "Tired of what? I have no idea what you're talking about."

"You know as well as I do." Hutch shifted through his clothes, throwing some into the suitcase at his feet, tossing others back onto the floor of his closet. His pajama bottoms slipped down over his hips, and he gave them an angry yank, pulling them back around his trim waist, catching a glimpse of himself in the mirror.

He would be forty-four next month, and women half his age still flirted with him so boldly it embarrassed him. He took after his father, Lucas Hutchinson, Sr., who, despite the loss of his mind before he died, had the body of a man twenty years his junior. Even now, Hutch could still haul a sack of cement over his head into one of the three trucks that had come to him with his father's small construction firm and outwork most of the men on his crews. Although he had inherited his strength and stamina from his father, he'd gotten his long-lashed eyes and tender nature from his mother. But he'd always hidden that gentle part of himself when he'd been a boy. He was his father's son, a rough-and-tumble boy who liked to fight and had won two medals for bravery when he'd been a medic in the last years of the Vietnam War. But it was his mother's nature that nurtured the dying and held the hands of those who writhed in pain. The tough kid won tonight. He slipped out of his pajamas and angrily yanked on his boxer shorts, jeans, and a rumpled sweater.

"I'm sick of all the lies we tell each other, Eva. I'm sick of how empty I feel, how empty we leave each other feeling. There's no joy between us. I just want out." He bent down and opened his suitcase, still wondering if he was doing the right thing.

Eva climbed out of bed and faced him, her anger written in a line across her pursed lips. "What brought all this on?"

A look of defeat settled on Hutch's face. "I don't know."

"You started this mess, getting me out of bed at this time of night with this foolishness, and you're saying you don't know why you're going? Hutch, what in the hell is wrong with you?" Hutch sank down on the bed beside her; their bodies barely touched. "Is this some kind of male menopause bullshit?"

Hutch studied the dimple on her cheek that deepened whenever she cried or laughed. The first moment he'd seen her, he'd fallen in love with the soft deep indentation that gave her face an impish look. It had seemed out of place on the face of such a serious, take-no-nonsense young woman. *Why do you always kiss me there?* She used to ask him, her eyes suspicious, questioning how someone could love her as much as he obviously did. And he had loved her then. But he didn't think he loved her now, not at this particular moment anyway, and he wasn't sure if he ever would again. He turned away from her and continued packing.

Eva moved directly in front of him, and Hutch felt his eyes water. He glanced away, turning his attention back to his bag, packing it efficiently and neatly, as if he knew where he was going. He had no idea.

"So you're saying that you're leaving me?"

"Yes." He knew her eyes were probably angry, so he spoke without looking at her.

"And you don't know why?"

"Yes."

"You're saying that now, all of a sudden, our lives together just aren't happy? That you can't stand to be around me, that you have to get up in the middle of the night—and go!" He noticed the hint of sarcasm in her voice, the note of mockery that made him prepare for attack.

"Yes," he said, realizing with a stab of embarrassment just how crazy the whole thing sounded.

Eva lit another cigarette and exhaled loudly and dramatically. "Is this the way you did it to Irene?"

Hutch stopped short. "Irene?" He said the name as if he'd never heard his ex-wife's name before, and then he went back to work. "What are you talking about?"

"Is this the way you did Irene and Steven? Leaving

them like this in the middle of the night with no warning, out of the blue like this?"

"You know that's not what happened. I didn't leave that woman out of the blue. Don't bring Irene into it. And I never left Steven. So don't throw that up in my face." God knew he'd told her the truth about *that* situation more times than she wanted to hear it, more times than he wanted to tell it.

"I should give Irene a call. I should tell her that you're pulling the same shit on me. I should—"

"That crazy witch doesn't know anything about me, so don't bring her name into it." Hutch said "witch" but thought "bitch." He'd been taught all his life not to curse in front of women, and old habits broke hard. Eva, who could outcurse a gangsta-rapper on steroids, swore enough for both of them anyway.

"I should give her a call."

"Suit yourself," Hutch finally said with some effort.

"Are you seeing somebody?" Eva said it calmly, but there was a quaver in her voice. He noticed that she watched his reaction carefully, peering into his eyes as if they would reveal the truth. Hutch shifted them to the ground, which he always did when he was uncomfortable about something. He was uncomfortable now even though he told her the truth, and he hadn't done that before.

"No."

"Liar." She turned away from him.

"This has nothing to do with another woman, Eva." He almost wished it did.

"So you're willing to disrupt our lives, toss everything we've worked for, and all of our friends, and Charley and Steven, everything we have together into the shitpile because you're bored. You suddenly feel like you deserve more out of life. Hutch, why are you doing this to me? Why?"

"Eva, I don't want to hurt you."

"Don't want to hurt me!" she screamed so loudly that Bama, their overweight cat, jumped off the foot of the bed where she'd been sleeping and ran underneath it.

Distracted, Hutch glanced down, then continued packing.

"This is like something out of a fucking movie! Hutch, I don't believe this! It's such a fucking cliché!"

"My whole life is a cliché."

Eva rolled her eyes. "So what are you going to tell Charley and Steven?"

Hutch stood up with a flat expression on his face.

"Have you forgotten about Charley? Have you forgotten about her wedding?" Eva snapped, her brow furrowed.

"You know goddamn well I haven't forgotten about Charley," he said, forgetting his home training. "This doesn't have anything to do with Irene or Charley or Steven or Charley's wedding. As for Charley's wedding, we haven't even sent out any invitations yet, so what are you talking about?"

"That's not even the point! What are we going to tell everybody? What are you going to say?"

Hutch realized with annoyance that she was more concerned about what people might say than about what he was telling her. He stooped down and snapped his bag shut.

"I'm sorry," he said to Eva, to his son Steven, to his stepdaughter Charley, to the friends and social ties they had developed together over the last ten years. Eva stood straight, like a soldier at attention. She held her arms rigidly at her side, and her lips were tight. Hutch felt dizzy for a moment, as if he might be sick. He felt a fleeting, momentary fear that maybe he was going through some kind of dementia. His father's personality had taken some weird lunatic turn a couple of months before he was diagnosed with Alzheimer's. He winced as his father's stern face flitted across his mind.

His father had not been a cruel man, but he rarely showed his feelings or affection. He had prided himself on his keen, straight-arrow sense of morality and knowing right from wrong. There were no greys in his father's world; there was black or white and "weakness of character" was a mortal sin. Hutch's backside bore the marks from the belt that had on many occasions taught him that particular lesson. This was the kind of action, irresponsible and spontaneous, that would have enraged his father. Eva stared at him, her eyes unflinching. None of the hurt and pain he knew she must be feeling showed in her eyes. She had gotten almost as good at hiding her feelings as he was. He felt a pang in his heart as he backed away from her.

"I just need to go, Eva." His voice was almost a whisper. "I just need to get out." He picked up his bag. It was heavier than he'd thought. He wondered if he should take less, and remembered that he hadn't decided yet where he was going. There was an Embassy Suites nearby. Should he go to his office? Or maybe he should go to his friend Donald Mason's. Donald had several guest rooms in that big-ass house of his. If there was one man in the world who would understand

and accept how he could leave a woman he'd sworn he'd loved for the last ten years, it was Donald Mason.

He opened the bedroom door, shoving his bag outside, and wondered for a moment if he should stop and get the cart in the downstairs closet, then decided to leave it where it was. He picked up his bag again, nearly tripping over Bama, who had come out from under the bed. The cat gave a squeal, looked accusingly at Eva and then sidled over to Hutch, rubbed against his leg and looked up at him beseechingly, as if she knew something was wrong and had made her choice. Hutch picked her up and stroked her soft black-and-gray-striped fur.

"Put her down," Eva said with a murderous glint in her eye. "Bama is my cat. Put her down."

"Eva, don't—"

"Didn't you hear me? Put my goddamn cat down!" Eva moved toward him, her eyes ablaze as she snatched the cat roughly from his arm. Bama, claws drawn, mouth open, lurched away, scratching Eva across her cheek as she struggled to get free. Eva cursed as she dropped the cat, who hit the floor on her large bottom with a thump. Bama struggled to her feet, glanced over her shoulder first at Eva and then at Hutch and shot out of the room with her ears bent back against her head. Eva watched her go and started to cry. Hutch stepped toward her. But he couldn't think of anything else to say, so he picked up his suitcase and quickly walked out of the house.

# Eva

### FRIDAY NIGHT, SATURDAY,

### AND SUNDAY MORNING

Ten minutes after Hutch left, Eva realized that she didn't feel anything. There was no scream, sob or catch in her throat. She was proud of her self-control for a moment and then ashamed. After ten years of marriage, she couldn't even work up a good cry. *I must be in a state of shock,* she thought as she lay back down on her bed and closed her eyes. When the cat scratch on her face began to sting, she went into the adjoining bathroom to spread some Neosporin on it.

"It would be all I need to end up with an infected cat scratch that grows into some kind of strange-ass keloid," she muttered, and then she covered her gray hair with her hands and squinted critically at her face in the mirror. "I should do something about this goddamn gray hair. I look like Grandma Alvia with this goddamn gray hair. No wonder the man left me."

Eva didn't have much gray hair but what there was

fanned down the side of her face in a solid silver streak. On good days, she thought it made her look smart and sophisticated. On bad days, she tried not to think about it. Except for a few unruly hairs that occasionally sprouted like crabgrass on her chin and which she immediately plucked out, and the slice of silver hair, she looked and felt the way she'd always looked and felt. She had just turned forty and was about average for her age and height. She'd inherited her quick smile and the dimple in her left cheek that Hutch always made so much of from her grandfather Charles, who died before she was born and whom her grandmother Alvia always claimed the dimple brought to mind. Eva would catch her gazing at it in starry-eyed recollection. Eva had mixed feelings about its value.

She had never thought of herself as pretty, although people often told her that she was, and she could almost see it when she looked at her daughter Charley, whom she had named for her dead grandfather and who looked just like her. When she was growing up, people would carry on about her flawless skin and "cute" nose, but Eva had never considered any part of her more valuable than any other part, the way some women feel about "great" legs, "high" breasts or "good" hair. What Eva liked most about herself was the fact that she was considered "smart"—she had always done very well in school and loved to read—and that she was an artist. Or at least she had been.

She wondered again if she should dye her hair, then scolded herself for not being more concerned about Hutch's dramatic departure. When she thought about it, she slapped down the toilet seat he'd left up with so much force she nearly cracked the bowl. Except for her stomach, which had begun to rumble in an annoying manner, she felt calm. She went back to the bedroom, dropped back down on the bed, lit another cigarette and glanced at the clock. It was two in the morning.

"Wonder where the hell he went," she said aloud. The sound of her own voice in the large silent room startled her, so she cleared her throat to make another noise. In all their years of marriage, she'd never known Hutch to act this way. He was the dependable one, the man whom everybody—from her dead mother Louisa to Charley to her stepson Steven—counted on to see them through. He was everybody's anchor. The quintessential Responsible Black Man. What had gotten into him?

*Could he be seeing somebody?* They hadn't made love in six months, and the last time they had, there had been such a lack of passion and excitement she caught herself wondering if the Bulls had beat the Mavericks and who had scored the last point. Not that he wasn't good in bed when he wanted to be. And there was certainly the possibility of another woman. God knew by the way the eyes of women on the make lit up when he strolled into a room that he had opportunities. And he had crossed that line once that she knew of, thanks to the influence and persuasion of his dog of a best friend Donald Mason. But Eva had never told Hutch that she knew.

She had told herself that the affair was brief and therefore meaningless, as far as she knew anyway, and she'd summoned up every bit of willpower she had to keep from reacting to it—she had too much pride for that. But who knew what influence Donald Mason still had? Eva groaned aloud when she thought about him.

Thank God the man was Raye Mason's problem and not hers. That fool never missed a pass a woman threw his way, and he would have loved for Hutch to accompany him on his forays into infidelity. Son of a bitch had even had the gall to make a drunken, tacky play for her one Saturday night when Hutch was out of town. She snuffed out her cigarette brutally, as if it were the top of Donald Mason's nappy head.

"I should have told Hutch," she said aloud, wondering again why she hadn't, except she didn't want to see that sad, dejected look that came into Hutch's eyes whenever somebody disappointed him. He could look more melancholy than any man she'd ever known. She loved him too much to call up that glance just to put Donald Mason in his place. So she'd kept *that* little nugget, like the one about his infidelity, tucked away in some wicked part of herself, ready to flick out if she ever needed it.

She was sure a glass of warm milk—with a slug of brandy in it—would help her sleep. Then when Hutch, sad-faced and repentant, crawled into bed whenever he finally made his way home, she'd be out like a light. Barefoot, she padded down the hall, headed down the carpeted stairs to the kitchen and flipped on the overhead fluorescent bulb, flooding her perfectly square kitchen with soft light. It was a pretty room, neat but crowded. Eva read the Williams-Sonoma catalogue like other people read *Essence,* and she had bought every imaginable spice, pan, pot or condiment that they had ever sold.

She chose a small glass saucepan from among the two dozen or so on her shelf, filled it with milk, heated it, then poured it into one of the oversize cups she'd picked up the week before at IKEA. She measured in a tablespoon of sugar flavored with the vanilla beans she kept stored in a tin, and topped it all off with a short splash of Courvoisier.

Something, probably a squirrel or a neighbor's dog, made a rustling sound in the backyard. Eva avoided glancing out the French glass doors that led to the deck and hurried back upstairs, pausing at the top because she heard what sounded like a door opening.

"Hutch?" she called out, her voice shaking. There had been a break-in two houses down a couple of weeks ago and she was frightened. When nobody answered, she marched bravely into the living room, turned on the alarm system, then went back to her bedroom and climbed into bed.

Their house was large and oddly designed, with three bedrooms on the second floor and a master bedroom on a landing three stairs up. There was a room for Charley before she moved out, one for Steven on his occasional weekend visits and a guest room with an attached bathroom. The house was too big for just the two of them, even when Hutch was around, although his presence made it seem smaller. It had been listed as a handyman's special when they'd bought it, which was a kind exaggeration. But Hutch—the handiest man anybody knew—had expertly put it back together, from the moldy basement floor which had become the rec room for Charley and Steven to the skylights in the attic that became her artist's loft, which was now filled with out-of-season clothes and books that nobody read. They'd bought the house ten years ago, the same year they'd married, combining the money she saved during the years she lived with Charley in her small rent-controlled apartment in Harlem and the money Hutch saved when he lived with his parents after he left Irene.

The house, a Colonial situated on a leafy street with other Tudors and Dutch Colonials of nearly the same age, was located in a New Jersey suburban town in a stable, *very* integrated neighborhood. There was no way Eva would ever have let Charley be the only black kid on her block. Thanks to her mother Louisa and her constant zeal for "bettering" herself, she had endured the painful drama of being the "first and only" when she'd been a girl and her mother had forced her father to move them up North, and she didn't want her daughter going through it.

Everyone, both black and white, had been friendly enough in the beginning, but as more black families moved in, more white families moved out, so the block was nearly all black now. Those whites who stayed were good neighbors, and some had become friends, hesitant and uneasy at first but closer as the years passed. Eva had been happier in this house than she had ever been anywhere in her life.

Steven and Charley, however, had mixed feelings about it. Steven, who had a mystical slant, swore the place was haunted. Charley, who was planted squarely in the here and now, had always dreamed of living in a sprawling, modern house with enough water pressure to ensure a hot shower in the morning and a dependable furnace that didn't go out in the dead of winter. But despite the house's idiosyncrasies and strange shiftings and creaking, Eva loved it. She turned down the TV now and cocked her ears for its latest noise.

"Hutch?" she called out again. *Silence*. She settled back on her pillow and made herself sip her milk.

What would he say when he finally strolled in, and how would she take it?

She didn't have much practice forgiving him because he never did much to be forgiven. They rarely fought. He never raised his voice. The angrier he got, the quieter and calmer he always became. She was the one with the temper, the one who screamed and cursed.

*There is no joy between us.*

What the hell was he talking about? Had he forgotten the joy they felt when they rented that villa in Ocho Rios four years ago? That was joy! God, she'd never felt so much peace in her life. They had sat for hours holding hands, with the breeze hitting their damp skin, watching the birds swoop and soar in the bright Jamaican sky.

*There is no joy between us.*

What about when Charley graduated from Spelman the year before last and Steven came out of Rutgers?

Angry again, Eva got up and locked the bedroom door. Let him knock to get back in, putting her through this shit at this time of night when all she wanted to do was fall asleep beside him listening to the buzz of the TV. Mewing pathetically, Bama poked her paw underneath the space between the door and the floor. Eva got up again, opened the door and scooped the cat up. The hall clock chiming like a foghorn made her jump.

"Like something out of Tales from the damn Crypt," she muttered, as she slammed the door, locked it and settled back down on the bed, stroking the soft space between the cat's ears.

"Yeah, you jive little sucker, you better make up

with me. I'm the one who feeds your fat little butt," she said to Bama, who scrambled out of her arms and onto the bed, glancing for a moment at her pillow and then flopping down on Hutch's, which made Eva think about Charley.

People always assumed she was Hutch's natural child. She walked, talked, joked like him. "It's good luck to look like your daddy," people told her so often that Eva was sure even Charley forgot that she didn't really come from him. But Eva never forgot. Charley had come from one of several tempestuous, passionate afternoons of lovemaking with her boyfriend of the time, a sensual nineteen-year-old named Jerry Winston, who had left no trace of himself on his daughter's face, her body or their lives. She thought of him sometimes, and remembered how sweetly they had loved, but she had no idea where he was, what he had done with his grown-up self or what he would think of her or Charley now, and what was more, she didn't care. Hutch had taken care of that. She glanced again at the cat. Through no effort of his own, Hutch had become the center of Bama's life, too.

They had been driving through Alabama when Eva had spotted the cat. Married less than three months, Hutch was bringing his new bride home to meet his extended family, who were old even then and seemed to be dying by the month, and a wedding—his favorite cousin's—was a damn sight better for meeting a wife than a funeral. Child-free (she had left Charley with her mother) and married at last, Eva reveled in her good fortune. After twelve years of losers, she had finally hit the number. Everything in her life seemed golden. Charley adored this gentle new man who gazed at her as if she were his own. For once in his life, her father Scoe Lilton was taking his pills, cutting down on whiskey and cigars and acting like he had some sense. No cancer had yet bitten into her mother's left breast. And there was no dead baby to haunt her dreams.

It was raining hard that morning, and they had stopped beneath a bridge. Cozy in Hutch's blue Volkswagen, Eva had spotted what she thought was a rat traveling fast and slinking into the shadow of the bushes, but then she realized no rat could be so thin. Without saying anything, she had jumped out of the car, grabbed the small wet creature and returned to the car, holding her close.

Hutch, an amused smile on his lips, had watched her silently and then patted the small animal gingerly with the tips of his fingers. After studying him for a moment, the cat leaped from Eva's arms and settled her small wet body next to him. They had named her Bama for the obvious reason. It was hard to see any trace of that scraggly kitten in the overfed cat who now stretched beside her, snagging her claws into the woven white bedspread.

*There is no joy between us.*

Where had their joy gone?

"Damned if I know," Eva said to the cat and flicked the channel to CNN. She mindlessly watched TV for a while, smoked another cigarette and glanced back at the clock, which now read three-fifteen.

Suddenly it occurred to her that something could have happened to him. Just as suddenly, she could hear her daughter's voice scolding her, *Mother! You always think the worst!*

*Mother.* It was Charley's word for her these days. Not "Mommy," like when she'd been a child, or even "Mom." But "Mother," with its distant, haughty ring. Eva had been Charley's age when she had started calling her mother by her given name, Louisa. Charley was four by then, and Eva's calling Louisa by her name with an amused irreverent affection had put them on equal footing. She felt that she had earned that right because of the hurt she had endured when her mother, furious at the thought of a grandchild out of wedlock, had thrown her out of the house. But then Louisa, overwhelmed by guilt and love for the grandchild she had denied at birth, had put aside her haughty, rigid ways and accepted Eva's title meekly, without a blink.

But "Louisa" had become "Mama" those last few months of her mother's life, and "Mommy" that last time she'd held her frail hand the night she died. But never, not even in the worst days of their strained relationship, had she called Louisa "Mother," spoken in the disdainful, superior way that Charley had of saying it. Charley never called Hutch "Father" like in those old TV shows in the 1950s. It was always "Daddy," spoken with little-girl charm, purred out. *D-a-d-d-y* and Mother.

*Mother, you're so negative. Mother, you always think the worst,* Charley was fond of telling her. *Mother, why can't you just let yourself be happy?* Eva rolled her eyes when she thought about that one.

" 'Let yourself be happy.' 'There is no joy between us.' Maybe I should just roll over and fucking die of feeling sorry for myself," she said to the cat.

*Did he go to his office?*

That was one place he always ran when he needed

somewhere to go. But there was barely enough room for a couch in the reception area, and Hutch had taken his suitcase, so that was out. Maybe a hotel? Since he took a suitcase he was probably going to stay longer than just tonight, even though he'd left close to midnight. But Hutch was too cheap for a hotel. That left Donald Mason.

*So when would he come home?*

The same rational voice that told her where he probably was told her he would be home in time for dinner tonight. She got back up and brushed her teeth again, the sour nasty taste from the cigarettes suddenly unbearable. Then she crawled back into bed, clicked to the weather channel, and then to CNN and finally settled on the food channel for a rerun of Julia Child preparing a country pâté. Snapping on the TV timer, she tried to go to sleep.

*I'll bake some French bread,* she thought, *easy to make and he likes it and I have that white wine that will go good with some fish, or maybe something drier if I pick up a small salmon, poach it and present it on one of the fancy platters, maybe do a light salad, that black bean and corn one was so good when I fixed it last week if I can get some cilantro or I'll make a dill sauce for the fish or maybe asparagus instead of the black beans, but Hutch hates asparagus, so maybe not. I wonder if I can get some nice strawberries . . .* Food and how she would cook it were Eva's last thoughts when she finally fell asleep.

A clap of thunder woke her up Saturday morning. She opened her eyes, glanced over at Hutch's side of the bed, spotted Bama's round, gray rump covering his pillow and shoved her off. She stumbled into the bathroom, washed her face and brushed her teeth without looking at herself in the mirror, then pulled on jeans and a T-shirt and went downstairs to make some coffee.

Although the weather had been hot, it was raining this morning and the house was cool. Eva went back upstairs to look for her favorite sweater, a worn cable-knit navy one that her mother had given her before she died. She'd stored it in the attic with the rest of her winter things, so she climbed the ten steep stairs to the attic—now a loft—that ran the length and width of the house. Even on a dreary day like this one, the light that shone in from the skylight gave the room a serene glow. Four years ago, Hutch had designed and built the loft for her, demanding that she keep out until he'd finished. When he finally let her see it, it took her breath away. They had opened a bottle of champagne, toasting his work and the work she thought she would do, then made love on the paint-smeared drop cloths that smelled like paint thinner. But then she couldn't paint. She hadn't picked up a pencil, brush or anything else in almost two years. It was as if the space he'd given her had killed her inspiration by placing some terrible expectation on her. She was always too tired when she got home from her job at the library. Or there was nothing she wanted to draw. Or she simply had something better to do with her time. It was as if the part of her that had always brought a sense of well-being and accomplishment had left without a trace. Nothing as far as she could see had changed in her life.

But Eva often missed what lay in front of her.

The sound of dripping water caught her attention. A

puddle had settled under the skylight. She found a rag and mopped it up, noting with alarm that it was not a new leak; a steady drip from the roof had worn the floor beneath to a dull yellow. She found an old tin bucket in the basement, carried it back upstairs and shoved it under the leak. Hutch could fix it when he came home. After dinner or breakfast. After they had talked. She went back to the kitchen and poured herself a bowl of cornflakes and another cup of coffee and settled by the window, sipping, munching and watching the rain. When the telephone rang, she rushed to answer it.

*It was about goddamn time.*

"Hutch?" Her anger turned her voice cold. There was silence on the other end. Eva filled it quickly.

"You may as well answer me. Yes, I'm still mad at you. Walking out like that last night, like you've lost your mind. And we have a leak in the damned skylight. What time—"

"Excuse me, Mrs. Hutchinson?" The voice, which Eva didn't recognize, was distant and overly polite. A thought came to her that made her pull her breath in so quickly it hurt.

*The police!* Hutch had been hurt. Or killed. Somebody had run him over. Or shot him dead. Her mouth wouldn't move for a moment, and if she had been able to open it, she would have screamed.

"Mrs. Hutchinson?"

"Oh, my God! Oh, my God!" Eva screamed. "Please tell me what happened. Oh, God."

"Mrs. Hutchinson!" The voice was concerned but firm.

"What?" Eva pushed all her fear into that one word. "What?"

"This is Isaiah Lonesome."

She paused, perplexed. "Who?"

"Isaiah. Isaiah Lonesome. I met you a couple of months ago, when Charley brought me by for dinner."

"Who?" Eva still didn't understand.

"Isaiah. I'm a friend of your daughter's. Was a friend of your daughter's," he amended. Eva's heart stopped pounding; her breathing returned to normal.

"Why the hell didn't you say so in the first place?" she asked, furious that she had shared her business with a stranger. She also recalled with embarrassment the unfortunate words that she had said to the man two months ago—when she had broadly hinted that he was not right for her daughter and should consider moving on—that had been indirectly responsible for Charley's leap from the nest.

"How can I help you?" she spoke formally now, trying for some dignity.

"Is, uh, your husband, Mr. Hutchinson, okay?"

"Everyone is fine, thank you."

He paused, "Are you sure?"

"That's what I just said, isn't it?" She tried to say it lightly, but her words had a nasty edge to them, and she could tell by the edge in his voice when he answered her back that he had picked up on that.

"I'm sorry to call you so early, but I . . . I needed to talk to Charley about something."

"Charley?"

"Your daughter," he said with a touch of sarcasm that annoyed her.

"You don't have to tell me who Charley is, Mr. Lonesome. I'll tell her that you called."

"Thank you. Please call me Isaiah."

"Isaiah." She doubted Charley would want to talk to him, considering the abrupt way that her daughter—obviously using her relationship with the man to prove a point to Eva and Hutch—had slipped back into her Black American Princess mode the moment he was out of her life. She'd also found Bradley—a more "appropriate" man in almost everyone's opinion—to become involved with. Charley had ditched Isaiah Lonesome so quickly and with so little fanfare, Eva found herself feeling sorry for the man. And what the hell kind of name was "Lonesome" anyway? Knowing Charley, she probably realized after her initial infatuation that "Lonesome" was not a last name *she* wanted herself or her kids to be saddled with for the rest of their lives. And there was *no* doubt that Isaiah Lonesome, with his trumpet, avant-garde jazz and sad, pretty eyes, could ever present her with the two-carat diamond from Tiffany's (Charley had checked for the name on the inside of the band) that currently lit up the ring finger of her slender left hand.

"Charley doesn't live here anymore," Eva added. "If you'd like I can give her your message, Mr. Lonesome."

"Isaiah. Thanks. I hope it's not any trouble. Giving her the message, not calling me Isaiah."

"I wouldn't have offered if I didn't want to do it," Eva snapped and then chastised herself for being a bitch so early in the morning. Hell, it wasn't Isaiah Lonesome's fault that Hutch had walked out last night.

When he gave her his number, Eva repeated it slowly and earnestly as if she had actually written it down and then promptly forgot him, his number and everything he said the moment he hung up. On impulse, she picked up the phone again and pressed the speed-dial button to call Donald and Raye Mason, and then slammed down the phone when she heard Donald's voice on the other end. All she needed was for that cheating bastard to hear the desperation in her voice if Hutch wasn't there. She could almost hear the snide, sleazy turn his voice would take as he hinted that Hutch was as much a dog as he and that their marriage of ten years was as corrupt and weak as his own.

But maybe it was.

*There is no joy between us.*

Where had he picked that one up? It didn't even sound like something Hutch would say. And what the hell was joy anyway?

She stared at the soggy bowl of cornflakes, picked up a spoonful, then dumped the gloppy mess into the garbage disposal. She poured another cup of coffee, sat back down in front of the window and watched the rain come down.

What should she do now on this lazy Saturday morning? What did she usually do on a Saturday morning? Talk to Hutch, mostly, clean a little, read the paper, take things to the cleaners, watch some TV, shop for the week, start dinner around three. Maybe she should start the bread now. It would give her something to do. He'd probably be back around six, she could bet that, just in time for dinner. Maybe with some flowers. A bottle of red wine. Hutch liked white. But he'd pick up red because he knew she preferred that. Maybe she should forget about the salmon and make some chowder. The house was still chilly, and something comforting and welcoming that she could serve in bright blue bowls garnished with parsley

would make up for those harsh words they had exchanged.

So Eva mixed the flour, yeast, water and salt,
kneaded the bread and let it rise while she was in Fresh
Fields picking up fresh clams for the clam chowder.
She punched down the bread when she got home,
rinsed the clams, peeled potatoes and then some apples
for a pie, punched down the bread again, baked the pie,
shaped the bread, got everything ready to make the
chowder, set the table and had a glass of wine. At eight,
she baked the bread, and gobbled down a slice straight
from the oven spread lavishly with butter and gulped
another glass of wine. At ten, she screamed, "Fuck
you!" four times at the top of her lungs, tossed everything for the chowder into a pot and cooked it at a
rolling boil. She nearly choked on one of the rubbery
clams when she wolfed it down twenty minutes later.
She cleaned the kitchen in a rage, watched three bad
movies on HBO and then fell asleep.

She was still mad late the next morning, when her
ringing phone woke her up.

"Hutch?" She knew her voice was desperate. She
didn't give a damn.

"Are you okay?" Charley asked on the other end.

"Yeah."

"I spoke to Daddy yesterday, and he told me what
happened. He asked me to call you to see if you were
okay."

"Humph," Eva grunted. At least she knew the man
was alive. "So he called you?" But of course he would
call his baby. "Did he say where he was?"

Charley paused for a moment as if she were afraid

of betraying a trust. "Over at the Masons'. What did you do to him?"

"What do you mean, what did *I* do to *him?*"

"Did you-all have a fight?" Another pause. "Did— did you *tell* him to leave?"

"Why the heck would I tell him to leave? He left on his own."

"Why?"

"Maybe you should ask him."

"I did."

"What did he say?" Eva sat up straight, eager to hear the answer.

"He just said that . . . things had changed between you . . . and things needed to change."

"Needed to change?" Eva snorted as she reached for a cigarette. "Did he say exactly *what* needed to change?"

"No. He just said he loved me and that Steven and I had nothing to do with it. It was between you and him."

"Between me and him," Eva sneered.

"Is he coming back?" Was that fear in Charley's voice?

"I don't know." Eva didn't bother to hide the fear that was in her own. "Did you ask him?"

Charley hesitated. "Yes."

"What did he say?"

"He said he didn't know. Do you want him to come back?"

"I don't know," Eva said, her answer surprising her because she had no idea where it came from.

"Mommy?"

Eva smiled. She hadn't heard *that* in a while. "Yes, baby."

"Are you okay?"

"Fine."

"Are you going to be able to go to work tomorrow?" When Charley had been a child, Eva's going to work every morning had always signaled that everything was okay, that life hadn't kicked her behind hard enough to keep her from pulling on clothes, gulping down coffee and pouring just enough Cheerios into Charley's *Sesame Street* cereal bowl to allow them enough time to make the morning subway to the day-care center and whatever temporary job Eva had managed to secure. She had always worked, even though her current job paid little money and marriage to Hutch had offered her the chance not to.

"Of course I'm going to work tomorrow. It's Monday, isn't it? What would they do without me?" That was a lie, and Charley knew it, but Eva said it anyway.

"Do you want me to come over?"

"No. I'm okay, Charley, really."

"Do you have anything you want me to tell him?" Expectation had replaced Charley's fear.

"Like what?"

"I don't know. I just don't want you two to break up. Is there anything you want me to say?"

"No," Eva said firmly, but the lump in her throat was so big she had trouble saying it.

# Hutch

The morning after Hutch left Eva, Donald Mason leaned against the island in his spacious black and white kitchen, answered his phone, then shook his head in disgust when the caller (who happened to be Eva) didn't say anything.

"Whoever it was didn't bother to speak," he said to his wife, who was busy drying wine glasses, and to Hutch, who was sitting on a nearby stool drinking coffee.

"I thought that only happened to me," Raye Mason said pleasantly but the look Donald threw her told Hutch her words had hit their mark. Hutch dropped his eyes to his cup. "More coffee?" Raye asked sweetly as she poured herself some more.

"Not now. I'll get it in a minute." Hutch pulled up his eyes to glance at her. He'd always thought she was a pretty woman, with her heart-shaped face and generous lips that always seemed to smile, which Eva claimed made no sense at all considering the man she was married to. He knew—everybody knew—that Raye and Donald's marriage had its problems—namely Donald—but Raye always seemed contented, even happy.

Raye was older than Hutch by about three years, and although gravity and good living were catching up with her, if you didn't notice the gray that spiked through her short black hair, her face, which was a soft walnut brown, could have belonged to a woman in her mid-thirties. She wore a red and blue workout suit and new white sneakers. When she bent toward him to put a pan on the counter, he caught the scent of the sensual, subtle perfume she always wore.

"So what are you doing on this rainy Saturday morning?" he asked.

"Going to the gym."

"Hey, good for you!"

"I usually walk in the park in the morning, but—" she nodded toward the window with rain pouring down and shook her head in disgust—"rain or shine, you've got to do what you've got to do."

"Raye looks good for a woman her age, don't she?" said Donald. "She is one of the finest-looking fifty-year-old women I've ever seen."

"Fifty! You've got my birthday mixed up with your own," Raye added with a smirk passed off as a smile.

"Raye looks good for a woman *any* age, man," Hutch corrected him.

"Aw, man, I'm just playing with her. She knows what I mean, don't you, baby?" Donald gave Raye's behind a playful slap. Raye turned, quickly aimed the towel she was holding in the general area of his genitals and snapped it hard.

"Keep your hands and everything else to yourself, old man," she said playfully.

"That's *not* what you said last night." Donald shot her a lewd grin.

Raye rolled her eyes in disgust. "What am I going to do with this fool, Hutch? Shoot him?" she asked lightly.

Hutch laughed with her but it stuck in his throat. He knew only too well that if he picked up the newspaper one Sunday morning and read that Raye Mason, 47, had shot Donald Mason, 49, her husband of twenty-three years, in the back late Saturday night, he would not be surprised.

Donald Mason had bad manners, bad skin and a body that was woefully out of shape. The hair that framed his homely face was receding, and his bad feet forced him to walk in a stealthy, tiptoe rhythm, like a cat sneaking up on prey. But his looks were deceiving. Power dripped from the tips of his long manicured fingers and down the pants of his $3,500 suits straight to the heels of his handmade orthopedic shoes. He was the best-known, most influential, richest black lawyer in New Jersey. Eva staunchly maintained that his "juice" and bank account were the only things he had going for him, but Hutch knew there was more. He had the charm and bold self-confidence of a rake who knows he's wrong, doesn't give a damn and dares the world to call him on it. Women found him irresistible. And it cut both ways.

Donald Mason's women were as much a part of his life as his asthma and bad feet. He slept with every type of woman imaginable—tall, short, young, mature, white, black, stunning, plain. From investment bankers to waitresses to social workers, he was a woman's man who prided himself on his eclectic taste.

And he was shameless about it. Anywhere, anytime, any day of the week. As far as Hutch knew, Raye simply accepted his running around. Eva claimed she'd have to be dumb, deaf and blind not to, so she probably didn't give a damn. But Donald never brought any of his women anywhere near his wife, and Hutch was certain that as much as Donald could love anyone he loved Raye Mason. He had a generous spirit, and showed his adoration in the only way he knew how: a new Mercedes or Jaguar every other year, trips to Paris for the fall and spring collections, a month at a villa in Mustique or St. Barthélemy whenever she felt like getting some sun, and a liberal allowance tactfully sent into her bank account each month that he never saw, touched or questioned. He took "good care" of his wife, and if any of his women were dumb enough to think that he'd leave her for them, they were just plain too dumb to be in his bed, he'd told Hutch on more than one occasion.

"Hey, man, you can pour me another cup of that java while you're up." He waved his cup in the direction of Hutch, who was filling his own.

"Sorry." Hutch shook the empty pot. "Last drop."

"Man, ain't that just like a nigger. Come over here, sleep in my damn bed, eat my damn food, drink all my goddamn coffee." He shook his head in disgust.

"Are you okay in that room? I can tell Elena to switch you to the one near Donald's study," Raye said over her shoulder after giving Donald a neat peck on his lips as she picked up a large white and red L.L. Bean canvas bag and headed toward the door.

"No. I'm more than okay," Hutch said. "Thank you."

"Shut up before I punch you. You know you're always welcome in my house," Donald said.

"One of the few of his friends who is," Raye added.

"She means it, man. She ain't kidding around."

"Man, thanks. I don't know what I would have done if—" Hutch stopped, suddenly aware of the catch in his throat. *What the hell was wrong with him?* He took a quick gulp of coffee to swallow it down.

"Don't mention it, man."

"I'll see you two later. Hutch, don't let Donald give you any bad advice," Raye said as she left for the gym. Hutch nodded and grinned, but he knew that any advice Donald gave him probably wouldn't be worse than what he had given himself. He still wasn't sure why everything had suddenly become so intolerable. He just knew that all the sadness he felt seemed to be catching up with him. He'd had to get out. He'd known that, and if he hadn't left at that moment, he didn't think he would ever be able to do it.

After he left last night, he'd sat in his car in front of the house for a good hour, wondering if he should go back inside, apologize and crawl back into bed beside his wife like somebody with good sense. Yes, they had been fighting more these days than they used to, but Eva wasn't the kind of woman to hold what had happened last night against him. She would just have shaken her head with that funny look she had sometimes in her eyes, that expression somewhere between wonder and amusement, turned back over and gone to sleep. They would have gotten up this morning, she'd have made banana pancakes or muffins for breakfast, they'd have talked about nothing as if nothing had happened and spent this rainy Saturday like the countless other rainy Saturdays they'd spent together in the last ten years. But something within him couldn't let that be.

Instead, he'd called Donald from a phone booth on the Parkway, and Donald, as Hutch knew he would, had warmly welcomed him, no questions asked, no explanation needed. Hutch took another sip of coffee and glanced at his friend, who studied him with concern.

"Now that the women-folk is gone, let's talk," Donald said.

"Not much to say."

"Bug finally bit you, huh?"

"Bug?"

Donald cackled knowingly. "Bug, nigger, bug! Da Bug, that bites all us crazy motherfuckers when we been with one woman too long."

"What are you talking about?" Hutch pursed his lips primly.

Donald picked up an imaginary phone and dramatically dialed an imaginary number while Hutch looked on curiously.

"Mr. Undertaker?" he said with a scowl. "I got a goddamn corpse sitting up here in my kitchen drinking my coffee. Been bit by the bug and don't know it. Nigger *must* be dead."

"Aw, man, get out of here."

"You feel like a drink?"

"Drink? It's too damn early for a drink."

Donald studied him for a moment and then shook his head in dismay. "You looking bad, man."

"Jesus Christ, Donald, I just left my wife."

Donald chuckled. "A lot of men would be celebrating that shit. Your mistake was leaving *her*. You should have let her leave *you*. That looks better in court. We can do something with that—woman walks out on a good man, working man, don't treat her bad, don't be hitting her or no shit like that. You got a better chance of keeping what's yours if she leaves you with no real reason. You can get out of paying the *big* money if she leaves *you*. But on the other hand, your kids are grown, so that puts a different light—"

"Shut up, man," Hutch said. His eyes showed he meant it.

Ignoring him, Donald continued. "No, I'm serious. It is always better if they leave you. You get a lot of sympathy as long as you ain't done nothing to bring it on. And there ain't nothing better than sympathy pussy."

"Jesus, Donald. Don't you think of anything else?"

"Sympathy pussy," Donald reminisced. "Best pussy in the world. You can do anything you want with it."

"Jesus, man. Raye should have left *your* sorry ass twenty-two years ago."

"Raye got good sense, man," Donald said with a cocky grin. "I've never had nothing to do with a woman who didn't have a good head on her shoulders, and Raye is one of the smartest women I know. She knows what the real deal is."

"And that is?"

"I treat Raye good, and she knows it. But you and Eva? You should be concerned about keeping all the money you can keep."

"No. It's not about me and money. What you're really talking about is feeding your brethren sharks," Hutch said. "Helping them get their pound of flesh at three hundred dollars an hour on somebody else's misery, right? Things aren't like that between me and Eva."

"You left her, didn't you?"

"Yeah," Hutch said as if he were tired, dropping his eyes.

Donald studied him sympathetically. "Don't take it so hard, brother."

"How am I supposed to take it?"

"Let me get this straight. Maybe I'm not understanding something in this scene. Didn't you just tell me, aren't we discussing the fact, that you just left her, right?"

"Yeah."

"Then why you so tore up about it?"

"I don't know."

"Guilt?" Donald offered, and Hutch shrugged. "You and Cara on again?" Donald asked with real interest.

"Me and Cara were *never* on," Hutch said with annoyance. The mere mention of Cara Franklin, the one and only woman he'd ever had an extramarital affair with, made Hutch grimace. The affair, such as it was, had happened a year ago and Cara, an associate in Donald's firm, had been vain and superficial. Donald had goaded him so much about her, he'd almost felt obligated to sleep with her. He also had the uncomfortable feeling that Donald had set up the relationship so that he could experience it vicariously. All in all, that year had been a bad one for many reasons.

"A year ain't that long. I know for sure she probably wouldn't mind doing the do again. She's always asking about you. That's one good-looking piece of woman, man, with them long-ass legs and big, juicy tits. Good-looking woman."

"Why don't *you* sleep with her, then?"

Donald wagged his finger and shook his head as if in warning. "Nope. Not me. What they say, don't shit where you eat? My mama didn't raise no fool. Too many women out here for me to be getting into that."

"Well, don't mention her again to me."

"Don't be so sensitive, man. Just trying to cheer you up." Donald bugged his eyes innocently, but there was a mischievous light in them. "No kidding, though, man. All you got to do is think about the honey." Hutch glanced at him, puzzled. "That's what that brother said, didn't he? Show me the honey. Well, Hutch. All kidding aside, now. It's time for you to show me the honey. Show me the honey. Who is the honey you left Eva for?" Donald's eyes twinkled in expectation.

Hutch said, "You know damn well it's show me the money, not honey, and I don't have any honey to show your sorry ass."

Donald looked perplexed and then distressed. "You didn't leave with nowhere to go, did you?" Hutch shrugged. "Hey, man, this is Donald Mason you're talking to. I know you're a gentleman and all that shit, man. I'm a gentleman, too. You got to be these days or you won't get nowhere, but you're not telling me you don't have anywhere else to go once you leave here, are you?"

Hutch sighed deeply and sorrowfully. "Look, man, I don't want to put you and Raye out or nothing like that, I—"

"No, I'm not talking about that, you can stay here long as you want. But I mean, you've got a lady to go to, right?"

"No."

"Okay, brother," Donald said, a gleam of understanding coming into his eyes. "I know no straight-thinking man ever leaves a good woman *for* another woman, good or otherwise, that don't make no kind of sense, but you do have a honey parked away somewhere, don't you?"

"Except for those times with Cara, I've never

cheated on Eva." It came out sounding more sanctimonious than Hutch meant it to, and Donald smiled.

"Except for those times with Cara," he said in a malevolently teasing voice, and Hutch realized for the tenth time just how much Donald had riding on *his* infidelity. For Donald Mason, marriage without a "little something on the side" was as inconceivable as snow was to a camel. Hutch opened the refrigerator, pulled out a container of orange juice and poured himself a glass. Donald held his cup for Hutch to pour some into, and then went to the oak cabinet in the small bar near the kitchen for a bottle of vodka and splashed a generous amount into both glasses.

"So what are your plans now?"

"Well . . ." Hutch hesitated because he didn't have any. "I'd like to stay here for a couple of days if I can, if it's okay with you and Raye."

"Stay all year if you want to. We ain't got nothing in this damn house but room."

"Just a week or two, if it's okay. I'm going to start looking for a place later on this week."

"Don't worry about looking for a place. I got that place in the city, you know the one over on West Seventy-Second. You can stay there if you make yourself scarce when I need it and keep your mouth shut about it. Raye thinks I got rid of it six years ago. One of my frat brothers rents it for me."

"I just need to think things over—" Hutch had barely heard him— "maybe talk to Eva in a couple of days, see if—"

"Talk to Eva about what?"

"Just see her, talk to her." Hutch wasn't sure why himself.

"If you walked out on her, there's no reason to talk to her or see her. She'll know she has the advantage if you see her. Are you serious about leaving her or are you just bullshitting around? What happened anyway? Did you have a fight or something?"

"No."

"You just up and walked out the house?"

"Yep. That's what I did."

"No provocation. Nothing. Just left?"

"Yeah."

"And you're serious about leaving?"

"Yeah," Hutch said after thinking about it a minute.

"You really should have called me first. There are ways to leave a woman, and there are ways to *leave* a woman."

"We've been over this, Donald."

Ignoring him, Donald continued, "You may have put yourself at a disadvantage legally. I'm telling you, man, never do anything like that without talking to your lawyer—namely me—first."

"Oh, fuck that, Donald, just fuck it!" Hutch said, slamming the glass down on the table. Donald watched him for a few minutes without saying anything.

"And now you're talking about maybe going back?"

"I didn't say that."

"Didn't you just say you want to talk to Eva?"

Hutch sighed and shrugged.

"I can tell you right now that unless you plan on crawling back with your dick in one hand and your balls in the other, it won't do you any good. Now she'll have the advantage if you go back, and she'll know it. That's one thing I know about women. If you walk out, you better keep on walking. Don't expect her to take you back unless you beg her, and you'll pay for it for the rest of your natural life. You'll have to give her anything she wants. Now if she had walked out on you—then things would be different. Then you'd hold all the cards. Then she'd be coming back to you."

"I'll give it a few days, see if maybe Eva and me can talk, see if . . ." Hutch was talking more to himself than to Donald.

"Humph," Donald grunted.

"Today is Saturday. I just left Eva last night. I just need to relax. Do nothing. Think of what I'm going to tell the kids when I talk to them later."

"Tell the kids? They're grown. Don't tell them nothing."

"I've got to tell them something."

"Then tell them as little as possible. You never know who will take whose side when something like this happens. Blood means nothing. You can't even trust Steven. Charley may be loyal, but you did—"

Hutch held up both hands in protest and supplication. "Please, Donald. Just let me think. Shut up for once! Leave me alone!"

"Think all you want, just don't tell those kids, when you call them later on, anything more than they have to know. Here is what you *can* do. You can keep on paying the mortgage on the house, the car payments, the utilities, anything to show the judge when you finally go to see him that you're a fine, upstanding, responsible black man and not some shiftless Negro with nothing on his mind but loose shoes and tight pussy. Who do you think will handle it for her?"

"Handle what?"

"The divorce, man, when it gets to that. Just pray it's not sanctimonious Sam. I had to go up against him in court last month, and once a year with that fat black bastard is once too much. Sam Henderson will make it personal. Scrubs the floor with me every time I meet him. If we're lucky, she'll go with Bruenstein."

Hutch glared at him. "We're not there, Donald, we're not there. I just walked out. I'm not filing for divorce. Jesus, Eva isn't filing for divorce. We just need some time to—"

"Listen, Hutch," Donald interrupted in a low voice even though they were the only people in the house. "When it comes to this kind of stuff I know a hell of a lot more than you do. If you left her, there was a reason for it. You may not fully know it yet, but believe me, once you get out there and live a little, do some sampling, find out what you been missing, you'll know you made the right decision. Your gut instincts, survival instincts, led you right. They always do."

"I don't know man, I don't know. I—"

"Listen to me, brother." Donald grabbed him by the shoulders and shook him for emphasis. "We—you, me, some of the other brothers we know—are the first generation of black men to ever be able to live the way we want to. First generation to peek up over the top of that crab barrel they got us in, to push the cracker's foot from up our ass. Some of us got money now, and smarts, and he will never be able to beat us down like he did our daddies. We can fuck him as royally as he fucked us." Pausing dramatically, Donald poured some more vodka into his orange juice and shook his glass gently, staring at it as if in a trance.

"We're living in this goddamn country in the best goddamn time to live in it—and don't throw South Africa in my face, 'cause nobody knows what's gonna go down there once Nelson croaks. We can live the American dream like most of these broke-ass niggers out here never had a rat's ass chance of doing, and a piece of that dream—I mean just a little itty bitty edge of it—is living it with as many women as you want. That's one of the fruits of our labor." His eyes shining with excitement, he clicked his glass against Hutch's. "Soar, motherfucker, soar! The world and any piece of ass you want in it is yours!" He dropped his head as if in prayer, and Hutch, who had heard variations on this speech for as long as he had known Donald, sipped his drink meditatively for a moment, nodded respectfully and then excused himself to go back to his room to make some calls. Once he got there he slumped down on the bed.

Soaring was the last thing in the world he felt like doing, but Hutch had to admit that Donald was right about one thing: his generation was different from his father's. It had taken everything you had in his father's day just to live your life sane enough to make enough bucks to pay the man his rent each month and make sure nobody went hungry, to make it through life without killing some white man in rage. That was joy enough. Maybe he was spoiled like his daddy used to tell him.

He had been thinking about his father more in recent weeks than he had in the two years since he died. Even now Hutch could smell his Old Spice aftershave lotion tinged with a whiff of Wild Turkey. He could almost see his ghost rounding the corner just before he focused his eyes good. God, how he'd loved and feared that old man, as sour and demanding as he was. His daddy had built his construction business up with sweat, determination and grinning at white men who he knew would sooner see him dead than make a red cent. And he'd made it work and handed it down to Hutch, his only son, and never asked for anything in return except that he keep it alive, which Hutch had promised he would. He had taken care of his father like a baby in the end—feeding him, changing his clothes, bathing him. The duty of the only son of an only son. Like Steven was to him.

He picked up the phone and dialed Steven's number. When Steven didn't answer he called Charley, and was secretly relieved that neither was home, that he didn't have to have the conversation he knew he'd have to have later on that night, before Eva gave her twist to last night's events. But he didn't know what the hell he was going to say. He picked up the remote, snapped on the TV and watched CNN for a while, then switched to Headline News and called Steven again, vaguely wondering where he could be on a rainy Saturday afternoon. He felt a lump in his throat as he thought about him; there was guilt there too. He got angry again as he remembered Eva's crack—as if he could *ever* leave Steven. How could she have tossed that one out, knowing the guilt he felt about not raising him?

He was closer to Eva's Charley than to his own son, that was the truth of it. Irene had gotten the day-to-day pieces of Steven, the spelling lists and strawberry Jell-O and tears you could turn into giggles. It had been easy for him to replace Steven with Charley—to experience with her the things he wished he had been able to have with him. She was more his now than Steven was, and he wondered if he would ever get over the disappointment he saw in Steven's eyes because of it. He dialed his son's number again, listening to the sound of his voice on the recording that was now as deep as his own, as his father's had been. Steven was a man now and he'd missed the whole damned thing.

He hung up the phone quickly without leaving a message, waited ten minutes, then called again and left Donald's number. He watched TV for a while longer, and finally drifted off to sleep, lulled by the sound of the rain on the roof. An hour later, a knock on the door woke him up.

"You okay in there?" Raye asked.

"Fine." He cleared his throat.

"Feel like some soup? I put some on."

He washed up in the small adjoining bathroom and joined her on a stool in the kitchen. He didn't realize how hungry he was until he smelled the food.

"I'm not a real cook like Eva, it's just Campbell's," Raye apologized as Hutch gobbled it down. She poured some more into his bowl and watched him polish it off.

"Donald went out?" he asked between spoonfuls.

"Yeah, in all this rain, would you believe that? That damn Phi Omega Ki sees more of him than I do. They're giving some kind of fund-raiser tomorrow night, so he had to go to the hotel this afternoon to help get things under way."

*Right,* Hutch said to himself.

"So what are your plans for the rest of the day?"

Raye shrugged. "Nothing much. What about you? You going to stick around here for a while?"

"Nah. I've got some bookkeeping to do over at the office. Make some calls. Look over the figures on a new site over on Maple. I got to write up and send out some bids before the people think I'm just a trifling colored boy who don't want no work." He was thinking about Steven and Charley and what he would say to them when he finally got them. Raye studied him without saying anything.

"You're going to work on a Saturday, and on a day like this?"

"Not work. Just . . ." He shrugged without finishing.

"Hutch, why don't you tell me what happened?"

She had a way of holding his eyes and demanding an answer. He had always found it easy to talk to her, although in the years that he had known them, he rarely spoke to Raye without Donald being present, and then their conversations always revolved around him—how he was feeling, what he was doing, the court battles he was waging. When they did talk, just the two of them, they always spoke honestly, cutting to the chase as if they understood that they didn't have time to waste on superficialities because Donald would soon bust in and put his particular, jaded spin on everything that was said. Their intimate talks, and Hutch could recall each one almost word for word, always came at some traumatic, pivotal moment in his life. Raye's eyes could always shake loose his truth.

He'd talked to her the day before he left Irene, and when his father died, and after Lucas, his and Eva's baby, died shortly after his birth. He had cried with her that night because he hadn't been able to cry about it or even talk about it with Eva; it had hurt too much to see the anguish on her face. Raye had listened, saying nothing. Then she told him about the loss of her child, the one that Donald had never mentioned, that she and Donald had lost the first year of their marriage. It hadn't been a loss like his and Eva's, she'd explained, when the baby was a baby with a name, a body, a soul. Her baby had died in her womb, and as if cursing it, she'd never been able to conceive another and had found it hard to mourn it properly. She had grieved for his child and her own that night, crying for him until he was able to speak without weeping. And whenever they'd seen each other the next week or so, with Eva on his arm and her on Donald's, they'd embraced with a secret intimacy that hinted at the sorrow they had shared.

The last time they'd talked had been after his father's death. He'd shared his sadness, his relief and his guilt. She understood and listened in a way that Eva had never been able to, had never wanted to.

"What's wrong, Hutch?" she asked now, gently prodding him like some shy, lost child, like she always did.

"I don't know." He shrugged the way Steven used to.

"It's around the anniversary of his death, isn't it?" she started this conversation where they had left their last one, about his father. "Maybe that has something to do with it, with your leaving Eva like you did." Funny, when he thought about it, how these conversations with her never really seemed to end.

"I don't know."

"It was about this time, wasn't it?"

"Yeah. I guess it was." It had been June, and hot like this, too. He smiled for a moment as he remembered his father in his last days, running on about the South and his dead family, talking about buying Christmas gifts in June. He'd been dead by the end of the month.

"How are you feeling now?"

"I don't feel anything, I guess."

"You tacked that 'I guess' on pretty quick." He shrugged again. Steven's shrug.

"Do you love her?"

"I thought I did."

"What has changed?"

He sighed. "I have no idea. Everything just began to feel fake. Like we were pretending about our feelings, just lying to each other about everything." He thought for a moment and then added, "Maybe I'm expecting too much out of marriage. Out of love."

"Was there anything in particular that happened?"

He shook his head to tell her there wasn't, and said nothing for a while and then added as if he had just been thinking about it, "I just know I only have a couple of summers."

Raye looked puzzled. "A couple of summers?"

Hutch sat up as if he had just remembered something. "I mean, I think about Pop, maybe this whole mess does have something to do with him after all, but I think about him, and how he hit sixty, only about sixteen years from where I am now, when he came down with that shit, the Alzheimer's, and after that . . ." He sighed and shook his head in sad frustration.

"And your father's illness has something to do with you and Eva?"

"Hell, sixteen years isn't anything, Raye. Sixteen years ago Steven was six and I can still see that yellow raincoat he used to toss on the stairs when he came home from school. Sixteen years ain't nothing at all. Sixteen summers? Maybe thirty if I'm lucky?"

"You've only got tomorrow if you're lucky," Raye said with a slight smile. "How many years does anybody have?"

"I don't want to settle anymore."

"And you think you're *settling* with Eva?"

"I don't know."

Raye avoided Hutch's eyes. "Settling is part of being grown. We settle for little things all the time, Hutch. We settle for chicken if they're out of steak. We settle for a blue car when we really want red. We settle and compromise and try to be happy with what we've got."

*Like you have,* Hutch thought but liked her too much to say aloud. "I'm not like that, Raye. Being grown is knowing that you can't afford to settle anymore, that when you settle for nothing that's usually what you get."

"So those ten summers you spent with Eva are nothing, you settled for nothing and that's what you got." There was a nasty edge in Raye's tone, a weariness that made Hutch sad.

"I didn't say that."

"What are you saying, then?"

"That I know there's more. I need more."

"And you blame Eva for that?"

"I don't blame anybody."

"But you said that when you left Irene," Raye said. Hutch rocked back in his seat as if she'd tried to hit him, but Raye stared him down and he couldn't interpret what was in her eyes—whether it was anger, disgust or simple curiosity.

"Irene doesn't have anything to do with this," he said almost by rote.

"If you say so."

"I know so," he said with finality.

"Be careful, Hutch," Raye said more gently after a moment. "Summers go fast, but that Hawk flying around the corner in the middle of winter will knock you flat on your natural, grown-up behind if you're not careful."

"I know that, too," Hutch said.

# Charley and Steven

## SATURDAY, JUNE 28

Two weeks after Eva and Hutch broke up, Charley and Steven, their "grown" children by different partners, sat sharing a joint in Charley's studio apartment in a small New Jersey city that was close, but not *too* close, to the town where they had both grown up.

"So what did Daddy say to you?" Charley asked.

"Nothing. How about you?"

"Just that he'd left. He sounded real down about it, though. I never thought this would happen to them." Charley sucked in the smoke from the joint. "Did he give you a reason?"

"I didn't ask," Steven said. "Dana and I were headed out the door when he called, and I didn't want to go into it with Dana standing around. He just started the usual song and dance about how we never see each other, and I said yeah, and he asked if we could meet for lunch or dinner the Saturday after the Fourth. I'm supposed to call him back." He sucked his teeth in disgust. "He probably wants to put me through his corny father-son bonding bullshit again, and you *know* I don't want to hear that."

A seed from the marijuana sizzled, popped and fell into Charley's lap, burning a round hole in her red cotton robe. She brushed it off with annoyance. "Damn, Steven, who broke this weed up? . . . You shouldn't be so hard on Daddy."

Steven took the joint from her, drew the smoke in and held his breath as he spoke. "I'm not being hard on him, Charley. I'm being real. . . . Dana brought the shit back from Minnesota. It's homegrown."

"Minnesota?" Charley said in disbelief and they both laughed heartily, as they did whenever they were together and since they'd been kids and everything always seemed to strike them as funny.

Charley and Steven were fast friends from the day they met, telling those who didn't know better—nosy camp counselors, substitute teachers, annoying saleswomen—that they were fraternal twins, and most people believed them. It wasn't too far from the truth. At the very least, they were soul mates who discovered within each other the sibling they had yearned for. Although each looked like their respective mothers— Charley like Eva and Steven like Irene—they were the same age and nearly the same height and weight. They routinely borrowed each other's sweatpants and Polo sweaters and always knew the latest purchase the other made. They shared hip-hop and reggae CDs, hilarious gossip, the occasional joint and significant events in their lives. They critiqued each other's clothes, career choices and lovers and had been right so often about the other's business that they rarely did anything without consulting each other first. They sat side by side on the couch Charley had inherited from a college roommate. A box of Nabisco graham crackers and a bottle of Evian mineral water were on the beat-up footlocker that served as a coffee table.

"Want some Juicy Juice?" Charley asked as Steven rolled another joint.

"Naw. Too sweet."

She went into the refrigerator on the far side of the room, poured some grape juice into a large cut-glass goblet and settled back beside Steven, who lit the joint and noisily pulled in the smoke.

"This whole thing is wack," she said as she grabbed it away from him, took a quick drag and handed it back.

Steven shook his head. "He is such a fucking asshole."

"Don't say that about Daddy." Charley looked genuinely offended.

"Well, that's the way I feel."

"Don't talk that way about him, Steven."

"Don't forget, this is the second time he's put me through this kind of shit."

Charlie thought for a moment and sighed. "Did you tell Irene yet?"

Steven laughed. "My take-no-prisoners mother? Of course I did."

"What did she say?" Interest piqued in Charley's eyes. She had always been fascinated by Irene, a late-blooming civil-rights lawyer.

"She got that funny grin on her face that she always gets when I mention him. Then she shook her head and sighed and asked if I knew how E was taking it."

"What'd you say?"

"I said I hadn't talked to her yet."

"Then what did she say?"

"Nothing. She never puts him down in front of me. But I heard her talking about him to my aunt later. Just like in the old days."

"You think we should do something?"

"What can we do? By the way, how *is* E taking it?" From the beginning of his father's married relationship with Eva, Steven had called Eva "E" rather than "Mom." When Eva and Hutch married and the question came up as to what Steven should call Eva, he solemnly explained that a child could only have one mother and his was at home watching TV. Eva, who immediately agreed, told him he could call her anything he wanted, so he called her E, a shortened name he thought had a nice ring to it, and it had been that ever since.

"I talked to her two weeks ago, the Sunday after Daddy left. He called me Saturday night, and I wanted to get her side of the story."

"He always calls you first." Although Steven quickly glanced away, Charley saw the glimmer of disappointment in his eyes.

"No, don't take it there! He said he'd been trying to get you too, but you weren't home." Charley patted his arm reassuringly. "I spoke to her again yesterday to see if I could borrow that ice chest she keeps in the attic for the Fourth. She's seems cool. Daddy's been gone almost two weeks, and she's been going to the library every day like she usually does. Coming home. Watching TV. Doing whatever Mother does. I guess she's gotten used to him being gone by now."

"So she seems okay?"

"I don't know. You know how aloof Mother can be."

"Moth-thaw!" Steven imitated Charley in a broad voice that sounded like Bette Davis. Charley grinned and waved him away. "How do you really feel about it?" he asked a minute or two later, turning serious.

Charley shrugged like she didn't care, but her shoulders sagged. "I don't know. Maybe it hasn't really hit me. Maybe they'll get back together. I don't know." They shook their heads almost in unison. Steven draped his arm loosely around her shoulder.

"Well, I guess we're supposed to accept all this. We're supposed to be grown. We're not kids anymore."

"I don't feel grown," Charley said.

"Neither do I. I still feel like a kid."

Charley sighed in agreement and then grinned as if she had thought about something funny. "Speaking of kids, I dropped by my grandfather's house yesterday. He wanted me to meet his new girlfriend."

"Word? How's the old guy doing?"

"Roscoe's got a new lady friend," Charley said.

"A new woman? Wow." Steven shook his head in admiration. "My man is a *serious* player. Dude is never without somebody. He sees more action than I do."

"Than you used to," Charley corrected and they both laughed.

"What's her name?"

"Precious." They both giggled at the name. "She seems nice. An old-time blues singer. She used to sing at a place called the Key Club that used to be in Newark." They passed the joint between them for a moment, bobbing their heads to the Peter Tosh CD blasting from Charley's oversize speakers. "So what you doing for the Fourth?"

"Friday? Nothing much. Dana and I will probably roll into the city to check out the fireworks. But we'll definitely ease by your cookout before we go over. Do you need anything?"

"Some wine coolers, a few beers. We're doing it in Bradley's parents' backyard. Bradley is bringing a lot of stuff. I'm borrowing the cooler from Mother. She's bringing it over the morning of the Fourth."

"Ah, Bradley—Mr. Definitely Been Paid. That's nice of him. So he's not pissed about the way things went down?"

"Naw, we're still cool. Cool enough to have the thing at his parents' place anyway."

Charley picked up the CDs that were stacked on the trunk and sorted through them as she tried not to think about Bradley. She had broken off their engagement of six months the week after Hutch had told her he had left Eva. She didn't think the two things were related, but in some way she knew that they probably were. It still made her sad to think about the hurt in Bradley's eyes, and on some level she knew she still loved him. She was certain that he still loved her. But she had begun to feel enclosed by him—fenced in. "He'll get over it," she said, more to herself than to Steven.

"But will you?"

"I already have," she said, sounding sure of herself. Steven looked at her and shook his head, as if he could read through her uncertainty. Charley always acted far more sure of herself than she really was, and Steven was always stunned by how insecure she actually was. Charley continued, "Oh, yeah, I forgot to tell you. Guess who called the house looking for me a couple of weeks ago. Isaiah Lonesome, remember him? Mother told me yesterday, when I called her about the ice chest."

"Isaiah of the soulful eyes and sexy pecs?"

"You noticed?" Charley said in mock surprise.

"Is the world of music still kicking his ass?"

"Probably."

"What did he want?"

"He's looking for a place to live for a couple of months. His roommate is getting married, and they want to stay at his place while they look for something else. I promised him I'd check around."

"I'll see if Dana knows about anything."

"As fine as Isaiah Lonesome is, Dana might just kick your skinny little ass out!"

"Oh, forget you, Miss Bitch."

"Oh, fuck you, Steven! Speaking of fucking, just when do you plan to tell Daddy about Dana?"

"Tell Daddy what?"

"You know what."

Steven shrugged. "That *requested* lunch or dinner, I suppose. That's as good a time as any." He studied a poster of Bob Marley hanging on the wall across the room and blew out a stream of marijuana smoke.

Charley frowned at him. "Don't be looking away."

"I don't really have a choice anymore, do I? About Dad and Dana?"

Charley shook her head that he didn't. "I don't know why you've waited this long.

Steven shrugged. "You know me and bad scenes."

"Dana will be relieved."

"Yeah. Did you tell them yet about you and Bradley?"

"Daddy knows. I told him I had been thinking about

it when he called me that Saturday to tell me about him and mother. I called him last week at work and told him the whole story. I haven't told Mother yet, though."

"Moth-thaw! You'd better say something to E."

Charlie shrugged. "I'll get around to it. The whole thing was unreal anyway." Charley sighed as she thought about Bradley, a generous, soft-spoken investment banker she had met in college and who up until his relationship with Charley had been as careful with his heart as he was with his money. "I know he still cares about me," she said sadly.

"Do you care about him?"

"I don't know what the hell I care about anymore. All I know is I just want to be who I'm going to be. Not feeling any pressure. Live my own life for a change," she said dramatically.

"Who else's life do you think you've been living?"

"My thing with Bradley meant more to her than it meant to me anyway," Charlie said, more to herself than to Steven, not answering his question.

Steven said doubtfully, "So you're definitely going for your dreams now?"

"Definitely."

"But you're going to keep the day job?"

"I have to pay for this stupid place, don't I? But my nights are going to belong to me, baby. All mine!" Charley abruptly stood up, put her hands on her narrow hips and shook them dramatically in Steven's direction before she sat back down. "Everything has gotten so *overwhelming*. That's the way I feel, anyway." She stood back up and went to the cabinet to get another box of graham crackers. She tossed an unopened pack to Steven, then opened one for herself and crammed two crackers into her mouth. "Damn, these things are good!"

"It's the weed, Charley. It's the weed!" Steven opened his pack, carefully ripping off the top, then slowly taking each cracker out of the box, examining it and nibbling off the tip. Charley, who had wolfed hers down, eyed his hungrily. Grinning, Steven waved a cracker in front of her nose and when she snapped at it handed it to her and got another one out for himself. "What do you think he's going to say?"

"Who?"

"Dad."

"Don't worry about it."

"You think the race thing will come into it?"

"Race is the *least* of your worries!" Charley said and they both fell out laughing.

## Eva and Isaiah

**FRIDAY, JULY 4**

It was hot as hell, and the Fourth of July traffic on the Garden State Parkway was thick and slow. Eva was in a foul mood and had been in one all day. She had gotten used to the idea that Hutch probably wasn't coming back anytime soon, but she still missed him more than she cared to admit, even to herself. Loneliness and a low-grade depression dogged most of her days. Yet there were times, admittedly few and far between, when she actually enjoyed her solitude. Nobody grabbed the remote control and switched channels during commercials. She didn't have to cook unless she felt like it. Nobody tossed out snide remarks about her smoking. The toilet seat stayed down. After several weeks of fruitless waiting, Bama had thrown in her lot with Eva, who could now count on the cat's soft body on her side of the bed. Some nights it was still hard getting to sleep, but the warm milk spiked with brandy she'd fixed herself that first night had become a comforting habit, and she looked forward to it.

With the exception of the Masons, whom she assumed Hutch had told, and her boss at the library, Helena Levine, none of their friends and acquaintances knew. When she went down the list of people to whom she habitually sent Christmas cards, she realized that with the exception of her very best friends, there were few with whom she was ready to share her change in marital status. Eva had always been a loner in the smug clique of middle-class African-Americans to which she and Hutch loosely belonged. The group concerns—who got the best deal on a Lexus or Land Rover, whose bright, accomplished offspring got into Yale or Princeton, who was renting this place or that in Sag Harbor or the Vineyard—struck her as superficial. She didn't miss the idle gossip, prying phone calls or boring conversation. She was wary of deep friendships with people preoccupied with other people's business, so she had always been careful with details about her personal life. The good friends she'd made over the years lived in different cities, and the news about her and Hutch would keep until she was able to see them in person and have the kind of soul-searching conversation that required a long night and a bottle of good red wine.

At work, she hadn't even considered mentioning it to anybody besides Helena, a sixtyish, divorced redhead who regularly bummed cigarettes and offered advice, which Eva took because Helena usually knew what she was talking about.

Eva, always the artist, had shied away from getting a "real" job or establishing a career. She had had a number of McJobs—substitute teacher, saleswoman in a boutique, manager of a Starbucks—to give her the time to paint, which she never did. At her father's suggestion, she had started off at the library as a volunteer seven years ago, and two years ago when Hutch's construction business had taken a downturn and they'd needed extra money, she had asked for and been given a full-time job. She was surprised to find how quickly she learned to love it. She relished the peace and civility of the place and found that working there rekindled that studious, serious part of her personality she so often forgot. She enjoyed doing research and making knowledge easily accessible to those who under ordinary circumstances would never be able to find it. Helena said she was a natural librarian—gentle-hearted and patient, with a love for books and a respect for learning. Eva didn't know about that, but she did enjoy her job, even though, like most of her coworkers, she considered it a bridge over troubled waters—a place where you stayed until you could fully commit yourself full-time to your life's work—playing your music, writing your book, earning your Ph.D. For the most part, nobody ever asked about or cared to know anyone's personal business.

She glanced at the temperature gauge on the BMW with concern. The car was great from the end of March through the middle of June and from October to December, but she hated to drive it in extreme weather. Although the car was good for show and in car-years looked like a debutante, it was as temperamental and troublesome as a spoiled dowager. The air that only occasionally made its way out of the air vents was ice-cold in winter and dry-hot in summer. At first, she'd been grateful that Hutch had taken the old Volvo station wagon used for hauling supplies and left her the "good" car, but now she realized that he had probably remembered the hell-days of July and was having a last hearty laugh.

With renewed irritation, she thought about the last time she'd seen him. He'd come by the house on Monday, three days ago, to pick up his summer clothes, which said he would be gone at least until fall. Only by chance had she been at home. She usually worked on Mondays but had taken the day off at the insistence of Helena, to whom she had finally broken down and told about Hutch's leaving the Friday before.

"You just can't trust these damn men for anything, can you?" Helena had told her as she exhaled smoke through her nose. "It's just like with Stanley. Everything is fine, just him complaining like he always does, next thing you know, poof! Twenty years down the goddamn drain! You didn't have a clue, did you?"

"No," Eva had said, which was a lie. The clues had been Cara and the fact that she hadn't been sure enough about their relationship to confront him about it.

"How are you feeling?" Helena's blue eyes were big with concern behind her thick glasses that magnified everything, including the clumps of mascara on her lashes.

"I'm okay," Eva said, realizing that Helena assumed that the breakup had happened the night before, not three weeks ago. She didn't feel like setting her straight.

"I want you to take Monday off. Just take it off! Don't worry about anything around here. Take care of yourself. I also think you should think about going back to school and getting that degree in library science we've been talking about. I won't be here forever. I'll be retiring in another five years, and as much of myself as I've put into this place, I want to make sure it goes to somebody who deeply cares about it.

"You can't depend on men in this life. God knows that's one thing this job has afforded me. I have my own IRA, my own pension, my own savings now. The son of a bitch did me a *favor* when he left me. Maybe that's why men are put on earth, to show us that we really *don't* need them to survive."

Eva had nodded obediently. She wasn't sure how much she "deeply cared" about the library, but she could use a day off.

So Eva had been lying in bed last Monday when Hutch had dropped by. She was thinking about what Helena had said, wondering if maybe she was right. But it was bad enough to be turning forty without needing to think out a new direction for her life. She had always taken a vain, foolish pride that unlike many of the women she knew—black or white—she didn't *have* to work. Marriage to Hutch had given her the privilege of pursuing her true passion, which she never pursued. How could she have been such a fool? And now here she was, one of those pitiful, dependent women they warn you about becoming in women's magazines. No better than Raye Mason.

When she had heard Hutch come in, she rushed downstairs to confront him and followed him back upstairs, ranting and raving, demanding some answers.

"Can we just live with it for a while to see what happens, to see what we should do? We need more time," he had said. He looked embarrassed and rushed. It was clear that he had chosen this time of day deliberately, obviously hoping to avoid her.

"To see what happens! What the hell do you expect to happen?"

"I just have to find out some things. I need some time."

"What kind of things? What kind of time?"

"I don't know!"

"Don't expect me to sit around here waiting for you to come home! I have my own life to lead! I'm doing my own thing, the same as you!" Eva had threatened, but he was out the door, slamming it behind him before she could grab him or demand to know anything else.

"Goddammit," she said now as a blast of hot air from the car's air vent brushed her sweating forehead. The temperature gauge took a sudden leap upward, and Eva instinctively slowed the car down, cursing all the while.

The afternoon had been particularly unpleasant. After finding the ice chest that Charley had begged to borrow, Eva had dropped it at her daughter's fiancé's parents' house as requested, and Charley, always short of money, had asked to borrow her last ten dollars, which she'd given her with the notion of borrowing some money from her father when she saw him later that day. As luck would have it, Eva had run into her future in-laws as she was leaving their home. They had an hour to kill before they headed off to Sag Harbor, so they begged her to join them for a drink on their breezy patio. Not wanting to be rude, Eva sat down and tried to keep Hutch's name out of the conversation as she gulped down lukewarm pineapple juice and became increasingly annoyed as she watched them. They were a couple dangerously involved with each other—touching, smiling, glancing, cooing—like child-obsessed first-parents. They alluded to the fact that Charley and Bradley were "having some problems" but assured Eva with smiles and winks that the "loving couple" were sure to "find their way back to each other." Eva had no idea what they were talking about, and their saccharine confidence that love conquers all made her sick to her stomach. And her day got worse.

After leaving them, she'd headed to her father's place for a "barbecue" and to spend some "quality time," as he put it, with his new girlfriend Precious. That scene was one she didn't enjoy recalling.

Her father, Roscoe Lilton, who had always enjoyed the company of women, had been through at least a woman a year since her mother's death ten years ago. Except for his dangerously high blood pressure, which continuously worried Eva since *his* father Charles had died of a stroke, he was a remarkably fit seventy-two-year-old. He had worked most of his life as a librarian but read everything he could about the stock market and in recent years had managed to wisely invest enough money to provide himself a very comfortable retirement. Roscoe Lilton wasn't rich, but he was close to it.

From the moment Eva arrived, he gushed and fussed over his new love, grinning like a teenager as he handed Eva a glass of overly sweet lemonade.

"Isn't she something?" he whispered in her ear more than once. Eva found it disturbing that her father at this stage of his life sought and seemed to need her approval of this new woman, and she only begrudgingly gave it.

"Scoe is always talking about you," said Precious Andrews. Her tone was formal and her voice was low, husky and strong. Eva vaguely remembered her father mentioning something about the woman being a retired blues singer, and she looked as if she belonged on stage. She was wearing a silky turquoise pantsuit, which flowed unevenly over her ample body. Her face was as smooth and brown as a chestnut, and her hair was a strange shade of red. She looked to be in her early sixties. She struck Eva as standoffish and unfriendly, not at all like the others, who were overfriendly and eager to please. Her father had mentioned that she had been widowed twice and divorced once, which Eva found ominous. She had always been able to quickly categorize the women in her father's life—the brittle ex-teacher, the moody loner, the chic club woman. They had all had bits and pieces of her dead mother. But this one was different. Eva regarded her uneasily.

She and her father had never been as close as her mother and she, but since her death they'd managed to forge their own relationship. Eva had become as protective of him as her mother had been—keeping on him about his diet, reminding him to see his doctor and take his pills, nagging him to cut down on his drinks and to be wary of fortune hunters. Most of the women he saw these days had outlived their spouses and due to generous insurance policies were as well off if not better off than he was. Eva studied this new woman with a suspicious eye. She also glanced disapprovingly at his lit cigar and mint julep. But he rolled his eyes and poured Precious another drink.

After gagging down a bowl of the woman's lousy potato salad and some salty barbecued spareribs her father had bought at a nearby Pathmark, Eva made her excuses and left as soon as she could, so upset she'd forgotten to borrow some money.

But they did seem happy, she had to admit that. Roscoe Lilton at seventy-two was part of a couple, which was more than she could say for herself. Couplehood, she realized when she'd turned onto the Garden State Parkway, was one of the things she missed. This Fourth of July was the first holiday in ten years she hadn't spent with Hutch.

As the needle on the thermometer gauge rose, Eva moved to the far right lane, slowing down again and wondering if she should get off at the next exit.

"You stupid piece of junk," she muttered as she slowly downshifted, hoping that move would keep the car from overheating.

Eva didn't know a thing about cars—car maintenance had been Hutch's department, along with taking out the trash, doing repairs and mowing the lawn, and a sense of shame swept her when she thought about it. She was like some nineteenth century Southern white woman, dependent upon some patriarch for everything, forced to return to the home of her father when things went wrong—like she could ever return to Scoe Lilton's house.

The narrow black needle rose yet again and Eva realized with horror that its ups and downs had nothing to do with how fast or slowly she drove. When the needle soared into the middle of the bright red danger zone, she realized she was probably on the verge of doing some irreversible damage to the engine, so she snapped on her hazard lights, pulled over to the side of the road and stopped in the first spot she saw.

She sat in the car for about fifteen minutes, smoking her last cigarette, staring at the gauge and complaining to herself. Then she carefully put the key in the ignition, said a prayer and turned it slowly, hoping against hope that whatever was supposed to catch would and that the needle would stay where it belonged. For a moment the car purred in its usual tone, and the needle hovered within the safe range. She sighed with relief and thanked the Lord. But before she could put it into first gear, the needle again popped into the red zone. She turned off the car and let it cool for another fifteen minutes. Then she turned it back on and watched helplessly as the needle edged into the red again.

*Maybe if I open the hood and let the air hit it,* she thought. She got out of the car, amazed at how hot the body of the thing had become, and popped the hood slowly, half expecting a gush of white-hot steam to scorch her. When it was open, she realized again that she had no idea what she was doing. After about twenty minutes, she closed the hood and tried the engine again. Her heart sank as the needle made its slow, sure climb back into the red.

It was getting dark, and Eva realized with alarm that she could end up sitting on the Parkway all night before anyone realized she was missing. Charley was partying hearty with friends and her last ten dollars. Scoe was probably curled up somewhere drinking scotch with Precious. More than likely, Steven was in New York hanging out with Dana, whom he had recently introduced her to. And Hutch—God knew where he was. And here she was. Stuck on the Garden State Parkway, halfway between hell and the nearest exit, with the sun sinking in the sky, only loose change in her purse and no cigarettes to calm her nerves. She got out of the car, slammed the hood down with a vengeance and kicked the car's front tire as hard as she could.

"Goddamn you!" she screamed as she kicked and kicked. "You ridiculous, worthless little car! I hate you! I hate you!" She screamed at the car, at Hutch, at everything that had happened to her that afternoon. "Why me? Why me? *Why me?*" She railed at the sky and stars now visible. She walked around to the back and kicked that tire too. A streak of pain shot up her calf. She kicked it again with the other foot.

It was at that moment that Eva noticed a black Geo pull up about fifteen feet behind her.

"Thank God! A cop!" she muttered aloud. Eva didn't entirely trust the police, but under these circumstances she decided to have some faith. He was probably undercover, she realized—in that car he had to be. And she could see that he was a black man; that was a plus too. Embarrassed, she realized how she must look. She turned to face him squarely with a contrite smile on her lips, trying to look respectable and vaguely wondering why the police chose Geos as undercover cars. Surely they didn't go fast enough to catch anybody.

But her common sense took over as the door opened and he climbed out, and she realized with a jolt who he *really* must be. Here she was, a woman, possibly deranged, obviously alone, standing next to an expensive—albeit useless—car. The word "victim" was stamped across her forehead like a caste mark. A sudden terrible sense of vulnerability swept her. She quickly climbed back into her car, locked the doors, rolled up the windows, closed her eyes and prayed that whoever it was wouldn't shoot her before he demanded the keys she would gladly give. The occupant of the Geo approached.

"Hey, Mrs. Hutchinson! It's me, don't be scared."

Eva slowly opened her eyes. "Isaiah Lonesome," she said in utter astonishment, when she recognized the handsome young man who stood in front of her.

"Yeah," he said with a touch of irony.

"I seem to be having some trouble with my car," Eva said as she climbed out to face him.

"Tires acting up?" His amused smile told her he'd witnessed her madwoman act, and she cringed.

"Lost my temper." There was no sense in lying.

"Are you okay?" The man always seemed to be asking her if she was okay.

"Of course I'm okay. I'm fine."

"You sure about that?" There was that same note of condescending amusement.

"Thank you for your concern, but yes, I am," Eva said stiffly.

"Would you like some help?"

*No, I just want to stand here like a fool on the Parkway,* Eva thought, but said with a pleasant smile, "If it wouldn't be too much trouble."

"Not at all," said Isaiah Lonesome. He popped the hood open and bent over the car as if he knew what he was doing.

Despite herself and the mood she was in, Eva found herself noticing the cut of his sleeveless T-shirt and the way it emphasized the muscles in his chest and arms. He was wearing worn but obviously expensive jeans that fit his body nicely. He was also apparently one of these men who took working out seriously. She had always liked his eyes, which were slightly slanted and a strange, soft brown in color. When she'd met him before, his head had been shaved, but now he wore short dreadlocks, which fell fetchingly over his eyes while he worked and emphasized his face, which had good, classic angles. (The artist in her noticed that.) His lips were sensual, full, and he seemed to like touching them with his tongue. (The woman in her noticed that.) She could certainly understand what Charley saw in him, at least physically. Embarrassed, she snatched her eyes from the man's body.

*Is that what six months without sex has led me to?* she thought. "For crying out loud," she scolded herself aloud without realizing it.

"Excuse me?" he glanced over his shoulder.

"I just said, for crying out loud, what a bummer this car acting up like this. Do you know what's wrong?"

"No idea."

He stood back up and wiped his hands on his pants. "Better not drive it."

"Tell me something I don't already know."

"I'm sorry. I'm not a mechanic."

"That's obvious," Eva spoke her thoughts out loud before she realized it.

"Do you always have an attitude with folks who stop on the road to help you out?" That amused half-smile played on his lips again.

"No," Eva said quickly, momentarily shamed. "I've had a real bad day."

"Well, that's not my fault."

"It's not my fault either. I'm sorry," she said, looking him in the eyes again, which were not long-lashed and deep like Hutch's but more expressive. It was probably hard for eyes like that to lie. "Thank you for stopping."

"No problem."

They both stood uncomfortable with the silence, Eva unsure what to do or say next.

"Did you call Triple A?" Isaiah asked.

"Call Triple A?" Eva's eyes glazed over.

"No car phone, then?"

"Car phone? No," she said, cursing to herself for not listening to Hutch when he'd told her to get one. But even if she'd had it, her Triple A membership had expired. Although he continued to pay the mortgage, utilities and several other important bills, several minor ones—the Triple A among them—had not yet been paid.

Would he continue to put his checks into their joint account? Would he keep most of it for himself? He would have to if he rented a place. Would he consider the insurance on her car an essential bill, worthy of payment? What about the cable? Smaller bills had come in and Eva had just kept tucking them away, trying not to think about them, continuing to spend her weekly paycheck without completely facing the bleak reality of her new situation.

"Would you like me to give you a lift somewhere?"

"Huh?" Eva slumped back against her car, the weight of these realizations upon her. Hutch would fix the leaks, change the tires, give her the money so she could pay the bills, keep her living in the style to which she had become accustomed, even though she told herself—and it seemed true, to most outward appearances—that she was an independent, self-reliant, confident woman. It had all rested on Hutch, who could, willy-nilly, decide late one June night to disappear because he felt no "joy" in what they'd built together for the last ten years. And here she was, a dollar in change in her pocketbook and a Triple A card that had expired. Had she been in some kind of a daze for the past two and a half weeks—past ten years?

"Mrs. Hutchinson?"

"Eva."

"Eva." Her name had a different sound coming from his mouth. "Would you like me to take you somewhere, maybe to a phone booth or garage or something?"

Eva nodded that he could and without saying anything else checked the car locks on her car and turned on the alarm system (not that it mattered). She climbed into the passenger's side of Isaiah Lonesome's subcompact, thinking that it had been a very long time since she'd been in such a small car. Hell, it had been a very long time since she'd even sat beside a man other than Hutch in *any* size car, she realized, and she found that thought strangely distressing. She reached for a cigarette, remembered she didn't have one and took a deep breath instead, hoping it would quell her craving.

"Yeah, that definitely helps sometimes," Isaiah said.

"What?"

"Taking deep breaths like that, taking it in, letting it out. Let all your troubles go with it. Believe it will make you feel better."

*Spare me the wisdom of people under thirty,* she thought with irritation and vaguely wondered if she should ask him to stop so that she could pick up some cigarettes and then decided that she'd try to do without them. He probably wouldn't want her smoking in his car anyway. She'd heard that if you could get through that initial first craving for nicotine you could make it for at least an hour or two until the urge hit again. She took another deep breath. He took a quick look at his watch.

"Were you on your way somewhere?" she asked to keep from thinking about the cigarette. *But why else would he be on the parkway on the Fourth of July?* she chided herself.

"I've got a gig in an hour or so, that's all. But don't worry 'bout it. I'll make it."

"Where's the gig?" The word "gig" felt strange. She hadn't realized musicians still called it that.

"City."

Charley had mentioned he played sometimes at a club in New York. Eva glanced at the clock, which said eight. It was later than she thought.

"You can just drop me off at the nearest gas station, and I'll be fine. Thank you again." She wondered if she had remembered to give Charley his message and vaguely wondered what it had been. She hoped he wouldn't ask her about it. "So you're a musician?"

"Yeah."

"What do you play?" She tried to make conversation.

"Horn."

"What kind of horn?" There *were* a lot of horns in the world.

"Trumpet."

"Oh, like, uh, Miles Davis?" She had tried to think of somebody who was still alive but the only other horn player she could think of at the moment was Kenny G, whom instinct told her she shouldn't mention.

"In my dreams." He shifted his eyes toward her and smiled. He accidentally brushed the side of her pants leg, apologizing as he shifted the car into fourth gear, and she noticed his fingers, which were long and slender. A musician's hands.

"So you play music for a living?" she asked and then realized he had just told her that, and it was really none of her business anyway what, if anything, he did for a living

"Yeah, I guess you could say that. You're a librarian, right?"

"No!" Eva said it a bit too loudly. "I'm an artist," she added, then wished she hadn't.

"Hey, I didn't know that. Your daughter never mentioned that you were an artist. Wow, an artist! Are you showing anywhere?"

"Showing?" Eva said the word as if she'd never heard it before. "No." God, she should have left herself in the damn library. She spent more time there than in her studio. "Actually, I haven't drawn anything in a while."

"Hmm."

"Hmm what?"

"Hmm nothing."

"In other words, you're not an artist unless you can make a living performing or practicing your art?"

"No. I just said hmm, that's all." He glanced at her curiously. "I was just thinking that I know what you mean. I go through dry periods like that too. Don't be so defensive."

"I'm not being defensive."

"If you say so." He abruptly turned the radio to a jazz station, which marked the end of their conversation.

When they approached a gas station, he pulled into it. "Maybe they can help you out. I need to get some gas anyway."

"Thanks again. At least let me buy the gas." Eva sat with her hands crossed in her lap, thinking that she *had* been defensive.

"Thanks. Would you like me to go in with you?" he said after a moment.

"No, no. I'm sorry," she said, realizing he was waiting for her to get out of the car.

"Hey, quit apologizing. You have nothing to be sorry for."

"I've just got a lot on my mind,"

"Do you want to talk about it?" His eyes were solemn as they searched her face, like he really meant it.

"No," Eva said and got out of the car, anxious suddenly to be gone—in her car or in the gas station truck to the quiet protection of her own home.

The teenager behind the desk, eyes glued to the latest edition of *Vibe* magazine, ears covered by earphones attached to a radio that peeked out of his shirt pocket, barely looked at her as she came into the station.

"Help you?" he asked, his head bobbing to the beat.

"Yes, thank you. The gentleman in the car needs some gas. That is what you sell here, right? And I need a tow truck. My car is disabled on the highway."

"Huh?" Annoyed, Eva repeated herself.

"I'll get the gas but the tow truck is broke. Plus it's a holiday, and the guy who runs it went home."

Eva stared at him for a moment, and then collapsed into the chair beside the desk.

"What do you expect me to do?"

He looked at her with a blank expression on his face. "Beats the heck out of me, lady."

"Well, can I use your phone, then?" she asked, and he handed it to her. She held it for a few moments, trying to decide who to call. Against hope, she called Triple A, and found that what she'd feared had come to pass: the card had expired a week ago. If she had it towed, she'd have to use her American Express card, which thank God was okay, but she'd have to make sure she found a service station that took it, and when she looked around the office she didn't see any stickers. She called her father and then Charley, neither of whom answered. Desperately, she tried to remember Donald Mason's number, drew a blank and slammed down the phone.

"You okay, lady?"

*Why does everyone keep asking me that?* she thought. "Fine, fine." She said it twice.

"You still want the gas?"

Eva nodded that she did and followed him out to Isaiah's car. She watched as he put the gas into the tank and then, realizing she had offered to pay without having any money, climbed back into the car and slumped into the passenger's seat.

"So everything is cool?" Isaiah asked.

"I gave my last ten dollars to Charley, and they don't take American Express. I can't pay for the gas."

"Hey, forget about it," Isaiah said and handed the boy a twenty-dollar bill.

"They can't do it. They can't get my car. They don't have a tow truck." She watched the boy as he nonchalantly went back into the office and slammed the door behind him. She wondered how it could get any worse.

"Want to try another station?"

"No."

"What do you want to do?"

Eva sighed, sad and defeated.

"Want me to drive you home?" As he said it, Eva noticed that he gave a quick, furtive glance at the clock, which now read eight-forty.

"Just drop me off somewhere," she said wearily.

"Like where?"

"Anywhere."

"But where?"

Eva shrugged, and Isaiah pulled out of the gas station.

"So home it is?" He studied her as he kept one eye on the road. Eva didn't say anything. They drove in silence for about fifteen minutes before he spoke again. "So did you call somebody?"

"Nobody was home."

"How about your husband? He may be out here looking for you now. He must be worried as hell about you. Maybe he—" Isaiah stopped in mid-sentence when he glanced at Eva's face and saw the look in her eyes.

"My husband?" Her voice was a croak. "My husband? Are you talking about Hutch? Lucas Hutchinson, Junior?" She screamed the name out in a plaintive wail of pain and rage. Embarrassed, Isaiah fastened his eyes to the road. Eva buried her face in her hands and began to weep.

"Stop it! Stop it! Stop it!" she scolded herself between sobs. Isaiah pulled over to the side of the road.

"Hey," he said as he leaned over to comfort her. "Hey, hey. Nothing can be that bad. What about those breaths you were taking? Nothing can be that bad."

"It is that bad." Her nose was running, and she looked desperately through her bag for a Kleenex, finally tossing the bag on the floor of the car in desperation when she couldn't find one. Isaiah offered her a roll of toilet paper that he took out of the glove compartment. She wiped her eyes and nose.

"What's wrong?"

"Everything. Everything! My husband of ten years has left me for no reason that he's willing to say. My house is falling apart. I don't have any money. I'm broke. Here I am, a grown woman with about as much going for me as that trifling teenager back in that garage. I'm just trifling! I don't even have a job I can call a real job. My life is in shambles. Nothing is holding together! Everything is falling apart!" She screeched out the last part, and Isaiah watched her curiously. A slight smile came to his lips.

"Well, you've got your health."

Eva glared at him, her eyes narrowed in anger. "How could you say something like that to me? I've poured out my heart to you, and all you can do is come up with some trite-ass bullshit like that?"

"Well, what am I supposed to say? I really don't know you that well."

"Say *something*, I don't know! Something sympathetic. Something nice."

He shrugged. "I'm sorry. I wish I knew what to say to make you feel better."

"Just shut up."

"Well, it's the truth, isn't it? You're healthy. You're strong. You're smart. You can take it." Eva turned her back on him, dramatically squeezing around to face the passenger's-side window in the tiny car. "Hey listen, nothing ever seems serious to me. That's just the way I am."

"Well, maybe you should learn to keep your shallowness to yourself."

"Yeah, you're right. Maybe I should." They drove for a while in tense silence before he said anything else. "Hey, Eva?"

"What?" She glared at him out of the corner of her eye.

"Listen, I think I better make it into the city in time to do this gig. Wanna come?"

Without looking at him or turning him down, Eva suddenly remembered Janet Kujinski, the little blond girl who lived next door when her family moved from the warmth of the South to that hateful street where none of the kids said shit to her until the morning Janet peeked from her door and said the two magical words: "Wanna play?"

*Wanna play? Wanna dance? Wanna come?*

"Okay," Eva said, and for the first time that day she smiled.

# Eva and Isaiah

## FRIDAY NIGHT AND SATURDAY MORNING

Traffic being what it was, Eva and Isaiah didn't get to the club until nearly ten. On the way over, he warned her about the bandleader Sky Langston, an old-time piano player who had been famous in the seventies, obscure in the eighties and was on his way back up. He didn't like his musicians to be late, and he was bound to give them some lip.

"Where the fuck you been?" Sky Langston said the moment they walked in the door. His eyes roamed Eva's body lazily, and there was a know-it-all smirk on his ashy lips. He was a low-rent version of Donald Mason, and Eva disliked him on sight. Anger flitted across Isaiah's face.

"Sorry I'm late, man. I had to help a lady out."

"Is that what they call it these days?"

Eva dug her nails into the palm of her hand to keep it from flying across his face.

Isaiah reared back. "Mind your own goddamn business, man." There was an unmistakable threat in his voice and stance that Eva appreciated. Langston held up his long, thin hands in acquiescence.

"Sorry, man, but we got a show to put on."

"I'm here now." Isaiah's eyes flashed with anger.

"Hey, man, it's cool. By the way, miss, I'm Sky Langston," he said as he grabbed Eva's hand. "I didn't mean to insult you. I just got to keep these jigaboos in line."

"Eva Hutchinson." She saw that he'd noticed her wedding ring, which despite its age and worn condition, chose this moment to sparkle.

"Lefty, huh?" He let her know he'd seen it.

"All my life," Eva said stiffly as she jerked her hand back and glanced nervously around the room for a means of escape.

"Want to sit near the front?" Isaiah bent over and whispered; his warm breath in her ear startled her.

"Anywhere!" she whispered back desperately, and followed him toward the bandstand. She slid behind a small table, suddenly aware of the other musicians who were seated nearby and who had focused their attention on her.

"I'll be back in a minute. Get yourself a drink." Isaiah went to the edge of the stage and put his horn down. Eva nodded wearily.

*This is definitely a mistake,* she thought. She needed a cigarette, opened her bag to find one, then remembered she didn't have any. "Dammit," she muttered. A couple at a nearby table glanced at her strangely, and Eva shifted her eyes away and looked around the club.

The club, which was called Le Muse, was a hip,

cozy spot in SoHo, which, like its co-owner Sky Langston, had been famous once and was making its way back. It was decorated in dark colors—deep maroons, navy blues, chocolate browns—and the red walls were hung with photos of well-known jazz musicians blowing horns, sitting behind pianos and leaning on basses. There wasn't a big crowd tonight, maybe six or so at the bar, with groups of singles or threes crouched together around the rickety tables. Many of the patrons were white, as were most of the women seated near the stage. These seats, Eva realized with a jolt, must be the ones reserved for the musicians and their girlfriends, several of whom studied her curiously. She was suddenly conscious of her worn jeans and sloppy T-shirt. She wondered if she could find a car service that took American Express.

*But why in God's name should I care what people think?* she wondered. *I'm not with Isaiah Lonesome. We're not on a date.* Holding her head unnaturally high, she nodded haughtily at the women who scrutinized her, and then glanced around the room for Isaiah.

"Help you, ma'am?" A petite waitress with purple and orange hair popped out of nowhere to take her order.

"A glass of red wine, please."

"We don't have red wine by the glass."

"Then white."

"Chardonnay, Pinot Grigio or the house wine?"

"Whatever is cheapest."

"That's the house wine. Chablis."

"Pinot Grigio." Eva hated Chablis and was sick of Chardonnay.

"That's twice as much."

"Then give me the Chardonnay."

"I think we're out of that."

"Then bring me the Chablis!"

"Give her the Pinot Grigio," said a sultry female voice from the next table. Startled, Eva turned to face a thin white woman with flaming red hair, who was about thirty-five and dressed in a black turtleneck sweater. Tiny diamond earrings sparkled in her ears, and a matching stud was in her nose. "I'm Penny," she said. "You must be Isaiah Lonesome's new lady! He's a nice guy, isn't he? When did you-all start going out?"

"Penny?" Eva said the woman's name back to her as if she'd never heard the name before.

"Yeah. Penny Pedersen. He's a nice guy, isn't he, Isaiah? He used to go out with a friend of mine. Hey! Isaiah! Over here!" Penny, a bundle of energy, shouted wildly, and Isaiah, emerging with Sky Langston from a back room, gave her an enthusiastic wave.

"Do you take American Express?" Eva asked the waitress.

"Don't worry about it. I'll cover it," Penny volunteered.

"That's all right."

Penny shrugged. "They'll probably put it on Isaiah's tab, then. So when did you-all start going out?"

"We're not going out." Eva's voice was controlled as she glanced in the woman's general direction without actually looking at her.

"This is your first time out, then?"

Startled by the woman's nosiness, Eva answered without thinking, "No. He used to date my daughter."

An odd smile crossed Penny's lips. "Keep it in the family, huh?"

Mortified, Eva glared at the woman, and then shifted her eyes to the empty stage, her lips tight.

"What's your daughter's name? Maybe I know her."

"I really doubt that," Eva said and made a point of examining the small printed menu in front of her. Penny, taking the hint, turned back to her drink.

"You okay?" Isaiah said as he slipped into the seat across from her.

"Yeah." His knee brushed hers and Eva pulled hers back against her seat. "Maybe I'd better go home."

"Home? Now? Are you kidding?"

"Well, I mean, I can get a cab from here. Maybe a car service will—"

"What happened? You were doing fine when I left."

"I'm fine now," Eva said, resenting the patronizing concern in his voice, then added, "It was so nice of you to ask me over here, to look out for me. I really appreciate it. But I just don't want to be in the way. I'm really not into music much anyway."

Isaiah leaned back against his chair and studied her, a slight smile on his lips. "Not into music? How can somebody *not* be into music? That's like not being into spring or summer vacation."

Eva glanced at Penny, hoping she hadn't overheard the exchange, but she seemed to be minding her own business.

"I mean I don't listen to it much. I don't go to clubs or anything, I—look, I'm the reason you're late. I can catch a cab or a car service or the Path train to Newark and then take a cab home from there."

He looked at her as if she were speaking a foreign language. "Eva, you don't have any money. How are you going to take a cab? Relax. Have a drink—on me.

Enjoy the set. Take it easy. You've had a hard day . . . Eva." He said her name again, as if he enjoyed saying it.

The waitress brought her drink. Eva stared at it for a moment and then gulped it down in one swallow.

"Damn," Isaiah said, with unconcealed amusement.

"I'm not a lush."

"Did I say that?"

"I could see it in your eyes."

"Hey, baby, I don't judge folks. You're just a lady who has had a hard day."

Eva didn't know how she felt about the "baby" business. The man had gone from the reverent "Mrs. Hutchinson" to the casual "Eva" to the *too* familiar "baby" in less than three hours. She thought she'd better get things back on a formal level.

"I have to thank you again, uh, Mr. Lonesome." She'd paused as if it had taken her a moment to remember his name. "But I'm sure that either Charley, Steven or my father is home by now, and they won't mind driving into the city to pick me up. And I'm going to try that car service too. I'm sure I can find one that will take American Express. I don't want you to have to drive me all the way back to Jersey and—"

He interrupted her. "I live in Jersey too, *Mrs. Hutchinson.* For the time being anyway." He studied her for a moment, as if something were on his mind, and then shrugged. "Hey, suit yourself. It's up to you."

"Thank you for everything."

"Stop thanking me. Stop saying you're sorry."

"Stop telling me what to do!"

Ignoring her tone, he grinned. "Listen . . . Mrs. Hutchinson. I got to do this thing." He headed toward the bandstand and said over his shoulder, "Hope you're around after the set."

Eva settled back in her seat. Because she hadn't eaten since noon, the wine had gone straight to her head. She didn't feel like making her way over the laps of strangers, staring women and crowded tables to the phone at the other end of the room. *What madness has brought me here?* she wondered as she closed her eyes and tried to keep her head from spinning. *Was it anger at Hutch? Loneliness? Boredom?* The waitress plunked down a bowl of peanuts and she gobbled them down in handfuls. Temporarily satiated, she focused on the stage, wondering how long this "set" was going to last.

There were four other musicians besides Isaiah on the stage. Sky Langston, who was the oldest, sat hunched in front of his piano like an animal ready to feed. The drummer, a wisp of a man in a red vest who had surprisingly muscular biceps (Did they *all* work out? Eva wondered) swayed rhythmically in front of his drums. The bassist, who was white, middle-aged and dressed in a black suit and narrow tie nearly identical to the one worn by Langston, sat on a stool, his eyes dreamy, his bass resting on his knees. The tenor saxophonist, whose long, reddish dreadlocks weighed as heavily on his head as his horn around his neck, stared at Penny, who stared back at him. Responding to some subtle cue given by Sky Langston and missed by Eva, a hush suddenly went through the crowd, and the musicians picked up their instruments and began to play. Sound rushed into the room in a cacophony of brass, beats and cymbals. Eva, glancing around, noticed that with the exception of herself, everyone seemed caught up in it. To her, it simply sounded as if everybody were playing off-key as loudly and raucously as they could.

Penny leaned toward her. "Do you hear that? Do you hear it! It's great, isn't it? It's so now. So avant-garde!" Eva, stifling an impulse to put her hands over her ears, said nothing. "Isn't Isaiah great? Shit. He's such a fucking talent! He's such a fucking talent."

Eva nodded politely but kept her eyes on the stage. The music stopped as suddenly as it began, and the room exploded in applause. The musicians paused for a beat or two, and then rushed into the next number, which started off slowly and ended up the way first had begun. By the third number, Eva was amazed to find that she too was caught up in the energy, which wasn't surprising because it electrified the room.

"He's going to step out with a solo in a minute," Penny whispered. Eva wondered if Penny was talking about the tenor saxophonist she had been eyeing, but then realized she must be talking about Isaiah. "Listen, listen," Penny panted, her eyes fastening on him. Her lips parted slowly as if she were in the throes of an orgasm, and then she closed her eyes and slowly opened them.

*What the hell is wrong with this woman?* Eva thought with irritation. But she knew: Black Male Exotica. She flashed back to some of the white girls she'd known in high school who couldn't get enough of the black football players—all fine and gleaming with sweat as they strutted off the football fields in their red and white jerseys. They were the same boys who wouldn't speak to her or any of the other black girls when they saw them in the halls, and who the white girls would never take home to meet their daddies, and who would cry rape if Daddy ever found out. Nothing but studs, those young brothers had been. Walking, swaggering black dicks. Eva's old rage came rushing back, her anger about black men who only slept with white women. She swallowed it down hard.

Was Isaiah Lonesome one of those men who always went to the other side, always found white women more desirable, more appealing than the ones who looked like their mamas? Maybe that was why Charley, who was far too proud to admit she'd been beaten out by a white woman, had actually broken up with him. Eva eyed Isaiah suspiciously as he performed, wondering what he thought about this woman who obviously had a thing for black men—or one black man anyway.

*But what the hell is it to me?* Eva scolded herself. *Why should I care?* Yet like every other woman in the room, her eyes were pinned on Isaiah Lonesome. The quintet had slipped into a slow, sensuous ballad, and he stepped forward to play. He was clearly lost in his music. His eyes were closed, his body swaying rhythmically, his lips and tongue pressed deeply into the mouthpiece of the horn—and he did have some pretty lips. When he played he gave everything he had over to the music. Eva went with him, coasting with the sound that came out of his horn, captivated by him and the music he played.

*He's* really *good*, Eva thought, even though until that moment she hadn't been sure what *really* good playing was. But maybe it was like it was in the world of visual art, she realized, each musical choice marked with its own clarity, meaning and elegance. Penny glanced at her with an I-told-you-so smile on her face, and despite herself, Eva returned her smile. Applause broke out at the end of his solo, and Eva clapped too, smiling up at him as he nodded a respectful thanks.

"Oooh, go on, brother, blow that thang," Penny squealed, destroying any momentary camaraderie Eva had felt with her. But in the spirit of the music, Eva let her annoyance go. That is what good music did, she realized, took you outside yourself, to a place beyond pettiness and false divisions.

The next piece was like the first, up-tempo with no easily recognized structure, but Eva was into it now, waiting for Isaiah's solo, which came near the end in a cascade of screaming high and moaning low notes that brought the whole composition together in a seamless wall of sound. *Where did he go to find it?* Eva wondered. What part of himself had he wandered into? She could tell by his concentration that the beautiful sound that seemed to pour so effortlessly from his instrument was the culmination of several gifts: the strength in his agile fingers; the skill with which his full lips played in the metal mouthpiece; the way his body seemed to reach into the melody and pour it back out. He played with an ease and a graceful intensity that grabbed her, wouldn't let her go. When the rest of the band took over, she listened only for the sound of his horn, oblivious to everybody else.

Sky Langston introduced the band members in the middle of the next piece, and they ended with a ballad—"If I Loved You." Isaiah's solo brought tears to Eva's eyes. It reached deep into her, stroking a part that went beyond reason or good sense; it was almost sexual. Penny glanced over at her, her eyes gleaming too.

"He's so-o-o good. He's the best one up there, isn't he?"

"He's definitely talented."

Penny studied her with a question in her eyes. "So you're here because he used to date your daughter?"

"We're also friends," Eva said, catching that attitude she'd dropped earlier because it was none of the woman's business.

The group took a quick break, and the musicians went into a side room to confer with Sky Langston. They came back and played a shorter, lazier set and finally, exhausted and sweating like those football players Eva remembered, piled from the stage to greet the women who waited for them. Isaiah, amid pats on the back and hugs, made his way back to the table, beaming with excitement. Penny popped up the moment he arrived, gave him a long, body-clinging hug topped with a fleeting kiss and then left. Through the window, Eva saw her and the saxophone player climb into a waiting black Mercedes—S-Class, she couldn't help but notice. Isaiah dropped down in the chair opposite Eva and ordered a Sprite.

"Did you like it?" He searched her face. Eva was lost for a moment in his eyes.

"It was incredible."

"So you won't go around saying you're not into music anymore?"

"No, I guess not."

"I was playing for you." Embarrassed, Eva dropped her eyes and stared at her glass. Isaiah, embarrassed now too, shook his head as if still in wonder. "Yeah, that was something else."

"You've got a real fan in the woman with the nose

stud who was here a moment ago. The redhead," Eva said because she couldn't think of anything else to say. She watched him closely for his response.

"Penny?"

"Yeah. I think she left with the—"

"Saxophone player." He filled it in and laughed. "Penny, yeah. She's something else too."

"You used to go out with one of her friends, she said. Was she white?" Eva, realizing the question made her sound like a bigot, regretted it the moment it left her mouth. "Not that it matters," she stammered out. *Not that it's any of my damn business one way or the other either.* Isaiah looked puzzled, gave a short shrug and didn't answer.

"Well"—Eva cleared her throat—"I can still probably get that cab if—"

"Hey, we're all going to grab something to eat. But if you want, I can still drive you home now. Your choice."

"You don't mind if I go?"

"If I didn't want you to come, I'd take you to get that cab you were talking about earlier."

They walked to a twenty-four-hour diner a few blocks from the club. Eva ordered the Pancake'n'Sausage special, and gobbled down the sausages as greedily as if she hadn't sworn off pork three years ago. Their booth was a narrow one, and she was conscious of how closely they were squeezed together. She let her body ease into his. She was used to Hutch's soft and hard places, and Isaiah's were different. It was strange yet titillating to sit so close to him, feeling his body move, studying his body movements with her own, and she liked the way it felt. She liked the way he laughed too, and the way his eyes would turn sad suddenly without explanation, and then sparkle again. He was as easy to read as Charley or Steven. His eyes would always give him away. And they were some of the prettiest eyes she'd ever seen on a man—expressive and gentle. But the chin that she'd seen him thrust out with arrogance when he played eclipsed any girlishness that might creep into his face. And then there were those lips.

Eva was glad nobody at the table could read her thoughts, even though she suspected everybody assumed the worst about their relationship. They were all too friendly, too accommodating, and it was clear that they had made the same assumption that Penny and Sky Langston had made. What else could they assume? But nobody asked any questions, and soon Eva actually felt comfortable enough to bum a cigarette from the drummer, and he felt easy enough to offer her a drag off his joint, which she politely refused, when they drove him uptown.

The morning sun was shining by the time they drove through the Lincoln Tunnel back to Jersey. Isaiah pulled off at the exit where she'd abandoned her car, and Eva gave the car another try. The cooling-off period had obviously done it some good; it started with its familiar purr. Eva said a prayer of gratitude.

"You better have a mechanic check it out as soon as you can," Isaiah suggested, and Eva wondered where she would get the money for that. The thought of asking Hutch turned her stomach. She sighed without realizing she'd done it.

"I'll follow you home to make sure it doesn't give out again."

"No. Go home. You've done enough already. Do you live close by?" She had no idea how far he had to drive. He'd said Jersey, but for all she knew it could be Atlantic City.

"Just down the Parkway. For the time being anyway. If you feel like a spin on the wild side again, give me a ring," he said as he jotted down his telephone number on the back of somebody's card and handed it to her.

"A spin on the wild side?"

"You know what I mean." He shot her a mysterious grin, climbed into his car and drove off into the morning. But Eva wasn't sure what he meant, and she turned his comment around in her mind all the way home.

The house was dark when she got there. Pausing at the door, she listened for any strange sound and then entered cautiously. She tried to snap off the burglar alarm and then realized that she must have forgotten to turn it on. She was slipping. She quickly turned on the kitchen lights and the radio, thought for a moment about her neighbor's experience with the break-in, and then put it out of her mind. Bama dashed down the stairs to greet her, then stopped short and glared at her.

"I've been *out,* if it's any of *your* business," Eva said sassily as she opened a can of cat food and dumped it in the cat's glass bowl. The cat turned up her nose and walked away. "Starve, then!" she said as she got down her favorite cup and made herself a cup of the warm milk with the splash of brandy in it and went into the small sunroom off the living room.

She felt oddly exhilarated and stimulated at the same time. Like a kid before Christmas. But it didn't take long for the depression to creep in again. It was the silence in the house that brought it on. The unnatural stillness. She had always been uneasy being alone in the place. She still missed Hutch terribly, but she only allowed herself to admit it late at night or early in the morning, before her day started and as it was ending.

Cup of milk in hand, she settled by her favorite window. She had always loved sitting here. The yards nearby were all filled with ancient oaks at their greenest and fullest and summer flowers—scarlet rosebushes, white impatiens, peonies as pink as sunsets. She could catch the scent of her neighbor's honeysuckle through the open window when she breathed in deeply, and it brought back her own childhood. She breathed deeply again, her eyes closed, listening to the kids on her block who were up early and calling to each other as Charley and Steven had once, their high-pitched voices filled with excitement and summer's glee. It hadn't been that long since Charley and Steven had been out there too, shouting, arguing, laughing. Summers—years—passed too quickly.

Charley was older now by three years than Eva had been when she'd had her. She couldn't remember her own youth without Charlie being a part of it, clinging to her body like some delicate appendage. Had she ever been as carefree as Charley seemed now? As Isaiah Lonesome seemed tonight?

He must be in his late twenties, older than Charley but not by much. Had she ever been so intense, so serious about her work or anything in her life as he was? She had been about Charley, never about her art. Maybe that was her problem.

It was Saturday, and she had nothing to do, nowhere to go, nobody to see. The warm, brandy-flavored milk began to make her sleepy, as it always did. She would take a bath, she decided, just warm enough to put her to sleep. She'd nap for a couple of hours. Make herself some dinner. Watch some TV. Go to bed early and try to get back on schedule in time for work on Monday morning. *At the library.* Without a thought about her studio upstairs. If she'd ever had any real talent, she didn't have it anymore. Maybe she *was* just a librarian. Maybe she should just go back to school, get her degree in library science like somebody with some sense so that she could make a living and pay the bills that she would probably have to pay by herself.

Nearly three weeks without a word from him, without a call to inquire if she was alive or dead, to see how the house was holding up, to see how she was doing. Just that one time, dashing in to get his things and then out again. How could he have ever said he loved her?

*The hell with him.*

She soaked in the tub for a good half hour, savoring the fragrance of the lilac bath oil and the warmth that crept up her thighs and back. Using her big toe, she turned on the cold water to cool down. She drifted off to sleep for a moment, then got out, dried off quickly, pulled on a T-shirt and crawled into bed.

# Eva and Charley

**L**ater that same day, Eva awoke to Charley screaming in her ear.

"Mommy!"

"Huh—what?"

Charley grabbed her shoulders and shook her. "Are you all right?"

"Of course I'm all right!"

There was a suspicious glint in Charley's eyes. "What are you doing still asleep, Mother? It's four o'clock."

*Back to Mother.* "I can't sleep until afternoon if I feel like it? What are you doing here?"

Charley paused. "You didn't answer the door when I rang the bell, so I used my key. I brought the ice chest back. And, well, something important has happened to me. I've made a life change."

"If it's something about your father, I'm sick of talking about him."

"I said it was a life change. It's about me."

"What about you?"

Charley swept Bama off the foot of the bed and settled against Eva's knee. "I'm almost afraid to tell you. I don't want you going into some kind of hysterical thing. But my life has changed forever!"

Eva was swept with a sense of dread. She was awake now but not fully, and she recalled with trepidation the talk she'd had with her own mother eight months before Charley was born. Could this be what this "life change" thing was about? She remembered how she'd roused her mother out of bed, her own delight mixed with panic, her secret guilty joy over the small being who was part of her. She had prayed that her mother would understand and accept this "change" in her life—was that how she had put it?—and she had been devastated by her mother's cruel reaction. That day she had made an oath to herself that if a daughter of hers ever came to her with such a mixed blessing, the reaction she had faced that day would never be her own.

She studied her daughter carefully. She had known this body inside her own. She knew every part of it: the mole below the left breast, the scar on the knee. She was sure it was too early to tell, but she studied her anyway for the roundness of breast, softness of belly. At least Charley was older than she had been. She had finished college and was well on her way to independence. At least Bradley wouldn't desert Charley like Charley's father had her. They were getting married anyway. After the initial shock, his parents would be as ecstatic as she would be—after she got used to the idea. Maybe this was the problem they had alluded to. Hutch would be overjoyed.

"So how far—"

Charley's expression made her stop midsentence. "How far what?"

"Well, how, uh, how are you feeling, Charley? Have you—"

"Feeling about what?"

"Well, you . . ." Eva hesitated and unconsciously dropped her eyes toward her daughter's womb.

Charley's eyes widened as she cut her off. "Oh, my God! You think I'm pregnant, don't you?"

"No! Of course not—" Eva stammered and sank back into the bed, wondering what in the name of heaven had made her assume such a thing. Charley glared at her mother, then lowered her voice to a growl.

"You always think I'll do something wrong, make some mistake, shame you in some way! You don't believe in me. You've never believed in me!"

"Oh, Charley, you know that's not—"

"All my life you've thought the worst of me!"

"No, Charley! No!" Eva sat back up now, shaking her head wildly in denial and wondering what she had done to make her daughter so angry at her and wondering if she *did* assume the worst about Charley. "I just thought . . ."

Charley bent forward, her eyes suspicious, daring her mother to speak. "Thought what?"

"Never mind," Eva said, giving up.

"Thought what?" Charley demanded, not letting it go.

Eva threw up her hand helplessly and reached for a cigarette. "I honestly don't know what I thought, Charley," she said, beaten into submission.

"Well, I am certainly *not* pregnant!" Charley lifted

her head and tossed Eva a disdainful glance. "Believe it or not!"

Eva rose from her bed, went into the bathroom and closed the door.

"Good!" she shouted at Charley through the closed door. She sat down on the commode with her head in her hands. She could never get it right with Charley; everything she said always came out wrong.

She took her good time brushing her teeth, showering and dressing. Finally after about fifteen minutes, she came back into her bedroom. Charley sat on the bed, dangling a string in front of Bama, who swatted at it furiously. She glanced up at Eva when she came in. Eva sat down beside her on the bed.

"Sorry I yelled at you."

"I'm used to it."

"Oh, Mommy, don't be such a victim."

"Sometimes you make me feel like a victim."

Charley rolled her eyes dramatically. Neither woman said anything for a while.

Charley broke the silence. "Do you want to know what I had to tell you?"

"If you can tell me without being nasty."

"I've made two decisions, and I wanted you to know about them."

"What are they?" Eva's heart beat fast. God knew what the girl was about to say.

"Well." Charley smiled shyly. "First of all, I'm not going to marry Bradley." Eva drew a quick, short breath. So that's what Bradley's parents were talking about. Charley continued, "Maybe I will in a couple of years or maybe I won't, but I'm calling it off. I don't think he's what I'm looking for. Second, I've decided to forget about law school. Yeah, I did good on the boards and all that, but I really don't think I'm a lawyer at heart. When I think about lawyers I think about Mr. Mason, and I don't think I'm like that."

"He's not the only role model there is for a lawyer," Eva said.

"I'm not cut out to be a lawyer. I know that now. But I've had a taste of what I want to do, and I've decided to pursue it." She took a deep breath and let it out slowly. Eva was reminded of Isaiah's advice in the car. "I want to go into show business," Charley said. "I've decided to become a comedian. A stand-up comic."

"A what?" It took Eva a minute and a half to find her voice.

"A stand-up comedian."

"A stand-up comedian?"

"That's what I said."

"Charley, what in God's name makes you think you could become a stand-up comedian? You're not funny!" Eva spoke the first and truest words that came into her mind. The look on Charley's face made her wish she'd lied.

"That's right! Smack me down like you always do. Trample on my ideas! Rain on my parade! I knew you weren't going to support me. I knew it! And let me tell you this, Mother, you're the only one in the whole family who hasn't. The only one!"

Charley had always had a flair for the dramatic. As far as she could remember, Eva had never in her life smacked Charley down, trampled on her ideas or rained on her parade, but she thought it best to keep her thoughts to herself. Instead she said, "You've told other people this?"

"Of course!"

"Who?"

"Daddy, Steven, Bradley."

"And they've told you that you have what it takes to become a stand-up comedian?"

"Yes."

"Charley, they're lying to you. They don't want to hurt your feelings. Listen to me. I'm your mother. It is my responsibility to tell you the truth. You're a lawyer, not a comic!"

"That was *your* dream for me, not mine. Why don't you stop expecting me to live your dreams?" Eva stopped short, and a chill went through her. *Hadn't she said that to Louisa once?*

"What do you know about comedy anyway?"

She turned back to Charley and could see the hurt in her eyes. "Not a damn thing. You're right, honey," she said, forcing a smile. Changing directions, she bravely continued, "Actually, the more I think about it, they used to say your grandaddy Charles had a strong sense of humor. He was very dramatic too. Your grandmother used to say he belonged on the stage. You've got his dimple. Maybe you got his talent too. And you used to tell jokes good when you were little, and—"

"Drop it, Mother."

Eva threw up her hands in exasperation. "What do you want from me?"

"Your advice."

"I gave you my advice. Go to law school!" Bama snatched the string that hung from Charley's hand and scurried out of the room. Both women watched her go without saying anything.

Charley took a deep breath. "I just want you to give me your blessing. Wish me luck."

"Charley, you always have my blessing, don't you know that? Whatever you do is okay with me. I just want you to be happy. That's all I've ever wanted." Eva felt her eyes brimming with tears of confusion and distress. She was disappointed about Charley's new career plans and at the same time angry with herself for not being more supportive.

Charley studied her doubtfully for a moment, and then continued cautiously, "I want you and Daddy to be there. I'm starting to gather material for my act."

"What kind of act are you going to do?" Eva pasted on what she hoped was an encouraging smile.

"I'm not sure yet. Stand-up comedy is kind of like meditating. It's a way of life. It comes to you in bits and pieces. You have to wait and see what kinds of funny little things come across your path that you can use as material."

"So where's the show going to be?" Eva made her voice sound excited.

"Club Resurrection in Fort Greene, Brooklyn. They do amateur nights and I'm scheduled to go on the first Saturday in October. I had to audition for it. It's not like just giving somebody the mike, it's like the real thing. Agents might be there and everything. I know I'm going to make it. Will you come?'

Charley's eyes were shining with excitement. Eva forced another smile. "I wouldn't miss it, sweetheart. You know that." She searched for something supportive and encouraging to say, but Charley spoke before anything came to mind.

"So where did you say you were last night?"

Feeling guilty for her earlier discouraging words, Eva spilled out the truth in a torrent. "The car broke down on the Parkway. That friend of yours, that guy Isaiah Lonesome, happened to drive by and he was going to give me a ride home, but he didn't have time so I rode with him to this club in the city and he drove me home afterward."

Charley looked at her skeptically, but there was mischief in her eyes.

"So you were out all night with Isaiah Lonesome."

"You know I didn't say that!"

"Yes, you did."

"The man gave me a lift home, that was all."

"And you went to hear him play."

"Well, it was on the way home."

"Right. Well, I guess *your* opinion of Isaiah Lonesome has changed, hasn't it?" The mischief in her eyes turned to amusement.

"I never had an opinion about the man one way or the other. I just told you he was inappropriate."

"Wait till Steven hears about this!" Charley was grinning now.

"There's nothing for Steven to hear about," Eva said as evenly as she could.

"Well, Mother," Charley said, still teasing, "your business is your business, but at least you could go out with somebody your own age. You broke up with Daddy and now you're hanging out with Isaiah Lonesome." Eva got up, edged Charley off the end of the bed and began to make it up. Charley settled into a side chair across the room and with a sly smile on her face watched her as she worked.

"I won't even dignify that statement with a response," Eva said after a few minutes, taking things more seriously than she needed to. "I'm not going out with Isaiah Lonesome. The man was kind enough to give me a lift and that was that. Why did you say you broke up with Bradley?" She tried to shift the conversation back to Charley, who wasn't buying it.

"So are you going out with him again?" Charley was having fun now.

"We didn't go out, I told you that."

"But you went to a club with him, right?"

"Charley, you're not still interested in the man, are you?"

"Come on, Mother, get real!" Charley turned serious.

"Tell me the truth, Charley." Eva, sensing her daughter's discomfort, was having some fun of her own.

Charley studied her mother for a moment and then shrugged. "Too broke. Why are you so concerned?"

Eva gave a shrug she hoped was dismissive. "No reason. What happened between you and Bradley?"

Charley turned serious again. "Bradley is too dull, Mother. My life is like something out of a boring book. Nothing exciting happens. I've never really done what I wanted to do. You never let me take chances as a kid. This is a chance."

Eva sighed. She knew in some ways that Charley had it right. She had always protected her, especially when it was just the two of them. In those early years, she had worked jobs that were going nowhere and meant nothing to her—part-time waitressing, office clerking, anything she could get to scrape together a living for the two of them. She had gone to school at night when she could, and after six years of City College had managed to earn an undergraduate degree in art history that got her nowhere. Later there had been checks from Scoe Lilton, generous ones that came fairly often. Her father also hinted that Aunt Delia was "spinning her some spells." But it had been up to her to make her own way and her own luck. She had done the best she could do.

She had learned to be good with money, buying cautiously only the necessities she couldn't beg, borrow and, on one shameful occasion, steal. Life during Charley's first ten years had been the toughest she'd ever lived, and any surprise, any small unexpected, upsetting thing could turn everything upside down. She had learned that life was better and happier when everything was planned out safely. She had learned to leave nothing to chance because both of their lives depended upon it.

"I just want to live my life to its fullest," Charley said, a dreamy look in her eyes. Eva knew that her sacrifices had given Charley the right to claim such a thing, but it still made her uneasy.

"But Bradley is a good man. You can count on him," she heard herself say and then chastised herself for saying it. How often had she heard that about Hutch? "Are you seeing somebody else?"

"Like who? Isaiah Lonesome?" Charley quipped with a smile. "I'll bet he made you pay for the ride, huh? He never has any moolah!" she rubbed her forefinger and thumb together. "The last thing I need in my life is a broke-ass musician. All he cared about was that stupid horn. Plus he was too old."

"How old is he?" Eva was curious but cautious.

"Twenty-eight. Too old not to have it together."

"Have you heard from your father?" Eva made another stab at changing subjects.

"I thought you were sick of talking about him."

"I just asked if you'd heard from him."

"No." Eva could tell by the tone of her voice that Charley had heard from him, but wasn't going to admit it. Eva sensed that she was still angry about the breakup and still blamed her for it. Charley remembered those hard days when there had been just the two of them, and she couldn't forgive Eva for putting her happiness—and security—at risk again, even though now she was a grown woman and Hutch was the one who had put it at risk.

*Always blame your mama.* That was what it came down to.

They talked about safe things for the next fifteen minutes—the summer sales at Bloomingdale's, what was happening on *General Hospital*, Charley's pedicure. Eva avoided mentioning anything dangerous— the broken engagement, Charley's new career, Isaiah Lonesome.

But after Charley left, those dangerous things were all Eva could think about. It was the final straw. She hadn't realized until Charley told her it was off just how much she'd been looking forward to Charley's marriage to Bradley. Her dreams for Charley had been *her* dreams. It had become *her* girlish fantasy, the wedding she had never had, a chance to indulge herself in thoughts about flowers, gowns and caterers. When Charley had begun sporting the huge diamond ring Bradley gave her, Eva felt that Charley was finally on her way: she would have a life with a man who could afford to give her anything she wanted. She had envisioned her daughter's future as solid and protected: big wedding to a good man from a strong, stable family. Graduation from law school in three years; a nice salary as a lawyer, then maybe working part-time when she had her first child. What was Charley thinking? What had come over her?

But what had come over everbody?

The phone rang and Eva let it ring for a moment before she answered. To her absolute surprise, it was Hutch.

"Hey, uh, Eva. It's me." Eva couldn't find her voice. She sat up straight, her body stiff, her mouth in a tight line. "I just called to see what was up. How you're doing?"

After weeks of separation, this was all he could come up with? Eva was suddenly filled with a seething rage. She stood up, walked as far as the extension cord on the bedroom phone would allow and then flopped back down on the edge of the bed.

"What do you mean, you just called to see how I'm doing?"

"Just wondered how things were going. How life has been treating you."

*What is he talking about?* "How the hell do you think things have been going? You walked out on me with no excuse. Not even a decent warning or goodbye. How the hell do you think things are going?" For a moment she thought he had hung up, but then she realized she could hear him breathing.

"Oh, well, uh, listen. Just called to say hello." The words sounded trivial, stupid.

"Just called to say hello!" She repeated his words in a mocking tone, scarcely believing what she heard.

"Well, uh, Eva, I—"

"As far as I'm concerned, Hutch, it's over between us. You can do what you want to do. Live where you want to live. Sleep with whoever you want to sleep with. You can go straight to hell!" Eva slammed down the receiver, as angry as she'd ever been with anybody in her life. She reached for her trusty cigarette, lit it and sank back into the bed. Who the hell did he think he was, calling after all this time with that kind of bullshit?

The phone rang again, and she snatched it out of its cradle. "Didn't I tell you where to go?"

There was silence on the other end for a beat. "Eva?" said a surprised voice.

It took her a moment to place the voice. "Isaiah?"

"Did I get you at a bad time?"

"That goes without saying."

"I was just calling to make sure you got in all right. The car was okay and everything."

"Yeah. Thank you." After that brief, hateful conversation with Hutch, this seemingly authentic concern for her welfare touched her. There was a long, uncomfortable pause on the other end.

"Listen, Eva. There's something else I wanted to ask you about too." Another pause.

"What?"

"Yeah, well, uh . . . The dude I share my crib with just got hooked up a couple of weeks back, and he and his old lady are looking for a place, but I wanted to give them some privacy for a while, you know what I mean, so I thought I'd move out till they find something. Only thing is, I can't find anybody who is willing to rent a place, like a room, for a month or two."

"No," Eva said firmly.

"How do you know what I'm going to ask?"

Eva paused. "Go ahead, then."

"Well, this may sound strange, I guess the word is presumptuous, but I was wondering if you—"

"No!" Eva said again. "Out of the question." She didn't know how she knew but she did. She was surprised to hear him chuckling on the other end.

"What do you think I'm going to ask?"

"I'm not looking for a roommate."

"Boarder. Tenant. Not roommate. I'll keep out of your way. I work at night, practice during the day, you'll hardly know I'm around. There's nothing for the length of time I need it. Nobody wants to rent for a couple of weeks. Plus, we're compatible. I'm not compatible with a lot of people."

"How do you know we're compatible? We hardly know each other."

"I can tell after ten minutes with a person, believe me. We know each other well enough," he said, but then added, "Hey, if you're worried about, uh, me, uh, taking advantage of you or anything, don't worry. I got a lot of people who will vouch for me, for my character and shit. It will be just straight-up business. On the up and up. You're the only person I've met in the last six months who I like who has space, and you said yesterday that your house was falling apart. My daddy was a master carpenter. He taught me everything I know—except how to play a horn."

"I don't think so, Mr. Lonesome." Eva heard the chuckle again.

"Think about it, Mrs. Hutchinson. Talk to you later."

After he'd hung up, Eva stared at the receiver as if she were looking at his face.

But she was surprised to find that she did think about his proposition. Maybe it was because Hutch's call—the triteness of it, as if everything were as it should be and that she should be taking his departure as casually as he obviously did—had enraged her to her very core. Maybe it was because everything else in her life had taken such a turn into craziness—Hutch leaving like he did, Charley becoming a stand-up comic—that the crazy notion of taking in Isaiah Lonesome as a boarder seemed perfectly sane. And when yet another skylight began to leak and the knob on the bedroom door came off in her hand, she considered it again. It crossed her mind when the water, town tax and gas bill came in the mail the same day, and she found herself thinking about him when she heard Miles Davis playing those first few notes of "How Deep Is the Ocean" on the radio late one night.

By Thursday afternoon, the idea didn't seem ludicrous at all, and by Friday morning she was fantasizing about how Hutch would react when her new tenant opened the front door. And tenant he would be, there was no question about that. Their relationship would have to stay on that level, that was for sure. After all, she reasoned, she wouldn't be the first homeowner to take in a boarder for the extra money, and what was it that Aunt Delia used to sing when she got vexed about what folks were saying? *Ain't nobody's business if I do!*

So when Isaiah Lonesome called on Sunday morning and asked if she had reconsidered his proposal, she said that she had thought about it, and since he had so generously helped her out when she needed it, she had decided that she would help him out too. And if he was still interested in moving in, he could pay one month's rent and one month's security for kitchen privileges and the use of the guest bedroom beginning on the first day in August. At least until he found something else.

# Hutch and Steven

Hutch, his muscular frame squeezed into a rattan chair, waited impatiently in a restaurant called *Beans 'n' Sprouts* for his son to arrive. It was the long-awaited Saturday after the 4th of July. The restaurant, which had been Steven's choice, was hung with green and white wallpaper decorated with dainty alfalfa sprouts and dancing lima beans. The floors were covered with sisal mats and the windows were shaded by overgrown spider plants. Hutch glanced self-consciously around the small, interracial crowd of trim, fit couples earnestly sipping herbal teas and munching seaweed crackers, and wondered if they could sense his gnawing desire for red meat and wine, despite the July heat.

There was only one other single man in the place, a good-looking young man in tan chinos, Birkenstock loafers and a lime-colored summer sweater. He had longish blond hair and was about Steven's age. He smiled at Hutch when he caught his eye. Annoyed, Hutch looked in the opposite direction. All he needed, Hutch thought with irritation, was for some gay man to be flirting with him when his son walked in. Like many of the men he knew, he didn't know any gay men, and if he did, he didn't want to know about it. He didn't like to think that he was homophobic, but he knew on some level that he probably was. He never understood how one man could physically love another and found the whole idea troubling and mildly disgusting. When the man nodded in his direction, Hutch, narrowing his eyes and scowling, glared back to discourage any assumption about his sexual orientation. The man quickly shifted his eyes to the menu. Hutch summoned the waitress and ordered a tea called Ease Your Mood, which he figured he needed.

He had been in a bad mood ever since the Fourth. Holidays depressed him, and this one had been especially bad. At the beginning of the week, Donald had announced that he was taking Raye to Bermuda for the holiday—a surprise trip brought on more by guilt than generosity, Hutch suspected. The two of them had headed out a week ago, leaving Hutch bored and alone in the empty house. Before he left, Donald had made the unwelcome suggestion that Hutch should consider renewing his short-lived affair with Cara. It had only been a year, Donald reminded him. The house would be empty, and his time was his own. He needed something young and firm to fight his loneliness. The thought of it had made Hutch slightly ill. He realized now that he had been egged into the affair in the first place by Donald and was filled with a renewed sense of self-disgust whenever he thought about it. Donald, a combination of the sly older brother and warmhearted father he'd never had, was nobody's idea of a role model, but Hutch had found himself more influenced by Donald and his suggestions than he probably should have been. The year of his affair had been one of the worst of his life. His father had died at the beginning of it, and the construction business had entered a nearly fatal slump. He'd had to borrow money from Donald (the only man he knew who could write an interest-fee check for $50,000 and never mention it again) and the bank for the first time in his life. Eva was out of sorts and distracted. Cara had been the antidote to depression. But he'd felt empty and deceitful after sleeping with her, and seeing her again was out of the question. Things were getting better. Business had improved, and this month was particularly good. Hutch had gotten a sizeable down payment on a job he'd put in a bid for and had been able to give his crew the weekend of the July Fourth holiday off.

After Donald and Raye left for Bermuda, he'd had nothing but time on his hands. He'd sat around the house watching TV, drinking Donald's expensive scotch, and enjoying his solitude. Out of habit more than anything else, he'd gone to his office in the middle of the week, talked to the architect in charge of the project, paid some bills and then gone to a movie he didn't particularly want to see. The morning of the Fourth, he'd awakened at dawn, gone for a long walk in the woods behind Donald's house and soaked in the Jacuzzi. Around three, he went to see Eva because he couldn't get her out of his mind.

His heart was beating fast when he rang her doorbell. He had no idea what he was going to say. He didn't know whether he should apologize and beg her forgiveness or pretend that he had come to pick up a forgotten piece of clothing. He wasn't sure what damage he'd done and if she would hug him or slam the door in his face. He wanted to ask her why she'd turned off the answering machine, and if she'd gotten the messages he'd left for her at work. He wanted her to know that he was willing to try to work things out if she was.

He hoped that she would tip her head the way she always did, and that her dimple would peek out at him and no words would be necessary. He was sure that at some point he'd have to offer some explanation and it would have to be a good one. But he also knew that whatever the explanation was, he could now say in all honesty that he still loved her.

When Eva didn't answer, he timidly unlocked the door, turned off the alarm system and stepped into the kitchen.

"Eva!" he called out so she wouldn't be alarmed. Bama dashed down the stairs at the sound of his voice, nearly running into the leg of the kitchen table. "Hey, Bam, how you doing?" He picked the squirming animal up as she made a pass for his face with her tongue. He scratched her around the ears and put her back on the floor.

"Eva?" he called out as he rinsed the cat's dish out and filled it with dried food. The cat greedily gobbled it up. Feeling like an intruder, Hutch made a tour of the house while calling Eva's name. Although nothing had been changed, everything seemed unfamiliar, as if Eva had rearranged the furniture in his absence. He wan-

dered up to the third floor, examined the leaking sky-
lights and the water stains on the floor, made a mental
note to offer to fix it and wandered back downstairs.
After a while, he dozed on the couch with Bama
perched on his chest. He woke up with a start after an
hour, realizing that he'd forgotten to turn off the water
sprinkler on Donald's lawn. Still wondering where Eva
could be, he drove back to Donald's without leaving a
note.

He'd broken down and called Eva the next afternoon but froze at the sound of her voice. Their conversation had been one of the most painful he had ever
had with her. The rage in her voice had paralyzed him,
and he had stuttered and stammered like a fool. Every
word he'd said had sounded callous and inane, and he
was still haunted by them. Why hadn't he just told her
how much he missed her and begged her forgiveness?
Except maybe some part of him was still afraid, and
that when all was said and done, after a month or two,
they might be right back where they started. He heard
the rage and intransigence in her voice when she told
him to go to hell, and realized that maybe nothing had
really changed. He would probably leave her again.
There was still no connection, no intimacy, no joy.

He took a sip of the Ease Your Mood tea, which
burned his tongue, and then stirred in a generous glob
of honey, waited for the tea to cool down, and glanced
again at his watch. Steven was half an hour late. The
boy was always late. He took after his mother, Irene.
Eva was rarely if ever late, and he had immediately
liked that about her. They were as different as two
women could be. Irene, a former social worker, had
gone for and received her law degree shortly after di-

vorcing him, and was now a full-fledged attorney, which she'd always told him had been one of her dreams. Eva, on the other hand, dreamed of being an artist. But when they'd been married, Irene had settled into social work the same way Eva had settled into being a librarian. Guilt swept him as he wondered yet again if maybe he was responsible for Eva's lack of growth as an artist. She'd been painting seriously when they met, sure of herself and of where she was going with her work. Was there something about him that robbed the women he loved of their potential? Was he some kind of human black hole, drawing in light, letting nothing seep out? He sank back into his chair, caught the eye of the blond man again, and shifted his view to the lima beans kicking up their feet on the far wall.

"Dad!" Steven's voice startled him, and Hutch rose quickly to greet him, the happiness he felt whenever he saw his son flooding his body.

"Hey, man, how you doing?"

"Fine, Dad. How about you?"

"Fine. Fine." They hugged, sat back down and grinned at each other.

"It's good to see you, son."

"Yeah. You too, dad."

Hutch reached across the table and knocked his son's shoulder, giving him the short, gentle punch that had served as a greeting between them since Steven had been a boy. "Nice place," he said because he couldn't think of anything else to say.

"I like it."

"Yeah, I like it, too." It was an obvious lie that begged his son's approval. Hutch hoped that Steven wouldn't see through it, which he did.

"Right, Dad. Like this is really *your* kind of place."

"No, I like it."

"Stop lying."

"Well, if you knew it wasn't a place I'd enjoy, why did you suggest it?" Hutch tried to soften his tone with a tight smile, but the damage was done. They were already off to a bad start.

"Because it's *my* kind of place."

"Great." There was an awkward silence as both men studied the menu. Hutch loved his son more than he loved anything or anyone in the world. Why could they so seldom find common ground?

"So what's good here?" Hutch, making his voice sound pleasant and nonjudgmental, tried again.

"I like the tofu and rice casserole. The veggie salad is good, too. They make a nice vinaigrette. Lot of garlic. But *you* should probably get the eggplant parmigiana. You'll like that." Steven grinned, taking a leap of faith. Hutch grinned back. Things were agreeable again, and his heart leaped.

They placed their orders and talked for a while about the Mets and the Yankees. When their meals came, they talked about the food. When they'd finished eating, they avoided each other's eyes, and Hutch wondered as always why he found it so hard to talk to his son. Finally, he broke the silence.

"Seen Charley recently? What's she's up to?" From the time Charley had entered their lives, her comings and goings had always offered them a safe, amusing topic of discussion.

"You heard about the stand-up comedian thing?"

"Yeah, she told me." Both men shook their heads and laughed. "Who knows, she might make it. Far be it from me to be negative. She's really committed to it."

"How did Eva feel about it?"

Steven froze at the mention of Eva's name. "You haven't talked to E, then?"

"No, not recently. How's work been going?"

"Why don't you say what's on your mind, like why you left this one?" Steven said irritably. Hutch shifted uncomfortably in his chair and dropped his eyes. He'd had no idea that Steven would jump so quickly into the topic of Eva and why he had left her. He gulped his tea.

"I don't know why," he finally muttered.

"Were you *that* unhappy, to just walk out on her like that?"

"It was things piling up, son. Nothing we did seemed to make either of us happy. It seemed sometimes like we couldn't connect, we were just going through the motions." *There was no joy*—but why did he have to go into this with his son?

"And that was a reason to leave?" Steven's voice was accusatory. Hutch sighed.

"Can we drop this, please?"

"No. You asked me to lunch, let's talk about something real for a change."

Hutch paused and then gave in. "I felt like, well, I felt like because I left your mother, I couldn't settle for less with Eva than being happy. Is that real enough for you?" He was surprised by the truthfulness of his own words. Irene, in her own way, had been part of this departure too. Leaving Steven and his mother had been the hardest thing he had ever done, and once he'd done it, settling for anything less even from Eva was unacceptable. He had to be as happy as he had once thought he could be or he'd thrown everything—his life with Steven—away for nothing. Steven looked distant for a moment.

"Mom always said you left her because you-all fought all the time."

"She fought with me. I closed down."

"What do you mean, you closed down?"

"I turned off."

"So you just up and left?" His eyes condemned Hutch, and Hutch didn't like the feeling.

"My God, Steven. That was a long time ago. Can we just let it be, let it go?"

"Gone!" Steven, his voice dripping with sarcasm, whisked his hands in the air dramatically, as if dismissing a person or a thought.

"I couldn't stand to see her unhappy. To see you unhappy," Hutch went on to explain. Maybe he was right. He had never really talked with his son about why he left. Not as an adult anyway. Maybe it was time. But this was hardly the place.

Steven rolled his eyes. Hutch felt a pang in his heart.

"So are you going back? I mean to E?"

"I don't know." For a moment, Hutch thought he might cry. He could feel his eyes water and a lump forming in his throat. He could tell by the softness that suddenly came into Steven's eyes that his son knew it, and he was glad that his sadness could still touch his son.

"Dad?"

"Yes, son." Hutch's voice shook. He took a swallow of tea.

"You okay, Dad?"

"Yeah." They were silent for a moment, each lost in

his own thoughts. Hutch wondered how he had managed to lose control of the conversation, how it had veered into areas that he had no intention of talking about or even thinking about. But maybe it was for the best. Maybe.

"You've got to know why you left before you can go back." Steven broke the silence, and his voice was forgiving, momentarily kind, like that of a parent giving a child much-needed advice. Hutch was strangely overcome with gratitude. "I know you love her. I know you don't want to hurt her." Hutch nodded his head, numbly listening. "Maybe you should just give it some time. People who really care about each other always find a way back. It may not be on the same terms that they left, but they'll usually make something that works better."

Hutch nodded his head enthusiastically, as if he had just received some piece of wisdom from a sage. He grabbed Steven's hand and held it for a moment. Sometimes things could be so sweet between the two of them, so gentle and loving. "So you're grown enough to be giving me advice?"

"Somebody'd better." Hutch smiled at that, and Steven did too. They ordered some more tea, saying nothing until it came. "Maybe you should talk to somebody about it. Like a therapist or something," Steven said after a while.

Hutch smiled shyly. "You know a good one?"

"As a matter of fact I do, when you're ready—"

"When I'm ready?" Hutch joked, then added more seriously, "Thank you, son." Hutch had no intention of seeing a therapist or anybody else, but he was touched that Steven cared enough about him to advise him to do it. He knew that his son often resented him, and he was never sure what to do about it.

Steven shrugged. "No big thing. I'm sorry if I made you uncomfortable."

"You didn't make me uncomfortable."

"You never tell the truth, Dad. You always lie. You're so out of touch with yourself."

Hutch chose not to respond to his comment. Instead he said, "You know you're my life, Stevie. Do you know how much I love you?"

The depth of Hutch's feeling caught Steven by surprise, and his eyes were the ones to water this time. Hutch felt the lump come back into his throat.

"I love you too, Dad. Don't worry. Things with E will work themselves out, one way or another. And if they don't . . ." Hutch looked dismayed at the thought. Steven grinned a loopy grin. "You've still got me, right?" He asked it in a mock little boy's voice, like the one Hutch hadn't heard in fifteen years, maybe since he'd last called him Stevie. He gazed at his son, conscious again of how much he had changed yet remained the same. Steven had always been an old soul, as Eva's Aunt Delia had told him once when she was alive, and he had grown into a man with a benevolent spirit, the kind of man who, with the marked exception of Donald Mason, Hutch usually chose for a friend.

"Thanks for meeting me, Stevie. I don't see enough of you. I—I miss you." Hutch had never meant anything more in his life.

"Next time it's your choice, Dad. Steak 'n' Ale, maybe?" Steven's grin was mischievous, and both men laughed as they finished. Hutch thought how good it felt to laugh with his son. He closed his eyes, holding on to this moment. Savoring it. He opened them again, and glanced at his watch out of habit more than anything else, since he didn't have anywhere to go. But he found that he was surprisingly anxious, as if he should leave while feelings between them were still good.

"Well, son. I guess it's time for me to go. I've got a few things at the office I want to——"

"Dad!" The urgency in Steven's voice caught him short.

"Stevie, what's wrong?" He said it like he'd used to say it when Steven had been a boy, even though he had tried to take the apprehension out of his voice.

"Nothing is wrong. Everything is right for once in my life, but—but there's something I'd better tell you, that I need to share with you." Steven's voice broke, and Hutch noticed he was out of breath. He also noticed Steven was avoiding his eyes, but then, as if getting courage from somewhere, he looked straight into them, smiling uncomfortably. He drew in a breath. "I knew this wouldn't be easy."

"Take your time, son." Could Steven be ill? Had he been arrested for something? Had he gotten some girl pregnant? Hutch's heart beat fast for a moment, but then he made himself calm down. Whatever it was, they would face it together. Whatever it was, he would be glad to hear it, and he was glad Steven felt comfortable enough with him for once to open up about it. Maybe even to share this confidence with him first instead of with his mother. For once. Steven cleared his throat, a delaying gesture that Hutch unconsciously used himself from time to time and that asked for more time. Hutch was glad to give it. Taking the pressure off, he leaned back in his chair, forcing himself to strike a relaxed pose.

He studied the wallpaper and idly wondered why it would occur to an artist to feature dancing lima beans on wallpaper. Had the name come first or the wallpaper? He glanced around again, noting the couples who had just come in. A little boy about the same age as Steven when he had left Irene came hopping in behind his parents. He gave Hutch a smile, and Hutch smiled back. The next time he had a child that age in his life it would be a grandson, from Steven or Charley. He'd always heard that grandchildren were easier than children. Sheer pleasure, he'd heard it described. God knew, the little Steven had adored his father and touched a part of that hard old man that he'd never known he had. He wondered what his father would say if he were alive now. How gratifying it would have been to be sitting here with the two of them. But his father would not have put up with these grains and sprouts. Red meat for him.

Hutch noticed with annoyance that the young blond man who had been staring at him when he came in was now gazing at Steven. Feeling as if some intimate moment between them had been violated, Hutch felt an immediate surge of anger.

"Goddamn freaks," he said under his breath and nodded toward the blond man nearby. "That goddamn faggot has been checking me out ever since I came in the goddamn door. What the hell does he think we are?" Steven's face froze. Hutch knew at that moment that he had said something unpardonable, something that had changed things between them forever.

He couldn't remember the last time he had even said

the word "faggot," maybe not since he'd been in Nam, and for the life of him he couldn't figure out why he'd used it this time, except it seemed to provide an opportunity to connect with his son in some shared bond of masculinity, to create the *other* and secure the emotional bridge they'd just forged. It was something that men did to remind themselves who *they* were, and that they were not weak and soft like women.

"What did you say?" Steven's voice was strangely controlled. The pitch of it demanded Hutch's attention.

"I—I—don't know, I—"

"You called him a faggot, didn't you? Well, I'm a goddamn freak too! I'm a goddamn faggot." Hutch stared in disbelief at his son. "Let me introduce you to another freak, another faggot. Dana"—Steven gestured to the blond man at the table—"you can come over now." Steven's words were spoken in a low voice, but his tone was smoldering. The young blonde rose slowly and self-consciously and came to their table. Hutch, more miserable now than he had ever felt in his life, felt his face freeze. He couldn't get his mouth to move. He couldn't even force a polite smile. Steven stood up; his eyes, cold and unblinking, bore into his father.

"Dana Allen Willoughby, this is my father. Lucas Hutchinson, Jr. Successful building contractor. Unhappy husband. Faggot's father." He grabbed Dana's hand and held it defiantly.

Stunned, Hutch was still unable to speak.

"Goddamn it! We're lovers, can't you say anything?"

"Why?" Hutch asked, realizing even as the word left his mouth that it would make no sense to anybody but himself. But it was the first and only word that came into his mind. *Why* did this happen? *Why* did you become gay? *Why* are you telling me this now?

"What do you mean, *why*?" Steven glared at him. His eyes had narrowed and he spoke in a whisper. Hutch gazed at his son, and shook his head as if in shock.

"Can't you even say anything?" Steven demanded. Several diners glanced in their direction. "Are you so unwilling to see or accept this about me, like everything else in my life—like everything else in your own damn life—that you can't even speak?" Steven's voice trembled slightly. Hutch dropped his eyes and stared at the green and white tablecloth.

"This was not a good idea, Steve, I told you this wasn't the way to do it. I told you this wouldn't work," Dana said in a quiet voice.

"This is between me and my father!"

"But *I'm* here now too. You should have waited, like I told you to."

"Let me handle it my own way."

Dana backed off. "Suit yourself."

"Dad, I'm gay. I'm in love. Why can't you at least say something? At least acknowledge that you've heard me?" Steven's eyes, voice and every move of his body begged him for some reaction.

Hutch could plainly see the pain in his son's eyes, the plea for some positive response. But he was unable to give it. He was unable to say anything. He let his eyes drop.

"You have never accepted me for who I am. Never! If it hadn't been for everybody else—my mother, Charley, E—I probably would have killed myself when I was fourteen!"

"Oh, God, Steven. Don't say that." He finally found his voice.

"Why? It's the truth."

"Oh, please, son, please—"

"My mother is right about you."

"Oh, Jesus! Don't bring her into——"

"All my life I've tried to please you, all my life, to be something that you wanted me to be. But I'm tired of it now, Dad. I'm just sick of being something I'm not just so you'll love me!" Hutch could see his son was close to tears. He reached out for him, trying to pull him back down to the table.

"Who am I, Dad? All these years and you had no idea? Why don't you open your eyes and see what's in front of you?"

"I—" Hutch finally managed to say a word.

"You what?"

"I'm sorry——" Hutch stood slightly and looked helplessly around, beginning to realize even as he said it that he was apologizing for everything at once. For not being able to speak. For the fact that he hadn't known or guessed. For the fact that he had failed his son once again.

"Sorry? Sorry for what? Don't be sorry for me, be sorry for yourself. As far as I'm concerned, you're just one sorry-ass bastard!" Steven's words, spoken so loud and publicly, pushed Hutch back into his chair. Turning to Dana, Steven kissed him full in the mouth, and Hutch, conscious of the looks that had now turned to frank stares from surrounding tables, fastened his eyes to the teapot on the table. Still holding Dana's hand, Steven marched from the restaurant, and Hutch hurriedly paid the bill, ran out to catch them to say something, to explain the stunned silence that had been his first response at Steven's news. But it was too late.

It was late afternoon by the time Hutch got to his office, the place where he ran when things upset him. It was housed in a nondescript red brick building on a commercial street about thirty minutes from the restaurant. The sign on the door said HUTCHINSON & SON in large black block letters and looked strong and assertive—take-no-nonsense like his father had been. He could still recall every detail of the day his father had bought this place. Even the smell never changed, no matter how much air freshener he sprayed around.

He walked into the small reception area with its worn gray rug and collapsed into one of the secondhand chairs. As he brushed off the dust that had accumulated on the ancient coffee table, he reminded himself to get somebody in to clean. His mother had done it when she'd been alive, but Eva rarely visited, and when she did, she wasn't about to clean it. He couldn't even imagine asking her to do it; it was out of the question now. He got a paper towel from the bathroom and wiped off several surfaces, then went into the inner office where he and his father had once spent so many of their days. He used to bring Steven here when he was Stevie and watch him out of the corner of his eye as he colored in his *Sesame Street* coloring book or made imaginary animals out of Play-Doh. The summer before he'd left Irene, Stevie had come nearly every day, playing UNO and checkers with his grandfather or watching the tiny TV they kept in the corner just for him. They'd order pizzas for the crew for lunch, and Hutch would sit outside in summer drinking with the men, kidding about their women, bragging about their kids, betting on football or basketball, while Steven and his grandfather sat at the window, his father gazing at his grandson as if he were the most precious thing on Earth. Hutchinson and Son.

He sank down into the olive green leather chair behind the big desk, the one luxury his father had allowed himself, and closed his eyes, trying to forget his encounter with Steven, and then went to the small refrigerator and pulled out two beers, snapped one open and returned to the chair, gulping it down.

He felt better now. This dim, quiet room always made him feel in control of his life. They had always worked in silence, he and his father, crammed into this small space, grunting rather than talking, nodding occasionally. When they worked outside with the crew, they said even less. It was men's work. Hauling, sawing, hammering, measuring, cutting, anticipating each move the other would make. After a job was finished, they'd drive by and look at the work that was done, proud that it would stand longer than they lived. Their own monument to immortality in brick, wood and glass. It had been the two of them for so long and then finally Ernie Griffin, Sam Anderson, Jack Wilson, one or two teenagers, sons or nephews of the regulars, home from college or just out of high school. This business his father had built made it possible for men to own their own homes, take care of their women, send their kids to school—or drink it up and play it out at the tracks if that was what they wanted to do. His father had given this legacy to him.

But for all his respect and love, Hutch was uneasy in his father's presence. His approval had been the only thing he had ever wanted or needed and never fully got. He could never drive a nail straight enough or saw a plank even enough or paint a wall smoothly enough. He was always just a little bit off, never perfect or as disciplined as his father had wanted him to be.

*All my life I've tried to please you.*

Like father, like son. Would he end up as disappointed in his son as he had always feared his father had been in him? Would that be his own unhappy legacy?

*How did he* really *feel about what Steven had told him?* Steven was the same boy he'd raised and loved. He tried to tell himself that there was nothing wrong with being gay, yet he had been profoundly shaken by Steven's news.

He tried to think about the gay men he'd seen on the street, the ones he'd seen marching on the news in the gay rights parades or for the rights of AIDS patients. He had never held the contempt for gay men that some men he knew had; as a matter of fact, he'd always suspected men who were too vocally anti-gay were harboring fears about their sexuality. He had always regarded gay men with indifference, a vague sense of superiority. He was a man, and they were not. They were to be pitied rather than accepted. Men who were not like him or any of the men he knew. And that was fine. As long as they kept their distance. But that was not true anymore. It would never be true again.

Hutch knew he was now vulnerable in a way he had never felt before, as if he'd been dragged into some new space that he had never wanted to enter or even know about.

"Why?" He said the word that he'd said to his son

out loud now in the silent room. *Why was he gay?* Was it something he had done or not done? Was this an indication that he had failed him as a father? Had he failed him as a man?

And suddenly he was afraid for his son. The world of men despised gay men. Without even thinking twice, he himself had shown contempt for them—and for Steven—because that was what men did. Gays were not what men were supposed to be. There were men in this world who would kill Steven because he was gay. Men who would hate him, discriminate against him and ridicule his ideas, never give him a chance to prove how good he was. Hell, it was bad enough being a black man in this world, but at least he could show his son how to protect himself in that world, how to shield himself from their scorn and defend himself mind, body and soul. But what did he know about being gay? How could he tell him about that?

Hutch polished off the second beer in a couple of gulps and went to the refrigerator for another one, wishing that he kept something stronger in the office. His father, who hated liquor, had always forbade it inside the building, and it was only in the last few years that he'd kept them in the office. He felt a slight buzz. He thought about his father. What would his father have done if he had come to him with such news? There would have been no discussion because Hutch never would have told him. It would have been the end of their relationship. His father would have cut him out of his life forever. End of story.

But he was not his father. He had never wanted to be like his father. Never.

He closed the blinds, turned on the desk lamp and made himself study the figures for the project he was working on and type up some orders for building supplies. He went to the driveway and checked the supplies he'd had delivered to the small prefab building he used as a warehouse behind the garage. Then he came back inside, turned on his computer and took an inventory of the supplies he needed to buy for a job he was doing in December.

Still unable to get his son off his mind, he'd called his ex-wife Irene at 8:00 P.M.

"Well, you certainly screwed that one up, didn't you?" Irene said the moment she heard his voice. Ever since their divorce, there was either mild derision or slight contempt in her voice whenever she spoke to him.

"What was I supposed to say? I had no idea."

"You should have said *something!*" So Steven had told his mother everything that had happened.

"But what did I do wrong?" Hutch wailed into the phone.

"Nothing, you fool! Our son is self-confident and loves himself. We did everything right! Why don't you try accepting him for the intelligent, handsome, high-achieving, *gay* male that he is?"

"But I have no problem with the fact that he's gay!"

"Now that's a lie and we both know it," Irene snapped. "If you didn't have contempt for gay men you wouldn't have called his lover a faggot. That's like white folks casually calling somebody a nigger and insisting they don't despise us."

"What should I do?" Hutch begged Irene for advice, which he hated to do.

"Steven thinks you're dishonest. Admit to him that you have mixed feelings about the fact that he is gay. Ask him to have some patience with you while you work through your stupid bigotry. Tell him how much you love him."

Hutch knew she was right, and after he hung up, he tortured himself with should-haves. He *should have* been glad that Steven had finally felt close enough to share his feelings with him. He *should have* rejoiced with his son for his happiness. He *should have* embraced Dana, the object of his son's affection. He *should have* found a way to laugh at his own narrow-mindedness and at the bigotry the two of them would face. He *should have* condemned and cursed those who hated. He *should have* applauded him for having the courage to stand up and live his life the way he wanted to live it.

But he had done none of that, felt none of it. He had been as silent and cold as his own father would have been. His father would say he had failed his son in every way that he could fail him, and he thought that was probably true.

At nine, he got up from his desk and drove back to Donald Mason's, stopping on the way for a cheeseburger and fries. He got home at ten and called Steven, who answered on the first ring, then hung up when he heard his voice. He didn't try again. At eleven, he fell into bed and after two hours of tossing dreamed of the sound of his son's laughter when he'd been a boy and they'd played ball near the house where they used to live. At three, he awoke and stared at the ceiling until daybreak.

# Eva and Isaiah

When all was said and done, Eva had to admit that any fool with two working eyes should have seen what was coming. It was bound to happen—and sooner rather than later, considering her state of mind. Yet it took her by surprise—just like everything else since that hot June night when Hutch had left. Isaiah Lonesome was more matter-of-fact about it.

"I knew the first time I saw you," he said. Although Isaiah reassured Eva that that first time was when he'd picked her up on the Garden State Parkway and *not* when Charley brought him home, and that his desperate search for a temporary home had nothing to do with where things ended up, Eva was still distressed by his words.

It all started out innocently enough, with a question about his music. Up until then, everything had gone as Eva had planned. So little seemed to have changed in her life, she hadn't even bothered to mention her new living arrangement to Charley or Steven. First of all, she was sure they would disapprove. Besides that, they were both preoccupied with living their own lives: Charlie with working and preparing for her October debut. Steven with Dana. Eva knew that one or the other was bound to stumble upon the truth at some point, and she'd do her explaining then. If she bothered to explain at all. Truth was, it felt good for once not to bother with what anyone—particularly her children—thought about her life. It made her feel free and completely independent.

As for her neighbors, they were neighborly enough to keep any questions they had about her new boarder to themselves. She spotted one or two giving Isaiah curious, appraising glances when he came home in the morning, but they were far too polite to ask her who he was or what he was doing there. Eva suspected that they assumed he was a college friend of Steven's, which was fine with her.

Things seemed to be going as Eva had planned. That first week they successfully avoided running into each other and that week established their pattern for the next two. Eva left at seven in the morning for the library just as Isaiah was coming home from the club in New York City. He left around seven at night, about an hour after she'd gotten home. She stayed in her room watching TV or he stayed in the guest room doing whatever he did until she was safely out of the house. When they ran into each other on the stairs or in the kitchen or garage, they would exchange a few pleasantries about the weather, the traffic or who would play in the World Series. He did all his laundry and made all of his calls from his apartment in Jersey City while his roommate and his new wife were at work. There were never dishes left in the sink or trash cans left unemptied. When Eva peeked into the guest room, she found that the bed was neatly made, the floor swept, and the guest towels in the small attached guest bathroom arranged on the towel rack in a tidy row. When she got home from work one Monday, she noticed that the lawn, which had begun to resemble hay, had been mowed and the newly repaired water sprinkler was shooting out rainbows of water. He paid two months' rent in cash when he moved in and always replaced any food that he took out of the refrigerator. There were times when Eva almost forgot he was there. But then she picked up his horn.

It happened on a Wednesday afternoon during the third week of his stay, almost two weeks before Labor Day. Because of a power outage at work, Eva's shift ended two hours early so she'd come home at three instead of six. She heard Isaiah's trumpet the minute she pulled into the driveway. The sound was so pure, she thought at first that it was a recording, but when he repeated the same phrase a dozen times with a new emphasis and a fresher line of sound each time, she realized he must be practicing. She opened the back door, pausing to hear the mellow tones that greeted her, and still holding her bag of groceries, was as lost in his music as she had been the first time she heard him.

He played scales, rapidly gliding through tones that were vaguely familiar, and then dashed off a riff. Transfixed, Eva sat down and listened as he settled into a sensuous, bluesy wail and then a haunting melody that made her feel wistful and melancholy. When he stopped playing, Eva anxiously waited for more. Then she put the milk in the refrigerator and headed to the sunroom, where he had been playing.

There were two entrances leading into the sunroom, which ran the length of the dining and living rooms, and as she stepped through one door he left through the other. Eva suspected that he'd heard her come in and was as anxious to avoid her as she was him. He'd left his trumpet, however, which lay in an open carrying case on a small side table.

The case was made of well-worn brown leather and lined in plush maroon velvet. The horn gleamed as if it were made of gold. Hesitating for a moment, Eva touched it with her fingertips, as if it posed some threat or would snap at her hand. Then she picked it up and examined it. It was heavier than she thought it would be, and she wondered how he could hold it as effortlessly as he did. As if in a trance, she put the instrument to her lips, curious about how it felt and where the sound came from, wondering what kind of skill it took to make music come from it like Isaiah did. For some odd reason, she expected it to be warm like skin.

"Why don't you try it?" Isaiah's deep voice coming from behind her startled her, and she nearly dropped the horn on the floor. She quickly placed it back in the case where it belonged and turned to face him, catching the scent of the lavender soap that she kept in the guest bathroom. She had bought the soap a year ago in Sag Harbor at a tiny perfume store that offered overpriced items for the "luxurious bath and bed" and had gone through her box in a month, showering and bathing with each bar until it was little more than a sliver. Until this moment, she'd forgotten she had any more.

He was dressed in jeans and a royal blue cutoff T-shirt that showed off his smooth chestnut skin and his well-developed arms and shoulders. She noticed for the first time a jagged tattoo high up on his arm that encircled it like barbed wire. Eva hated tattoos but found herself staring at this one in fascination. His short black dreadlocks, which had curled up tightly from the moisture of his shower, still held tiny silver droplets of water, and one drop dripped down the side of his face like sweat. He wiped it away impatiently.

"Go ahead. Pick it up and try it."

"No. I don't think so."

"Go ahead."

Self-consciously, Eva brought the mouthpiece to her lips again, and cautiously blew through it.

"Did you blow?"

"Nothing happened."

"Try it again."

She blew again and a squawking sound, somewhere between a note and a grunt, came out. She handed the horn back to Isaiah.

"How do you do it?"

"It's all in the lips and the tongue and the way you work them." He took the horn and blew a few notes, followed it with a very fast riff and then something slow and moody. Captivated, Eva watched him, noticing how tenderly he held the instrument, almost as if it were alive.

"What were you playing earlier, before you went upstairs?"

"You could hear me?" He glanced at her sheepishly. "I hope it wasn't too loud. I don't want to freak out your neighbors."

"No. It's okay. Nobody has said anything. What was it?"

"Well, uh, you know, I compose sometimes. Play it, then write it down later. The music you heard? It was something I wrote. I'll write it down or something when I go back upstairs."

"Will you play it again?" Eva wasn't sure where that came from, asking him to play what he'd played, but she was curious, even though she knew how artists were about a work-in-progress and their hesitancy about sharing it until it was finished. She knew how she had been. She also noticed the shyness that had come into his eyes. "Well, you don't have to play it if you don't want to," she quickly added.

"No. That's okay." He picked up the horn and blew the notes he'd played before, but they were shrill and rushed. Eva wondered if she had trodden into a place she shouldn't have gone. "It sounds different every time I do it," he said, apologizing.

"Where does it come from?"

He looked puzzled as he put the horn down. "Where does what come from?"

"Turning a thought into sound. Where does it come from?" She had wondered about that from the first time she'd heard him play, from the moment he'd stepped away from the band and blown that solo that had taken her and everybody else prisoner. He had what she had lost, that was for sure. It didn't have a name, and she couldn't see, feel or touch it, but she could hear it when he picked up his horn, and she knew she had had it once, but she didn't know where or why it had gone.

His eyes questioned her. "I don't know where it comes from. I just blow. "

"But how?"

He looked perplexed. "I don't know how. I just do it."

As if explaining, he picked up his trumpet and played something short filled with riffs and short blasts of sound. Then he smiled, shrugged and handed her the trumpet.

"Try it."

"You know I can't play like you."

"Just try it. Hold your lips like this." He pursed his lips together. Eva wondered if he was trying to change the subject, but she did what he said.

"Like this?"

"No." He pursed his lips again, demonstrating, and Eva tried it until hers came close. "Now you put it to your lips." Eva timidly took the horn and held it against her lips. "Now hold it this way," he said, pausing for a moment as he turned her body away from his. His arms encircled her body as he showed her how to grasp the horn, gently touching her underarms and gliding past her breasts as he held her in an embrace that wasn't quite an embrace. Eva stiffened, and then allowed her body to shift into his. She caught her breath. She liked the way he made her feel, so fragile and in an odd way protected. She could feel his body moving closer to hers, and his smell, blending subtly with that of the lavender, was inviting and dangerous. She drew back, aware suddenly that maybe she was enjoying this too much. But it was too late.

He nibbled very lightly on the back of her neck, his lips gently traveling upward to the base of her scalp, and then slowly and evenly back down again as far as they would go until they were cut off by the top of her collar. He stroked the curve of her neck and her chin and then gently caressed her breasts. Eva lost her breath and collapsed against him with a sigh. He took the horn from her hands, dropped it into the case, turned her toward him and kissed her fully and deeply, his tongue touching hers. Eva, completely aroused now by his touch and the surprise of it all, felt the rumble of sexual desire (which she hadn't felt in the better part of eight months) stir violently in the pit of her stomach. She pulled back.

"What's wrong?"

"I don't know!" She could hear the panic in her own voice.

He smiled that mischievous smile that she was never quite sure what to make of and nodded toward the stairs.

It was as if they did some Star Trek transport thing, it seemed to her when she thought about it later. She remembered being in the living room surprised that he was kissing her, and next thing she knew she was lying in his arms, completely nude in the guest bedroom. She couldn't remember negotiating the stairs or opening and closing the door to the room. She vaguely remembered seeing and entering it. The room was small and oblong with two windows, a hanging rhododendron and a ceiling fan, which whirred softly. But strangely enough, it was as if the room wasn't part of her house. Although she'd changed the linen before he came and had obviously bought it, she couldn't remember ever seeing it before. The whole room seemed unfamiliar, as if she were in the middle of some erotic dream and had never picked out the cream-colored wallpaper trimmed with blue cornflowers or the blue fake Persian rug or the glass IKEA vase filled with dried flowers that sat on the bureau. She didn't remember taking off her clothes or crawling next to him between the cool sheets. She remembered hearing the whir of the ceiling fan and thinking how good it felt against her naked skin, and how nice that it was on, but she didn't remember the time of day or whether it was dark or light or day or if she'd locked the front door.

His body was thinner than she had thought it would be, but muscular, and Eva was momentarily self-conscious about her own. But her desire for him quickly outweighed any embarrassment, and she realized she didn't give a damn one way or the other how she looked. When he'd pulled back the summer quilt, a cream-and-lace-covered number a friend had given her as a wedding gift, she felt a twinge of momentary guilt, but then realized she didn't give a damn about that either. She was too aroused to worry about anything but how good his smooth lean body felt next to hers. His obvious excitement was contagious, and she was overpowered by her need for him.

He opened her lips with his tongue again, kissing her fervently until she found herself with tongue in his mouth, wanting to touch and taste every part of him. His lips on her mouth and face, her eyelids, her neck, then all over her body, felt to her as if he were playing some long, sweet song. He followed the lines of her body with his hands, reading each piece of her with his fingertips and palms, as Eva touched, nuzzled, kissed every part of him that she could reach. He found new parts of her to touch or stroke—parts of her that she'd never known could be so quickly aroused—the small of her back, the tiny space between her breasts, the slender area near yet not touching her pubic hair, and finally gently teasing her clitoris with his tongue and bringing her to the edge of orgasm before he pulled away.

She wanted to devour him. She couldn't get enough of the salty taste of his neck on her tongue as it zipped down to his lips or the solid feel of his chest against the flat palm of her hand. Her fingertips slid over the muscles in his shoulders and upper arms. The ragged tattoo had fascinated her when she'd first spotted it and now she ran the bottom of her tongue down and across it, thrusting her face into his shoulders and arms, playing in the tight curly hair under his arms, around his belly button, and gliding down finally to slide his penis into her mouth as he buried his face into her stomach. And then finally, facing each other, pausing for a moment to gaze with stunned amazement into each other's eyes, as he thrust himself into her. Eva reached her first orgasm effortlessly, and then had a smaller, less intense one before he rolled onto his side, exhausted. And it was better the second time.

But the first thought that came to Eva's mind when they finally lay quiet and still beside each other was, *What have I done?* She tried to get up. Isaiah pulled her back down beside him.

"What's wrong?"

"Stop asking me that!"

"Tell me."

"When I figure it out, I'll tell you."

"You don't regret this, do you?" He had read her mind.

"I don't know yet." It was an honest answer.

"Then let's do it again," he said with his mischievous chuckle, and they did, more leisurely this time, as if getting to know each other again in a less frenzied, more intimate way.

When it was over, they slept for an hour. Eva awoke to Isaiah climbing out of bed. Fascinated, she watched him move around the room. She had known each crevice and crease of his body with her hands and mouth and now she studied him with her eyes, noticing how completely at ease he was with himself. He glanced up at her and smiled his strange amused smile.

"Come on, let's take a shower."

"Give me a minute." Eva, her passion spent, was self-conscious again about the years between them, those little sags and wrinkles that would show up in the late afternoon sun that was streaming unfiltered through the window. *How could I have done something like this?* she wondered. Somewhere between the passion when they first hit the bed and the first time they made love, she had reminded him to use condoms, and she now said a prayer of thanks for *that* presence of mind. Nevertheless, she felt like an irresponsible fool.

When she heard him turn on the shower, she grabbed her clothes from the floor where she'd stripped them off and dashed out of the room and up the stairs to the safety of her bedroom. She closed her door, buried the impulse to lock it and jumped into her shower. When the water hit her body, she thought about Isaiah again and desire for him tore through her body with the sharpness of pain. She turned on the cold water, letting it drip down her back and breasts, opening her mouth to it, letting it run down her throat, tasting it the way she'd tasted him. Then she dried off with a rough towel, slipped into a caftan and went downstairs.

Isaiah was sitting at the kitchen table, fully dressed, sipping a Sprite. When Eva sat down on the opposite side of the table, he offered her the can. Avoiding his eyes, she took a swig and handed it back to him.

"So where did you go?"

"Back upstairs."

"Why?"

"I wanted to shower in my own bathroom."

"Oh." He shrugged. "I was thinking about what you asked me before," he said solemnly after a moment.

"What did I say?" *God knew what she'd screamed out.*

"About how I play my music. How I *create*. Don't you remember?"

Eva thought for a moment, and then nodded. *That conversation certainly belonged to another age.*

"Well . . ." He paused. "I start with a note. One note. And I'll blow until it's as perfect as I can get it, and then I go back and blow another, and another, until finally the whole thing is done. Nothing miraculous. Just one note at a time. That's the way I do it."

Neither of them said anything for a while after that. They just passed the Sprite can back and forth until it was empty. Then Isaiah glanced at his watch and said it was time to go to work, and he'd catch her later on that night. After he left, Eva sat at the table with her head in her hands and wondered what in the hell she'd gotten herself into.

# Eva and Isaiah

## SUNDAY, SEPTEMBER 28

What Eva had gotten herself into those last weeks of August and well into September was a new set of expectations. She would wake at six-thirty, stagger into the bathroom to shower and dress, make it down the three stairs that led to the guest room on the second-floor landing and then pause, ears alert for any sound or movement. Clothed only in his briefs, Isaiah would snatch her into his room, thrust his tongue into her mouth as if searching for some treat between her lips and pull her clothes off in half the time it took her to put them on. They'd make love until Eva could tear herself from his arms, shower, pull her clothes back on and slide into the library late yet again.

Sometimes they would meet for "lunch." On those days, Eva would peek into the the cheery staff-only room, where the others chatted as they opened bagged lunches and snapped soda cans, and spout the lie that she had some miscellaneous errand to run. Then she'd race home at breakneck speed in time to catch Isaiah emerging from his shower, water dripping from his towel-clad body, rainbow droplets gleaming in his dreadlocked black hair.

More than once she wondered if she should save time by simply sleeping in Isaiah's bed, nude and ready to go in the morning when they woke up. But she realized she needed the separation and space her own bed provided. She wasn't ready to give Isaiah, who had touched every inch of her body, access to every part of her life. She needed the distance, insisted upon it. So he never climbed up the stairs to the master bedroom, and she never invited him.

Eva was puzzled by this new aspect of her personality. She wondered how much of the artist-librarian, whose life once consisted mainly of fretting about her lack of artistic inspiration and cooking for her children and husband, still lived within this lustful woman who took Isaiah's body into hers with such ravenous abandon, so she tried not to think about it. But some things were impossible to hide.

"Well, congratulations! On you and Hutch!" Helena from work said with a mischievous wink one afternoon when she stopped by Eva's cubicle to bum a cigarette. Eva's lunch—a box of Ritz crackers and an open jar of peanut butter—sat on her desk, and she was sipping apple juice from a cardboard container as she shifted through a pile of overdue notices and book order forms.

"Thanks," Eva muttered back, completely confused.

"The separation obviously did you two some good. You look like a woman in love! You positively glow in the morning . . . and those late lunches!" Helena rolled her eyes and grinned with delight. Eva stared at the computer screen. Helena settled into the chair across from her, obviously eager to discuss the finer points of the reconciliation

"Can we talk about this later?" Never comfortable lying, Eva impatiently threw away the straw, tore open the container and gulped the apple juice down.

"Oh, God, I'm sorry. I didn't mean to pry. I just thought you might feel like talking."

"It's just too . . . too soon." Eva, lying easily now, dropped her head demurely. "I'm just not ready to talk about things yet."

Helena patted her hand reassuringly. "Listen, these things take time. I'm just happy you-all have worked things out. But if you need a good marriage shrink, I have one. She didn't help me and Stan much, but it might do the two of you some good to talk to her."

Eva dutifully jotted down the woman's name and number as Helena read it from her electronic organizer, and Helena, satisfied that she had done her good deed for the day, returned to her office humming. More determined than ever to keep her relationship with Isaiah Lonesome a secret, Eva slumped into her chair, dispirited. The very thought that Helena, her coworkers or other acquaintances had guessed the truth about her morning rituals and lunchtime rendezvous sent a chill through her. She decided then to change her pattern—anything to keep that telltale glow off her face.

So she avoided Isaiah during the next few weeks, arriving at work before anybody else and eating lunch with her coworkers in the staff room. She listened sympathetically as Sheila complained about the incompetence of her dissertation advisor, and comforted Marvin when he whined about receiving another rejection letter from an editor. If Helena asked about Hutch and the progress of their relationship, she smiled and lied. When Isaiah tried to pull her into his bedroom in the morning, she claimed she had a mandatory meeting or dry cleaning to pick up, promising they would "talk" on the weekend. He'd simply shrug, smile and amble back into his room.

But Eva found his lackadaisical attitude disturbing too. *How much do I really mean to this man?* she wondered. Each time they made love she became more conscious of the dangers and pitfalls of a middle-aged woman involved with a man nearly the age of her daughter. Isaiah seemed to need little from her—no conversation, no emotional commitment, no financial help—nothing but sex whenever she was willing to give it.

And when they did get around to *actually* talking on the weekends, Eva found the emptiness of their conversations unsettling. He was evasive when it came to intimate details about his life. Although music was an important part of their relationship now and the playing of his favorite musicians—Miles Davis, Roy Hargrove, Clifford Brown, Lee Morgan—inspired their lovemaking and was always somewhere in the background, he rarely talked about the club, and he practiced when she wasn't home. He did mention that Sky Langston had asked him to lead the band on alternate weekends and that he had sold out to a new partner, but didn't say when he would be playing or who now co-owned the club. But Eva continued to be curious about him—who and what he came from and where he was going.

"What is your mother like?" she demanded to know when they were together late one Sunday morning about two months into their "arrangement," which was what she'd taken to calling their affair. Isaiah sat on a stool next to her in the kitchen, wolfing down the banana pancakes she fixed for him on Sundays because he claimed that nobody had ever cooked for him. He was dressed in tight cutoffs that rode low on his waist, just below his belly button. Eva could see silky tufts of hair whenever he moved or shifted, and she stifled an impulse to run her finger through it. Between her deliberately missed mornings and his late nights, they hadn't touched each other in a week and a half. "Your mother, Isaiah, what is she like?"

"Why do you want to know about my mother?" he asked, suspicious.

"Just curious."

He grinned the grin that Eva found irresistible. "Do you think that *you* remind me of my mother and that's why we got involved?" There was amusement in his eyes, as if he didn't take her seriously. But Isaiah never took anything but music seriously.

"No. I'm just curious."

"Do you really think I could have *this* kind of relationship with a woman who reminded me of my mother? Come on, cut me some slack. Cut yourself some slack. How could you possibly remind anybody of his mother?" He made a playful grab for her, and Eva let him hold her for a moment, feeling strangely grateful for his words and enjoying the feel of his quick, hard erection against her thigh. She thought about unplugging the coffeepot and suggesting that they go upstairs.

But she said instead, "Well, I'm somebody's mother." Isaiah let her go and returned to his stack of pancakes.

In the two months they had been together, this was the first time either of them had mentioned Charley. Eva hadn't talked to her daughter since Charley had called two weeks before to remind her about the performance at the Brooklyn club next week, the first Saturday night in October.

"Why do you let this age thing mess you around? I just like women. I don't care how much older they are than me."

"I wasn't aware that I was letting this age thing mess me around," Eva said, aware that that was exactly what she was doing.

"You always bring it up."

"No, I don't."

"It's always on your mind. You're so easy to read."

"That's more than I can say for you."

"Cut it out, Eva. I get tired of you always trying to figure me out."

"Well, what is she like?"

"My mother? She's like somebody's mother, that's all. I never think about that kind of stuff, how somebody is, what's on her mind. Don't you know that about me by now?"

"What is there to know? You never tell me anything about yourself."

He looked annoyed. "Don't start that again. You make me sound like I got something to hide."

"Well, do you?"

He turned away from her, his mouth poked out, and Eva, recalling her last argument with a man she cared about, decided not to push it. She got some juice out of the refrigerator and poured herself a glass, to avoid saying anything else.

But after a moment Isaiah added somewhat defensively, "I told you about Sky Langston and Le Muse, didn't I? That's something."

"You didn't tell me what weekends you're playing or who bought the club." Eva noticed his eyes shift away from her but chose not to mention it.

"Is that really important?" he asked, still avoiding her eyes as he stuffed a forkful of banana pancake into his mouth.

"And anyway, I don't care about Langston and his new partner, whoever he or she is. Is your mother still alive?" Eva continued.

"Back to that. Yeah. She lives in Jersey City with my stepfather," he said, finally giving it up.

"Then your parents are divorced?"

"Jesus, Eva. Give it a break! My dad died fifteen years ago, when I was a kid. She married again. I can't stand the dude; he can't stand me. My mama takes his side, okay?"

Eva thought, *Fifteen years ago I was a grown woman who was praying for a good man, and Charley was still losing her teeth. Fifteen years ago you were a kid who was crying for his daddy.*

"You're still a kid, Isaiah," Eva said as if she were talking to herself. Isaiah looked surprised, then annoyed and then he grinned.

"You think so?" He pulled her body into his with one hand, and unhooked her bra with the other as he ran his lips over her throat and downward, unbuttoning her robe and taking her nipple into his mouth, flicked it with his tongue.

"So you do have a mama thing?" Eva teased as he brought his lips back to her mouth, and they went upstairs and made hot, fast love on top of his bed.

Afterward, as she lay beside him listening to his breath, satisfied but somehow not, she sighed almost inaudibly as her eyes roamed the room. He was everywhere now. His clothes pressed against Charley's and Steven's winter sweaters and coats hanging in storage bags in the closet. His weights were piled like toys next to the bathroom door. His red T-shirt and worn denims were casually tossed over the white rocking chair and nearly covered the crisp green and white gingham pillow that she had inherited from her mother. Sometimes when he was away, she would lay on the rumpled bedclothes, taking in his smell and remembering how they'd made love that morning. Even now, the thought of him inside her aroused her again. She stretched and moved closer to him, closing her eyes for a moment, and then opening them to watch the rise and fall of his chest.

*Why have I become so involved with this man and what does it mean?* she asked herself.

This relationship between them had happened so quickly she had scarcely had time to reflect upon it. Maybe it *was* just sex, but maybe that was all you could count on sometimes. After ten years of conversation, routine and predictability, what had she really known about Hutch? She moved close again to Isaiah, kissed the top of his ear, then ran her tongue down the outer edge of it. He stirred and ran his fingers up and around her thighs, crossing her buttocks.

There was a gentle, persistent scratching on the closed door, and Eva glanced toward it with annoyance. Fiercely loyal to Hutch, Bama never entered any space that Isaiah had come into but would simply sit on her plump gray haunches outside the room, scratching or mewling until Eva came to fetch her. Eva usually tried to ignore her, but Bama, whose cry could go from a gentle purr to a raucous growl, was persistent. She meowed pathetically now, her voice as grating as fingernails against a chalkboard. Eva kissed Isaiah lightly on the lips, slipped on her clothes and picked the cat up, and then realized with a pang of guilt that she'd forgotten to feed her. She headed downstairs to the kitchen with the cat at her heels, opened a can of cat food and watched as the cat greedily gobbled it down. Then she began to clean up the breakfast dishes and load them into the dishwasher.

"Your cat doesn't like me," Isaiah said when he came downstairs about twenty minutes later. The moment he came in, Bama turned tail and ran. He was dressed casually in a sports jacket and open shirt, but there was a studied elegance about his clothes and the way he carried himself that made him look mature, more responsible. Eva figured this must be one of those nights that he was filling in for Sky Langston.

"Bama is shy. It takes her a while to warm up to people. Don't take it personally."

Isaiah shrugged. "Hey, it's just a cat. I don't take it personally; I don't really care," he said over his shoulder as he blew her a kiss and closed the door behind him. Eva watched him get into his car and drive away, thinking how good-looking he was, and how young. After he'd gone, Bama crept back into the kitchen and rubbed against her leg, and Eva picked her up.

"Did you hear that? You're just a cat. You may as

well be nice to the guy; he may have to feed your simple little butt someday," she scolded. The cat squirmed to get away, and Eva dropped her back on the floor.

A draft blew in through an open window in the living room, and Eva shivered, wondered if it was some kind of omen and then put it out of her mind. Labor Day was three weeks past and the leaves had begun to turn; she could smell winter in the air. She paused for a moment, thinking about how quickly the summer had gone, and then closed several of the windows, checking to see if the storm windows were working. For the last five years, she and Hutch had spent Labor Day weekend with friends in Sag Harbor and had toasted the end of the summer with champagne. In September there were bulbs to buy and plant, bird feeders to fill and ratatouille to cook, which Eva only made in fall with its surplus of eggplants, zucchinis and the last of the tomatoes. It was one of Hutch's favorite dishes, and they'd eat it for two days with red wine and freshly baked French bread. Next week would be the first week in October, and November would be here before she knew it. She had so many things to do before it got cold, things that Hutch usually took care of: check the furnace, have the gutters and fireplace cleaned, put the fertilizer on the grass, have the trees around the house checked for loose branches. She hadn't even finished sorting and packing away her summer clothes yet, and there were her winter clothes to take from the cedar-lined trunk in the attic.

That was one of those tedious seasonal chores she hated, and she always put it off until the last moment. She went to her room, showered and dressed and then went into the attic, glancing at the newly repaired skylight as she passed it. One Sunday afternoon about a week after they'd made love the first time, Isaiah had brought some tools and showed her how to fix it. They had worked as a team, chatting and joking, the first and last time they did anything together besides make love. Isaiah was an able carpenter, but the job was not that of a skilled craftsman. She had lived with an expert long enough to know good work when she saw it. *How old was Isaiah when his father taught him to work with his hands?* she wondered. She tried to imagine him as a boy, picking up a hammer and nails, examining them the way Charley used to examine Hutch's tools, and she felt sad at the memory. Charley had loved to work with Hutch when she'd been young, but Steven had never showed the slightest bit of interest, which hurt more than angered Hutch, and Charley soon lost interest too. That was one thing they'd joked about when she'd been pregnant with the baby they'd lost, how this one would take on the family business, this one would be the architect—a combination of the artist in her and the builder in him. This baby would belong to the two of them. That dream died with the baby and neither of them had talked about the baby or the dream since—or even how much they had lost. Another conversation they had never had.

Lucas Hutchinson III. The inheritor of precious, forgotten dreams. Their gift to each other.

She sighed loudly as she thought about that child and then put him out of her mind. Autumn always made her wistful—the coming winter, the death of summer. Winter had always brought death into her life. Her mother. Her baby. She settled next to the trunk on the floor with another sad, long sigh. Bama, who had followed her upstairs, licked her hand, and Eva scratched the cat's ears.

"You miss him, don't you?" she said as the cat arched her back. "I miss him too," she said, admitting something to the cat that she hadn't been able to admit aloud to herself. Although it had been more than two months since she'd heard from Hutch, she alternated between nearly calling him at Donald Mason's house and a firm determination never to speak to him again. More than two months without a word from him, not since that trite conversation, if you could even call it that, which they'd had after the Fourth. Not a call to inquire if she was alive or dead.

Had she underestimated the seriousness of his affair with that woman Cara? Was she the source of that lack of joy he had claimed to be feeling? Hell, he'd left Irene for a younger woman—maybe he'd left Eva for a younger woman still. Maybe this was Hutch's pattern, to pull up stakes every ten years or so and find somebody younger and firmer. She could understand now the pull of youth with all its wild, unfocused energy. Had Cara been for Hutch what Isaiah was for her? Maybe what was good for the gander was good for the goose.

She went downstairs and filled a laundry basket with summer clothes from her bedroom closet and brought them back upstairs, folded them, packed them into the cedar-lined trunk. She examined her winter clothes—flannel shirts, sweatsuits, a robe from L.L. Bean and thick socks. The smell of cedar reminded her of her mother, that and this season that always brought her back. She held a sweater rich with the scent of it close to her face, trying to bring her mother back again, just for an instant.

*What would Louisa say?* The thought of it made Eva cringe. There had been a hard side to Louisa, a fierce determination that never let anything rest. That had been the Louisa who had thrown her only daughter out because she was pregnant, the Louisa of snobby women's clubs and pretentious aspirations on a librarian's salary. The one who had bitched and bellyached until Roscoe Lilton, weary of his wife's complaints, had carried them up North, leaving the "messiness" of his family—Aunt Delia with her spells, chants and unguents—back where they belonged in South Carolina. There had been nothing of the southern black woman in Louisa. She was as hard and tough as a Newark street, and she'd been proud of it.

But there had been another side to her mother too— the part that had dreamed big dreams for her daughter, that had stayed on her about school, and getting into a "good" college to become the professional woman circumstances and the South had never permitted her to become.

An abortion would be an easy choice, her mother had hinted, never quite saying or suggesting it was a way out, especially since she'd been careless enough to get pregnant in the first place. But carelessness shouldn't ruin a woman's life. Women had made that choice before, and it was a wise one when there was no connection with the father, when there were other things she wanted to do with her life. At this point it was the simplest choice to make, the least complicated. And then—with no shame—she could continue college as Louisa wanted, become the woman Louisa knew she could become, and Eva had loved and wanted to please her mother. It might have been the right choice for another daughter or even for herself at another time, but she knew something that her mother didn't. This one *had* to be born. More than her own life, she loved this baby she carried within her, certainly she loved it far more than pleasing her mother, and as young as she'd been, just shy of nineteen, she'd walked out of her mother's house without a glance back and never for a moment regretted it.

*What would Louisa say?* How many times in her life since her mother's death had that question haunted her? Eva brought the sweater to her nose to smell the scent once more before she packed it away. What her mother would say about the choices she made filled her dreams sometimes and occasionally her nightmares.

"Mommy!" The sound of Charley's voice screaming up from the downstairs landing startled her. Eva shoved the sweater into the box. "Are you there?" Eva's heart quickened as she took the steps downstairs two at a time.

Charley, a strange expression on her face, stood in front of the guest room—Isaiah's room. Eva focused on the space above her daughter's head, avoiding Charley's eyes, not ready to see what was in them. *I have nothing to be ashamed of*, she said to herself. *I am a grown woman. Charley is not a child.* Finally she made herself look at her daughter, willed herself not to flinch.

But the eyes that stared out at her were not her daughter's eyes but the accusatory eyes of her mother, large with disapproval and unblinking. Eva reached behind Charley and firmly closed the door to the guest room, but her hand was trembling.

"How could you do something like this, Mother?"

Charley said. Eva reached for the cigarette she didn't have in her pocket and then forced herself to turn and walk downstairs toward the living room without saying anything. Charley trailed behind her, like she used to do when she'd been a little girl begging for candy in the A&P.

"This has nothing to do with you, Charley. This is none of your business."

"Isaiah Lonesome's shit is everywhere! My ex-boyfriend is living here, and you don't think it's my business?" Charley looked wounded as she slumped down on the living room couch, but her voice was low and controlled, not hysterically high as Eva had expected it to be. Eva was surprised and relieved; it was a blessing. *Maybe Charley will be more accepting of this relationship than I've given her credit for. Maybe everything will work out.* Eva felt a surge of relief, a release of tension. She could catch her breath.

Leaving Charley alone on the couch, she went into the kitchen in search of a cigarette. She found one in an emergency pack she kept hidden away in a drawer in the kitchen. She had managed to cut down to four cigarettes a day—the first in the morning when she had her coffee, the second when she joined Helena for their midmorning smoke, the third when she got home from work, and the final one at night just before she went to sleep. She pulled in the smoke now from the emergency cigarette, as if it were the last breath she would inhale, and then went back to join Charley on the couch.

"I guess this is a new stage for us, isn't it, Charley?" Eva's voice was hopeful, philosophical, as she settled next to her daughter.

"New stage? What do you mean?" Charley eyed her suspiciously.

"Well, maybe we're both learning to accept each other for who we are, as complete, independent women. Grown women who love, honor and respect each other despite all of the quirks and crazy passions we each know that we have—"

"Quirks and crazy passions?" Charley narrowed her eyes, suspicion now in her voice. Apprehension snaked its way up the back of Eva's neck.

"Well . . ." Eva shrugged her shoulders, forcing herself to act casually, naturally. Charley, wrinkling her nose, moved to the wing chair across from the coffee table that separated them.

"I hate cigarettes, Mother. You said you were stopping."

"I'm down to four a day, but sometimes I feel like I need one. Like now," Eva smiled self-consciously.

"How could you smoke? Nobody smokes anymore. It's like . . . well . . . vulgar. Kind of rude. Look what you're doing to your health!"

"You sound like your father."

"What's wrong with sounding like Daddy?"

"Nothing," Eva said quickly, stuffing out the cigarette. The first draw was the only one that counted anyway. "There, satisfied?"

Charley sighed. "Thank you. Aren't you scared people will get the wrong impression?" Puzzled, Eva regarded her daughter without saying anything. But a sense of foreboding made her back stiffen. "And what did you mean when you said that stuff about quirks and crazy passion?"

Eva shifted her eyes nervously and took a breath. "I

don't know quite what to say, Charley, except these things just happen. I'm not even sure how or why, but sometimes the physical attraction between two people is so strong, so overwhelming, that you just have to accept it, give in to it, live with it for a while and see where—"

Charley's eyes grew big with horror. "Oh, my God!" she said, enunciating each word very slowly. Eva's heart began to pound. "Do you mean to tell me that you and Isaiah . . ." Eva regarded her daughter with alarm, realizing that until this moment Charley had thought that the extent of her relationship with Isaiah Lonesome was that she had simply offered him a place to live.

"W-well, yes," she stuttered out.

Charley took a sharp breath in and exhaled loudly as if she couldn't catch her breath. "I don't believe it! My mother is *fucking* my ex-boyfriend! My mother! Oh, my God, I don't believe it!" Dramatically, she threw her hands up in the air.

Eva slumped back against the couch. "Please don't use language like that in my presence," she said. It was a ridiculous thing to say, since Charley had heard her use the word herself in a fit of anger on more than one occasion, but it offered her a momentary sense of control.

Charley continued to stare at her in wide-eyed disbelief. "Isn't that what you're doing, for Christ's sake? Is *that* all you have to say for yourself? Yell at me for saying 'fuck'?"

Eva stood up, sat down and then stood back up again. Anger flashed through her at the tone of Charley's voice, but she didn't know what to do. For a moment she felt like slapping her daughter across her face, something she had never done in her life. "I don't have to say *anything* for myself," she finally said and sat back down, covering her face with her hands.

Neither woman spoke for a very long time. Eva closed her eyes for a moment, trying to draw on the strength she knew she must have in reserve, and then took her hands away from her face to look at her daughter, who stared straight ahead.

"I know this must be a shock to you, but—"

"Shock!" Charley screamed as she shook her head. "Is 'shock' the only word you can come up with? Do people actually know about this? People like the Abbots and Hammersmiths and Mr. and Mrs. Mason and Mrs. Lennox?" Charley's eyes grew wide again as she named their immediate neighbors, Donald and Raye Mason and the respected mother of one of her best friends. Eva didn't say anything. "Does daddy know?" Charley's voice was a plaintive wail. "How do you think he is going to feel?"

"Don't criticize what you don't understand!" Eva managed to mutter. She knew it sounded weak, but it was the only thing she could think of to say. Bama entered the room and jumped into Eva's lap. She hugged the cat in a surge of gratitude for easing, at least for a moment, the tension in the air. A lump formed in her throat. Charley watched the two of them and shook her head in disgust.

"Why Isaiah? I mean, what's *he* got that's so irresistible?" Eva noticed that curiosity and sarcasm seemed to have momentarily replaced Charley's anger, but she couldn't trust herself to speak. She pulled Bama toward her and then let the cat squirm out of her lap. "Are you in love with him?"

"No! Of course not," Eva answered quickly; that was one thing she was sure of. She was old enough not to get good sex mixed up with love.

"Then why?"

Eva couldn't bring herself to admit the obvious to her daughter so she avoided her eyes.

"What do you see in him?" Charley's eyes were watering and her voice was tight. Eva hoped that perhaps her daughter was trying hard to understand something that seemed incomprehensible. She didn't say anything, afraid she'd make things worse.

"What?" Charley's voice was harsher now, demanding an answer. Eva realized that she was daring her to say or hint that what she had with Isaiah was based purely on sexual pleasure.

"We're friends," Eva muttered weakly. She guessed maybe that was true. Charley rolled her eyes with another exasperated shake of her head. "Please tell me what you're feeling, Charley," Eva said, but even as she spoke, she knew she was actually trying to understand what she herself was feeling. She was numb. She was embarrased. For some strange reason she felt humiliated.

Charley studied her mother's face for a while and then answered like a hurt, pouting little girl, "I don't want to tell you how I feel."

"Just say it. I need to know."

Charley sighed, and then looked Eva straight in the eye. "I feel betrayed. I feel like maybe you were lusting after him the whole time I was going out with him. Like maybe you've always seen me as some kind of competitor instead of a daughter, like maybe you don't like who you are and really want part of me, part of my life, to make up for the hole in your own. The whole damn thing is kind of . . . well, frankly, it's sick and incestuous!"

Eva cringed and her eyes watered. "Do you have any feelings for Isaiah now, Charley? Please tell me if you do and I'll—"

Charley interrupted her with a scowl of indignation. "Have you forgotten? I broke up with him! He got on my nerves with that dumb horn and all his weird music. All the time. It would be different if he were into hip-hop or reggae and making some money or something, but jazz? You don't have to worry about anything between me and Isaiah Lonesome. What did he say about me?"

"We've never discussed you. Our relationship has nothing to do with you," Eva said. "Why do you feel betrayed when there was nothing serious between you?"

"Because you are my mother," Charley said quietly and emphatically, and then added with new bitterness, "I feel like I don't even know you. Like we're really not even mother and daughter. Like we're not even related. Your relationship with Isaiah Lonesome is— well, it's inappropriate." Charley had used the word that she and Hutch had used to describe Isaiah's relationship with her, and Eva wondered if she remembered it.

"Life is often inappropriate," Eva said quietly.

"I have nothing more to say to you."

"Charley, please—" Eva pleaded for she wasn't sure what, but those were the only words she could utter before Charley picked up the wool sweater she'd gotten from the closet in the guest room and left the house without looking back.

\*    \*    \*

"Just how deep was your relationship with my daughter?" Eva asked Isaiah later that night. They were standing on the landing between the second-floor bedrooms and the stairs that led up to the master bedroom, headed to their separate spaces. It was late, and they were both tired.

Isaiah didn't answer for a moment and then said, "Are you asking as Eva or as Charley's mother?"

"Is there a difference?"

He smiled his enigmatic smile. "Of course there is, but I don't think you're ready to admit it yet."

"So your answer would be different?"

"Same notes, different beat."

"Give me the mother beat first."

He cleared his throat, and spoke with exaggerated seriousness.

"Well, Mrs. Hutchinson. I, uh, respect your daughter very much and all that, but we have *nothing* in common. You think I don't talk to you; there wasn't even sex between me and Charley." Eva flinched, but Isaiah continued. "We don't have the same values, we don't like the same things, and, in case it really matters, I've been with maybe *five* women since I've been with her, so it's not like I jumped from her bed into yours. But why are you so worried about Charley all of a sudden?"

"Because she found out about us," Eva said miserably.

An amused smirk settled on Isaiah's face, yet his voice wasn't cruel when he spoke. "Did you actually think that she wouldn't?"

# Hutch and Raye

Anxious to share her news, Charley called Hutch the first thing Monday morning.

"I've known since Labor Day," Hutch said in what he hoped was a calm, self-assured voice, but which came out sounding sour and shaky.

"That was three weeks ago! Why didn't you tell me? Can you believe it? And with Isaiah Lonesome, of all people! Isn't it disgusting?"

"Isaiah Lonesome?" Hutch repeated the name. His stomach dropped as he placed the face of the man he'd seen Eva with when he'd gone to the house on Labor Day. "Isn't that the saxophone player you used to date?"

"Trumpet player. Yeah, that's him."

Hutch groaned involuntarily, then mumbled, "However you feel about this, Charley, remember, this is your mother's business, not yours or mine." He was mouthing what he was sure Eva had said to her daughter, if she had said anything at all. Parental instinct told him that, despite the circumstances, when it came to their children he and Eva should present some kind of united front. Besides, he really didn't want to hear the sordid details of Charley's encounter. He quickly changed the subject to her upcoming comedy club performance and grunted occasionally while she rambled on about the material she was preparing. But he wasn't listening. His mind was on Eva and Isaiah. With the exception of the time he spent with Raye Mason, that was where it had been for the past three weeks.

After Charley hung up, Hutch settled back on the rented brown tweed couch in the furnished apartment where he'd been living for the past three weeks. He wondered what Charley—or Steven, for that matter—would say about the turn his life had recently taken. "Disgusting" might be the *kindest* word Charley would use. But maybe his situation was as inevitable as everything else that had happened since that hot June night when he'd left. Maybe he was as destined for this change in his life as Eva obviously had been. But *he* was nagged by an overwhelming sense of guilt. He knew the worst was yet to come, but there didn't seem to be anything he could, or wanted to, do about it. If only it hadn't been for that chance encounter with Eleanor Hammersmith, his nosy, overbearing neighbor, in the cashier's line on Labor Day, things would be different. He might have remained in sweet ignorance, and the inevitable confrontation that he now dreaded would never come to pass.

\*　　\*　　\*

He had been shopping on Labor Day in the early part of the evening in a convenience store he was glad he found open, his cart filled with soaps, shaving lotion, dental floss and toothpaste, when he felt Eleanor's persistent tap on his left shoulder.

"Hutch?"

"Eleanor! How nice to see you!" He turned to greet her, noticing with alarm her critical glance at the items in his cart. Desperately, he tried to think of a graceful way to escape her questions. He picked up a copy of the *Star-Ledger*, which he'd already read, and leafed through it, hoping she would take the hint.

"I was so sorry to hear about you and Eva." Resigning himself to what was coming, he folded the newspaper and tucked it back on the shelf.

"Yeah. We're trying to work things out, and I'm sure we will. Thanks for your concern." He stared at the bald head of the man in front of him, hoping she'd sense his mood and leave him alone. No such luck.

"There must be something going around. Did you know that the Levins, three houses down from you and Eva, just separated?"

"I hadn't heard," Hutch said, studying the man's head. Did the woman sit all day with a pair of binoculars trained on her neighbors' windows? he wondered.

"But good things are happening too. The Browns' daughter is getting married next February. There's nothing quite like a winter wedding ceremony! All that red velvet and buttered rum punch. I heard Charley was engaged."

"They broke up." One more piece of juicy gossip for Eleanor to thrust on some defenseless soul.

"Well, she's very young."

"Yes, she is. Well, it was certainly nice talking with you, Eleanor." He nodded, smiled and picked up a copy of *Newsweek*.

"Yes . . ." Eleanor paused uncomfortably as if she were trying to think of something else to say. Hutch toyed with the idea of getting out of line on the pretense of having forgotten something, but before he could make his move, Eleanor grabbed his arm. "Well, I certainly hope you two will work things out. You are such a lovely couple. Such a nice family. And it was certainly nice of that young man—I guess he is a friend of Steven's—to help out around the house. I've never seen the grounds look so beautiful, I—"

"Friend of Steven's?" Hutch closed the magazine, frozen.

"Yes. A very good-looking young man. Drives a cute little black car."

Hutch was puzzled for a moment, but then realized that the car must belong to Dana. Eleanor Hammersmith, good, color-blind neighbor that she was, had politely left out the fact that Steven's friend was white. So Steven and Dana had moved in with Eva. He felt a surge of relief and then joy. Now, finally, he knew where he could find his son.

Hutch had not spoken to Steven since his son's harsh words—and his lack of them—at Beans 'n' Sprouts. He had been calling Steven every single day for nearly a month, and Steven never returned his calls. Hutch had even stopped by Steven's apartment and been rudely told by the superintendent that his son had moved out in July. Irene had been unsympathetic. After their initial conversation the night that it had happened, she refused to speak to him again about it. He knew he had been living with his son's anger for too long. He had to talk to him and explain his feelings, and let him know how much he loved him and that whoever he was—gay, straight or in-between—Steven would always have his love. He needed to make peace with his son, whatever it took. But first he had to find him. And now Eleanor Hammersmith and her big mouth had given him his opportunity. It was the chance he'd been praying for. He turned anxiously toward her, eager to listen.

"So Steven and his friend are there all the time?" He wondered off-handedly if Eleanor had guessed that Steven was gay, and decided that she hadn't. If she knew, she would have found a way to work it into the conversation.

"Well, I haven't actually seen Steven, but his friend is certainly there. Jim sees him leaving for work every evening."

"God, that's good news. Great!" Hutch nearly shouted. Eleanor Hammersmith glanced at him curiously and then rambled on. Hutch scarcely heard her; he was too busy planning his next move.

He was giddy as he drove toward his old house, plotting things out, imagining Steven's surprise and what his reception would be. He worried for a moment if they would be home. It was a holiday, but he would have to take that chance. At the very least, he now knew where Steven lived. Steven couldn't avoid him; he would have to listen to what he had to say. And if he didn't, Hutch would just keep coming back until he did. He'd sensed a peacemaker's spirit in Dana that day in Beans 'n' Sprouts and was sure he'd be a sympathetic ally. And maybe Eva would be too.

This would also be an opportunity to talk to her again, something he hadn't dared do since that short, nasty conversation the day after the Fourth of July. But maybe now he could make things right between them. The boring, exhausting life he was now leading was hardly the "joy" he had been looking for. All he did now was work, talk to Raye and drink scotch with Donald when he was around, which was seldom. His midnight departure, which had seemed so desperate and necessary in June, seemed laughable now. What in God's name had been on his mind? Why had he left? He didn't care anymore. He just wanted to go back home.

When Hutch saw the black Geo parked in the driveway, his breath caught in his throat. Thank God! They were there. There were no parking spaces in front of the house, so he parked across the street two houses down and sat in his car for a moment or two, collecting his thoughts. According to Eleanor, Dana spent more time at the house than Steven did; it might be easier to approach him first. Get right to the point. Tell the man how happy he was that he and his son were in love. Ask him to help them reconcile.

He had gotten out of his car and was happily walking toward the house when he spotted Isaiah Lonesome leaving it. Hutch stopped dead in his tracks. For a moment, he wasn't sure what to make of the young man, trumpet case in hand, who sauntered down the driveway like he owned it. Stunned, he tried to make sense of the situation. Then, his heart in his throat, he stared in disbelief.

The exchange between Eva and Isaiah was short and sweet.

"Hey," Isaiah said with a nod toward Eva, who stood at the back door and whose quick smile told Hutch more than her words could say. "Later on, okay?"

"Okay," Eva said coyly, returning his smile.

Hutch had never before realized that the word "okay" could hold such sexual promise. There was a sensual playfulness in her smile and in the toss of her head, and a hunger in the way the man leaned against his car and watched her go back into the house that told Hutch everything he needed to know. If he had had any doubt left, it disappeared when the man ogled the subtle swing of Eva's hips as, glancing over her shoulder at him, she sashayed into the house. She was wearing the white rayon robe with blue piping that Hutch had seen a dozen times before, but always in the bedroom, never in the kitchen, never standing on the porch, saying "okay" and grinning at a stranger.

Only later was Hutch thankful that they had been so involved with each other they hadn't noticed him, mouth agape, straining to hear what they were saying. Transfixed, he had watched the man climb into his car and drive away. For a moment, Hutch considered pursuing him, catching him, cursing him out, beating him up. He could almost feel the man's flesh go flat and bloody against his fist as he pummeled him to the ground. But then he realized that it was pathetic enough for him to be spying on the two of them. The only thing worse than looking like a fool was proving himself one by trying to fight a man twenty years younger and thirty pounds lighter who could obviously kick his behind.

Feeling nauseous and slightly dizzy, Hutch returned to his car and sat in it for the next ten minutes, trying to get himself together enough to drive back to Donald's. He played with the idea of barging into the house and confronting Eva, demanding to know what she was up to, where she knew this guy from, how long she had known him and if he was the reason their sex life had gone into the toilet. Was he somebody who worked at the library? But what could she possibly say to make him feel better? It was obvious what was going down.

He had driven back to Donald's house in a daze, feeling so many emotions at the same time that he couldn't sort through them. But mostly he felt hurt and humiliated—those two feelings he was sure of. When he got to Donald's house he went immediately into his room and like a whipped child crawled into his freshly made bed to sulk and think of what to do next. Finally he got up, splashed cold water on his face and went in search of Donald for counsel and sympathy. Donald had again been proven right—if only he had listened! Donald had warned him to start thinking about himself, to forget about going back, and to heed his instincts about his marriage. Those instincts had been correct after all. Donald would know what he should do.

But Donald was nowhere to be found. Instead, Hutch found Raye sitting in the small room that adjoined the master bedroom, leafing through a magazine. After hesitating a moment, he walked in.

"I've had a terrible blow," he said. Raye looked at the expression on his face, placed her hand over her mouth, stood up and moved toward him as if prepared to catch him, then sat back down.

"My God! The kids! Did something happen—"

"No. Nothing like that. It's Eva."

"Eva? Is she okay?"

"Yeah. She's fine."

He was out of breath. He closed his eyes for a moment and then opened them. He made himself breathe in and then out. Taking it slow. Relaxing. Forcing himself to take in his surroundings.

This room, which he'd never been in before, was unmistakably Raye's. It was small and neat, with pale yellow walls and ivory trim. Willowy ferns floated in the large open windows. The heady scent of the perfume Raye wore was everywhere. Hutch found the room strangely comforting, as if he'd wandered into some serene oasis. It was hard to imagine Donald cursing, bragging, tossing back scotch in this soothing space. He settled down beside Raye on the narrow divan covered in white Haitian cotton. As usual, her eyes demanded the truth, and he poured it out.

"She's seeing somebody. I think he's living with her."

"Eva?" Raye, her eyes big with disbelief, took off her reading glasses and dropped them into her lap. "Are you sure?"

"Yes, I'm sure," Hutch said miserably, dropping his head into his hands. Raye got up and came back with a snifter filled with brandy, which she handed to Hutch, who gratefully took it and swallowed it down, feeling like he was playing a scene from a 1940s movie about some sorry-ass husband whose heretofore faithful wife had just run off with the plumber. Raye was playing the role of his old wartime buddy.

"I don't know what to say," Raye said finally. Hutch shook his head helplessly and she added, "Did you recognize him? I mean, is he a friend of the family? Somebody from work?"

Hutch was breathing hard again. He took another gulp of the brandy and swallowed it, ignoring the way it burned his throat. "He's young. I know that. He looked familiar."

"How young?" Raye asked skeptically. "He's not the paperboy or somebody like that?"

"Raye, when was the last time you saw a boy deliver the paper? Old retired guys who can't find anything else to do deliver newspapers now. He's Steven's age."

"Hmmm." Raye fell back against the couch and watched Hutch sip his drink. "What are you going to do?"

"Do you mean, am I going to pull some crazed jealous husband bullshit or something like that?"

"I guess if you were going to do that, you would have done it by now," Raye said with a philosophical shrug, answering herself, and Hutch sighed.

"What can I do? What right do I have to do or say anything? *I* walked out on *her* remember?"

"Hmmm," Raye said again, and Hutch glanced at her with annoyance.

"What does that mean, that hmmm you just said?"

"Which one? The first or the second?"

"The first. About the son of a bitch being Steven's age."

"That puts him in his twenties, right?"

"Yeah."

"Don't worry. She'll get bored fast. Once the sex is—"

"Oh, God!" Hutch interrupting her, doubled over as if in pain, but Raye continued, seemingly oblivious.

"I've heard they're never good lovers, guys that

young. What can they do? Get it up fast, make it last forever! No technique, no—"

"Jesus Christ, Raye! What are you trying to do, make me feel worse than I do?" Throwing her a dirty look, he walked to the other side of the room and then came back and collapsed beside her.

"I'm sorry. I didn't mean to hit a tender spot," Raye said sheepishly.

Hutch shook his head in exasperation. "What kind of a man am I?" he said as he finished off the brandy in a gulp.

Raye, trying to make up for her earlier insensitivity, said quickly, "You're a very good man. Fine. In terrific shape. Smart. Successful."

"No. I don't mean like that," he said impatiently and dropped his head into his hands. "What kind of a man lets his wife do this to him?"

"It's not your fault."

"It must be my fault. My wife isn't supposed to be screwing around with some fool young enough to be her son. This isn't supposed to happen."

"Well, it happened."

"Eva is mine!"

Raye's voice was firm. "What the hell are you talking about? You don't own Eva. It's not your decision. It's hers. You have nothing to say about it."

"She's my wife."

"So what?"

"It's *my* house!"

Raye narrowed her eyes. "That's bullshit and you know it. That house is Eva's too, so don't pull that tired-ass I-am-man-hear-me-roar crap."

Hutch settled back into his chair and smiled at her

despite himself. "I'm not the only one who has a tender spot."

Raye, ignoring him, continued, "Have *you* ever been unfaithful to Eva?"

"No! Of course not," Hutch lied quickly and easily. The brandy had done its job, and he felt himself relaxing, fortified. He was beginning to appreciate why they gave men a swig of brandy before a battle or after a shock.

But why was he lying to Raye?

"What are you feeling now?"

"I feel fine."

"You're not fine. You just found out the woman you love is sleeping with another man, a younger man. Why do you lie about your feelings?"

Where had he heard that before?

"I don't know." Hutch felt his eyes water and he couldn't trust himself to speak. If he'd had a pair of sunglasses he would have pulled them out and put them on. The stern face of his father came to mind, and he cleared his throat to chase it away, but felt his nose twitch the way it always did before he wept, and he realized there was no sense hiding it. He looked Raye straight in the eyes, letting her see what she would. There was no use lying to her anyway.

"How did you get so wise?" he asked after a moment.

Raye looked surprised, and then tilted her head to the side like she did sometimes. He noticed that her eyes were shining too, as if she had tears in them. "I'm not very wise, Hutch. Most days I look in the mirror and wonder where Raylene Jackson went. I wonder what happened to that smart, ambitious little twenty-one-year-old girl who thought she was God's gift."

"I can tell you what happened to her. She just gets better each year. Prettier, smarter, wiser. What kind of perfume is that you always wear, anyway?" Hutch couldn't believe he'd said that, didn't know why it had tumbled out of his mouth as it had. It was the kind of thing Donald would say to some attractive woman he was left alone with for two minutes. He felt himself blush, even though asking a woman the name of her perfume wasn't exactly like asking her if she'd sleep with him. But he had needed to compliment her, say something that would make her feel better, change the sudden melancholy shadow that had come into her eyes. He wanted to forget his own anguish.

"It's called Joy."

"Joy?" he asked, thinking how ironic the name of the perfume was.

"Supposed to be the most *expensive* perfume in the world. Donald used to buy it for me by the quart when he started to make big money. He has always used gifts as a sign of his affection." She gave a slight, self-deprecating chuckle. "I was at one of his office parties recently and this pretty young thing came up, trying to be nice, I guess, gave me a hug and said, 'You smell so good. My grandma used to smell like you!' I didn't wear it for six months after that, and then figured, what the hell. I probably knew her grandma at Howard, or her mother anyway."

"No. It's classy. Like you. Like you've always been." *Jesus Christ, what is wrong with me?* Hutch thought after he'd said it and then tried to figure out why he had. Maybe he was more like Donald than he thought. *Call your son's lover a faggot, make a half-assed pass at your best friend's wife. Anything to reas-*

*sure yourself that you are still a man.* He added quickly, "Hey, uh, where is your better half, anyway? I haven't seen him in a couple of days." He was on firm ground again, away from any unintentional compliments or unexplained sadness.

"Out with one of his women, of course. Where else would he be? Certainly not with me." Raye said the words evenly, but he could hear, feel her bitterness. In all the years he'd known her, in those brief, precious moments when they shared some private misery, she had never once brought up Donald's affairs. There had always been some unspoken rule against it, a silent pact. And, amazingly, he had never questioned what Donald's ways had cost her. "Do you know where he is, Hutch?"

"No. Of course not!" he answered readily, feeling the need to say something quickly. God knew he'd wanted to change the subject, but not to this. At least Donald hadn't bragged about the latest "honey" he was probably shacked up with tonight. The last time Hutch had talked to him, Donald had actually thanked him for staying at the house and keeping Raye company and out of his business. "I *do* know how much he loves you, Raye. How much you mean to him. You're his life." The words sounded fake, and Hutch could tell by the look Raye tossed him that she gave them about as much credence as they deserved.

"You wonder why I stay with him, don't you? A *wise* woman like me."

He hesitated before he answered, knowing he was about to step into a minefield and wondering how much if any of this he should be discussing with her, how much was Donald's business and had nothing to do with her. He desperately tried to think of a way to gracefully change the subject back to his pain, even to Eva's betrayal. But he didn't really want to talk about that either. He stared straight ahead, not looking at her. But Raye wasn't going to let him off the hook. "You have wondered, haven't you?"

"Yeah, occasionally. But not much. Frankly, it's your and Donald's business." There. Maybe that would do it.

"I stay with him because it's easier than leaving him. Do you know what kind of coward that makes me?"

"I don't think—"

"I'm embarrassed to join any women's social club or do any charitable work. Every time I meet a strange woman or make a new friend, I wonder if Donald has slept with her."

"Raye, I—"

"Do you know what that has done to me, Hutch, socially, personally, on every level imaginable?"

"Maybe, I—"

"You wonder how I deal with it, don't you?"

"Actually, I—"

"It's gotten to the point where it doesn't bother me anymore, Hutch. Isn't that sad? I deal with it like he has some kind of lingering disease, like his asthma. I can even smile about it occasionally, rationalize it, even joke about it with him in some vague, witty way. But then he'll do something outrageous, something so beyond the pale that every little bit of pain that I've pushed down will rise to the surface again.

"So I'll go away for a couple of weeks, maybe even a month, to the islands, on a cruise, to Europe, and I'll cool out for a while. I'll buy some ridiculous expensive nothing that I don't and never will need, and when I come back, Donald will be attentive, pamper me, tell me how much he loves me, and I *won't* catch him in a lie, so I let down my guard, allow myself to trust him. And lo and behold, the cycle will start again."

Hutch wasn't sure what to say to her. He looked straight ahead, silently cursing Donald for putting him in this position with a woman he cared so much about. And, strangely, he was beginning to feel her betrayal by Donald almost as deeply as he did his by Eva. Donald and Eva. Two of a kind.

He realized suddenly that his pain had given her permission to express her own.

"I'm like a battered woman, always waiting for the next swat or punch."

"I wouldn't say you're exactly battered, Raye," he said finally, realizing that he should probably say *something* in Donald's defense, if for no other reason than he was living in the man's house.

"That's the way I feel."

"Have you told him how much it hurts you? I know how much he loves you; maybe he'd try to get some help."

"How do you tell a liar the truth?"

"If you're so unhappy, Raye, then maybe you should leave him. Maybe you're as bad for him as he is for you." It came out sounding more harsh than he'd meant it to, and he wished for a minute that he hadn't said it, but then was glad that he had. It was the most honest thing he could say in a dangerously dishonest conversation.

"Right, Hutch. Leave Donald, and leave behind

everything Donald has worked so hard to attain," she said sarcastically. "I'm not that much of a fool. Sooner or later, I'll get mine too."

They didn't sound like Raye's words, but he knew that this was what she probably told herself when the pain got too deep to handle. It was a side of Raye that he didn't like seeing, and he was sorry that he had. "So you stay with him for his money?"

"Correction. *Our* money. No, I'm not that callous. If I were, I would have figured out how to get the better of him years ago. I stay with him because I love him. I honestly don't think he can help himself. He loves me the best way he can." Hutch averted his eyes, embarrassed by her outpouring of feeling and afraid to pour out his own. "I guess you must find Donald hard to understand?" she asked after a moment.

"What do you mean?"

"You've never been unfaithful to Eva. Our whole arrangement must seem—"

"No, Raye, that wasn't the truth. I had an affair last year," he interrupted her, realizing he didn't want her to think he was better than he was.

"Did you tell Eva?"

"No! How could I?"

"You should have. You might turn into Donald."

"It was really none of her business. She has no idea it happened. I didn't want to hurt her."

"If it's over, I think she has a right to know."

"I don't agree."

"If you start lying in a marriage, sooner or later it comes out or it will just eat away at the core of everything you have, no matter how good the two of you are. Do you really want a marriage like mine?"

It was a rhetorical question, and Hutch glanced away, knowing she didn't expect an answer. "He put you up to it, didn't he, cheating on Eva?" she added with a smile that really wasn't one.

"No, of course not," Hutch said too quickly. "I'm a grown man, Raye. How could Donald make me cheat on my wife?" It was a question he'd asked himself. "Have you ever cheated on Donald?"

She waited so long before she said anything that he was surprised by her answer when it came. "No. I never have."

"Why?" Hutch was genuinely curious.

"I don't know why. God knows I should have as often as he has cheated on me, but I could never bring myself to do it. Maybe I'm so used to it at this point I let it roll off me. Maybe I don't think I'd be good with anybody else. Maybe I'm just stupid?"

"No, Raye. Not stupid," Hutch said quietly.

There was a lengthy, awkward silence. Raye finally broke it. "You know why he took me to Bermuda over the Fourth, don't you?"

"Well, he said he wanted to get away. He was anxious to surprise you. I assume—"

"Don't you start too, Hutch, lying like he does. You're too good for that." Hutch didn't defend himself. "I suspect that he's fascinated this time with some ambitious, pretty young woman in his office. God knows where that will lead."

"Cara?" So Donald had broken his cardinal rule about sleeping with the help. He wondered what kind of perverse delight Donald had taken in encouraging him to start up with Cara again. Donald knew him too well. He had been absolutely sure that he wouldn't do it. Or maybe he was testing Cara. Or the power he had over both of them. Who could tell, with Donald Mason?

"How did you know?"

"Wild guess."

"Obviously he's mentioned her to you."

"I met her once, and she fit your description."

"Did he tell you he was interested in her?"

"No."

"You're too good for that too, Hutch. Making excuses for him."

"So are you, Raye."

She visibly flinched, and he was sorry he'd said it. He hadn't meant to hurt her. He stood up to go, and Raye stood too. Some impulse made him reach for her, to embrace her. He wanted to soften the impact of that truth. God knew it wasn't the first time he'd hugged her to make her feel better. In an odd way, he knew her body almost as well as he knew Eva's.

But this time it was different, and they both knew it. Maybe it was because of what he'd seen that afternoon at Eva's or maybe because her honesty had pushed them past some line. Maybe it was the sensual claustrophobia of her room, a safe refuge within Donald's house. Maybe he simply missed the presence of a woman in his life, and he needed to feel her close to him to reassure him that he was still a man who had something worth wanting. Or maybe that gentle, nurturing part of him that he so often tried to beat down sensed how much she needed his comfort.

He was aware this time of her body as he had never been before, the way it molded into his. He was aroused by her perfume as he'd never been touched by the scent a woman wore before. He was lost in the carnal possibilities of their embrace; he didn't want to let her go. Raye drew back in surprise, gazed at him for a moment, a question in her eyes, and then reached for him with her lips, her tongue flitting between his lips, demanding more and gently getting it, until it settled into his mouth as if it belonged there.

Hutch moved out and checked into a hotel that night. The next day he rented a small furnished apartment five miles from where he worked, which was where he was sitting when Charley called Monday morning. In the three weeks that followed his leaving Donald and Raye's home on Labor Day, Raye visited him as often as she could, and they laughed, wept, talked as they always did when they were together. Finally they made love.

But Donald's presence hovered like a ghost outside the door.

# Hutch and Raye

The first time Hutch made love to Raye Mason, he knew his bond with Donald had been severed forever. Friends don't sleep with friends' wives; such a transgression was unforgivable, and Hutch was wracked with guilt. On the other hand, Raye's betrayal of her husband could be easily understood and forgiven. Donald had cheated on her more times than anyone knew and on some cosmic level it served him right. She owed it to herself to find happiness in any way and with anyone that she could. But Hutch knew his betrayal of his oldest friend, surrogate brother and running buddy was another matter—the type of behavior that was indefensible. Yet he had done it anyway.

When Hutch thought about it later, he realized that the reason could probably be found in his dreams. The night he left Donald's house he dreamed about his mother. He always slept uncomfortably in hotels, with their musty sheets and sagging mattresses, and that night he'd tossed and turned in a fitful sleep filled with strange, disjointed images. Raye, disguised as a small, lost animal with large unblinking eyes, had appeared in the dream, as had his mother, younger than she'd been when she died, and dressed in the drab army-green housedress she always wore. She'd smiled conspiratorially, then nodded at him the way she used to when giving him tacit permission to defy his father. Her smile had awakened him, and he'd lain in bed for a while, unsure of where he was, still aware of her dream-presence and missing her more than he had in years. His mother rarely crept into his dreams; it was always his father, his face in its perpetual scowl, his eyes staring angrily, his arms locked tightly across his chest.

Hutch recalled the dream later that morning in his office as he waited for his crew to report to work. There was little of his mother in that place, just a white china vase she'd once kept filled with flowers, an ancient, tattered copy of *The World of Gwendolyn Brooks* and a crystal paperweight shaped like the Statue of Liberty he'd picked up for her in Atlantic City when he'd been a teenager. He reminded himself to buy some flowers for her vase, something no one had done since her death, and settled back wondering why he'd dreamed about her in the first place.

He'd read somewhere that the dreamer is each character within a dream: the executor and the executed, the lover and the beloved, the master and the slave. Perhaps he was both his mother and Raye Mason—the nurturer giving himself permission to nurture some part of him that needed care. In a burst of insight, he wondered if he was calling forth that piece of himself he rarely acknowledged, the mother's boy rather than the father's son. So when Raye called him in his new apartment at the end of the week, he remembered the dream again, and knew it had been a message from his mother. There was still enough of his southern roots in him to recognize a sign when he heard, saw or dreamed it. Raye Mason was a wounded woman in need of tenderness. Hutch was beginning to realize how badly she had been hurt by her husband, his friend.

Raye's shy kiss had stayed on Hutch's mind when they made love that first time, and he had responded to her the same way—as if he wasn't quite sure about things to come and was traveling in strange, unfamiliar territory. There had been an undeniable need for kindness in the timid way she brought her body to meet his. He sensed her mistrust. She was self-conscious and embarrassed when she undressed in front of him, even though Hutch made it clear that he thought she was beautiful, soft and full where Eva was firm and sturdy. She trembled when he entered her that first night, as if she were afraid, and he thrust his body into hers as gently as he could, fearful in some strange way that he might hurt her, as if it were her first time, as if she were a virgin. Raye brought out his need to offer protection more than any woman he'd ever been with. He felt that he had to defend her against her own self-doubt and find ways to reassure her about how appealing and desirable she was. Each time he touched her and saw the sadness that lay so deep in her eyes, he was reminded how much Donald had hurt her. He wondered how and why he had been unable to see it before.

The following week when they made love again, he had asked her, "Why do you let him hurt you like this?" It was the first time either of them had mentioned Donald, and Raye jumped, as if he'd just peeked into the room. Hutch pulled her toward him, kissed her throat under the chin and then let her go. They were lying on the king-size bed that nearly filled the small, narrow bedroom in his new apartment. The sheets, which Raye had brought from home, smelled like her perfume. His apartment consisted of the bedroom, a modest living room painted a dull mustard yellow and containing a rented brown tweed couch. There was a tiny kitchen off the living room filled with a table and three chairs and a tinier bathroom. The first night she came she had replaced the seventy-five-watt bulbs in the ceiling light in the bedroom with soft pink ones, which gave the small stark room a dreamy, hazy glow.

"I don't know. I must be a masochist," she replied.

"You're definitely not a masochist."

"It's my own fault, though."

"Why do you say that? He must know how destructive his affairs are."

"But I set the rules. If I had left him the first time he betrayed me, I would have set the boundaries. But I kept ignoring it, making excuses for him. He's like a kid with no limits who runs over you until you slap him, and I never slapped him."

Hutch had kissed her lips at the edge of her smile and nodded that he understood. But he wondered what kind of man could treat a woman like Raye with so little regard and what kind of compulsion sent him dipping from woman to woman like some crazed bee flitting down a line of honey pots. Hutch knew he was not like that. He never had been and never wanted to be.

After Raye had left that night, he thought about Cara for the first time in a long while and how little she had meant to him. They had barely talked. He could recall nothing about her—no memorable part of her face or body—like Eva's dimple or the corners of Raye's lips. He had no idea what she liked to eat, how she had grown up or where she had gone to college. Even their lovemaking had been by rote. He could also tell that she had faked her orgasms, and he'd wondered why she'd felt the need to lie about such an intimately shared experience.

He had made love to Cara four times—after six costly lunches, two canceled rendezvous, and five hot, sexy phone conversations, three on the downsize phone when Eva was asleep about what they would do for each other when they finally got together. When he'd finally come to her tiny, chic apartment, he'd been struck by what little of her was there—no photographs of family or friends, no clothes flowing out of drawers or newspapers folded on the couch. He'd also been shocked by her young body, flinching when he realized she probably wasn't that much older than Charley. But he'd made love to her that first time and after that despite it, knowing each time even as he performed—and they were performances—that he was making a grave mistake. Cara Franklin was a pretty, sexy young woman. Donald's protégée, and he had Donald's approval and encouragement—man to man. She had been a trophy, a gift from Donald Mason, and the thought of that now made him cringe in shame. She'd floated into his life and left nothing of herself on his mind or with his spirit.

Why had he risked hurting Eva? What had he been trying to prove? Was he trying to prove something now?

He pondered again his relationship with Raye Mason from every angle, wondering if he had gotten involved with her to get even with Eva, and if his feelings for her were nothing more than an attempt to deny his rage, replace his pain with pleasure. Yet when he was with her, the rough spots in his life seemed smoother—his anxiety about his relationship with his son, his worries about work, his discomfort at being away from his home. Raye's presence in his life had quickly become indispensable. Within ten days, her elegant style was reflected in his humble apartment. Roses and mums were placed in jars in his dreary bedroom and lackluster living room, so dabs of fragrance and color sprouted from unexpected spots. Her costly ecru sheets and matching embroidered duvet made his bed feel luxurious. Her perfumed oils and lotions sat on the sink and counter in his drab bathroom. Her lemon verbena soap replaced the Dial in his soap dish. Whenever she came, she bought the cheeses, pâtés and wines that he loved, knew nothing about and would never buy for himself.

By the fourth time they made love, he could feel a difference in her response. She was surprised and delighted by his touch. Although she was still self-conscious about her gracefully aging body, she had begun to accept how desirable he found her. She yielded to his touch, and every move she made—the shy, self-conscious ones, the free way she laughed when they joked—delighted and charmed him. The fragrance of her cologne lingered on his sheets, and after she left him he would sleep with her scent in his nose and mouth; he could almost taste her soft, sweet skin against his tongue.

Donald was in London the fifth time they made love on the last Friday in September, so Raye stayed through the weekend. Monday morning they showered together, and when Hutch soaped her back with the lemon soap, playfully painting fanciful, sudsy designs on her back, breast and thighs, he wondered if he was falling in love with her. Forgetting about work (something he'd never done, particularly on a Monday morning), they'd gone back to bed and made love again, giggling like kids sharing mischievous secrets, as he tried again to taste the delicious fragrance on her skin.

But fear seized him after she left. He wondered where things were heading and worried how things would end. It was as if they were lost in a timeless void in the space of his apartment. Nothing else existed—certainly not his father's harsh judgment, Eva and the hornplayer or Donald's inevitable wrath. And Hutch didn't care. He sensed that Raye was essential to any healing his soul had to do. He belonged to her now, and not to her husband.

This new reality was on his mind Friday night when Raye called just before he locked up the office to go home.

"Hey, what's going on?" He was pleased yet surprised to hear from her. When she'd left Monday morning, they'd agreed that they wouldn't see each other until the following week. Donald would be back in town, and Charley's long-awaited comedy debut at Club Resurrection in Brooklyn was tomorrow night, and he had promised to drop by tonight for her final rehearsal.

"It's Donald." Raye's voice was anxious.

Hutch's breath stopped in his throat. "Does he know?" He could barely speak the words.

"I need to see you tonight. I need to talk to you."

"Does he know?" Hutch demanded again. He tried to make his voice calm, tried to take out the panic. What would he say to Donald when the inevitable confrontation came? He knew it was bound to happen sooner or later, but he wasn't ready for it tonight.

"No. He's too selfish and self-absorbed to even wonder where I am when he calls."

"Don't bet on that," Hutch said, more to himself than to her. "What's wrong?" Her voice caught when she answered him, and Hutch could tell that she had been crying.

"It's just so damn humiliating. It's the last straw. The last one." She was barely audible.

"What, Raye? Tell me!"

He could hear her breathing hard on the other end, and then he heard her sigh, as if collecting her thoughts. Her voice came out calm, like the Raye he'd gotten to know. "I've made a big decision. Or maybe it's been made for me. Can I come by tonight?"

"Is Donald back?"

"He won't be back until Sunday."

"Yeah, of course."

"Half an hour?"

"I'll see you then." He hung up, called Charley and told her he wouldn't be able to come to the club. He stood in the middle of the office for a few minutes, feeling strangely out of sorts, wondering what Raye was going to tell him. Then he drove home to meet her.

The leaves were beginning to change and the air had a bite to it, a telling sign that winter was close. It was already dark when he parked in front of his building, so he waited outside. Although his building was in a stable neighborhood, he was still wary. He'd spotted a group of teenagers sitting on the stoop of the building next door who looked like they had nothing on their minds but mischief when he'd come home from work the night before. He listened for the expensive purr of Raye's sleek black Jaguar and watched her pull up to the curb and park amid the aging Hondas, Camrys and Jettas. She was dressed in a gray knit skirt and sweater and looked chic but distracted. He could see that she was nervous. She'd forgotten to turn on the car's security system, so he took the keys and armed it, pressing the button until it beeped, and then handed them back to her. Her eyes were red; it was clear she had been crying. He wondered if Donald had called from London and told her he was leaving her or if one of his women had called to taunt her. They walked into his building and into his apartment in silence.

Raye sat down on the couch, her face tense and her mouth tight. Hutch wondered if it was possible that she'd been seized by some late-breaking sense of guilt. Maybe Donald had somehow sensed her independence and made some last-ditch effort from afar to bring her back under his spell. He studied her face, trying to read her emotions, then he went into the kitchen and poured some brandy into a water glass, came back and handed it to her.

A spark of amusement popped into her eyes. "Haven't we played this scene before?"

"I'm doing your role," Hutch said solemnly, and when the smile edged itself onto her lips he bent and kissed each corner and then sat down beside her. He took her in his arms and held her for a moment. He could feel her heart beating like that of some frail timid animal whose life and limb depended on his mercy. He relaxed his hold on her, and she sighed and took a sip of the brandy, then put the glass down on the table.

"I feel so humiliated," she said quietly.

"What did he do?"

She laughed but the sound of her laughter was hollow. "It's such a strange thing to be discussing. I've never been comfortable talking about a person's will when the person is alive. But lawyers always say, look at them before it's too late. Maybe I'm lucky." She glanced up at Hutch, a question in her eyes. "Do you know how wealthy Donald is?"

Hutch, wondering where the conversation was going, shook his head. He didn't, although he had a vague idea.

"He's worth at least six million with his practice, his property, his substantial investments—" She put her hands over her face. "God, I hate to talk about this kind of stuff." She took another sip of the brandy.

"Just say it."

"You know how Donald loves his damn fraternity brothers. I guess he feels they've done God knows what for him and now it's his turn to pay them back. Or maybe he feels like he's protecting me and my interest in some stupid way by asking them to take care of me." She shook her head as if she were mystified.

Hutch noticed that her left eye had begun to twitch and then stopped, as if she had willed it to be still.

"Who did he leave it to?" He cut to the chase, almost wishing he didn't have to know.

"Phi Omega Ki," Raye said, closing her eyes and pausing between each word. "He left all of the money to his goddamn fraternity. Everything he does, every deal he makes he does through his corporation, which is in his name, and he left the money, the business interests, the investments, the property—some of which I had no idea he had—all of it, to Phi Omega Ki. Everything except our house, which my poor dead mama with her dying breath shamed him into putting in both of our names."

Hutch didn't know whether to weep with Raye, which she had begun to do openly again, or laugh out loud at the absurdity of it. For a moment he couldn't find his voice, and when he did it came out in a croak of disbelief. "Are you telling me that Donald made Phi Omega Ki his chief beneficiary?"

Raye's voice was a whisper as she slumped back beside him, her hands still covering her face.

"They are his *only* beneficiary. Oh, he's definitely instructed them to take care of me, to provide me with a generous allowance that will keep me living in the style to which I've become accustomed, but the money is clearly theirs. He probably thinks he's protecting me from inheritance taxes."

"He can't do that, can he? You're his wife. He can't cut you out. Aren't you legally entitled to inherit?"

"Sure. I could sue his frat for a third under New Jersey law, but he doesn't think I'll bother. He thinks I'm too timid to want the aggravation of facing his frat brothers in court. He assumes that I'd be perfectly content to sit on my ass and let that bunch of fools take care of me for the rest of my life."

Hutch slumped back into the couch too now, unable to speak. She began to tremble and he held out his hand, which she took without looking at him. He watched her pull in her breath, exhale it slowly and then pull it back again, her eyes closed so tight he could see small lines forming under them. She shook her head so hard that her short graying black hair hit the side of her face. He could barely hear her speak, and when she did her words came out in a hysterical laugh. "It serves me right," she said.

"Don't say that."

"It serves me right for living for so many years with a man who has so little respect for me that he has fucked any breathing object with breasts." She shook her head slowly now, as if trying to shake some bad thought out of it. "I sold my soul, Hutch. I sold my soul to live the way I did so I would never be poor again. I gave up my self-respect and my dignity, and this is what I get. *This* is what I deserve—to live out my last years, to end up a doddering old woman, dependent upon the goodwill and generosity of the Phi Omega Ki fraternity. I have reaped what I have sown!"

"Are you sure about this?"

"Yes."

"How did you find out?"

"Somebody from his office messengered a copy of his will over this afternoon, and I had to sign for it. I had no idea what was in the envelope. The messenger was carrying it with about five other letters and a couple of packages, and dropped it in a puddle on the way up the driveway. I saw that it was from his lawyer, and good little wife that I am, I didn't want any dirty water to soak through before he got back. I thought it might be something important. I opened the package intending to dry it off and put it on his desk, but there it was, Donald's last will and testament, spelling everything out, in that stupid legalese. I thought I was going to be sick. I *was* sick for a while. Then I called you."

Neither of them spoke. Hutch heard a car alarm go off, wondered for a moment if it was Raye's Jaguar, stood up to go check on it and then sat back down when he heard somebody turn it off. A phone rang loudly in another apartment. A boom box blasting from somewhere faded into the background. He heard teenagers laughing and shouting to each other in the street. Then all was quiet.

"Maybe he found out about us and that's why he did it," he said.

"The will was drawn up in July. He probably thinks he's protecting me."

"Did you call him in London to confront him about it?"

"No."

"When did you say he would be home?"

"Late Sunday. Early Monday." She started to cry again, but when Hutch tried to comfort her she waved him away. "It's not that I want him to die or that I was waiting for him to die or anything like that. It's just that . . ." She paused to collect her thoughts. "I understand now that he has no respect for my intelligence, my integrity or even my ability to survive without him. It's like he thinks I'm one of those women from some primitive society who should be thrown on the funeral pyre along with her husband because she has nowhere else to go. How could Donald live with me for so long and know so little about me?"

Her voice begged for an answer, but Hutch had none to give. "Donald has very little respect for anybody else's intelligence or integrity," he finally said, seeing yet another dimension to this man he had called friend. Raye went into the bathroom. He heard the water running, and when she came back he saw that she had washed her face. He caught the scent of the lemon soap as she sat back down beside him.

"I want to divorce him. I need to take what belongs to me while I can still get it without fighting his fraternity for it," she said quietly. Her face, clean of tears and makeup, looked fresh, almost like a child's. But her eyes were the weary ones of a very old woman.

"Are you sure?"

"I am almost fifty years old. I will not spend another year of my life with a man who holds me in such contempt."

"Maybe you should wait and think things out, don't decide too hastily, you don't know—"

"What I know is that if Donald Mason should choke to death on a Dorito, I will spend the rest of my life either waiting for his fraternity brothers to pay my grocery bills or in court fighting them for money that belongs to me. It's the most demeaning thing he has ever done to me, almost as bad as the women. I'd almost gotten use to them."

"Is it just about his money, Raye?"

Hutch was startled by the amount of bitterness and hurt that was in her eyes when she answered him. "I told you once before, Hutch, that it is *our* money," she said, her voice surprisingly composed and cool. "I put the bastard through law school when I was twenty-two. Money that *my* mother gave me from *my* daddy's insurance policy paid for that first, tacky little storefront office he had over on Broad Street in Newark. *I* was his goddamn legal secretary and research assistant for the first five years he practiced law. My youth was his seed money, and I was his sole investor. I want my fair return."

Hutch let her words settle for a moment or two, embarrassed that he'd asked it because he knew better. Donald himself had said as much on more than one occasion. Ironically, it was one of the things that he most admired and cherished about his wife: her unselfish giving of all that she had.

"I'm going to start looking for a lawyer," Raye said.

"How about Sam Henderson?" Hutch suggested, remembering the name of the lawyer that Donald had said he least liked to meet in court, and Raye smiled. "But don't let Donald know you're angry about the will. Don't let him know you're ready to leave until you're ready to do it. Don't give him anything to be suspicious of because he'll use it against you." He was trying to think like Donald, and she would have to do that too, if she was going to win. He thought about mentioning the apartment in New York City and the names of some of the women he knew Donald had gone out with, but said instead, "It might be a good idea to hire a private investigator. Do you have enough money?"

"I *always* have enough money. In his own way, Donald is the most generous man I've ever known." There was a wistful note in her voice, and Hutch noticed that the anger that had been there a moment ago had softened; only sadness remained.

He held her for a moment, taking in her fragrance, letting her cry against his shoulder. When she stopped he led her into his bedroom and made love to her, and when they finished, they lay together somewhere between sleep and wakefulness.

"Charley invited me and Donald to her show. Will I see you tomorrow night?" she asked. "I don't want to be there by myself." Hutch thought about it for a moment, unsure what to say. Everybody would be there—Steven, Roscoe, Eva. "I need to be with you." She turned her head toward him, and her eyes begged him for an answer. He nodded that he would see her there, and kissed her throat and the tender spot under her chin.

"You've redeemed me, Hutch," she said as she rolled over full into his arms, snuggling close to him. Her face was peaceful now, and her eyes were closed.

"We've redeemed each other," Hutch whispered into her ear.

# Eva and Charley

Club Resurrection, where Charley was staging her comedy debut, was on the first floor of an aging building in Fort Greene, Brooklyn, that had once been a shoe store but had been "resurrected" by a crew of earnest young black entrepreneurs into a club that featured aspiring poets, wannabe hip-hop musicians and avant-garde plays. The October night was cool and rainy, but the club was packed, filled to capacity with the friends and family of the performers. It was an odd mix of well-dressed single black women in their forties, artsy-looking white couples in their thirties, and hip-hop kids of all races and ages. Several young children, obviously awake beyond their bedtimes, whooped, hollered and ran around, which gave the place the sound and fury of a schoolroom before recess.

The stage was an elevated wooden square at the

front of the room that resembled a butcher's block and was surrounded by tables and chairs three rows deep that looked as if they'd done hard time in a church basement. The walls were a dull shade of gray, which, along with the dim reddish lights that peeked from the ceiling, gave the room a grungy, slightly dangerous look. The place smelled vaguely of marijuana, rose-scented air freshener and roasted peanuts.

Eva squinted her eyes as she entered the club and searched for a place to sit down. Charley's various friends and family members filled most of the tables near the front of the stage, and she recognized a girl Charley had known since high school and three of her best friends from Spelman. Hutch, who looked tense and uncomfortable, sat alone on the far right, nursing a drink. Roscoe and Precious were two tables up from Hutch, and Steven and Dana sat a row across from them. There was an empty table near Hutch with a hand-printed RESERVED sign on top of it. Eva wondered if Charley, in some vain hope of forcing a reconciliation, had saved the table for her, and she watched anxiously as Hutch glanced around the room. She hadn't heard from him in months, and she played with the idea of casually walking over and saying something cordial to him.

He did look good tonight, but then Hutch always looked good. He was wearing a well-made gray sports jacket that she hadn't seen before. He'd gotten his hair trimmed, and he had obviously found a new barber. The cut had more style and shape than usual and made him look younger, yet more sophisticated. She watched as he scanned the room, and their eyes locked for an instant. He nodded coolly, a formal sign of recognition. Eva returned his curt nod, as if they were two old enemies forced to acknowledge each other's presence in an ongoing battle. *How have things gotten so bad?* she asked herself. She wondered if he knew about Isaiah. She was certain Charley hadn't been able to keep it to herself, but then she had always been protective toward Hutch and careful of his feelings— advising him on his wardrobe, cheering him up when he looked like he needed it, begging him not to work so hard. He always chuckled appreciatively when she gave her advice, and the give and take between the two of them had always delighted Eva. The memory of it tonight made her feel sad. He dropped his eyes for a moment, and then shyly glanced back up at her. God, she knew this man so well, she thought. Something was bothering him, she was sure of that. She wondered if she should approach him. Maybe that table *was* for her; maybe *he* had asked Charley to reserve it.

But in the next moment, he shifted his glance from Eva to a spot just behind her, and a slow, easy smile came to his lips. Eva turned to see Raye Mason wave in his direction and move swiftly toward his table. She wondered where Donald was tonight and why Charley had bothered to invite them at all. But Charley had known them since she and Hutch had married, and had always considered them part of her extended family. Since the club charged a minimum cover charge plus two drinks per head, she had probably invited everybody she knew to make sure she was invited back.

Raye Mason was dressed as elegantly as ever. She wore black merino-wool knit pants with matching turtleneck and cardigan teamed with a thick gold bracelet that sparkled dramatically from her wrist. Although Eva liked clothes as much as the next woman, she didn't make a fetish of it the way she was sure Raye Mason did. Although she would never acknowledge it, Eva occasionally envied Raye's taste and style. Raye was always beautifully turned out, the perfect wife for Donald Mason. But Raye had always struck Eva as one of those shallow black women whose main concern in life was what she should wear, where she should wear it and if anybody else had one like it. Yet Eva had to admit she was a good-natured, kindhearted woman who basically meant well and did nobody any harm. Eva had always felt sorry for her, married for as long as she was to a man like Donald Mason. But Raye and her philandering husband were more Hutch's friends than hers, and it didn't surprise Eva that she hadn't heard from either of them since Hutch had walked out. Truth be told, she didn't miss the friendship.

She watched Raye slide into the seat beside Hutch. Her heart jumped when she saw him lean toward her, touching her cheek tenderly as he whispered something in her ear. Raye blushed a schoolgirl's shy blush, and even from where she stood, Eva could see the light come into her eyes. Eva noticed with alarm that the smile he gave her was one she hadn't seen in a while, and one he had never given to another woman. Her heart pounding, she watched him whisper something that made the sad, pensive look on Raye's face disappear. Eva knew Hutch well enough to know that there was something very serious going on between them. Yet there was something about the way they discreetly exchanged glances and words that told her that Donald Mason didn't know about this change in their relationship yet. She felt dizzy suddenly, and dazed, as if she had just awakened from a disturbing dream.

"E, you want to sit with me and Dana?" Steven's hand on her arm startled her, and she turned to face him. "Mom is running late, but she promised she'd be here sooner or later, probably later." Eva dropped her eyes, hoping to conceal what she knew was in them. But Steven could tell that something was wrong, and he quickly demanded to know what it was.

"Nothing. I'm just very tired," Eva said as she forced a yawn to prove her point. Steven glanced over her shoulder at Hutch. Eva followed his eyes and then quickly looked away. Hutch was staring in her direction again, but at Steven this time, his eyes filled with a sad, mournful longing.

"I'm not speaking to him these days," Steven said, focusing on Eva. "And I don't feel like getting mad all over again, so don't ask me why."

"I wasn't going to ask you why."

"So you want to sit with us?" He changed the subject back to his original question, obviously uncomfortable with discussing his father.

"No, thanks, sweetheart. I promised Roscoe I'd sit with him and his friend." She didn't particularly want to spend the evening with Irene, so despite her misgivings about Precious, sitting with her father seemed the safer bet.

"Are you ready for Charley's act?" Steven's eyes settled on her with an odd intensity.

"As ready as I'll ever be," Eva said lightly. Bending down, Steven gave her a peck of a kiss on her cheek and then walked her to her father, who stood up when she joined him.

Roscoe Lilton always displayed Old World, gentleman's manners, which struck Eva as pretentious but usually amused her. He always stood when a "lady" came or left the table and was a stickler for which fork went where and was used with what. He knew the best places and most expensive places to eat and had put many a snotty wine steward in his place with his vast knowledge of wines and how to serve them. When she had been a girl, Roscoe would tap her elbows with the blade of his knife if she put them on the table or forgot to use her napkin. He was dressed tonight in his usual elegant fashion: conservative brown Harris tweed sports jacket, dark slacks, well-starched shirt open at the neck. He looked and smiled as if he had just stepped out of a Ralph Lauren ad in *Modern Maturity*.

Precious, on the other hand, looked as if she were getting ready to perform. She wore a navy suit made from a silky material, with rhinestone buttons that matched her earrings. A dark ratty fur that might once have been mink swung on the back of her chair. A reddish brown tendril of hair had escaped from the navy turban she wore, giving her the look of an overdressed fortune-teller. Her perfume, which was musky and sensual, floated over the table in a fragrant cloud. Everything about the woman was so radically different from Louisa—whose clothes were always tailored and whose manner was as unfailingly proper as her husband's. Eva wondered if her father was becoming senile. But she managed a smile when her father gave her a hug.

"What do you want to drink? Whatever it is, keep in mind that you've got to have two," Roscoe said.

"Maybe I should stick to seltzer. I haven't had anything to eat since lunch."

"They don't count that; I already tried it. Some wine won't hurt you. Precious, you ready for another one?"

Precious nodded and held out a glass that held the remnants of what looked like scotch and water.

"I'm glad you're sitting with us tonight," she said to Eva. "We hardly had a chance to talk on the Fourth." Eva thought that her smile looked genuine, and that she seemed warmer today than she had when they'd last met. Although she wasn't in a smiling mood, Eva returned her grin without much effort. "You must be so proud of Charley."

Eva, on the alert for any hint of sarcasm, decided to take the woman at her word and tell her the truth. "Frankly, I'm hoping she'll forget about all this foolishness and go to law school," she said.

"But we have to let people we love be who they are going to be and live their own dreams. Especially children. We raise our children to make choices. You give them life, but you have to let them live it themselves. That's the biggest gift you give them," Precious said with a knowing nod.

"So how many kids do you have?" Eva asked.

"Never been blessed."

*Then shut up because you don't know what the hell you're talking about,* Eva thought and then was ashamed of her thoughts.

"Raised more than my share, though," Precious added as if she could read Eva's mind.

"Precious raised her second husband's four kids after he passed," Roscoe said as proudly as if he had had a hand in it.

"Well, that certainly makes you an expert, doesn't it?" Eva said with a pleasant smile that she hoped masked the hint of sarcasm that had seeped through in her tone. *Why am I being such a bitch?* she asked herself. But she knew it was because of the way Hutch's eyes had lit up when they settled on Raye Mason, and the way Raye's had turned happy when he whispered into her ear. *I should have brought Isaiah,* she told herself, but even as she thought it, she knew *that* would have been a disaster.

"Scoe says you're an artist," Precious said, filling a lull in the conversation.

"I work in a library. But yes, I like to sketch."

"What do you like to draw?" Precious's eyes questioned her with the blunt demand for an answer.

"Nothing in a while."

"Eva's muse has taken a break, but it will come back." Roscoe gave her a nod of support, and Eva tried to remember when she had mentioned her dry spell to her father. Roscoe called for another round of drinks. He ordered a Jack Daniel's neat for himself—for which Eva tossed him a disapproving scowl—a Dewar's and soda for Precious and vinegary red wine for Eva, and they settled back to wait impatiently for Charley to make her appearance.

The first comedian wasn't funny, which Eva thought boded well for her daughter; the evening couldn't go anywhere but up. He was a scrawny young white man with a sallow complexion, who was dressed all in black and spoke with a western twang that sounded fake. His feet barely touched the floor when he settled awkwardly on the barstool placed in the middle of the stage, and he was obviously nervous, taking long, noisy swallows from the glass of water that sat on the table near the stool. His hands noticeably shook. His smirk, which had a dirty-old-man look about it, made Eva uncomfortable, and his material added to her discomfort. It was drawn mostly from problems he had with his digestion and relied heavily on bathroom jokes—his problems with constipation, the impact on his social life of broccoli and beans, the pleasures of self-administered enemas. Most of the laughter in the room came from the few children present and the far corners of the club, where Eva assumed the majority of his friends sat.

"Nobody wants to know about what that man does in the bathroom," Roscoe said with disgust as the man left the stage. "Redd Foxx told bathroom jokes, but *he* was good. If you're going to talk about going to the toilet, you would *want* to be funny." Precious, her lips pursed, nodded in silent agreement. "I sure hope Charley doesn't do anything like that," Roscoe added with a shudder.

The second comedian was better than the first but not much. She was a plump, middle-aged black woman with a pleasant face who was dressed in a black leisure suit. Her jokes all revolved around being a plump middle-aged black woman with a pleasant face who liked to wear leisure suits. Several of her stories were funny, and the woman delivered them with a good-natured grin that made her appealing. But at the end of her routine, she made an unfortunate turn into cursing and exaggerated "Ebonics" that destroyed the crowd's goodwill and had several older members of the audience tittering with disapproval.

"She was funny till she got carried away," Roscoe

observed with a disappointed nod. "Charley said there were only three acts, so she must be next. Maybe we can get out of this place before midnight," he added as he glanced at his watch, and as if on cue, Charley sauntered across the stage.

Eva's eyes watered with pride when she saw her. They always did whenever Charley made a public appearance, from the first time at five, when she'd read a poem at a PTA meeting, until the valedictorian speech she'd delivered at her high school graduation. She stole a glance at Hutch, who was gazing proudly, and she remembered with a painful jolt how he would squeeze her hand whenever Steven or Charley performed some public function—holding the flag, collecting the church offering, reading a winning essay. Their children always seemed so sure of themselves, so serious about their responsibility, so determined to make their parents proud.

Black seemed to be the color of the evening, and Charley was dressed accordingly, in tight black jeans and a casual black T-shirt. Eva wished she had worn blue or red. Black always made her look stark and thin, not at all like herself, and she wondered with annoyance why Charley had felt the need to dress like everybody else. She watched nervously as Charley took her time strolling across the stage and gracefully positioned herself on the stool, as if she had all the time in the world. She slowly poured water into a glass and took a slow, leisurely sip, then smiled as if letting the audience in on a joke. Unlike the other two, she seemed completely at ease and sure of herself, as if she were enjoying the audience's anticipation, and her obvious comfort made the crowd comfortable, as if they had just dropped into her living room for an intimate chat. By her third sip of water, there was a cough or two of impatience, but everybody was curious about her.

"There are certain things in this life that you *don't* want to know," she drawled as she stabbed the air with a pointed, red-nailed finger and crossed her legs, which were ensconced in thigh-high black leather boots that made her look like a weary dominatrix in a soft-porn video.

"Like, you do *not* want to know what some of these loser dudes would do to you if they had you alone, right? And they always got to tell you something— here you go, walking down the street, minding your own damn business, and one of these motherfuckers is going to tell you what he'd do, what he'd do it with, and where he'd do it. Right?" There were some giggles of recognition, and a laugh or two in anticipation.

"Like, a couple of days ago, there was this loser standing next to this chick in front of me at Kmart." Eva, who knew Charley would no more stand in line at Kmart than fly to the moon, chuckled to herself, but saw also that it was not so much what Charley was saying, but *how* she was saying it. Her delivery and pacing were irreverent and funny and gave an old joke a new meaning. Her long, raunchy description about the "loser dude" and his "tired-ass rap" brought derisive shouts of recognition and agreement from the younger women in the audience, and when she ended with a punch line delivered in the girl's "ghetto-fabulous" voice about having one asshole and not needing another—Eva laughed despite herself. Charley seemed to get energy from the audience, like the call and response country preachers got from an excited congregation, and she was thriving on it.

Roscoe shook his head in admiration. "She's funny, but where did that child learn to curse like that?" He tossed Eva a critical glance.

"Hell if I know!" Eva quipped, in good spirits now, and they both laughed heartily as Roscoe held up his hands as if to ward off Charley's salty language. But it was clear that he was delighted and proud of his granddaughter.

"You know my father Charles Lilton used to dream of being on the stage," he stage-whispered to Precious. "Charley's named after him."

"Really? Did he ever perform?" Precious's eyes were bright with interest.

"Heck, yeah! He made his living as a train porter going North from Charleston to New York City. Used to say he did so much bowing and scraping and acting for the white folks on those trains he could have been Paul Robeson if they'd given him half a chance. Talked about it till the day he died."

They laughed uproariously as if it were the funniest thing either of them had heard. Roscoe turned to Eva, laughter still in his eyes. "I told you Precious used to be a singer, didn't I?"

Her eyes sparkling, Precious grinned at Roscoe. "I did the Key Club, the Cadillac, all of those old jazz clubs in Newark before they closed down. That was where I met your daddy, at the Cadillac."

They both giggled, and Eva's heart skipped.

Had he known this woman when her mother was alive?

"I always did like singers. My mama, Alvia, used to

sing." Roscoe said. His eyes focused on Precious with dreamy fascination.

"Did you ever think about going on the stage, seeing that this show biz stuff seems to run in your family?" Precious asked.

"You know, I always wanted to dance, now that you mention it," Roscoe's eyes got a faraway look. "I always liked them hoofers. The Nicholas Brothers were my favorites. Man, those boys could cut up the floor. Glide, spin in the air, float like they had wings. And always looked like they just got back from the tailor. Poetry in motion, that's what they were. That's where I learned to dress, studying those two brothers. I always dreamed of dancing like they did."

Eva looked at her father in surprise. This was the first time she'd heard about *that*.

"How did you end up in the library?" Precious asked him.

"I always liked books too. Good way to make a living. They were hiring colored librarians back then. Money was okay. Respectable job, kind of like being a teacher. You could learn stuff, too. That's where I learned to invest. Sitting in that library, reading all those newspapers and magazines all the rich white cats were reading. Money don't know no color."

Eva glanced at the two of them hovering together in a mutual swoon and felt like the third wheel on a bicycle. She wondered if she should have taken Steven up on his offer to sit with him, Dana and Irene, who still hadn't arrived.

"We both got show business in our blood," Roscoe said thoughtfully.

"That's pushing it, Dad."

"Well, you remember all the things I told you about my father."

Although Eva had heard bits and pieces about her grandfather all her life, he'd been long gone before she was born. But maybe Roscoe was right, she realized. Charley did seem to be a natural, despite her initial misgivings. With a sultry toss of her head, she told another joke, drawling her lines and pointing at the audience, and they roared back with delight. Eva snuck another look at Hutch, who beamed with pride. Raye's eyes were fastened on him.

Eva made herself think about Isaiah. What time would he be getting home from work? she wondered. They had settled into a routine, spending time together on weekends but still talking about nothing very important. She didn't really know that much more about him than she did when he'd moved in. What she did know she'd learned from observation and her own intuition. He said he didn't have to talk because he talked through his music, and she'd decided that maybe that was true. She still loved to hear him play, and he played for her whenever she asked, but he did his serious practicing and composing when she wasn't there. The mornings when they made love were still as delightful as ever, but she was usually asleep or too tired to do much but talk at night.

She had taken Helena's advice and enrolled in a course in library science at a nearby university. She found it interesting and challenging, and had decided to work toward a degree. Strangely enough, Isaiah seemed as excited about her going to classes as she did, and they talked about that sometimes. He said at one point that he had thought about going back to school himself, and she encouraged him to think about that more too. But his music seemed enough for him, and they both knew that that was the only thing that really mattered to him. She wasn't sure where their relationship was going, if anywhere; she had made herself stop worrying about it one way or the other.

The sex was as good as ever—better, even—and whenever she was bored she would imagine the way his hands or mouth felt on her body. It was embarrassing how quickly just thinking about him could arouse her. Some small innocuous thing would remind her of him—a snatch of music on the radio, a glimpse of a man who shared his build—and she'd be nearly overcome in a rush of sexual excitement. Sitting in the library with nothing particular on her mind one day, she'd picked up a pencil and without even realizing it, sketched the hard strong lines of the curve of his back and torso, and then his face with its angular yet surprisingly gentle lines. The drawing was quickly and crudely done, but the process had been effortless, and it was the first time she'd sketched anything in a very long time. She felt that day as if she were filled with some delightful secret that she wasn't ready to share with anyone else, and that Isaiah, unwittingly, was part of it. She'd folded the paper in quarters and stuffed it in her bag, where she'd kept it for several days like a good luck charm. But then she hadn't been inspired to draw anything else.

Although Isaiah had been politely curious about Charley's performance tonight, they had an unspoken agreement that he wouldn't show up after he finished his set. Maybe in a year if they were still together they would go places as a couple—or whatever they were—

although whenever she thought about it there was no place where she really wanted to go with him. The places she had occasionally gone with Hutch—the museums and galleries, the restaurants, the bookstores—held no interest at all for Isaiah, and she had begun to enjoy going to these places alone. She could be alone with her thoughts and reactions and stay as long as she wanted without worrying about somebody else's feelings or schedule. She could go out for a drink or coffee afterward, stopping on the spur of the moment whenever she wanted to. She also found that she enjoyed eating alone, finding a corner table far away from everybody else, sipping a glass of wine while she read a book or went over her lessons for class.

Her life seemed calmer than it had immediately after Hutch had left. Things had settled down. Although she hadn't talked to or seen Charley since that day at the house at the end of September, she was sure that somehow things would work themselves out. Things usually did if you gave them enough time.

She turned her attention back to Charley and smiled. She hardly recognized her daughter. Eva had never seen her so relaxed and in control of a situation. Maybe the showman genes *had* popped up again in her daughter. It could be worse. The genes Charley got could have been Aunt Delia's.

"What are you thinking about, kiddo?" Roscoe asked, noticing the faraway look on Eva's face. Every so often her father would ask her that question phrased in just that way. Kiddo was a name he'd called her since she was a child.

"Nothing much."

"Still not telling me your business, eh?"

Although she and her father were close in their own way, they both knew her real connection had been with her mother—until she had "betrayed" her mother's dreams by bearing out of wedlock a daughter of her own. Her eyes lingered on Precious for a moment, as different from Louisa as Hutch was from Isaiah. What would *Louisa* have said about this woman? She turned her attention back to her daughter.

"Well, here's another thing I'd rather *not* know," Charley began again. Eva settled back in her seat and picked up her drink.

"I dropped by my stepmama's place last night"—the hair stood up on the back of Eva's neck—"and here she was fucking my ex old man—" Screams of mock horror and disgust rose from the audience in a wave. Eva's mouth fell open.

"Like I said, there are certain things you'd rather not know." Charley continued to drawl out her tale in exaggerated, X-rated language with colorful descriptions about her evil stepmother's reaction and her exboyfriend who dressed in red leather, rode a black motorcycle and had a way with his long, agile tongue.

Eva couldn't breathe; she felt as if she had been slammed against a wall. She wondered for a moment if she was on the verge of having a stroke. "My God!" she repeated again and again, hardly aware that she had said anything out loud. A concerned Precious watched her for a moment, then picked up a glass of water and offered it to her.

"Eva, what's wrong with you?" Roscoe demanded, leaning toward her.

"Did you hear what she said?"

Roscoe looked puzzled.

"What's wrong, baby?" Precious asked.

"Oh, come on, Eva," Roscoe said, patting her hand as if he'd just gotten the joke. "Nobody thinks the child is talking about you any more than people think she really overheard that mess in Kmart. It's all part of her act." He looked amused and slightly smug, like he had when she was a little girl and he'd try to convince her that there were no witches hiding in her closet. There was concern in Precious's eyes, however, and something else that Eva couldn't read. She avoided looking at her.

"The girl shouldn't be talking about her mama in public even if it is her stepmama and it's only a joke. *We* don't talk about *our* mamas in public." Precious spoke to Roscoe above Eva's head, which had dropped to her chest. "I think you'd better have some words with that granddaughter of yours, tell her to get *her* act together."

Roscoe sucked his teeth. "Oh, come off it, Presh," he said defensively. "You been in show business. The girl has her act together and that's what it is. Nobody is taking that girl seriously. Anybody who knows Charley knows she doesn't have an evil stepmother and that Eva would never do something like that. Nobody is listening to what that girl is saying up there on that stage. It's a joke! Lighten up on my grandbaby. You got to know when to take a joke in this world."

Precious tilted her head to the side as if she were considering something, then shook her head and sighed. "What's wrong, baby?" she again asked Eva, who hadn't found her voice yet.

How could Charley humiliate her like this in public? What had she done to deserve this? Eva closed her eyes. Her head was throbbing, and the cheap wine on her empty stomach was making her nauseous. She was sure she was going to be sick. She picked up her head and quickly glanced around the room, looking for the restroom. Charley had gone on to another joke—something about not wanting to know where somebody's hand had been before they prepared her cheeseburger—another lie; Charley had been a vegetarian since she'd turned eighteen. Unsteadily, Eva stood up.

"What's wrong, baby?" Precious asked.

"Don't ask me that again," Eva warned. "I'm sorry," she muttered in the same breath.

"That's okay, baby. That's okay! Whatever it is you've done, if you did it because you needed to, then you've got nothing to apologize for," Precious said in a low voice. There was a kindness in her tone and face that Eva hadn't noticed before.

"Something I ate earlier disagreed with me, that's all!" Eva muttered in her general direction. "Please excuse me. I'm going to look for the ladies' room." Her father stood up, a look of concern on his face now too, and held out his hand as if she might need some help, but Eva brushed him aside; all she needed was to be escorted from the room as if there were actually some truth to Charley's story.

As if in a dream, Eva got up from the table. She could make out a hand-painted sign with the word BATHROOM scribbled on it in the far side of the club, and she headed toward it. As she passed Steven and Dana's table she recalled the look in Steven's eyes when they'd talked earlier, and threw him a hurt look. He dropped his eyes. Did everybody in the whole damn room know about her lover? The thought half-formed itself in her mind.

She tried to avoid looking at Hutch, but then caught his eyes as she nearly tripped over the back of a chair as she passed by his table. Hutch rose from his chair as if he were going to stop her, a worried look in his eyes, but then he sat back down. Eva focused on the restroom sign like a beacon of hope as she pushed forward, hardly seeing anything else. She passed the edge of the stage and vaguely heard the audience chuckling and guffawing at Charley's latest joke. At last, she saw the glimmer of the bathroom light and she followed it, slamming the door and locking it behind her as soon as she got inside. Only then was she able to catch her breath.

# Eva and Charley

As Eva stood in the bathroom of Club Resurrection, she was conscious of nothing but the closeness of the room and her own breath. She badly wanted a cigarette, but managed to put the craving out of her mind; she'd gotten good at it. She leaned over the sink as if she might be sick, then turned the water on and let it run. It was something she had done since childhood when she was upset. The sound of running water had always made her feel calm, more in control. Who had taught her that? Her grandmother Alvia? Louisa? No, she had been far too practical for that. She gazed at herself in the mirror, then wet a paper towel and wiped the smudged eyeliner from under her eyes. Her face looked pale and drawn, and she badly needed some lipstick. She cursed out loud when she realized she'd left her pocketbook at the table in her rush to get away. Cupping her hands, she filled them with water,

then slurped it up, wiping her wet chin with the back
of her hand.

*We don't talk about our mamas in public.*

Had she failed to teach that one essential lesson that
black mothers teach their daughters—to respect,
honor, never defy them? Black women didn't talk
about their mothers in public. But *good* black mothers
didn't sleep with their daughter's ex-boyfriend. Her
own mother would no more have *flirted* with one of
her ex-suitors than she would have done a striptease in
church.

*Why was she involved with Isaiah? What need was
he fulfilling? Was he worth all this?*

Charley had been exaggerating what she said she
had witnessed in her confrontation, but Eva knew
there had been a kernel of truth in her jokes, and the
crowd had certainly voiced their common judgment on
such a woman, such a mother—evil stepmother—that
she was.

Yet Eva could not make herself feel guilty about her
relationship with Isaiah Lonesome. He touched some
part of her that needed to be touched and that had
brought its own particular brand of healing; she had finally been able to accept that much about their relationship. And there was the pure sexual joy of it. She
could not remember ever making love to a man the
way she did to Isaiah Lonesome. Even Hutch. It was
pure, uncomplicated passion, and she had permitted
herself to feel that way only once before, with
Charley's father before she knew any better. She
wasn't about to give it up.

What were those words Precious had uttered?
*Whatever it is you've done, if you did it because you*

*needed to, then you've got nothing to apologize for.*
But had she sacrificed her relationship with her daughter for some vague notion of sexual fulfillment? Eva was certain that Charley no more really cared about Isaiah Lonesome than she really stood in line at Kmart. (As a matter of fact, Eva reminded herself, *she* had stood in line at Kmart so Charley wouldn't have to.) But she was obviously still very angry, and she wasn't sure what to do about that.

*Our relationship has nothing to do with you. Why do you feel betrayed when there was nothing serious between you?*

*Because you are my mother.*

There was a knock on the door. Eva's heart jumped. "Go away! There's somebody in here," she said.

"Eva, it's me. Raye."

"Oh, Christ!"

"Hutch asked me to . . . to check on you."

"Tell Hutch to go to hell!"

"Eva, I just wanted to tell you, I—I think it was very cruel of Charley to, well, to—" *Does everybody know?* Eva wondered. She unlocked and opened the door before Raye could finish her sentence.

She gave Raye a quick once-over as she stepped into the room, noticing in a glance the pearl and gold earrings that studded her ears and the chic leather clutch bag she'd seen in the *New York Times* for a ridiculous eight hundred dollars. She turned from Raye to study her own as well as Raye's face in the mirror. The harsh lights made them both look tired and pale, but Raye looked worse, Eva decided, which made her feel better.

"So you know about me and Isaiah?"

"Hutch told me. Several weeks ago."

Involuntarily, Eva drew in a short, sharp breath. So he'd known about her and Isaiah even before Charley. *When did he find out?* She met Raye's eyes in the mirror.

"So what did *he* have to say about it?" She made her voice sound as calm and unconcerned as she could.

Raye sighed a weary sigh. "Not much. You must know how much he loves you. He always has, and he always will. That much is obvious, so he was very hurt. Hutch loves very hard."

"And I'm sure you know about *that!*" Eva snapped. Raye's face was both surprised and alarmed, which made Eva smile; she had hit her mark.

"He's a very good man, Eva."

"I'm sure you know about *that* now too." Raye flinched again. "So tell me, where is Donald Mason, Esquire, tonight? Your dear rich husband and my estranged husband's very best friend?" Eva realized that she was enjoying seeing Raye squirm. She felt like Bette Davis in a 1940s movie. *The joy of being a bitch is definitely underrated*, she thought.

"I'm not sure what you're—"

"Oh, cut the crap," Eva said with disgust. Looking slightly dazed, Raye dug in her bag and pulled out a leather case containing a comb, which she raked through her hair several times before putting it back. Eva felt triumphant. She'd been hurt by Charley, and it felt good to strike out at somebody else. But the feeling was fleeting. Raye's face and composure had begun to crumble, and despite herself Eva began to feel sorry for her. "If you're afraid I'm going to tell Donald, don't be. As far as I'm concerned he deserves whatever he gets. My business is mine, and Hutch's business is his," she added, but her words sounded unconvincing.

"Thank you."

"Please don't thank me. The last thing I need in the world is your gratitude."

Neither woman said anything for a while, and the silence was tense and awkward. Raye was the first to speak.

"He loves you very much, but he also has his pride, Eva."

"So do I."

Again there was an uncomfortable silence, and Raye began again. "I have to tell you the truth. I've never been any good at lying. There are things going on in my own life, between me and Donald that are—well, that Hutch is helping me through." Her eyes begged Eva's for understanding. Eva, not ready yet to offer her any sympathy, glanced away. "You know what Donald is like," Raye continued. Eva could see her eyes watering again. "You're so strong. You would have to be, for a man like Hutch to love you like he does, I'm just learning; and Hutch, well, he has helped me so much, to see—Oh, God—" she said, as if realizing that she was saying too much.

Eva stared at her, making her eyes as hard as she could as she tried not to let any understanding seep through. "What do you expect me to say to you?"

"This isn't coming out like I expected it to. I don't know what I expect you to say. Why I even came in here, except. . . ." She shook her head in frustration.

Eva jumped in quickly. "You came in here because Hutch told you to. You're doing like he tells you to do, the same way you do what Donald tells you to do. Don't be such a fool, Raye. Hutch will end up walking over you the same way Donald does." Eva spoke as cruelly as she could, even though she knew the words were a lie; Hutch was incapable of deliberately hurting anybody as vulnerable as Raye obviously was. But on the other hand, he'd hurt her, hadn't he? She could see the sadness come into Raye's eyes, and then something else. She realized it was determination.

"Anybody in there? Hey, this is a public bathroom. Take the lock off the door. I need to get in there," Charley's voice, loud and cheerful, boomed from outside.

Raye glanced at Eva, alarm in her eyes, but Eva remained calm.

"Would you leave so that I can have it out with my daughter?" she said quietly.

"What do you want me to say to Hutch?"

"Tell him whatever you want to," Eva said with a weary shrug. "I don't even care anymore." And Eva realized she really didn't. She didn't want to think about Raye or Hutch, especially not together. Charley was on her mind now, and anger had begun to replace the humiliation she'd felt earlier. She realized with sudden insight that her confrontation with Raye had prepared her for the one with Charley; it had brought out the fighter in her.

It took Charley a good five minutes to decide to come in. Eva wondered for a moment if she'd changed her mind and decided to avoid the whole scene by wearing her stage clothes home, which didn't seem likely. But then the door slowly opened and Charley shyly peeked into the room. Eva recognized the expression on her daughter's face as a cross between defiance and dread. In one guise or another, she had seen a variation of the look since Charley had been a toddler. Eva didn't speak for a moment or two. She simply glared at her daughter and then said in a calm, bewildered voice, "Why?"

"I didn't do anything wrong, Mother. I didn't mention you. The act was about my 'evil stepmother.' You're not an evil stepmother. Everybody knows that. It was part of my act, that's all." Defensiveness sparked in her daughter's eyes, which were also wide with innocence as she stammered out her reply. Eva recognized that look too. She tilted her head a notch higher and said in a quiet, dignified voice, "There are many things that you could have chosen to joke about, Charley. But my relationship with—"

Charley's eyes turned bright with anger. "You are making such a fool of yourself, Mother, can't you see that?" Eva's mouth went dry. She hadn't expected *that*. Charley continued, "Here you are, a middle-aged, respectable woman—fornicating"—Charley said the word and paused as if waiting for a reaction. Eva rolled her eyes—"with a man half your age. Your daughter's ex-boyfriend, at that! You should be ashamed of yourself!" Charley lifted her head sanctimoniously, her eyes narrowing in judgment. Eva shrank from her daughter's gaze.

"We don't talk about our mothers in public," she said without conviction, amazed to hear Precious's words spouting from her mouth.

Hardly hearing, Charley barreled on. "I still can't get over it. A woman of your age and station!"

*Age and station! Where the hell did she get that?* Eva wondered.

"Don't you have any dignity? Don't you have any pride?"

"Shut up, Charley. You left the stage fifteen minutes ago," Eva snapped, but her heart dropped as she saw again the contemptuous look on her daughter's face. "I don't want to fight with you, sweetheart," she added more gently. "Please, let's not fight."

But Charley continued, "And you've hurt everybody. You really hurt Daddy. I can tell by his voice."

"He seems to have recovered without missing a beat," Eva smirked.

Charley looked puzzled for a moment but went on. "You've been destructive and selfish!" Groaning, Eva rolled her eyes again as she recognized words she'd said to Charley more than once. "And you've hurt me too," Charley added quietly, her eyes leaving Eva's face.

"But why should my relationship with Isaiah hurt you, Charley? Why?"

Charley raised up her eyes and glared for a moment without answering, which told Eva she had to think of an answer. She went into one of the stalls, and Eva could hear her changing into her street clothes. She came out again and without looking or speaking to Eva she filled the sink with water, squeezed some soap out of the soap dispenser, lathered it up, then washed and rinsed her face.

"Didn't you tell me that Isaiah means nothing to you?"

"Right."

"Well?"

"Like I told you once before, that's not the point. You are my mother. And frankly, I don't like to see you making a fool of yourself."

Eva's sigh was long and sorrowful. "I don't think I'm making a fool of myself."

"You can't see yourself."

"And you can?" There was slight amusement in Eva's tone.

"Obviously better than you."

Eva watched her daughter rinse and scrub her face again with the soap and then said, "Don't use that stuff on your face, Charley. It's too harsh. It will break you out." She said it because she wanted to move her daughter; she needed to touch her and make her listen by connecting as she always had in the past, and the easiest way to do that was to become the caretaker again. Eva, the protector. Eva, the shield. But Charley wasn't buying it.

She stopped washing her face and glared at her. "I can't tell you who to fuck; don't tell me how to wash my face."

Eva gasped at the words and the tone of her voice. Charley turned to leave the room, and Eva grabbed her daughter's arm, pulling her around to face her. In a flash, she remembered how, when Charley had been a toddler, she had once grabbed her arm in such a pique of rage and frustration that she had bruised it. Eva had spotted the tiny dark marks on her daughter's thin arm when she bathed her that night, and she had cried out loud with guilt and shame. For months she had been haunted by it. Was she capable of abusing her child? she'd wondered. Had her own mother been right about her, that she wasn't ready yet to raise a child? She pushed the memory out of her mind.

"I have given you everything I can of my life, and now I want something back for myself," she said. The anger in Charley's eyes was replaced with astonishment. "I'm going to tell you this once and for all. If you can't be kind, keep your thoughts to yourself, and if you can't accept what I do with my life, then maybe you should stay out of it until you can. Just stay away from me, Charley. Stay away!"

Charley snatched her arm away. "All this over a man!" she said with a haughty shake of her head and a loud sucking of her teeth. "And as for staying out of your life, Mother, you don't have to worry about that!" She picked up her bag of clothes and slammed the door as she left the room.

After she had gone, Eva collapsed on one of the commodes. The full weight of her words settled down on her. Her own mother had once said similar words to her, and she too had left her house, slamming the door behind her, not seeing her mother again until Charley was four.

*What if Charley took her at her word and stayed out of her life?*

The humiliation and anger she'd felt earlier turned into despair.

*Was it all really just over a man?*

Without meaning to, without even realizing that she had done it, she had ended up speaking the same words her own mother had said to her, making war with her daughter as her mother had made it with her.

*Was she trying to resolve some battle with her own dead mother?* It sometimes seemed that she was acting out some ancient drama that had nothing to do with anything or anyone except what had passed before her. Had she created this situation with Isaiah to prove something to herself?

*I have given you everything I can of my life, and now I want something back for myself.*

The words had a primeval ring to them, as if spoken by someone else. But there had been truth there, too. *Had Louisa ever said those words to her?* She searched her memory, trying to call them forth. But it had been different with Louisa. She had wanted Eva to live a life she had dreamed for her, and when she hadn't gotten it she had thrown her out. Unborn baby and all. But hadn't Eva expected the same of Charley? She felt confused and for some reason ashamed.

There was another knock on the door, and her heart skipped a beat.

"Charley?" Eva cried out in excitement as she rushed to open it.

"No. It's me, kiddo. You okay? You look a little green around the gills," said Roscoe.

"Black people don't get green around the gills."

"Then whatever you ate that disagreed with you went down or came up?"

"That's one way of putting it," Eva said.

"Charley flew out of here a minute ago like a bat out of hell. Anything you feel like talking about?" Her father had always been able to read between the lines, even when her mother was alive. Eva wondered if he knew or guessed the truth.

"I'm surprised Charley didn't tell you."

"Tell me what?"

"I don't feel like going into it." The last thing she needed was Roscoe's opinion about her parenting skills.

"Feel like some coffee? The waiter says they serve coffee until the bar closes, so we have about forty minutes. I've got a couple of things I need to talk to you about." He handed Eva her pocketbook, which he'd brought from the table.

"Actually, I'm tired. If you don't mind, I really want to go home. Where's Precious?" Eva glanced around the nearly empty club.

"She went home. She has some church stuff to do early tomorrow morning."

"She doesn't strike me as the churchgoing type."

"Precious is a very spiritual woman. One of the most spiritual I've ever known. Come on, let's talk. It's important to me." Dutifully, Eva followed him back into the room. Club Resurrection was nearly empty now, and the stark room lights, which had been turned on, brought the place back to its humble origins. They sat down at a table next to the bar, and a young man took their orders between yawns. Eva ordered a cappuccino, Roscoe an Irish coffee.

"That's not good for you," Eva said with disapproval. Roscoe ignored her as usual.

"So what did you eat that made you so sick?" Eva glanced up at him and noticed the playful smirk on his face that told her he wanted more of the truth than she'd given when she left the table.

She sipped her coffee. "I was in shock."

Roscoe nodded with understanding. "Charley told me about you and Hutch. I was sorry to hear it. I didn't want to say anything until you brought it up. But I thought that happened over the summer. Why does seeing him still have such a strong effect on you?"

Eva still didn't feel like talking, but knew her father well; he'd keep digging until he found out something, so she gave him a piece of the truth. "Hutch and Raye

Mason are having . . . I think they're involved," Eva said, telling him less than he obviously wanted to know.

Roscoe shook his head in disgust. "Man, now I've heard everything. A man like Hutch betraying his wife *and* his friend! He must be going through some kind of thing. Good-byes don't always mean gone. He'll be back.

"How old is Hutch now? Mid-forties? The forties are funny, Eva. Strange things happen to folks when they're in their forties. You get the urging to shake things around, take another look at your life, stir things up. Now fifty—that's nice. Calm. You look around you, set things in order, throw things—and people— you don't need out the door. Sixty, now, that's something else again. Kind of scary. You can see the end coming round the bend, and every party you go to seems to come after a funeral. Seventy, well, you're just happy to get there, so every day is a blessing. Eighty, I guess you probably just sit around worrying, hoping the Grim Reaper won't knock on your door. Seems like the even decades—twenties, forties, sixties, something strange happens to you. Funny isn't it? You'd think it would be the other way around, the odd—"

"Did you say you had something important to say to me?" Eva scowled at her father impatiently as she interrupted him.

"I don't know if now is the time, since you hit me with that stuff about Hutch. Well, Charley said the man left, but I figured that he was just taking a little break; involved with another man's wife like that, I don't know—"

"Did Charley tell you anything else about me?" Eva interrupted again, searching her father's face.

"You? No, not really. But Precious said something that struck me as odd. Asked if you were involved with a younger man. I told her not as far as I knew. I didn't want to go into the whole thing with you and Hutch before I talked to you, but—"

"Oh, God!" Eva groaned. "What did she say?"

"Well . . ." Roscoe took a gulp of his Irish coffee and then shook his head irritably. "They don't put no whiskey in these things anymore. Time was you could order an Irish coffee and it tasted like it had some Irish whiskey in it. This thing is as weak as tea! Well, the way you bolted out of your chair, Precious said she thought maybe something Charley said had struck a nerve."

Eva forced herself to shrug as if she had no idea what he was talking about and emptied her voice of concern. "No. Nothing like that," she said, collecting her bag and coat, getting ready to leave. "Well, Dad, if you'd rather not talk now, let's get together for—"

"Wait." Roscoe put a restraining hand on her arm. "I'm thinking about asking Precious to marry me." His eyes gleamed with happiness. "I haven't asked her yet, but I wanted to talk it over with you first." Eva's mouth dropped open, and she stared at her father in disbelief. Roscoe's smile faded. "Obviously you don't approve."

"Does it matter?"

"Yes, it matters," her father said quietly. "You're my daughter. I want your blessing."

"You're seventy-two years old. What do you need with my blessing?"

Roscoe looked lost for a moment. "Just tell me what you think."

"You really don't want to know what I think," Eva said solemnly.

"Say it. Better now than later."

"She's not your type, Dad. She's nothing like my mother, like Louisa."

"Maybe that's a good thing."

Eva's breath caught in her throat, and she studied her father with surprise, but he didn't waver. "No. It's not a good thing. Not at your age. I think it's a mistake."

"Why?"

Eva tried to think of a way to say something kind about the woman without lying, but she couldn't.

"Go on."

She took a breath and plowed on. "Well, for one thing she has buried three husbands. That should tell you something right there. She's obviously not good for your health. You drink too much when you're with her and don't think I haven't noticed. You're also smoking more cigars than you have in years. All that Jack Daniel's is bad for your blood pressure. And I'll bet you haven't been taking your pills."

"Go on."

"You know how important it is for you to take your pressure pills. You're not a child. I don't have to tell you."

"Those damn pills slow me down. They interfere with my—well, you know . . ." he said shyly.

"I'd rather *not* know to be honest," Eva said disapprovingly, "but maybe it's time you slowed down. Marriage to Precious whatever her name is—"

"Precious Andrews."

"To Precious Andrews would be a mistake. She's

too—well, just too everything. And why in God's name did you tell her about your investments? That was one thing you should have kept to yourself. I know *you* don't think you're rich, but a lot of people who don't have anything might. Did any of her three husbands leave her any money? She's probably broke. And let's face it, Dad, you are a good ten years older than she is. Golddiggers come in all sizes, shapes and—"

"Just shut up! Stop it right there! You've grown up to be every bit as judgmental and harsh as your mother was," Roscoe said angrily.

"And speaking of my mother, did you have an affair with this woman when my mother was alive?" Eva snapped, furious at him for criticizing Louisa. "I heard that little quip about meeting you in that club."

"That's none of your damn business," Roscoe said, finishing off his coffee in one gulp. "I'm not saying if I did, and I'm not saying if I didn't," he said like a cagey child.

"Well, I think you're making a fool of yourself," Eva said, realizing with a jolt that she sounded just like her daughter.

"I thought you'd be happy for me. For us."

"You asked my opinion and I told you." She knew on some level that her harshness toward her father was the result of her painful evening—her angry encounters with Charley, her new knowledge of Hutch's relationship with Raye—but she couldn't seem to help it; this insight didn't make a difference. She couldn't remember the last time she and her father had argued. It had been years, she realized. She suddenly felt like crying.

"Well, you've said your piece," Roscoe said. "Thanks for nothing."

"Well, don't ask me next time." Eva tried to say it gently, but it came out wrong. Roscoe summoned the waiter, paid for their coffee and without another word between them they walked to their cars.

The drive back from Brooklyn, which usually took an hour, took Eva forty-five minutes. She tried to concentrate on the road, but her thoughts were on her family, and most of all on Louisa and how she still haunted them. Charley's response to her had been her response to Louisa. There had been no "joy" in Roscoe and Louisa's marriage either; she was certain now of that. There had been respect weighed down with duty and a simmering silent anger, but no real communication. Her mother's dreams had been tied up in her, and if her father dreamed at all it was of the magic and music he left in the South with Aunt Delia and the others. It made her sad just thinking about it.

Bama greeted her when she walked into the house. She picked up the cat and hugged her, letting her fur tickle her nose. She filled the cat's bowl with dried food, at which Bama turned up her nose and gazed up at her expectantly. Eva checked the cupboard for canned food and slammed it closed when she didn't find any. She heard Isaiah's car pull up, his car radio blasting some late-night music from a jazz station.

"Hey, you still up? How did it go?" he said when he walked in. He dropped his case down on the table, went to the refrigerator, took out a carton of milk and poured himself a glass. Closing the door, he leaned back against it, a smile on his lips as he waited for her answer.

"It's been a very bad night," she said. She made herself stop thinking about her family and concentrate on Isaiah. He wore cargo pants and a dark brown cable knit sweater that looked like cashmere. Eva imagined how it would feel to run her fingertips through the soft nap as she stroked his chest and back.

"So Charley bombed, huh?"

"No. Charley was very good. I underestimated her."

"Parents always do." He smirked as if speaking from personal experience and polished off the milk.

"So your mother underestimated you, too?" Eva's voice was testy as she took the carton of milk from the table where Isaiah had left it and put it back in the refrigerator.

"I didn't mention my mother, don't take it there," Isaiah warned. "Don't make me pay for your fucked-up evening by analyzing me."

"Why do you avoid sharing your life with me? Why won't you let things between us get any deeper?" Eva watched him drink his milk for a moment or two and then said quietly, "You're never going to let me in, are you?" Isaiah rinsed his glass out, placed it on the rack and then turned to face her.

"Hey, come upstairs." He nodded toward his room, ignoring her question.

"No. Not tonight," Eva said, raising her voice slightly, like a weary mother telling a toddler she didn't want to play his favorite game. The level of strain and annoyance in her own voice surprised her. Bama, who despite Isaiah's presence had crept back into the kitchen, looked up at Eva and meowed.

Isaiah picked up his horn. "You sure? Make you feel better."

Eva shrugged.

"Come upstairs," he ordered, more seriously this time, bluntly challenging her refusal. Eva suddenly remembered the last time they'd made love and the memory shot through her body like wildfire. Their meeting on the stairs that night had been unexpected. She was on her way to class, and he was on his way to work. Their lovemaking had been impetuous and almost savage in its intensity, and no words had been spoken at all. His eyes told her that he remembered it, too.

"Okay," she said.

Taking two steps at a time, he bounced up to his room, whistling the tune that had been playing in the car. Picking up the cat, Eva strode slowly behind him. But then, pausing for a moment in front of his bedroom door, *what was the point,* she wondered. After they finished, they'd continue on their separate ways, thinking their own thoughts no closer really than they'd been an hour before, six months before. Did she really need Isaiah on those terms tonight, on *his* terms, in his way? No, she realized that she didn't. So she continued to her own room instead, closing the door behind her.

# Hutch

## WEDNESDAY, DECEMBER 24

**E**va stayed on Hutch's mind long after he saw her
at Club Resurrection. For weeks afterward, he
thought about calling her, even though he had no idea
what he would say. He couldn't forget the look on her
face when she swept past him on her way to the ladies'
room. His first impulse had been to rush to her and
sweep her into his arms in a comforting embrace. The
humiliation he had seen in her eyes had broken his
heart. There was nothing that she had done—not even
her relationship with Isaiah—that deserved that kind of
public embarrassment, especially from her own daughter. He'd had no idea how she was feeling, and he was
worried about her. Raye had said nothing when she returned to her seat.

Charley told him little when he met her for lunch the
following week, even though he sternly lectured her
about the cruelty of her material. Hutch rarely inter-

fered in Eva and Charley's quarrels, but this time
Charley had gone too far. Yet she only balked, made
feeble excuses and left the restaurant with her mouth
poked out. Hutch even called Roscoe Lilton to check
on Eva's state of mind, but Roscoe had given him a
piece of his own, advising him in no uncertain terms
that he should "get your ass back where it belongs." He
did say, however, that Eva had been devastated by his
departure and probably wanted him back, which surprised and delighted Hutch. Every time he thought
about that white silk robe and the look on Eva's face
when she'd smiled at the horn player, he was sure that
things were over between them forever. The memory
of that night still stirred a primal rage within him. He
was haunted by that scene almost as much as he was
by his guilt about Donald and the knowledge that a
confrontation was probably inevitable.

Yet Hutch was amazed by how smoothly Raye managed her new situation. He had been prepared for
nights of frantic late-night phone calls and tears of regret and self-doubt but none of those had been forth-
coming. He found it unsettling how easily she could
pretend to still care about Donald in his presence while
expressing nothing but contempt for him behind his
back. She talked about Donald like a dog, and more
than once Hutch had found himself cautiously rising to
Donald's defense. He was constantly astonished by
Raye's cool ability to deceive. But then Donald had always told him that about women:

"Ain't you learned that yet, nigger? Women have
*never* been the weaker sex. They're twice as tough as
we are," Donald would say in his jaded, humorous
way, which Hutch found himself missing. "People talk

about how clever I am; if Raye had gone to law school she'd be kicking everybody's ass. Truth is, I married the woman so I'd never have to face her in court."

Raye had freed herself of Donald with a serene detachment that Hutch found stunning. He knew he could never be free of Eva—never want to be free of her—with such finality. Raye smiled sweetly as she continued to attend social affairs, entertain Donald's clients and make sure that everything in his life ran smoothly. She was, she said, biding her time, counting the hours and waiting for the best day to make her final move.

But each day that passed in the six months since Hutch had left Eva made him realize that he loved her more. He'd read somewhere that the pain of separation, be it due to death or separation, is always worst during holidays, and he could testify to that. Each one had brought its own special agony. The memory of his falling asleep on the couch in the empty house on the Fourth of July and then making that asinine telephone call the next day made him flinch with embarrassment whenever he thought about it. He would never forget the humiliation he'd experienced on Labor Day. And the latest holiday to pass, Thanksgiving, had been a disaster.

The Wednesday before Thanksgiving, Donald had called to invite him to the house. Hutch had firmly turned him down.

"But why?" Donald had wailed into the phone. "I miss you, man! Where you been?"

Hutch had cringed with guilt. "You're never around, Donald." He could think of nothing else to say.

Donald had chuckled lecherously, as if recalling the reasons for his absences, then added, "I told Raye to call you two weeks ago so you would get your rusty butt over here for some turkey. She forgot to ask you, didn't she? I love that woman, man, but I swear she is losing her mind! She say anything to you about what's been bothering her?"

"Listen, brother, I got to go. Somebody at the door. Got to get to work. Talk to you later!" Hutch had begged off as quickly and convincingly as he could, feeling the weight of his betrayed friendship once again.

He'd made several attempts to get in touch with Steven to offer to take him and Dana out to dinner, but his calls had, as usual, not been returned, and even Charley, always game for a free meal, coolly explained that she was cooking Thanksgiving dinner with friends. He was left to celebrate by himself.

He'd bought a small turkey with the notion of roasting it, but the thought of sitting in his gloomy apartment eating turkey and watching the football game by himself was more than he could bear, so he'd shoved it into the freezer. Unwilling to inflict himself on any of his employees, who, knowing of his current marital status, had all invited him to their homes, he'd hunkered down in the office to pay some overdue bills, go through some proposals and watch the football game on the small TV there. Later that night, he'd picked up some Chinese food, gone home and washed it down with two bottles of Heineken.

He had sorely missed Eva's cornbread stuffing and heavenly sweet potato pie. He nearly wept when he remembered the times that he and Steven had watched the game together, drinking sodas and laughing while Eva scolded them about not helping her get dinner ready. He imagined the horn player chomping down on a turkey leg while eyeing Eva lecherously, and then forced the scene out of his mind. Around midnight, he'd driven to her house with no idea why he was going or what he would say if he saw her.

November was drearier than ever, and the night had been wet and unpleasant. A layer of snow had fallen earlier in the day, and the night was bitterly cold. To Hutch's relief, Isaiah's car wasn't in the driveway when he drove up. *Have they broken up?* he wondered. He sat in his parked car for about fifteen minutes, wondering what he should do. Finally Eva came outside to put a bag of trash in the can at the curb, and his heart leaped. But just as he opened his car door to get out, he heard the hum of the Geo as it turned the corner. He slammed the door shut, dropped down into his seat and watched as Isaiah, radio blasting, pulled into the driveway. They strolled back into the house together.

It was nearly two by then, too late for Thanksgiving dinner. But the man was obviously still living there. Hutch imagined him devouring the pie that rightfully belonged to him and energetically making love to Eva in their big king-size bed until morning. Defeated, he drove home.

That night he polished off the better part of a fifth of scotch and fell asleep on the couch in a sorrowful, drunken stupor. The next morning, his head raging and his stomach flipping, he pulled himself up, showered and, after forcing down a pot of strong black coffee and several slices of unbuttered toast, stumbled to work and threw himself into his day, losing himself in the trivial details of contracts. Later that evening, Raye dropped off some turkey sandwiches and leftovers from their dinner on the way to some social event but said she couldn't stay because Donald was waiting for her in the car. And that had been his Thanksgiving weekend.

Determined to accept things he couldn't change, Hutch had managed to put Eva and her horn player out of his mind through the end of November and into the first weeks of December. But then Christmas carols began to play on the radio and the daily countdowns to Christmas began. Unwillingly, Hutch found himself pulled into the Christmas spirit. He also got an idea.

Christmas, he realized, presented him with the opportunity he needed to get back in touch with his son—and maybe even with Eva. But unlike Labor Day, now he knew what he was dealing with and there would be no surprises. The Christmas season always brought out the charity in his family. Eva loved the season and even after the kids were grown, they all got together to decorate the Christmas tree, open their gifts together and eat Eva's Christmas goose or duck. Arguments and differences were set aside. Nobody refused a kindness. Everybody was in good spirits. Gifts were generously given and graciously received, so Hutch decided that he would come to the house bearing them.

Charley was always losing or breaking her watch, and this would be a good time to buy her a new one, Hutch reasoned. Months before the disastrous lunch at Beans 'n' Sprouts, Steven had admired a gray cashmere sweater advertised in an old Brooks Brothers catalog. At the time, Hutch had chastised him for wanting to spend hard-earned money foolishly, but now he called the store and tracked down where he could buy one. He knew he could get back in Roscoe's good graces with a bottle of good whiskey. And he'd find something for Eva as well. Something tasteful and expensive. Something she couldn't resist. And on Christmas Eve, he would casually drop by her house with his presents. Maybe she would invite him in for a drink, and if the horn player wasn't there he'd take her up on it. And maybe he'd go in even if he was there. He had known and loved this woman for ten years, and nobody could object to their sharing a drink together on Christmas Eve.

The more Hutch thought about the possibilities of Christmas Eve, the more confident he became. No, he hadn't seen Eva since Charley's performance, and they hadn't actually spoken since July, but there was no reason why they couldn't now. Enough time had passed. Six months was a long time. They could at least begin to talk civilly to each other again. It was time for him to admit that he had made a mistake. And despite his relationship with Raye—maybe because of it—he was sure that it had been a mistake. If it weren't for the horn player, he was sure he would be home, where, in Roscoe's words, "his ass belonged." He needed Eva back in his life.

So, three days before Christmas, Hutch found himself in the curious position of buying extravagant gifts for people who weren't speaking to him. He bought Charley not only a watch but also a silver necklace from Tiffany's. He bought Steven not one but three cashmere sweaters in various shades of gray and blue. Remembering what he could of Dana's general size, he bought him a pair of black leather gloves; then, fearful that he might misconstrue the choice of black leather as some crude, stereotypical comment on being gay, he'd kept the gloves for himself and gotten him a hundred-dollar gift certificate from Bloomingdale's. He bought Roscoe not one but two bottles of Jack Daniel's and a bottle of Veuve Clicquot champagne. And after a long frustrating search for something appropriate for Eva, he settled on a luxurious hand-knit red shawl and a case of expensive Bordeaux. He fretted at first about buying the wine. There was a chance that the horn player would end up slurping it up like so much malt liquor. But there was also the possibility that Eva might open a bottle on the spot and share it with Hutch. The important thing was that he would get to see her again. Talk to her. He was sure she would let him in— even Eva, as angry as she was, couldn't possibly turn him down laden with gifts.

He went to work Christmas Eve but left for home early, stopping by CVS to buy some foil wrapping paper and elaborate bows with which to wrap Roscoe's liquor and Eva's wine. He fretted about the best time to drop by. If he came too early, she might not be home; too late could mean running into the horn player. He finally settled on eight-thirty, which seemed reasonable. He groomed himself carefully, ignoring Raye's lemon verbena soap (it wouldn't do to show up smelling like another woman's toiletries) in favor of his faithful Dial. He put on the navy lamb's-wool sweater Eva had given him last Christmas. He splashed on some Obsession cologne, then panicked when he remembered that she'd once complained that every teenager who came into the library was drenched in it, so he scrubbed it off, patting on his usual, generic aftershave lotion. He kept an eye on the time and at exactly ten minutes past eight set out for the house.

With his heart pounding, he searched for the black Geo, and when he didn't see it, parked his car and went to the front door. Although it hadn't snowed since Thanksgiving, the air was brisk and cold. He noticed that the railing on the front porch as well as one of the eaves on the roof had been repaired, two things he'd planned to do this fall. He also noticed that a line of smoke was curling from the fireplace. He'd never known Eva to build a fire; she always claimed that she could never lay the logs down properly, and that it always went out before it really got going. He anxiously looked around again for the horn player's car and then took a deep breath and rang the front door bell.

He heard the familiar chime, and leaned toward the door to see if he could hear anyone inside. He heard Eva's footsteps coming into the foyer from the living room. She paused at the door as she checked the peephole, and his heart jumped when he heard her turn the lock.

# Hutch and Eva

### DECEMBER 24

Eva didn't say anything when she opened the door; she just stared at him.

"Merry Christmas! Thought I'd drop these by. Wasn't sure I'd catch anybody home . . . Here!" Hutch forced a nervous grin, making his voice sound casual as he thrust the two shopping bags brimming with presents into her arms and hauled the case of wine in from the porch. Startled, Eva took the bags and smiled. *God, how he'd missed that smile!* His eyes were drawn to the dimple that he'd always loved. He quashed a reflex to bend down and kiss it, forcing himself to stand up straight and look respectable.

She did look beautiful, though. She'd trimmed her hair into a no-nonsense cut that emphasized her eyes and beautiful skin, and the gray streak, just a bit wider, was as bewitching as ever. A pair of jazzy reading glasses hung from a woven chain around her neck. He wondered when she'd bought those; she'd never needed them before. What other small things had he missed in the months he'd been gone? How else had she changed? He glanced over her head into the house. He could smell and hear the fire burning in the fireplace and was swept with nostalgia. He also picked up a whiff of pine. So she had put up her tree. He wondered if she'd decorated it by herself or with the horn player. He forced that image out of his mind.

"Thank you, Hutch. How thoughtful of you." Her eyes were smiling now too. How long had it been since he had seen her eyes smile? They stood awkwardly at the open door for a moment. Hutch wondered if he should leave. He took a step back, prepared to go.

"Well, I—I just wanted to stop by, drop these things off, tell you—well, you know, Merry Christmas, Happy New—"

"Would you like to come in?"

"Oh, sure! Thanks. Yeah!"

The question seemed easily asked, and was quickly answered. Feeling like a child who has finally been allowed to enter some exciting, forbidden space, Hutch felt his muscles tighten with a combination of anticipation and anxiety.

"Let me take your coat. Come on into the living room." Eva was gracious. Her voice was friendly, welcoming.

"Thank you, Eva." Hutch was overwhelmed with gratitude as he handed her his coat. He saw her eyes light up momentarily when she noticed his sweater. He thanked God that he'd thought to wear it.

"Wow, the weather has really gotten cold," he said, relying on the old tried and true conversation starter as she led him into the living room.

"It *is* December."

"Yeah, already! Do you believe it?"

Nothing had changed. The long, plush brown velvet couch still sat in front of the fireplace flanked by the two matching chairs of the same fabric. The low ebony coffee table that they'd bought when they first got married was still in front of the couch. Two kilims, both in subtle shades of gold, black and brown, still lay on the polished wood floors. The crackling fire made the room cozy and inviting.

"Great fire." Hutch couldn't help mentioning it.

"Thanks. I finally got the hang of how to build a decent one."

"You built it?" He didn't disguise his surprise.

"Yeah." Eva gave him an amused, tolerant look.

"I see you got your tree up." It felt good to be back in the house. Hutch walked through the living room into the adjoining sunroom, which was brighter and more casual than the living room and where they'd always put up the tree. It was smaller than the ones they usually bought, but he recognized the old decorations—crystal balls, silver snowflakes, chocolate-brown cherubs, ebony Santa Clauses.

"Steven and Dana helped me. They did a nice job, didn't they?"

At the mention of his son, Hutch felt a lump in his throat. "Nice," he muttered. He stooped to pick up a glass ball that had toppled to the floor. "Looks like Bama's been in here," he said as he placed it back on a lower branch. As if on cue, the cat dashed into the living room. "Hey, girl, how you doin'?" Laughing, Hutch stooped down and scooped up the cat. He rubbed her head, mashing down her ears, and the cat buried her head into his chest and dug her claws into his sweater in their traditional greeting. He carried her back into the living room and sat down on the couch. From her perch on his lap, Bama sat regally studying Eva as if reprimanding her. The cat had been the last thing on Hutch's mind when he thought about coming home, but the warmth of the animal's greeting touched him. He hugged her again. Eva watched, amused.

"And you, the person who used to hate cats!"

"Bama's not a cat. Can't you tell?"

Eva laughed "Well, whatever she is, she has obviously missed you." The cat jumped off his lap and glanced at Eva, who sat in one of the chairs across from the couch.

"Is she the only one?" It was a question that seemed to follow naturally, even though if he'd thought about it before he asked, he wouldn't have for fear of the answer. Eva smiled a thin, noncommittal smile.

"I'm not the one who left," she said. Her biting words, though gently delivered, were meant to sting. They were a clear statement of how she felt, and his heart dropped. They avoided each other's eyes.

Eva broke the silence after a moment or two. "So let me see what Santa brought." Her voice, though cheerful, sounded false. She picked the first gift out of the bag that sat near her feet.

"For Charley?" Sorrow instantly came into her eyes, and she put the two small packages back into the bag. "You'll have to give this to her yourself. I haven't spoken to Charley since—well, since." Her voice faded. Hutch, wanting to comfort her in some way but not knowing what to say, took the presents from her and put them back in the bag.

"I'll give them to her when I see her. I brought something for Steven too," he said quickly. "I know you'll see him."

Eva brightened, eyes thanking him for that. "I *am* speaking to him," she said as she took the gifts out of the bag and put those on the floor beside her.

*"He's* not speaking to me!" Hutch said. They looked at each other and started to laugh. It was a good laugh, hearty and cathartic, and Hutch realized he hadn't laughed like that with her—or with anybody else, for that matter—in a very long time. "And something for Dana too." He handed her the silver-foiled gift certificate.

"Good idea! I wasn't sure what to get him. He's a very nice kid. Have you met him?"

"Yes, I have. Got something for your old man too." Hutch said, changing the subject in a hurry. He didn't want thoughts of the Beans 'n' Sprouts incident to spread a pall over this moment.

Eva frowned, but her eyes were still amused. "Hutch, you really shouldn't have."

"Maybe not, but he's always been like a father to me. I—"

"I mean you shouldn't have gotten him booze! He'll love you for it, though."

"How's he doing?"

"Okay, I guess." She hesitated for a moment, and he knew something was wrong, but then she continued. "We keep missing each other. I've called him once or twice. He hasn't called me back. I—I don't know." She shook her head in frustration, and the sadness was back in her eyes. Hutch hoped that Roscoe knew about the horn player and had told her what he thought about him.

"You'll probably see him before I do," Hutch said with a smile. "Keep it for him, okay?"

"Okay."

Eva picked up the box that contained the shawl, and her eyes widened slightly like a little girl's, Hutch thought. He was glad that he'd paid the extra money to have it gift-wrapped so elaborately.

"Hutch?" She tilted her head to the side like she always did, and he found himself grinning like a kid.

"Open it, go ahead."

"You didn't have to do this." She glanced at him shyly.

"I know. But, well, it's Christmas . . ." He couldn't think of anything else to say. He watched her open the box, tearing the fancy paper off anxiously. He chuckled when he saw the delight in her eyes.

"Thank you!" she said as she spread the shawl around her shoulders, hugging it to her face as if it were a mink. "It's really *really* beautiful."

"You always did look good in red, Eva. Remember that poem I used to say to you? *When Susanna Jones wears red/Her face is like an ancient cameo/Turned brown by the ages/Come with a blast of trumpets, Jesus!*" They both laughed at the shared memory. Hutch continued seriously, "That's you Eva, Susanna Jones. It had your name written on it." He paused for a moment. "You don't have to thank me. Never. For anything."

She glanced away quickly, and Hutch, embarrassed now too, ducked into the foyer where she'd left the wine, opened the case and brought back a bottle.

"Here," he said almost shyly.

She gasped when she read the label.

"You *really* didn't have to do this Hutch. I don't even want to guess what you paid for a case of it."

"You've always been a lady who knows a good bottle of red wine when she sees one. It's no big thing," he added modestly. The truth was, Hutch had no idea that a case of wine—good or otherwise—could cost so much money. But he'd forked it over without a second thought.

"Would you like to taste some of what your hard-earned money bought?"

"Yeah. Great! I'd love to!" Hutch could hardly contain his joy. Obviously the investment had been worth it.

Eva went into the kitchen, and he heard her moving about, rattling glasses and opening drawers. He made a quick, critical survey of the living room while she was gone, noticing that the knobs on the French doors that led to the patio had been replaced. He tried them, and they worked perfectly. Whoever had done it had known what he was doing. Eva came back into the room carrying a tray crowded with two glasses, crackers on a plate and a generous wedge of Roquefort cheese. He took the tray from her and put it on the coffee table. They sat down next to each other on the couch in front of the fire.

"I see you're admiring my handiwork."

"*You* did that!" He was surprised but relieved. He'd assumed it had been the horn player. He regarded Eva with undisguised admiration.

"And I fixed the knobs on the bedroom doors as well. You remember the ones that kept coming off? And the bathroom and kitchen sinks—I put in new washers and a new sprayer," she added, as she poured their wine. "I've been taking courses in home repairs at the adult night school. I'm also going to take a course in car repairs."

"How's the car doing, by the way?" Hutch took a sip of wine.

"It's fine now. But it had some rough days this summer."

"Why didn't you call me?"

"It worked itself out," Eva said with a pleasant smile, and then continued, "I may try some carpentry. I think it satisfies my creative urge."

"Have you started drawing again?"

"No." Eva focused on her wine, and Hutch wished he hadn't said anything. That had always been one of the uncomfortable subjects. "But I've been busy. I've decided to get a master's in library science. "

"Good for you." Hutch raised his glass as if to toast her. "Your father's influence or Helena's?"

"Both."

Hutch studied her face as she sipped her wine. She did seem happy. Calmer and more sure of herself. He wondered if it was the horn player's doing. He hoped it wasn't. But maybe he was better for her than anybody would have guessed. "You look so beautiful, Eva," he said before he knew he'd said it.

"You just haven't seen me in a while." Eva chuckled self-consciously.

"No. Really. You seem . . . well, serene. More peaceful. Just different." He hesitated before he said it, but then said it anyway. Why not just tell her the truth?

"Well," Eva said after a moment. "The serenity probably comes from the lack of nicotine in my body. I finally stopped smoking about two weeks before

Thanksgiving. I'm taking yoga classes at the YWCA on Saturdays, and I love doing that too. I'm just learning to *be* by myself." She giggled self-consciously again. "I know that sounds hokey but I have. I've been doing pretty good."

"Hey, that's great!"

"I still want a cigarette every now and then, but I just chew gum or take a drink of water or brush my teeth or something and the urge disappears. It's getting so I can't stand the smell of them anymore."

"Wow. Congratulations!"

"Well, at least I'm not rushing from one cigarette to the next. Living my life through my butt," she added with a wry smile, and they both chuckled. It was a saying that he had always tossed out at her. He was glad she remembered, but how could she forget it? He'd said it often enough. He watched her lean against the couch. The bronze in her skin was highlighted by the fire and the red shawl that she still wore around her shoulders.

The earlier tension had disappeared. Hutch, however, was still wary, and he tried desperately to think of something to say that would keep the conversation on this even keel.

"So how have things been going at work?" Eva asked something she knew he liked to talk about, and he realized that she was feeling the same way he was. She was wary too, and cautious. Slowly he began to catch her up on what was happening at work. He eagerly told her about his new projects and what was going on in the lives of men she knew on his crew— who had a new baby, who was going back to school, who was getting married. She seemed genuinely interested, and Hutch was instantly transported back to those early days of their relationship, when each small thing, no matter how insignificant, seemed fascinating and novel. He asked her to tell him what it was like to go back to school and how she enjoyed it and what the classes were like, and she filled him in.

They had more wine, nibbled at the cheese, and in silence watched the fire burn, and when it burned down, Eva gave it an expert poke, and it crackled back to life. The fire and the wine made Hutch feel warm and sleepy. The clock chimed and he counted the strikes. It was ten, the shortest hour and a half he could remember in his life. He was reminded again of what he had walked away from, what he had thrown away.

"What are you thinking about?" Eva asked him after a while. She could still read him so well.

He told her the truth. "You."

They were silent again for a while, but it was comfortable. Familiar.

"Are you happy, Hutch?" she asked.

"Sometimes."

"Where are you living now?" He glanced at her face for any hint of sarcasm, but saw just concern and simple curiosity.

"Not where I want to be," he answered honestly. She deserved that from him, and she smiled, a reticent smile. Hutch continued, "I got a place off Livingston. One of those old buildings that have been renovated. You remember Tony Guirdello? I did some work for him a couple of years ago. He knew the guy who is doing the work, and I was able to get a place quickly. Overnight. It's close to the office, that's the main thing I like about it. The only thing."

"When did you move?"

"Almost four months ago. Right after Labor Day." He avoided her eyes as the scene from that night came back, and he forced it out of his mind. He told her about his apartment instead, describing the neighborhood and some of his more colorful neighbors. He talked about how lonely he felt sometimes. How he knew he was overworking. He told her he felt like he was becoming his father. They were both silent when he said that. Hutch was lost in his own thoughts for a moment.

"What are you going to do about it?" Eva asked finally, bringing him back, her eyes wide and concerned.

"About being like my father?"

"Yeah."

"I don't know yet," he said. "I feel like I've got to get in touch with some part of me that is gone. My mother's spirit, maybe."

Eva laughed as if she knew what he meant. "We all have to get in touch with our mother's spirit from time to time," she said, and Hutch nodded that she was right.

They sat for a while longer, and when she poured them both some more wine, he thought about reaching for her hand and holding it. He wondered what she would do if he did, if she would pull it back or let him hold it. He wondered what she would do if he tried to kiss her.

"Do you think you will stay where you are for a while?" she asked.

"Yeah. For a while," he said. Maybe she would come to visit him, he thought. Maybe they could get back together step by step. One day at a time.

"So you're comfortable there, at least for the time being?"

*Is she going to ask me to move back in tonight?* Hutch hoped against hope.

"I wouldn't say I'm exactly comfortable," he said, and he gave her a breakdown of each room, and they both laughed as he told her. "Everything is rented," he continued. "My bed, the couch, the TV set. I guess I'm not ready to invest in any furniture yet. Actually, the place is pretty depressing. If it weren't for Raye, I—" he stopped in mid-sentence.

Raye's name had tumbled out of his mouth before he'd even thought it, almost like a habit. He knew immediately that he'd made a terrible mistake. He made himself finish the sentence. It would be worse to leave things unspoken. "If it weren't for Raye *and Donald* giving me some kitchen things . . ." His voice trailed off and he gulped down the rest of his wine. "Damn, this stuff is good!" he said, raising his glass as if he were doing a wine commercial. Absurdly, he hoped that Eva hadn't noticed the mention of Raye's name. But of course she had.

In that split second between the cordial conversation about his new living arrangement and the mention of Raye Mason, everything had changed. The room was thick with tension again. Eva shifted her body away from him, turning her head so she wasn't looking directly at him. Hutch cleared his throat uncomfortably.

"So if it weren't for Raye Mason your life wouldn't be worth shit," she said quietly. He knew at that moment that Eva knew about him and Raye, and what a mistake it had been to send Raye into the restroom at Club Resurrection. *Why the hell didn't Raye tell me*

*Eva knew?* He wondered. *Why didn't Eva ask me about it before this?* He bit his lip.

"I didn't say that."

"Well, that's what you meant."

"I didn't say that."

"Well, that's the truth, isn't it?"

Suddenly Hutch was sick and tired of lying. He looked into Eva's eyes. "Yes," he said. "That is the truth. Raye is leaving Donald. Yes. She has made living in that disgusting little hole where I live bearable. I don't know what I would have done without her." There, it was said.

Eva, still holding her glass poised in front of her, turned to face him, her face like stone. Hutch wondered for a moment if she was going to throw the wine at him. But then she placed it very carefully on the coffee table. The fire crackled. Hutch glanced at it and then back at her.

"Was Raye Mason the reason you left me?" There was hurt and more sadness in Eva's eyes than anger.

"Oh, Christ! No!" he yelled in protest, his voice much louder than he had meant it to be. "Of course not! No! I—Raye—we—" Hutch sputtered for a moment or two, trying to collect his thoughts.

"When did you start seeing her?"

"After Labor Day," he said guiltily, and then wondered why he felt guilty.

"Why don't you tell the truth for once in your life?"

Bewildered, Hutch stared at Eva, not understanding what had happened and why she had turned on him so completely. And suddenly he was angry too.

"You want to know the truth about me and Raye, Eva? Then I'll tell you. I was hurt. I've never hurt so

much in my life. I came by here to make up with you
on Labor Day. To beg you to let me come back, and
what do I see? I see you and some jock with a horn
parading around my property like he owns it." With
each word Hutch uttered, every bit of rage he'd held in
since Labor Day came pouring out. He stood up, suddenly too angry to remain seated.

"*Your* property?" Eva said, sounding like Raye.

But Hutch didn't hear her; his anger had taken over.
"My God, Eva! What in the name of heaven has gotten
into you? How could you do something like this?
Carry on with some . . . some musician young enough
to be our son! One of Charley's boyfriends, for Christ's
sake! What kind of menopausal craziness is that?" He
heard himself ranting, and he couldn't seem to stop.
Something had been unleashed, and it felt good to finally get it out.

"Menopausal *craziness*?" Eva said.

Hutch noticed that Eva's mouth had dropped open
in astonishment and that all the color had drained from
her face. He sat back down on the edge of the couch
and tried to calm himself, but it was no use. "How
could you betray me like this, Eva? How could you betray my love like that?" He could feel tears welling, so
he shut his eyes tightly, trying to stop them.

"I don't fucking believe this," Eva said, turning
away from him and toward the fire as if speaking to it.
"He walked out on me. He walked out on me!" She
gestured in the air as if addressing some unseen presence who had just dropped into the living room. But
then she turned to face Hutch, her eyes blazing, and although she was still sitting down, her body was tense
and ready to fight. "Isaiah. That's his name. Isaiah

Lonesome. Yes. He was a friend of Charley's! Yes, he is younger than me. But that makes it very interesting, Hutch. You should know that better than anybody else, don't you agree?"

"I have no idea what you're talking about!" Hutch said indignantly.

Without warning, Eva suddenly jumped up. "Get out!" she screamed, pointing toward the door.

Hutch, startled, stood now too. "I'm on my way!"

"Now!"

"You don't have to tell me twice," Hutch said. His face tight, he headed for the foyer.

"Betray? You have the nerve to say that word to me!" Eva screamed as she followed him out of the room.

Hutch turned to confront her. "Yes, I do," he said calmly, acting the part of "the adult." "Betray!"—he said the word again louder, turning suddenly into a child, with a mocking teasing, voice. "Betray! Betray! Betray! Betray!" He shouted the word into her face.

Eva's lip curved like that of a rabid dog. Startled, Hutch realized he'd never seen that look before. He turned into the foyer and headed to the closet to get his coat. "I don't want to fight with you, Eva," he said evenly, as he snatched his coat from the rack.

"Cara!" Eva spat out the name as if it were a curse. Hutch stopped dead in his tracks. "Cara. You heard me! *Cara!* You've heard that name before, haven't you? And I know how you lied to me all those times for all these years. Those late-night calls."

Hutch's stomach dropped. "Oh, God," he said. He let the coat drop to the floor. "All this time, Eva, you knew? Why . . . ?"

"You are the one who betrayed me, who lied to me," she interrupted him, her voice triumphant.

Hutch thought about how Raye had acted out her days and nights with no indication of her true thoughts or feelings. Had he become Donald Mason after all?

"Why didn't you tell me that you knew about Cara?" he asked in a small voice.

"What would have been the point?" Eva screamed.

"But she didn't mean anything to me!" he cried, not wanting to believe what he was hearing. "She meant nothing, means nothing!"

"How do I know that?" Eva said. "And do you really think at this point, after all we've been through, that it makes any difference? And now there is Raye Mason! Were you sleeping with her before too? Playing me and Donald Mason, of all people, for fools?" Eva was indignant now.

"But that's still no reason for you to start sleeping with some no-account musician . . . that's no reason to . . . to!" Hutch sputtered out meekly in frustration.

"I don't have to give anybody, least of all you, a reason for anything I do! You walked out on me! Have you forgotten that?"

He tried to think of something to say to that but couldn't, and Eva, sensing an advantage, pressed on. "And you were right, Hutch. We did have nothing or we wouldn't be standing here yelling at each other like this. Everything was a lie. You were right to leave. There was never any joy between us. Now that I know what *real* joy is!"

"And you think *joy* is what you have with that asshole of a musician?" His voice came out in a squeak, but Hutch didn't care.

The doorbell rang. Startled, they both turned toward it. Eva peered through the peephole and threw up her hands in frustration. "Like I need this!" she murmured in disgust. Hutch stooped to pick up his coat from where he'd let it drop. He assumed it was the horn player and was thankful that he was on his way out. *The hell with her, then! Let her be with him if she wants*, he told himself. When Eva opened the door, however, he uttered a curse of his own.

"Merry Christmas! Happy Kwanzaa!" Irene Hutchinson said cheerfully as she stepped into the foyer.

Irene, Hutch's ex-wife, was a soft-faced, sloe-eyed woman nearly the same age as Raye. Her short, natural hair was liberally sprinkled with gray and was paired with dangling cowrie shell earrings, which gave her an exotic, ethnic look. She smiled easily, and the gap between her front teeth made her face appear both charming and impish. She was dressed casually in jeans and a red turtleneck under a fashionable black wool coat subtly trimmed with Kente cloth.

"And what are *you* doing here?" she asked Hutch bluntly when she saw him, and he prepared for attack. Her gentle eyes and easy smile gave her a sweet look, but he'd felt the lash of her sharp tongue more times than he cared to remember.

"He was just leaving," Eva answered for him.

"I should ask *you* the same question," he said to his ex-wife.

"Well," Irene said with a charming smile, "I'm dropping off a little something for Charley. I missed her performance at Club Resurrection, and it was so sweet of her to remember me. How did she do?"

Nobody said anything. "Well, I can't stay," Irene

said quickly, sensing the mood in the room and wondering what had caused it. "I'm on my way to Steven's. He and Dana invited me over for a Christmas toast, and I'm running late. Eva, it's always a pleasure to see you. Hutch." She nodded curtly in his direction.

"Steven?" Hutch couldn't hide the longing in his voice.

"Would you do me a favor, Irene?" Eva asked.

"Depends on what it is."

"Since you're going to Steven's, would you mind dropping some gifts off for him and Charley? I know he will see her before I do, and it will save me a trip."

"Sure. No problem." Eva promptly went into the living room to get the presents, and Hutch faced Irene in the light of the foyer.

"You're going to see Steven?"

"What's wrong, Hutch?" Her eyes, which usually looked at him with suspicion, were filled with concern. He shrugged indicating that there was nothing wrong and avoided meeting her eyes. "Would you like to come with me?" Irene added after a few moments. "Maybe it's time," she added more to herself than to him.

"Thank you," he said, and he could tell by the way her eyes softened that she had noticed the tremble in his voice.

Eva came back into the room with the shopping bags as filled to the brim as they had been when Hutch brought them. The red shawl was folded neatly into a square and laid on top of one.

"These are for Charley, Steven and Dana," she said to Irene. "I've added my own gifts in with the others." She turned to Hutch. "I'm really not comfortable giv ing my father liquor, with his blood pressure being so high. He doesn't take his pills, and he is at risk for a stroke. Since it's your gift, you should be responsible for it. Give it to him yourself." Her voice was toneless and matter-of-fact. He couldn't bring himself to look at her. He felt dazed, as if he'd been drugged.

Nobody said anything. Irene made a point of shuffling the packages around in the bag as if she were straightening them out. Eva stared at a space somewhere behind Hutch. He felt like the world was running in slow motion.

"Let's hope this new year is better than the last one obviously was," Irene said quietly.

A slightly crooked smile formed on Eva's lips. "My Aunt Delia used to have a saying. She used to say that sunshine follows darkness like mushrooms do rain. I hope she was right."

"What?" Irene looked puzzled.

"Sunshine follows darkness like mushrooms do rain."

Irene laughed. "Haven't heard that one before. But the sunshine has always seemed to follow the darkness in my life, and those wise women usually knew what they were talking about." Both women chuckled, as if they were old friends sharing a joke.

Hutch shifted uncomfortably. He was sure that in some veiled woman-speak way they were talking about him, comparing his presence in their lives to darkness and the sunshine to his departure. Without looking at or saying anything to either woman, he snatched the bags from Irene and headed out the door.

When he got to Irene's car, he set the bags on the ground and took the red shawl from the top of the bag. He held it against his face for a moment and then he slipped it around his neck. The night was colder than when he'd come, and Hutch could feel snowflakes dampening his nose and cheeks.

"Looks like it's snowing," said Irene, who had quietly walked up behind him.

"Yeah."

She opened the trunk and put the two bags into it. "Looks like you're leaving with everything you brought."

"Yeah," Hutch answered without looking at her.

She studied Hutch for a while and then gently took the shawl from around his neck and tossed it into the trunk on top of the bags. Then she put her arms around him and hugged him. Hutch let his body ease into hers, and for a few moments she felt as familiar and comforting as she used to when he was in love with her. He rubbed his cheek against the rough fabric of her coat, catching the scent of the essential oils she used on her skin. She stood on her toes and kissed the top of his forehead. He knew he had tears in his eyes. He hoped that she couldn't see them.

"Let's go and see our son," was all she said.

# Eva

### DECEMBER 24

Eva stood by the window and watched Hutch and Irene drive away in their separate cars, and then went into the living room and collapsed on the couch. Her emotions had been whipped around so much in the last few hours, she needed to sit down before she fell down. She had experienced a wild mix of feelings, the strongest being anger.

When Hutch had begun his sanctimonious rant about the "jock with a horn," it had been all she could do to keep from slapping him square in his mouth. Although she'd known about Hutch and Raye since Club Resurrection, seeing the way his eyes lit up when he'd mentioned her name had released a wellspring of anger and envy within Eva that she'd managed to repress until tonight. And there was Cara. He'd been so sloppy with his stuff, so careless and indiscreet with his whispered phone conversations, stray credit card receipts, secret meetings. It was almost as if he were daring her to find out. Maybe deep down she'd been afraid to confront him about it, afraid she would force him to make a choice. And his choice would not be her. That had been part of it too, she now realized, her own insecurities. It had seemed easier then to simply forgive and forget. And she had done neither.

She felt regret about tonight too. She regretted how badly things had turned out. She'd been overjoyed when she'd opened the door and he'd been standing there so bashful with his bags of gifts and case of wine. The mere sight of Hutch, even after all these years, still brought a smile to her lips. It probably always would. And she was sorry that he'd found out about Isaiah the way he had. She wondered if he had been spying on her, although that certainly didn't sound like Hutch. Funny thing was, she couldn't even remember what she had been doing Labor Day and if Isaiah had even been around. She also regretted adding that last crack about joy that she'd tossed at Hutch as he was leaving. She had indeed been trying to intimate that she was finding the "joy" with Isaiah that he'd left her to look for, but that was certainly a lie. Isaiah and she shared some good things—good sex being foremost—but that kind of "joy" was not one of them. She was most joyful these days when she was by herself—walking through the park and savoring the winter changes; jotting down random thoughts about her life in the journal she'd begun to keep; strolling through the museums she'd begun to visit on weekends. That was joy to her, allowing herself to be overwhelmed by beauty whenever she saw it.

She picked up the tray with the empty glasses and half-eaten wedge of cheese and took them back into the kitchen. Without thinking twice, she'd pulled out her good wine glasses, the ones her mother had given her on her wedding day, the year before she died. She'd had to climb up on a stool to get them, tucked away as they were in the back of the pantry, but it had seemed fitting, somehow, serving Hutch's costly wine in her best crystal. How often had she used them? Thanksgiving, two years ago? Last Christmas? Maybe twice in the past year. Had he noticed? she wondered. Probably not. She carefully washed and dried them, then packed them back where they belonged. Then she filled a kettle with water and went back into the living room to wait for it to boil.

He'd worn her gift, she noticed that the moment she saw him, and he'd bought her a shawl in her favorite color. He'd also quoted lines from that Langston Hughes' poem. But he hadn't quoted that last stanza.

> *And the beauty of Susanna Jones in red*
> *Burns in my heart a love-fire sharp like pain*

She smiled when she thought about it because she knew he remembered it too. God knew he'd quoted those lines often enough in the past. He'd made an attempt to reach out to her tonight, and she'd reached back. But neither of them could stretch far enough to get through the anger. It was still too easily stoked, and it had gotten the best of her. And of him. But would it always? She felt her eyes begin to water as she thought about how he'd held the shawl he'd given her against his face. Why had she given it back? It had been cruel of her to do it. But she was so angry, she hadn't thought twice about it.

She wept now when she thought about him. She knew it was because she was still high from the wine—crying in your beer, her father would have called it. And because it was Christmas, and she was by herself.

She let herself cry for a good fifteen minutes, and then she made herself stop and sit perfectly still. She took in a breath, held it and slowly let it go, as if letting go of pain. She was strong, she reminded herself. Stronger than she had ever been in her life. She could get through anything if she had to. The clock struck eleven, and the sound made her smile. She thought of that night last summer, the night Hutch had left, and how loud the clock had seemed each time it chimed and how much it had frightened her. Very few things frightened her now, certainly not a clock in a big, empty house. Certainly not being alone.

This house was filled with memories, mostly good. It was part of her, almost flesh and blood in a strange way. She knew each room so well, and everything that happened within it—the way the light filtered in from the kitchen, the sound of the trees as they hit each other outside. She knew every crack in the wall and ceiling, every window that didn't quite shut and floorboard that squeaked. But she had begun to wonder if this place was too big for her now, and if it was time to move into something smaller. She thought for a moment of how it would be to live in New York City, in a neat, sunny apartment on a quiet street near good restaurants and galleries. She could still commute to Jersey every morning, going in the opposite direction of everybody else. It might be fun for a while. A new twist in her life. Eva laughed out loud at herself and her thoughts. It was too early in the year to make such big decisions.

Yet just thinking about a radical change like that in her life made it an option. And life was full of options and that made her feel happy. It also made her feel free. She was free to do whatever she wanted to do. Free to be happy. Especially to be happy.

That was what it took sometimes, she realized. Deciding to be happy despite everything else. And it *was* a decision, she was sure about that. You could always count on life to throw you curveballs when you least expected to get them. But the way you caught them was always up to you. Happiness was knowing how to grab them before they knocked you down. It was a choice you had to make, and she had made it.

She stood up, right where she was in front of the couch, and stretched out her body as tall as she could. She liked to feel her muscles flex and relax, to sense her own power. Breathe in, breathe out—Isaiah had said something like that the first time they were together, and she smiled now when she thought about it. She wondered where he was tonight. He was spending more time away from the house these days. But so was she.

The kettle whistled, and she went into the kitchen. She took loose chamomile tea out of a tin in the cupboard, spooned some into a tea holder and placed it in the fancy teapot that had once belonged to her mother. On impulse, she took out one of the three remaining matching cups. It had been an exquisite Christmas tea set, Lenox china, fine and translucent, trimmed with gold and holly. Louisa had loved beautiful things, and she had given this one to Eva on Christmas, the last before she died. Her mother had always had good taste. Louisa loved fine china, good food and the very best wine. With her small treasures, old family recipes and what she thought was good advice, she had tried to pass the best of herself down to her daughter, as Eva had tried to pass her best on to Charley. Always the best that you had to give.

Eva closed her eyes and said a prayer of thanks to her mother. She'd been doing more of that recently when she thought about the women who had come before her and left any goodness that they could. Each day, she seemed to discover she owed them more, and she made herself stop and thank them on the spot. It felt good to do it, this small quick offering of a prayer of thanks, remembering to be glad for each day. She placed the cup, teapot and honey on the tray and carried it back into the living room, setting it down on the coffee table. The fire had died down again, and she tossed on another log and gave it a poke. It roared itself back to life.

It was funny how those strange words about mushrooms and rain had come back to her the way they had. Had they really been Aunt Delia's? They certainly sounded like something she'd say, but they could have been spoken by her grandmother Alvia or maybe even Louisa in one of her playful moods. She took a sip of the tea, stirred in some honey and licked it off the spoon.

*Sunshine follows darkness like mushrooms do rain, and right ain't always what you take it to be.*

*And right ain't always what you take it to be.* She'd forgotten that part of it until just now, the most important part. With the exception of Aunt Delia, she couldn't think of one of those old women who would think that Hutch leaving her the way he had or her love affair with Isaiah Lonesome was "right," but both had been right for her in their own way, even though she hadn't known it at the time. She laughed aloud again, liking the sound of her voice in the quiet house. After all these years she could still recall those old sayings. Nothing ever really left you; everything stayed tucked somewhere in your soul until you needed it.

The clock struck midnight. Christmas Day. Eva thought about all the other Christmas Days she had spent when she'd been a girl and Charley had been young and they'd been struggling to stay alive on Cheerios and chicken wings on 137th Street. If she made herself remember, she could call up so many memories, so many vivid scenes. Her grandmother's pies, so tart with lemon her tongue still curled when she thought about them. The smell of Aunt Delia's creepy old house that still made her shiver deep down in her bones. That ugly Cabbage Patch doll she'd struggled so hard to buy for Charley for Christmas that year. The black sapphire engagement ring Hutch had dropped into her glass of champagne the night he asked her to marry him. Her eyes went damp, just from the remembering. Especially about Charley.

Eva had reached for the phone more than once to call her. But she'd always stopped. It was up to Charley to reach out to her this time. It was Charley's turn to apologize, and she would just have to wait until Charley got grown enough to do it. She was tired of always being the one to forgive and forget her own pain so others wouldn't have to feel theirs. It had taken its toll on her, and she wasn't going to do it again, not even for the person she loved best in the world.

What would she do today? She wondered. She

sipped her tea and the flower-scented steam soothed and relaxed her. Isaiah wouldn't be here, of course. He'd be working as he had on Thanksgiving. She'd gotten used to his not being around.

Maybe she would do the same thing she did three weeks ago on Thanksgiving. She'd gone into New York City that night and found a small Greek restaurant in the Village where she didn't need reservations. The maître d' had been a kindly man in his late sixties, who'd brought her champagne on the house.

"I've always loved artists, especially pretty ones," he'd said in his rich Greek accent.

"But how did you know I was an artist?" Eva had asked. He'd just winked and attended to another customer. She'd been home by midnight, in time to chat with Isaiah, who had come in at two, and she was relieved that he didn't expect her to cook. But he never expected anything from her. And she hadn't missed cooking, not one little bit. Maybe that place in the Village would be open on Christmas. Or maybe she'd just walk around until she found something else that was. Or just take her chances.

She watched the lights twinkling on the tree, glittering like tiny stars. She had loved Christmas trees for as long as she could remember. Louisa would shake her head in frustration as she accused her daughter of loving the symbols of the holiday more than the meaning, and Eva would just laugh. "Heathen," her mother would scold and shake her head, but there was laughter in her eyes when she'd say it. Bama had pulled a silver snowflake off the tree, and Eva picked it up. It was one she bought the first year she'd been married, when she'd gone all out and no ornament had seemed too extravagant. She'd bought crystal balls, filigreed snowflakes made of sterling silver and delicately painted china stars. It had taken them three hours in the freezing rain to find a tree that suited them, and Charley and Steven had stood in stunned wonder when at last they had turned on the lights.

Eva held the ornament tight in her hand, as if she could bring it all back. Her mother had been alive then, her breast cancer not diagnosed. Or maybe she just hadn't told anyone; that was always a possibility with Louisa. Had she had it for years and been silent, Eva wondered, letting go only when she knew her daughter was in safe, strong hands? And Hutch's hands had been so safe and so strong. All Eva had wanted in the days after her mother's death was to have a child, a piece of her mother brought back to life. And they had tried so hard, made love nearly every night, and nothing had come. Then finally, after six years, she had gotten pregnant, and it had been an easy birth. And an easy death. Ten hours later. Before he'd lived good, pulled in a decent breath. Something within him hadn't grown as it should, the doctors told her, explaining everything thoroughly and clearly, and she had heard nothing they said.

He would have been four if he had lived. He would be sitting beside her at this moment, chatting about what Santa would bring him. He would have taken his bath and put on his footed pajamas that smelled like Downy, and they would have had a bedtime snack— hot chocolate—because it was Christmas Eve, and he would have gone back upstairs and brushed his teeth, then sneaked back down for one last look at the tree and how it sparkled in the dark. Four years old was young enough to believe that life always turned out the way you wanted it to, and she and Hutch would have done everything in their power to keep him holding on to that belief.

"Lucas Hutchinson the Third." When she said his name she realized it was the first time she'd spoken it aloud since the day he died. Why hadn't they allowed themselves to grieve together? She always sensed this baby was more important to her than to Hutch, and that had hurt her too. She'd turned thirty-six that year, and she'd wanted to give Hutch a child that was part of the two of them. She'd needed it for herself. But the baby had come and gone and they'd gone on with their lives. No ritual said, no formal bidding of good-bye. Charley and Steven had gone off to college. She had increased her hours at the library. Hutch had traveled his own road. Had his own troubles. Found his own solutions in his own ways. She and Hutch had been so careless with so many precious things. They had shared so little of what was important and so much that didn't really matter. And her baby from a Christmas that never was haunted her still.

Placing down her teacup, Eva went upstairs to her studio in search of her sketchpad and two soft pencils. She found the pad buried under some summer clothes and the pencils in a box near her easel where she'd stuck them long ago. Back downstairs by the warmth of the fire, she began to draw the face she knew so well yet had never really seen: the nose that she imagined would be so much like her own; the chin that Steven had inherited from his grandfather; Charley's dimple; her mother's bright eyes. She drew him playing, pouting, singing, crying, dancing to unheard tunes, running nowhere. She drew him as he would look lying in his crib, delivering papers, on his wedding day, and when she stopped, the clock chimed two. She caught her breath.

There were ten drawings in all, and each captured some element of her lost child. She studied them critically, dispassionately, and then went through them again, deciding which she would continue to work on, how she could expand in a different way or in a different medium or if it was complete in itself. And then she laughed out loud as it dawned on her what she had done.

*I start with a note. One note. And I'll blow until it's as perfect as I can get it, and then I go back and blow another, and another, until finally the whole thing is done. Nothing miraculous. Just one note at a time.*

Tears came into her eyes, and she closed the book, afraid to look anymore, but she knew that something had been shaken loose and had taken root. She said a prayer of thanks for this particular gift, to whoever had sent it: Louisa. Alvia. Aunt Delia. Lucas himself.

Eva was on her way up the stairs to bed when Isaiah came in the back door. Startled, he looked in her general direction and quickly away. Eva had seen that expression before. He came into the house and put his horn on the kitchen table. She came back downstairs to greet him.

"You're not waiting up for me, are you?" he asked.

"No. I was just sitting in the living room."

He glanced at the sketchpad she held in her hand. "Drawing?"

"Yeah."

"Can I see?"

"Not yet."

He smiled. "Good for you. Congratulations." He paused, then added, "I had an appointment. You know, hanging out with the new owner of the club." He got a glass, opened the refrigerator and poured in some milk.

"You don't have to tell me where you've been," Eva said, puzzled by his need to explain why he was late.

"I know," he said, and shrugged, but he still avoided her eyes. "So what you doing tomorrow?" He rinsed his glass and put it in the dishwasher.

"Nothing much. Maybe go upstairs, clean up my studio. Get things arranged again," she said and couldn't stop smiling.

"Good thing we fixed that skylight."

"Yeah, it is," Eva said. "You going to be around?"

"No. I got to work. I might go by to see my Moms, though, tomorrow sometime. Maybe take her out to dinner if she wants to go. I haven't seen her in a while."

Eva nodded with approval. "It's about time," she said.

He smiled his enigmatic smile and kissed her on the forehead. He smelled fresh, like soap, she thought. Very expensive soap.

"Merry Christmas," Isaiah said.

"Merry Christmas," Eva replied, and they went upstairs to their separate bedrooms.

# Hutch and Steven

**DECEMBER 24**

"Maybe I should stay in the car," Hutch said to Irene as they walked into Steven's building. Still reeling from his confrontation with Eva, he couldn't take being rejected again by somebody else that he loved. "Maybe he won't want to see me. Maybe I should just go home."

"Maybe you should just calm down," Irene said. They scrutinized the row of bells on the outside wall, and Irene rang the one that read HUTCHINSON/WILLOUGHBY. Hutch knew that Dana and Steven were living together, but seeing their names connected near the bell jolted him. He told himself that he'd have the same response if Steven were living with a woman, but he knew it wasn't the truth. "Damn! It's already eleven forty-five," Irene said, more to herself than to Hutch. She rang the bell again twice in quick succession.

"Maybe he saw me from the window and that's why he's not buzzing us in."

"Shut up, Hutch!" The buzzer rang and Irene visibly relaxed, and they stepped inside the building. They rode the elevator to the top floor in silence. "So what did you get him?" Irene asked as the door opened.

"Couple of sweaters. I got Dana a gift certificate. How about you?"

"We're not exchanging gifts this year," Irene said somewhat smugly. "He and Dana are volunteers in a group that works with children with AIDS, so I'm giving a donation in their names." Hutch was dismayed. Should he take the gifts back to the car? he wondered. He could donate money too. And time as well. He'd *make* time to do it. But it was too late. The elevator opened, and they walked toward Steven's door. Irene rang the bell. Steven opened the door.

"Hello, son." Hutch stepped forward, getting ready to give Steven a hug, but Steven offered his hand instead. Hutch grabbed it and held on for dear life.

"Thought I'd bring you a Christmas present," Irene said with a wink, and Steven glanced at his mother and shook his head in mock annoyance. She got the hug that Hutch wanted.

Hutch thrust the gifts in his son's direction without saying anything, and Steven took them and headed back into the apartment, and Irene and Hutch followed him.

The small, tight foyer led into an oblong living room with white walls, bamboo blinds and a couch and two sling chairs that Hutch remembered seeing at IKEA. He recognized several old pieces of furniture of Eva's that she'd brought with her from New York and kept in the attic, and an old Oriental rug that Irene had bought the year they were married—and which she'd made a big deal of keeping when they broke up. The bookshelves were also filled with books, which he assumed belonged to Dana, since most of Steven's were still in his room at Eva's.

Hutch, still feeling awkward, sat down on the couch. Whispering and giggling, Irene and Steven moved into the kitchen, and Dana ducked into the living room, a tight smiled pasted on his lips. Hutch noticed that he was wearing a turtleneck sweater Hutch had given to Steven several years ago.

"Would you like a drink, Mr. Hutchinson?" Dana's voice was overly formal. He was a good-looking kid with an open, frank face and an eager-to-please smile. Hutch wondered what his parents were like and how he had met Steven. Had he brought Steven into this lifestyle? He reminded himself to stop judging. It didn't matter how or when they had met. They were together now.

"Some coffee would be great if you have it," he answered.

"Great! One coffee coming up!"

When Dana went into the kitchen, Hutch picked up a thin volume of poetry that lay on the coffee table and quickly read the inscription scribbled inside. *To my only son Dana. May you always have the power of your convictions. Your Father.*

It was the kind of formal thing his father would have written to him if he'd been a man who bought books of poetry for his son. How did *this* man feel about his son's being gay? Hutch wondered. How did he feel about Steven's being black? Hutch was swept with a sudden sense of vulnerability and protectiveness toward his son. Dana came back into the room and set the coffee on the table, then turned to go back in the kitchen.

"Dana, can we talk a minute?"

"Sure." Dana sat down stiffly in one of the chairs, the expression on his face close to dread. Amused, Hutch smiled as he recognized the expression as one of Steven's.

"This won't be that bad," he said. They had the same spirit, he realized. Dana rocked forward in his chair slightly as if he were a student preparing to hear a lecture. *He is a polite kid,* Hutch thought, *well brought up.* "I just want to tell you that, well . . ." He paused for a moment, unsure of himself, but then realized all he had to do was tell it straight. Right from the heart. The way he felt it. He took a gulp of coffee and put the cup down on the table. "I'm ashamed of the way I acted when I met you in that restaurant in July," he said. "I know that I hurt Steven, and I hurt you, and I'm ashamed of that now. All I want is for my son to be happy, and you two seem to be. And that's all that counts." Hutch wished he were better at words and feelings, but he'd said what he wanted to say, and it was done. He picked up the coffee cup again. He noticed that his hand was shaking. Dana noticed it too. His eyes widened slightly, but then he smiled. "I'm not the one you should be telling," he said.

"I'm rehearsing," Hutch said without thinking about it, and they both laughed self-consciously because they knew it was the truth. Hutch put down the cup and held out his hand for Dana to shake it. Dana, looking a bit startled, took it and shook it quickly. He stood up, still slightly ill at ease. "Would you like me to get Steve?"

"Get Steve for what?" Steven said, coming back into the room with a plate of Christmas cookies in one hand and a glass of eggnog in the other. Puzzled, he glanced at Dana.

"It's okay," Dana reassured him and nodded almost imperceptibly toward Hutch.

"You sure?" Steven asked, not bothering to hide his apprehension.

"Yeah."

"Irene, how's my second mama?" In one smooth motion, Dana took Irene's arm and led her back into the kitchen. A bamboo curtain separated the two rooms, and Dana snatched it closed, which gave the illusion of privacy if not the reality. Steven sat down on the couch next to Hutch and scanned his father's face. Suddenly in a panic, Hutch picked up a cookie and bit into it. He avoided looking at his son's face and said as he chomped noisily, "Hey, these are good. Did you make them?"

"Same old dad," Steven said. "Still can't talk about anything real, huh? No, Dana made them. Did you come over here to talk about the goddamn cookies?"

Hutch was taken aback. "Could you bear with me?" he said. *Why did I pick up that damn cookie?* he asked himself. "Please, son?"

"Okay," Steven said after a moment. "I'm sorry. It's just—"

"Don't apologize to me, Stevie. I've come to apologize to you."

"Please, Dad, I don't feel like—"

"I don't think my father ever smiled at me," Hutch said quietly. He wasn't sure where the words came from or why he had said them, but he knew somehow that that simple fact was the crux of all of his problems. "I guess he loved me, but God knows, he was never able to say it. Criticism, yeah. He knew how to dish it out. And how to make me take responsibility. Or how to work until you dropped dead."

Steven shifted his eyes away from his father's face, but Hutch continued, not sure whether Steven's was one of impatience, anxiety or simple boredom. "Maybe that's why it makes it so hard for me to talk to you and to tell you how much I love you, because he could never tell me anything worth saying."

"Grandpa was never like that to me," Steven contradicted him, his voice tight. "I don't remember him that way at all. I remember him teaching me how to play checkers and letting me win. Buying me Baby Ruths when you said I couldn't have candy. Don't try to put your problems on my grandfather."

"You weren't his son, Steven. There are so many things about that old man that I loved and hated."

"Hated?" Steven stared at him in disbelief.

"I hated his rigidity. I hated his coldness. I hated the fact that he could never do anything but yell and tell me I'd done things wrong. I always felt like I had failed him. But I'm beginning to see how much of him is still a part of me."

Steven looked surprised but didn't say anything, and Hutch continued. "That's why when you said that to me, about never being able to please me, it hit me so hard. Do you remember when you said it?"

"I don't remember much of anything I said that day. I just remember what you didn't say." The hurt was back in Steven's eyes.

"Black men got so much shit we got to go through

before we can be ourselves. Half our lives we spend proving white folks to be the liars they are about us. The other half we spend proving it to ourselves. Being twice as good, twice as fast, twice as strong. The only time I saw my daddy cry was when he watched Jesse Owens run 'round that track like he did or Jackie Robinson hit those home runs. And when we're done proving everything we've got to prove, there's nothing left to give out, not even to ourselves—especially not to ourselves."

"Don't you think I've learned that by now, Dad?" Steven's voice was impatient, almost bitter, and Hutch was surprised by his tone. "What does this have to do with me and Dana?"

Hutch leaned over toward Steven and pulled him close. "I love you, Stevie," he said.

Steven pulled away. "Why didn't you say anything? At least you could have fucking said something. Anything," Steven said, and the tension was there again, as thick as it had been when he sat down.

"I don't know why I didn't say anything," Hutch said because he hadn't known then, and he didn't know now.

"To just stare at me like that, like I had told you something horrible. Like I had killed somebody or raped somebody or something. Like I had done something I should be ashamed of. All I did was tell you I was gay, and you acted like that." Steven's eyes begged him to understand. Hutch could see the anguish in his face again, and the anger from that afternoon creeping back. He took Steven's hand between his and held it the way he used to when Steven was a little boy. It was strange how that hand hadn't changed. It was bigger, stronger, definitely a man's hand, but it was the same. Hutch thought about how he'd held his father's hand the night before he died as he listened to him babble. He remembered how helpless he'd felt then. He felt helpless now.

"I'm sorry, son," he said.

"Is the fact that I am gay that shameful to you?" Steven continued, hardly hearing him.

"No," Hutch said, realizing again that the truth was all he had to give. "I have never been close to any gay men. I know I have a lot of prejudices and stupid assumptions about a lot of different things. About women. About love and marriage. About men who are different from me. I never thought I was a bigot. I read about men who beat up gay men, and I know they're the same animals who lynched us in the old days and would do it again if they could get away with it, and I hate men like that. I despise them for their brutality and their ignorance, but I realize now that I'm not that different from those men. I have the same evil in me. I'm a bigot too, and I'm ashamed of that. I've had to come to terms with that about myself over the last couple of months. I've had to come to terms with a lot of things."

He gazed at his son's face. The angles of the chin, the determined set of the jaw. Steven was more like Hutch's father than he remembered him being. He was growing into that face, his grandfather's face, which to Hutch so often seemed made of stone. But Steven's face was Hutch's mother's too. He could see the tenderness in the way his eyes brightened when he laughed, and in the spirit that showed through. He saw his mother now, in the forgiveness that softened his son's face, and he knew his mother had won.

"I love you, Stevie," he said.

"I love you too, Dad." Steven picked up a cookie and began to munch it thoughtfully. Hutch picked up one too. Without looking at each other, they went through the plate, cookie by cookie, until Hutch said thoughtfully, "Damn, the man can cook!"

"Yeah. Better than me."

A few moments later, Hutch said, "I really have failed you, haven't I?"

"You just did the best you could," Steven said. His voice was gentle.

"Dana seems like a nice guy. How long have you two been together?"

"Almost a year," Steven said with some pride.

"Is he the first person you've ever loved?" Hutch asked, wanting suddenly to find out everything he could about his son and this new part of his life.

Steven looked at him doubtfully, as if he were on the verge of telling him, and then changed his mind. "No," he said with a finality that Hutch knew was meant to put an end to his questions, and he decided not to ask anything else—not for now anyway. He reached into the bag that Steven had left by the couch and pulled out his gifts.

"Got these for you, son. And this for Dana." Steven took them and put them beside him on the couch. Then he went into his bedroom and came back with a gift wrapped in gold foil paper and handed it to Hutch.

Irene and Dana, chattering and giggling like old friends, came back into the room with a tray containing a pitcher of eggnog and four glasses.

"It's Christmas Day! Time for a toast!" Irene said.

"She really spiked it. Look out!" Dana warned.

"That's what makes it good!" Irene filled four glasses with the rich frothy mixture and generously ground nutmeg on each. She glanced at Hutch, and for the first time in a very long time, Hutch realized that her smile seemed genuine.

"Thank you, Irene," he said.

"I haven't given it to you yet!" she teased as she handed him a cup. "It was my pleasure," she said. Her eyes and nod of acknowledgment told him that she understood and accepted his thanks.

Steven picked up his glass, sipped, then waved at the glass as if waving away fumes. "Damn, Mom. This is strong."

"To friends and lovers," Dana said, suddenly serious, with a bashful glance at Steven.

"And fathers and sons," Hutch added, lifting his glass.

"And all of their mothers," Irene chirped.

Hutch didn't get home until nearly four in the morning. Steven and Dana had invited him and Irene to Christmas dinner that night, and he was glad to accept their invitation; he finally had somewhere to go. Irene had made other plans. Since Dana was going home, Steven said he would come to dinner at Hutch's place on New Year's Day and promised to bring Charley with him. With the exception of Raye, they would be his first visitors. Sad as it was, it was his home for a while, and this would make it feel more like home.

This would be his first Christmas without a woman in his life. There had always been his mother or Irene or Eva—to cook, wrap, cheer, decorate, civilize.

Women had always made his plans, often determined his mood, usually made things right. Maybe that was why men without women died so much younger than men who had them, he realized. Women were the ones who helped men feel, forced them to celebrate, organized their lives. And now he had to learn to do that for himself. He was alone now, and it was up to him to be his own nurturer, his own mother, his own wife. That was the only way he would survive.

He picked up the gift that Steven had given him and held it to his heart for a moment, almost as if it were his son. There was a note attached to it and he opened and read it quickly.

*Dad,*

*Mom gave this to me. I don't know when I will give this to you. Maybe Christmas. Maybe Father's Day. Maybe your birthday. Soon if we're lucky. I've always loved this. I hope you will too.*

*Your son*

Hutch unwrapped the gift carefully, folding the gold foil as if it were part of the present, and when he saw what it was, he took in his breath. It was an old photograph in a silver frame. Steven had just turned six, and Hutch's father was alive and robust. The three of them were sitting together; he and his father side by side, broad shoulder to broad shoulder. Steven was wedged between them, protected by them, and his eyes were shining as he held both their large hands in his small ones. They were all smiling. Same teeth. Same chin.

Same expression. Three generations of the same man. Hutch felt happy and then a brief, stinging loss and then regret. But mostly he felt happy, and he kept that feeling until he fell asleep.

# Hutch and Donald

**THURSDAY, JANUARY 1**

Hutch spent the week following Christmas in a state of elation. He and Steven were reunited at last. They talked easily during the week, and made plans to spend New Year's Day together. Charley agreed to join them, and Hutch was looking forward to the three of them being together.

Determined to celebrate New Year's Day in a traditional manner, Hutch decided to prepare dinner. He bought a cookbook for beginners that spelled out the basics, thawed out the turkey he had bought for Thanksgiving and settled on a simple holiday menu—turkey, stovetop stuffing, mashed potatoes, cranberry sauce and green beans. He was nervous about the turkey. Haunted by memories of the juicy birds flawlessly roasted by Eva, he began preparing dinner on New Year's Eve so if things didn't turn out right they could go to a restaurant. But he found cooking easier than he thought it would be, and as he worked he was transported back to when he'd been a boy helping his mother in the kitchen. He felt again as if he were reconnecting with her and some forgotten part of himself. He was in good spirits when he went to bed that night, and he was looking forward to New Year's Day.

Eager to taste the fruits of his labor the next morning, he sliced some turkey from the back of the thigh and slapped it on a piece of bread for breakfast. It tasted much better than he thought it would. He was munching on it thoughtfully when the doorbell rang. Assuming it was Steven or Charley, he opened the door without a second thought. To his surprise, it was Donald Mason.

"You got a few minutes?" Donald asked. Without waiting for permission to enter, he came into Hutch's apartment and collapsed on the couch with his legs sprawled out as if they'd been knocked from under him. "Got anything to drink?"

Speechless, Hutch stared at him. He had never seen Donald look so bad. His clothes were wrinkled, and his eyes were bloodshot. His face was swollen, and his hair had tufts of tiny feathers in it, as if he'd had a wrestling match with a down pillow. He smelled sour, as if he hadn't bathed, or had been up all night drinking.

"I don't know what I'm going to do, man." Donald covered his face with both of his hands. Hutch instantly felt the slap of remorse.

What had he done to this man? he asked himself. Had he been so blinded by his own pain that he had struck down his dearest friend? What in God's name was wrong with him?

He slumped down next to Donald on the couch.

"What you got to drink, man? I need the strongest stuff you got!"

Hutch went to the cabinet where he kept his liquor and poured Donald a generous snifter of brandy, but the smell of it brought back his brandy scenes with Raye, so he threw it out and got a bottle of the Jack Daniel's he'd bought for Roscoe. He poured Donald two shots in a water glass and gave it to him. Without looking at him, Donald took the drink and gulped it down like medicine.

"Raye left me, man," he said, his voice low and piti-ful. "She left me. Did you know anything about it? Did she say anything to you?"

Hutch sat back down on the couch, wondering what he should say. Should he confess? he wondered again. Should he clear his conscience? He decided again that he couldn't, but he wasn't comfortable blatantly lying to Donald either. He had never been a particularly good liar.

"Come to think about it, Raye did mention some-thing about being kind of, uh, . . . kind of unhappy," he finally said, treading very lightly on the side of truth.

"Unhappy?" Donald's face fell. "But why? I gave her everything she wanted. She knew how much I loved her. She had to know." He dropped his head in his hands again. "What did she say, man? What did she say?" His eyes pleaded for an answer. Hutch glanced away. Donald reached up and put his hand on his shoulder. "You don't have to worry about betraying Raye's trust anymore. It's over now. She's not coming back. She's out to destroy me, and there's nothing I can do about it." He stood up and began pacing the room, talking more to himself than to Hutch. "Man, I didn't have a clue!" He walked over to the window, glanced out absentmindedly and began pacing again.

"So we go to this New Year's Eve party last night over in Bergen County. White boy I know from the old days in Newark. Lots of big shots talking about running him for governor. Big-time party, right? You can count the niggers there on your right hand. Raye looked good too. Ever see her when she didn't? Half the dudes there wanted to fuck her. So we drink a lot of champagne. Eat some oysters, shrimp, caviar. Beluga by the kilo. The whole thing must have cost this motherfucker close to sixty grand. We get home around two. I take off my tux, get into bed, lay there waiting for her to join me, and she comes into the room all dressed up in a suit and says, 'Donald, I want to tell you something.' "

Donald shook his head as if still mystified and fell back down on the couch. "I just grinned at her, man. I thought she was going to tell me she wanted us to go away together for a couple of weeks, or maybe she wanted us to think about getting a place in New York City or redesigning the kitchen, so I say, 'Baby, it's New Year's Eve. Anything you *want* in this world you can have!' But I was wondering why the hell she felt like she had to wear a suit to ask me."

"And so she told you she was leaving you?"

"She says, 'Donald. I have loved you for as long as I can remember. I will probably love you for the rest of my days. But this is the beginning of a new year, and we're on the verge of a new millennium, and I am *not* going to begin either one with you.' Just like that, she says it! Then she says, 'My attorney is Sam Henderson, and he will be in touch with you within the next few days,' and she split."

Donald sank back against the couch as if all the air had been knocked out of him.

"I don't know what to say," Hutch said, which was the truth.

"You said a minute ago that she said she was unhappy. What did she tell you?"

"Well . . ." Hutch shifted uncomfortably on the couch.

Donald didn't wait for him to answer. "But why now? That's what I want to know. Obviously she's been planning this for a while." He narrowed his eyes suspiciously as if beginning to put things together like the lawyer he was. A chill ran up Hutch's spine. "So she left the house right after she told me, which means she had her bags packed in her car. She knew she was going to leave, and she must have known where she was going."

"I haven't seen her!" Hutch said too quickly, thanking God that she hadn't come to him. He'd been here all night cooking, and he would gladly have let her in.

Donald glanced at him skeptically. "Why would she come over here?"

"I just meant I haven't heard from her. You know, me and Raye talk a lot, but she . . . she didn't say anything about . . . uh . . . leaving you last night." She *hadn't* said last night.

"But she did say she was leaving me?" Donald was sitting straight up now, and Hutch sensed his lawyer's instincts were kicking into gear and that he was about to be cross-examined by the shrewdest lawyer in the state.

"Well, what do you expect, Donald?" he asked, taking the offensive. "You've been cheating on the woman for as long as I've known you both. Everybody knows it. You've earned yourself the reputation of a junkyard dog in heat. It's hard to meet a woman in the state of New Jersey who you haven't put the moves on. Raye has a lot of pride, man. Maybe she just got tired of your shit!" He hadn't meant to sound so sanctimonious and preachy, and he felt like a hypocrite and even more disgusted with himself.

Donald sighed. "Raye knows me. She knows who I am and that I've got . . . well . . . a weakness for the weaker sex." A rakish smile crossed his lips. "I appreciate the ladies, man, I can't lie about that. From the day I understood why they wore different drawers, I liked them. I love everything about them—the way they look, feel, smell, sound, taste. Raye understood that about me.

"Yeah. A lot of wives might see it as a fault, but Raye knows how much I love her. That's one of the reasons we were so good together, because she accepts me for who I am. No questions asked. As a matter of fact, I broke it off with Cara—did I tell you me and Cara had started up a thing after you said you didn't want anything else to do with her? Yeah, I stopped seeing Cara last month because Raye seemed like she had something on her mind, and I thought it might have something to do with Cara. Naw. This didn't have nothing to do with another woman," he said, more to himself than to Hutch. "And she got Henderson too. Of all the lawyers for her to get, she had to go and get him. He'll put everything he's got into this case just to jack me up, and Raye knows it. God, I hate that self-righteous son of a bitch!"

Both men sat for a while longer, and Hutch got up after a while and brought the bottle of Jack Daniel's back to the living room and poured Donald another drink and a short one for himself. They drank for a while in silence. After about fifteen minutes, Hutch stole a look at his watch, wondering how much longer Donald intended to stay. With each minute that passed, he grew more afraid that Raye might drop in. He stole a look at Donald, who was still sipping his drink meditatively with his eyes closed.

Hutch knew he needed to get away from him to be able to think. He got up from the couch and went into the small kitchen off the living room, turned the oven on low, took the potatoes out of the refrigerator and put them in a pot on top of the stove. If Donald would leave, maybe he could figure things out, think of the best way to tell him. Maybe he could make him understand. Donald joined him after a while, watching him work from the narrow doorway that separated the kitchen and the living room.

"So you cooking these days, man?"

"Yeah. Steven and Charley are coming over for dinner."

"Hey, that's real nice. Seen Eva?"

"No." Hutch decided to leave it at that.

"I envy you two, having kids. If me and Raye had had some kids, maybe . . ." His voice trailed off. Hutch stole another look and was saddened by what he saw.

"How are they doing?"

"Steven and Charley? Fine. Yeah, well, uh, I got to set the table, heat up some more stuff. You want to join us? I can set another place." He glanced at Donald, hoping he would refuse.

"Naw. I'm going to go home. Maybe do some work. Not let this get me down."

"You sure about that?" Hutch tried to be polite.

"Yeah. Thanks. Well, man. I can see you're busy. I guess I better let you get back to your *cooking*." A glimmer of the old Donald who loved to tease peeked through for a moment. Hutch dropped his eyes, saddened again by what had happened between them. What he had *let* happen between them.

Had it been worth it? he wondered. There was really no way you could put a value on it one way or the other. What he and Raye had shared had been worth it, he was sure of that; it had also been inevitable. He would not let himself be ashamed of it.

"I'm going to use your facilities, if you don't mind, man, then be on my way," Donald called over his shoulder as he moved away from the door toward the back of the apartment.

"Yeah. Go ahead, man. It's down the hall next to the bedroom, you can't miss it." Hutch glanced around the kitchen again, trying to figure out what he could do next, putting his mind somewhere else.

After Donald left he would figure this thing out. The best way to talk to him. The kindest way to tell him.

He threw himself into his kitchen work making himself concentrate so he wouldn't think about Donald or Raye or feel the sense of guilt that was so overwhelming it made him tired. He took the turkey out of the refrigerator and set it on top of the stove so it could warm to room temperature. Yet again, he read the instructions on the stove-top stuffing box. He fretted that he only had two wineglasses and that none of his plates matched. He recalled Eva's picture-perfect New Year's Day dinners: the gleaming china, the silver napkin rings, the pureed turnips, corn pudding and pound cake, and forced the image out of his mind. Absentmindedly he began to sponge off the Formica table.

He heard the toilet flush and Donald coming back down the hall. He heard Donald's footsteps stop at the bedroom door. And suddenly with a jolt, everything came back to him at once—the lemon verbena soap in the soap dishes, the ecru sheets and duvet still wrinkled on his unmade bed, the crystal bowl on his nightstand brimming with the potpourri Raye used in her sitting room. It was a short hall, not more than six steps would take you from the spot where Donald stopped to the kitchen, and Hutch counted every step. When Donald got to the kitchen door, Hutch studied the table he was sponging. Every muscle in his body stiffened.

Donald Mason had left the room a defeated man, and he was returning with the smug look of victory. The fight was back in his eyes. It was an expression Hutch had seen before on Donald's face—when he'd nailed some lying witness or held an ace in a poker game he was on the verge of losing. Donald was in his element now, he was in the flow, and he was taking no prisoners. He leaned casually against the side of the kitchen door with a crooked grin on his lips. Still sponging the table, Hutch tried to figure out his next move. The moment he had dreaded for months was finally at hand. When Donald spoke, his voice was even and matter-of-fact. There was no threat or menace, just total control. "So how long you been fucking my wife?" he asked.

Hutch tossed the sponge into the sink, suddenly realizing how foolish he must look holding it. He also realized how tight and narrow the kitchen was and that Donald was blocking the door. From somewhere within him, he found his voice. "What Raye and I do or don't do when we're together is none of your business," he said.

Donald flinched, but his voice didn't waver. "I'm going to ask you again, man. How long you been fucking my goddam wife?"

Hutch pulled in his breath and tried to make his voice sound calm and reasonable. "And I'm saying again, Donald. I'm not telling you her business. Or mine either, for that matter." It was out. Hutch could breathe again. He studied Donald's face, trying to sense what his next move would be. He was still conscious of the size of the kitchen, and suddenly he felt vulnerable and claustrophobic. He didn't like feeling uncomfortable in his own kitchen.

Donald looked lost. Hutch swallowed hard. "You know everything I'm going to tell you, Donald. I'm sorry that this has . . . has happened. I can't tell you how sorry I am. But I don't regret it. I have to tell you that too."

"You told her to leave me, didn't you? You're the reason, aren't you? I can't even think of anything low enough to call you. After all I've done for you. To pay me back like this!" It was Hutch's turn to flinch now as Donald stared at him, his eyes filled with contempt. "I let you move into my crib, you sorry motherfucker, and this is how you repay me. Fuck my wife behind my back in my own crib!"

Hutch asked himself again if any of it had been worth this. He dropped his head, unable to hide his shame. "Not in your house, Donald," he said quietly. "Never in your house." He had to tell him that, at least. *That* was his business. He knew firsthand how terrible even the thought of it was.

"So here? You fucked my wife here?" Donald scrutinized Hutch's small apartment disdainfully as if the humble surroundings made the act more troubling.

"Please leave, Donald," Hutch said as evenly as he could. "Please leave."

"I ain't going nowhere, motherfucker, until you answer my question." Donald advanced toward Hutch, who moved back a step and then hated that he had done it. He was again aware of how small the kitchen was. He also knew that he could not let somebody call him a motherfucker in his own house.

"Get out of my way," he said.

Donald didn't budge. "I asked you a question. I want the answer."

"I told you that you got the only answer you are going to get. Now get out of my way!"

"Well, tell me this, then. Why?" Donald's voice was an anguished whisper. Hutch could see the agony in his face, and he relaxed his stance. The tone of this question was different, and he wondered if in his own stubborn way Donald was softening. Hutch probed his face. Did Donald expect him to admit his own guilt? To apologize and beg his forgiveness? But he wasn't ready to tell him the truth as he saw it; yet things had gone too far for him to do anything else.

"I care about Raye as much as I do you. You were destroying her, man, killing her spirit. How can you make love to so many women and know so little about one? I didn't tell Raye to leave, but if our relationship gave her the strength she needed to do it, then I'm not ashamed of it. The only thing I'm sorry about, the only thing I regret, is that it took my sacrificing our friendship, because I love you like a brother, and I know you know that. All I did was remind Raye what she was worth. I'm not going to apologize to you or anybody else for doing that."

He searched Donald's face for change, and his eyes for any understanding. He knew that Donald had to realize that he was telling the truth, but there was nothing in Donald's eyes except scorn. He felt his own eyes water.

"This shit is because of what happened between me and Eva, isn't it?"

Hutch went numb. He wondered if something had happened that Eva hadn't mentioned, and why she hadn't. He also realized how desperate Donald was to hurt him, and that that was when he was at his most dangerous.

"You know what, man? I don't care what *you* say happened between you and Eva because I don't care."

"Ask me about it, then."

"I'm not asking you nothing about nothing because I know the truth."

"And what's the truth, then, since you're saying so much truth?"

"That Eva can't stand you, man. She has never felt anything but contempt for you because of the way you treat women. And if you start lying about her, Raye won't be the only woman who'll be hauling your ass into court."

Donald laughed a laugh that made Hutch wince.

"You *think* you know Eva like I *thought* I knew Raye. You don't know what she does, who she does it with or how they do it when you're out of the house. Do you?"

Donald never wasted words; they always found their

target. He hadn't mentioned the horn player, but Hutch was sure that he'd found out about him. He wondered who had told him. Not Raye, certainly. Or had she?

It took everything he had to make his voice sound as if the things Donald implied about himself and Eva hadn't touched him. He hardened his face and tried to give a nonchalant shrug of his shoulders. "Well, you know what, man? Eva's business is her business, same as Raye's. And if you and Eva had something going, well, I hope you both enjoyed it." With great effort, he added a tight smile which was meant to imply that he and Raye had certainly enjoyed what *they* had. It was a mean, petty touch, but he decided Donald deserved it.

Donald visibly cringed, which surprised Hutch, since he always managed to keep a cardsharp's face. "I think it's time for you to leave, man," Hutch said, taking a step forward. "We've said all we're going to say to each other." He didn't like the way Donald was blocking the door, keeping him trapped. Not in his own house. Donald still didn't move. "Get out of my way, man." Hutch took another step forward. "Let's act civilized about this," he said more gently. He noticed that Donald's eyes were watering too, and he tried to think of a way that they both could save face. "I wish this hadn't happened," he said at last. "I'm sorry." As he said the word he realized how weak it sounded, how utterly trite.

"It's too late for sorry."

"Let's go back in the living room."

"You don't want to hear about me and Eva, do you?"

"You have nothing to tell me about you and Eva, so why don't you just cut this shit out and go home, Donald?" Hutch said impatiently. "Don't make me have to throw you out of here. Please get out of my way." Hutch just wanted the whole scene to be over. He wanted to be alone with it.

"You're right, man," Donald said after a minute with a nasty sneer. "Truth is, I never had too much for women like Eva anyway. She looks good, with that nice ass and that cute face, but I like firmer tits. I like my women younger. Say you take Eva's face and ass and pin it on some young bitch, say twenty years younger, maybe twenty-two, twenty-three—now, that you can really have some fun with!"

Although Charley's name had not been mentioned, Hutch knew what Donald was trying to imply and he was seized with rage. He grabbed Donald by the shoulders and shoved him as hard as he could out of the doorway. "I told you to get out of my way, now get the fuck out my house! And if you ever come anywhere near my daughter, I will kill you," he said.

He had never in his life told a man he would kill him, and until this moment he had no idea that he could ever threaten another man's life. He knew that such words, once uttered between men, could never be taken back.

"Son of a bitch!" Donald muttered, getting up from the floor where he had landed. He ran toward Hutch, swinging at him with all his might. Hutch, who was in far better shape, ducked his attack like a fighter, and Donald swung again, twirling around like a dancer and falling from his own weight. Mortified, and with a killer's rage, Donald raced toward Hutch again. Hutch managed to keep out of his way by bending, swaying and ducking. A briefcase was the heaviest thing Donald had picked up in years, and he was sweating profusely and panting loudly. Hutch, hardly out of breath at all, stepped back and watched him for a moment. Somewhere in the back of his mind he thought what an irony it would be if Donald dropped dead right here in his apartment, putting his hated last will and testament into immediate effect. Donald Mason would certainly have the last laugh on everybody then.

"Man, just go home," Hutch said, shaking his head sorrowfully. "I don't want to fight you anymore."

Ignoring him, Donald pulled himself up once again and headed toward Hutch, who in a rush to get out of his way bumped into the end table near the couch and knocked off a lamp. Donald charged again. Hutch stood his ground, met his attack and shoved him backward. Donald fell again, smacking his face on the coffee table. His nose began to bleed.

"Don't make me hit you, man. It's over. Go. I'm not going to fight you. Go home!" Hutch said.

"Son of a bitch," Donald muttered as he examined the blood that dripped from his nose. "Son of a bitch! Son of a bitch! Son of a bitch!" Wiping the blood on his shirt, he flung himself at Hutch again, his arms waving wildly. Transfixed by the sight of Donald's blood, Hutch stood with his mouth open as Donald's fist connected with a loud wallop with his right eye. Donald, shocked by the power of his own punch, gazed at Hutch in astonishment. Hutch touched his eye in disbelief. Exhausted, both men cautiously watched each other. Hutch, catching his breath, suddenly became conscious of the state of the room—the broken lamp, the rug askew, the couch knocked out of place, the leg off the coffee table where Donald had fallen against it. He also heard the doorbell ringing and somebody banging on the door.

"Dad, are you in there? Are you okay?" Steven yelled through the door.

"Do you want us to call the police? Please let us in," Charley screamed. Her voice shook with fear.

Hutch and Donald looked at each other without saying anything.

"Just a minute," Hutch called out. His voice was trembling, and he was dizzy. He sat down on the couch for a moment to steady himself. Donald slid into a heap on the floor. Steadily avoiding each other's eyes, the two men began to put the room back in order. Donald clumsily tucked the leg back on the coffee table. Hutch pushed the couch back where it was supposed to be. Donald straightened out the rug. Hutch went into the bathroom and got two towels. Making certain they weren't ones that Raye had given him, he dampened them both, then came back out and tossed one to Donald. In silence, both men wiped the blood off their faces.

"Are you okay?" Steven yelled again.

"Yeah," Hutch said, and he opened the door.

Charley and Steven cautiously filed into the room. They stood in stunned silence for a moment or two.

"Wow," Charley finally said under her breath.

"Mr. Mason?" Steven spoke hesitatingly. Donald's nose had started to bleed again, and he dabbed it with the towel. Hutch could feel his eye swelling. Charley gazed at him without speaking.

"Hey, kids. How you doing? Happy New Year," Donald muttered as he picked his coat up off the floor. He quickly left, slamming the door behind him. Charley and Steven stared at Hutch, then at each other, and then back at Hutch.

"Looks like you need some ice for that eye, Dad," Steven said after a moment.

"Yeah. Look in the kitchen." Steven went into the kitchen and came back with ice cubes wrapped in paper towels, which Hutch took and held up against his eye. He sat down on the couch with Charley and Steven on either side of him, their eyes big. "Well, uh, me and Mr. Mason had a fight. And we'll just leave it at that," Hutch said in as calm a voice as he could manage.

"Well, that's a relief! I thought maybe you-all were into some rough sex or something," Steven quipped. Charley giggled with her hand over her mouth. Hutch glared at them both. Charley stopped tittering and her eyes filled with tears.

"Why were you fighting with Mr. Mason, Daddy?"

"Don't lie," Steven warned, as serious as Charley. "We were really scared, standing out there. I thought maybe somebody was trying to kill you."

"It's none of your business. I don't want to talk about it," Hutch said in the voice he'd used since they were children to cut off any further discussion. He went into the kitchen, got more ice out of the freezer, wrapped it in the towel and placed it on his eye. With the other hand he managed to slide the turkey into the oven to heat, put the potatoes and beans on the stove to simmer and take out the ingredients for the stovetop stuffing. As he was emptying the cranberry sauce from the can into a small dish, Charley and Steven joined him in the kitchen.

"You all ready to eat?" Hutch tried to sound cheerful.

"No. We're ready for some answers," Steven said bluntly. "And don't give us any bullshit about it being none of our business. Anytime we walk into a room and find our father in hand-to-hand combat with a man who has been like an uncle to us, we have a right to know what the hell is going on."

Hutch took a deep breath. He turned down the burner under the potatoes and put the cranberries he'd just poured in the bowl into the refrigerator. "Okay," he said. He knew by the looks on both their faces that he had no choice but to tell it from the beginning.

Nobody could have told Hutch that he would ever find it necessary to explain to his children how Donald Mason's betrayal of Raye Mason had in an odd way led him to *his* betrayal of Eva, which led her to Isaiah Lonesome, which led him to Raye Mason, which led to Donald Mason hitting him upside his head on New Year's Day. But he knew he had to tell them everything because the hard lessons he had learned about love, lust and the wages of a lie were just too important to keep to himself. Charley and Steven listened politely, every now and then shaking their heads in disgust and occasionally nodding with understanding.

"You cheated on my mother," Charley said in a small voice when he had finished.

"On our mother," Steven corrected, angry now too.

"Yes, I did, and I've paid for it. You asked me for the truth, and I've told you," Hutch added, realizing that this was the second time in a week that he had admitted his weaknesses to his son. But he'd read once that children can only truly become adults when they understand how much like children their parents were, and maybe that was true. Charley and Steven both avoided looking at him.

"This definitely goes under one of those things about your parents you'd rather not know," Charley said grimly. Steven glared at her and she added quickly, "Don't worry. I'll never do *that* again. I've learned my lesson about that."

"Maybe you should let your mother know," Hutch said, and Charley dropped her eyes.

Nobody said much as Hutch finished preparing dinner and while they ate it. Steven broke the silence.

"I finally feel grown," he said as the three of them were washing and putting away the dishes. Hutch nodded in agreement because he knew that Steven was right. Everybody had done some growing that night.

# Eva and Charley

*E*va's phone rang at seven in the morning, and she let it ring. When it rang again ten minutes later, she angrily picked it up. "What do you want?" she growled into the receiver.

"Eva?" a small, vaguely familiar voice said.

"Yes."

"This is Precious, your father's friend. Eva, it's your father; he's had a stroke. He's in the intensive care unit at Presbyterian Hospital. I think you'd better get down here as soon as you can."

Eva, completely awake now, sat straight up. She couldn't form any thoughts. The only thing she felt was fear, and that was overwhelming.

"Eva? Are you there?"

"Is he still alive?" From somewhere she found her voice.

"Yes. He's alive. Did you hear me, Eva?" Precious's

voice suddenly became demanding, commanding her to act.

"What happened?" She heard Precious sigh heavily on the other end of the line.

"Last night. About four in the morning he—"

"Four in the morning? What was he doing up at four in the morning?" Eva interrupted angrily, her voice accusatory. Why did this woman have her elderly father up at that time of night?

"He wasn't up at four in the morning. We were in bed." Precious's voice was firm but patient, as if she were speaking to an upset but spoiled child.

"Can you tell me what happened?" Eva closed her eyes, calming herself down.

Precious's voice broke, and there was a pause before she continued.

"We went to New York City last night, stayed until midnight. We got home around twelve-thirty. Your father wouldn't leave until then. It's Valentine's Day today. He's such a romantic." She paused again. "He wanted to wait until midnight to ask me. Your father asked me to marry him this morning, Eva, and I accepted."

"Marry him?"

"Yes." Precious continued, not giving Eva a chance to say anything else, "He was having trouble breathing. It was very labored, very heavy. I'd never heard him breathe that way before. When I tried to wake him up, his skin felt cold, very clammy. He couldn't speak. His eyes were open, but they were afraid. I've never seen Roscoe afraid before." She stopped again, unable for a moment to continue. "My second husband died of a stroke. I recognized what the symptoms were, and I called an ambulance. I was able to keep him warm until they arrived. He's very tired but he didn't lose consciousness and that is a good sign. But it's still touch and go."

"I'll be right there."

"I'll be waiting for you in his room."

It wasn't until her hand cramped that Eva realized how tightly she had been gripping the phone. She was too afraid to cry. She tried to make herself stop trembling. Could Roscoe be taken from her like this, with no warning? Each conversation they'd had since Club Resurrection had ended with her sniping at him about Precious and warning him of the mistake he would make if he married her. She was suddenly filled with shame.

If the woman hadn't been there last night, her father would be dead.

She got dressed without thinking, snatching yesterday's clothes from a hanger she didn't remember picking up from a closet she didn't remember opening. She stumbled down the stairs and staggered back up when she realized she'd forgotten her purse, and then back down again. She considered taking a taxi to the hospital, which was in a neighboring town, then remembered she didn't have any money. Barely conscious of what she was doing, she got into her car and somehow remembered how to get there. She parked the car by instinct and walked through the doors numb, not seeing or hearing anything. But when she got inside the lobby she stopped.

The smell and stark lights of the hospital immediately brought back the day of her mother's death.

*Was she about to go through that again?*

Her mother had died in a place like this. Eva had walked through a lobby like this to reach her and had sat all night at her bedside in her sterile room waiting for her to die. She had held her hand, trying to tell her how much she loved her, knowing that her mother couldn't hear her. Her mother's eyes had opened, then closed, unfocused and blank. Spittle had bubbled from the edges of her mouth and Eva had wiped it away with the edge of a Kleenex. She had talked, wept, prayed as she stroked her mother's forehead and cheeks, knowing as she did it she would never touch them again except in her dreams. Louisa had gained consciousness just once, just a few moments before she died, and Eva would never forget the look of absolute love in her eyes or the two words she uttered.

*"I know,"* she had said, and Eva had known instantly what her mother was telling her: that she knew how much Eva loved her and that she had forgiven her for any pain she had caused, that despite the misunderstanding and anger that had so often been between them, she loved her daughter with all her heart, and she knew that Eva would love her too, until the end of her days.

"I know," Eva said now as if uttering a prayer, bringing her mother back to her, giving herself the strength she needed to see her father.

*I know. I know. I know.*

And suddenly Eva did know what she would need to say to her father when she saw him. She would tell him that he could not die, that he had to will himself to live, that there were too many things on his horizon: A woman he had to marry. Grandchildren he had to hold. A daughter who had to make her peace.

Still numb, Eva walked to the intensive care unit but

was directed by a nurse to a regular wing of the hospital and told that her father was out of immediate danger and had been moved. The news made her want to sing. She rushed to the elevator and, when it reached the floor, dashed out of it and to the room where she could find him.

Roscoe lay in a narrow bed in the far right corner of a small room. Precious sat beside him holding his hand. The curtains were drawn, blocking the morning sun, and the room was dim. There was a tube in his nose and another attached to his arm. Eva stood at the door as her eyes adjusted to the light.

The room was a private one, and Eva was grateful that Precious had the foresight to get it. Roscoe, always fastidious about his surroundings, would have balked at sharing a bathroom with a stranger. She felt a lump in her throat when she thought about that and his countless other idiosyncracies. Precious knew him well. Eva stood at the doorway a few more moments, not wanting to speak to him until she knew there would be no trace of sadness in her voice.

Precious glanced up at her when she entered. "He's doing better. They have moved him in here, but they're still not completely certain what damage has been done." Her voice was barely a whisper. Gone was the deep-throated, blues-belting confidence that had defined it. "He is conscious, though. I know he's awake, although he can't speak." She bent down and kissed his forehead. Eva approached the bed, and Precious stood up and moved to the side, allowing her to sit next to him. Eva took her father's hand and held it gently. His hand was warm but the firmness that had always distinguished his grip was gone.

"Dad." She bent down and whispered into his ear. "Dad, I love you." She could feel his hand tightening just a bit, the movement so slight she was afraid that she had imagined it. "Dad, I'm here. I love you." His lips moved a bit, again so slight she wasn't sure she'd seen it.

"He can hear you. He knows what you're trying to tell him," Precious said.

Eva's eyes filled with tears, but she knew if she began to cry she wouldn't be able to stop. Precious rose and went to the doorway, gesturing with a nod that she wanted Eva to join her, and Eva, after bending to give her father a kiss, did.

"Thank you for taking care of him," she said to Precious.

"I'm not going to let this man die. He ain't getting out of marrying me that easy." There was just enough humor in her voice to make Eva smile. She could see the strength and warmth of this woman and wondered why she hadn't allowed herself to see it before. She wondered if Roscoe had mentioned her objections to their marriage but realized that he was too much of a gentleman to say anything. The truth was, Precious probably wouldn't have given a damn one way or the other. Eva closed her eyes and prayed silently, *Please don't let it be too late.*

"They're not sure how much was affected. They think he'll be able to talk again. He will probably have to learn to walk again. They think because he is older it may take him a while, but Scoe is strong and the youngest old man I've ever known," Precious said, her voice strong with affection. She was dressed today in her usual fashion—reds that didn't match and tennis shoes with stockings.

"I'm happy that you are with my father. Thank you for being with him," she said.

Precious continued talking to herself, seeming not to have heard or needed Eva's blessing. "Once I get him home, I'll be able to set up the house to make him comfortable. I'll have to move in earlier than we planned, I guess. We should be able to use that front room for a bedroom until he can climb stairs again. I may do some work in that garden he's let go, come spring. It will be nice for him to sit out there when it gets warmer. God knows that kitchen needs some work. I've never known a man to order food and have it delivered as much as Scoe Lilton. You'd think after all these years of being by himself he'd be able to cook himself a decent meal. I'm going to have to start doing that again, I guess. Never thought I'd be cooking for a man again . . ."

Eva nodded as if she understood, but only half-listened as Precious sorted out the details of caring for Roscoe. She walked back over to her father's bed and leaned down to whisper to him again. "She's good for you, Dad. You were right," she said.

She didn't know if Roscoe could hear her or how much of his mind would let him comprehend it. She didn't know how much of the man she had known all her life—the one who teased, joked and whom she had always taken for granted—would be able to smile at her again. Everything had changed. She studied her father's face—the skin nearly the same color as her own, the pattern of hair that grew on his beard, the lips that were parted and dry. She listened to each breath as it came and left. She closed her eyes, trying to make his fight her own, to put every bit of strength she had gained in the last few months at his disposal. Somebody touched her shoulders, and she recognized the touch at once, even though she hadn't felt his touch in nearly eight months.

"Precious called me this morning after she talked to you. He'll be okay, Eva. You know how tough he is. He's the strongest man I've ever known," Hutch said softly.

*Almost as strong as your own,* Eva thought, understanding now what Hutch had gone through and what she had never acknowledged, never truly grasped until now. She reached up and he took her hand in his. It felt good to have him touch her again, to have him close.

"Thank you for coming."

"You never have to thank me for anything." She remembered the last time he'd said that to her, and glanced up at him, wondering if he remembered it too. Somebody cleared his throat, not rudely, a gentle attempt to get her attention. Eva glanced up at a young doctor with curly brown hair and dark eyes nearly the same color. His eyes looked frightened. Panic seized her.

"Mrs. Hutchinson. I'm Dr. Salerno."

"Will my father be all right?" His eyes were kind; the kindness overshadowed the fear.

"It's hard to say," he said. "He's out of intensive care, but we don't yet know how much damage has been done. You have to remember he is . . . an older man." He glanced at his chart. "Seventy-six?"

"Seventy-two."

He glanced at her, puzzled, and then back at the chart, and Eva realized that her father had probably been lying to everyone about his age. "Seventy-six. He lies about his age." The doctor smiled. He had a nice smile, the kind that could make hard truths easier.

"It's difficult to say exactly what will happen." His voice was as gentle as his eyes, and Eva was thankful for that.

"But he won't—" She couldn't bring herself to say the word.

"No. We're reasonably sure he's over that particular danger. At least as far as we can tell. But there will be . . . a recovery period." He paused long enough to let Eva know that things would not be easy, and that Roscoe would probably not be the same man. Hutch still stood behind her, and Eva touched his hand as it rested on her shoulder.

After the doctor left, Hutch led her away from her father's bed to a chair on the far side of the room. "Are you going to be okay?"

"I think so."

"You don't sound too sure."

"I think I'll be okay," Eva said.

"Is there anything you want me to do?"

"No. Thank you, Hutch. Did somebody call Charley and Steven?"

"Precious did after she called me. Do you want me to call anybody else?"

For a moment, Eva wondered who he was talking about, and then realized that he was asking her if she wanted him to call Isaiah. She was grateful that he had asked and knew how difficult it must have been for him to do it, but Isaiah Lonesome was probably the very last person in the world she would need to get her through something like this.

"No. Nobody."

"Do you need me to stay?"

"No. I'll be all right."

"Are you sure?"

"Yeah."

"I'll be at work if you need me, then at home. Call me, Eva. The minute you hear anything, call me. Do you promise that you will?"

"Yes, I will." He jotted down several numbers on a hospital brochure and handed it to her, and Eva stuffed it into her pocket.

She looked up at him, touched by the concern in his eyes. "I'm glad you came, Hutch. I know how much you love him, how much he loves you."

Hutch nodded, and glanced away quickly. Eva knew that his eyes were watering. She also knew him well enough to know that he was trying to hide it. Suddenly she wanted to to pull him close to her, to feel the solid strength of his body against her. She heard her father stir in his bed, and they both went back to the side of his bed.

"Louisa," Roscoe whispered, and Eva froze. Was he saying good-bye to her now?

His breathing grew easier, less labored. A nurse came into the room and nodded for them to step outside, and they left to join Precious, who stood outside the door. Hutch put on his coat.

"Thank you for calling me," he said to Precious.

"I know how much he loves you, and I knew he'd want me to let you know what happened. Charley was here—"

"Charley is here? Do you know where she went?" Eva broke into the conversation.

"I'm sorry, Eva. I didn't notice. She was here with

Roscoe, and then she left, a few moments before you came in. I think she's probably still here in the hospital. She seemed very upset. I should have—"

"I'll find her. Don't worry. What did you tell me about not apologizing for things?" Eva was surprised how quickly the words came back to her; maybe they were developing a history. The two women went back into Roscoe's room. Eva glanced behind her to see if Hutch was following them, but he'd gone.

"So much of this is just waiting," Precious said, more to herself than to Eva. "Waiting to see if they're going to come through it. Waiting for the worst or the best to come. Waiting for hours sometimes." She turned to Eva. "Why don't you go and get yourself something to eat? Have you had breakfast yet? The cafeteria is on the first floor. Go sit down. Have some coffee. He'll be here when you get up, and if there is any change, I'll come and get you."

Eva knew that Precious was right. She needed time to herself to gather her thoughts, to sit among strangers and sort out her feelings. She found the elevator down to the first floor and looked for the cafeteria. There was a sign marked CHAPEL that pointed in the opposite direction, and on impulse she followed the arrows. When she reached it, she opened the door and paused for a moment before entering.

The room, which was large and modestly furnished, bore no resemblance to a chapel, save an enormous stained-glass window that bathed the area surrounding it in serene light. The walls were pale blue, which was obviously meant to soothe and comfort. There were photos of sunsets, waterfalls, and blooming flowers on the walls, and Bibles, the Koran and several inspirational books on a large table. On a smaller table nearby was a large vase of flowers with a sign indicating that they had been donated by a local church group. There were several sitting areas within the room, and as Eva entered she heard someone crying in one of the far corners. She recognized the cry immediately.

"Charley?"

Charley looked up, her face wet with tears. Eva felt tears come into her own eyes at the sight of her. She sat down in the chair next to her.

"How could that happen to him?" Charley reached out to Eva, who hugged her. She hadn't realized how much she missed the simple physical presence of her daughter, the way she felt, the smell of her hair. She rocked her gently like she used to when she was a child.

"I want to tell him how much I love him," Charley said.

"Then you should."

"But what if I'm too late?"

"It's never really too late."

Charley's eyes grew more sorrowful. "Sometimes it can be too late."

"Yes," Eva conceded. "Sometimes it can."

Charley pulled away slightly and fastened her eyes on Eva's face. "I don't want what happened to Granddad to happen to you. All of a sudden like that." Her voice was small, and her eyes were afraid.

"I expect to be around a while longer." Eva, slightly amused by Charley's dramatic show of concern, was also touched.

"But anything can happen anytime, can't it?"

"Yes, it can," Eva said, as she thought about her father and the words she hadn't said to him.

"I'm sorry," Charley said. "I'm sorry for what happened at the club. I'm sorry I hurt you the way I did. I'm sorry."

"I know," Eva said, her voice nearly as soft as her own mother's had been.

They held hands as they prayed for Roscoe's recovery and Eva said a silent prayer of thanks to Louisa, Delia, Alvia, all the women who lived within her child, and then, still holding hands, they left the chapel and headed back to Roscoe's room so that Charley could tell him what she needed to say.

# Hutch and Raye

Hutch had been profoundly shaken. Seeing Roscoe helpless and unconscious in the hospital bed had depressed him and made him acutely aware of his own vulnerability. He also felt guilty about their last words. Hutch knew that Roscoe saw his desertion of Eva as a betrayal of him as well, and that added to his sadness. So Hutch had gone to work after leaving the hospital and thrown himself into countless meaningless tasks. But the image of Roscoe, tubes running from his nose, his pale hands limp on the sheets, kept pushing itself into his mind and making him weak with worry and concern.

When he got home that night, there was a message from Eva on his answering machine, informing him that Roscoe had rallied at the end of the day and been aware enough of his surroundings to talk and assure them that he would be okay. Hutch had shouted out loud with happiness when he heard it. He immediately tried to return Eva's call, but she didn't answer her phone, so he left a message on her machine. He decided to call her first thing Sunday morning. Although few words had passed between them, Hutch prayed that maybe a hurdle had been crossed. Roscoe's illness had put things in perspective, at least for him, and he hoped that Eva felt the same way. For the first time in months, there had been no rancor in her eyes, and there had been tenderness in her touch. He'd gone to bed that night sure that things had changed between them. When the doorbell rang early Sunday morning, he jumped out of bed, eager to answer it, sure that it was Eva. But it was Raye.

Hutch was both pleased and surprised to see her. Although they often spoke on the telephone, he hadn't actually seen her since the confrontation with Donald. On the advice of her lawyer, they had avoided seeing each other until things with Donald were settled. They both knew that Donald would fight her with any weapon he could get his hands on; there was no sense adding fuel to his fire. But as the weeks passed, Hutch found that he missed her less and less. He thought of her only when he crawled into bed between her luxurious sheets or showered in the morning with the lemon soap. He smiled whenever she crossed his mind, but she was no longer essential. Something within him had changed after the fight with Donald, and although he didn't like to admit it to himself, he knew that it had soured some of what he felt for Raye. But he was genuinely happy to see her this morning, and her bright smile instantly told him that things with Donald were finally resolved.

She was dressed in tailored pants and a black leather blazer. As usual, she looked very chic, and the smell of her perfume instantly filled the room. "It's over," she said as she stepped into his apartment. She grabbed and hugged him tightly. "I brought the good stuff," she added as she took a bottle of Cristal champagne out of a wrinkled brown bag. "Will you help me celebrate?" Her voice was shy, like a little girl begging for a favor, but there was a teasing light in her sparkling eyes.

"Yeah, sure. Let me put on some clothes first," Hutch said, suddenly conscious that he was in his underwear and robe.

"I've seen you in less than that, Hutch!"

"Yeah, I know, but . . . this champagne deserves me at my best," he said weakly.

"You are at your best!" She giggled like a girl. Hutch realized he had never seen her look so carefree before. There had always been a shadow of sadness deep in her eyes, even during the months she had been with him. That was gone now, and seeing its absence made him happy too. He embraced her, wanting to share the happiness that he knew she felt and the simple pleasure of feeling her body next to his again. He felt aroused in a fast, hot wave and he pulled away, not sure if he should be feeling this way now.

He went into the kitchen to bring back some glasses. Then he popped the cork, and they sat down on the couch. As he watched her sip her champagne, he knew that even though it had been only a few short weeks there was a change in their relationship. She had needed him to free herself of Donald and now that she was free he wasn't sure where or how he would fit into her life. He wondered if she realized that too, and how she felt about it. Although he certainly cared about Raye, he had never had the aching longing for her he had for Eva. He loved her as a friend, but he wasn't in love with her and was sure he never would be. He hoped she understood that. And despite everything that had happened, Hutch found himself wondering how his old friend Donald was doing. He knew that their friendship was over, but it didn't prevent him from caring about him.

"Donald will recover," Raye said with an unconcerned shrug when he asked her about him. "He always does." Hutch wished that he could be as sure as she was.

"So things went the way you thought they would? Henderson worked out, and you're satisfied with the settlement?"

"More than satisfied." She took a greedy gulp of champagne. "Do you remember that Cara person I mentioned to you last fall?"

"Cara Franklin," Hutch said as if he weren't sure of her name. He had never told Raye about his relationship with Cara and saw no reason to do so now.

"Well, I was right. He was having an affair with her, but apparently he stopped seeing her sometime in November, about a month before I left him. Cara Franklin, it turns out, is a young woman with an agenda, and she was none too happy when he broke things off. She put in for a promotion, and when she didn't get it she threatened to sue Donald and his firm for sexual harassment. And you know who she got for a lawyer?"

"Sam Henderson." Hutch immediately felt sorry for Donald.

Raye nodded enthusiastically. "So we had a lot of things to negotiate with. Sammy also hired a great private investigator—a smart young sister based in Newark—who got everything there was to get on him. Donald even had something going on with Mimi Anderson, his junior partner's wife. Do you believe that?" Raye shook her head in disgust. "Donald was on his hands and knees begging us to settle, which we did. Things worked out, Hutch. I got everything I was entitled to and more. Much more than I had any right to expect."

"You got what you deserved, nothing more."

Raye sighed sadly. "Despite everything that has happened, though, I'll always believe that Donald loved me in his own way, and that in the end he wanted to do right by me. I still can't believe that he actually tried to beat you up over me. I've never had men fight over me before. I'm not sure whether I should be flattered or disgusted."

"Maybe both," Hutch said. "And you're right about him still loving you. At least you know that all those years weren't wasted, that there was really something there." Hutch was thinking about his own relationship, and his feelings were in his voice. He knew even without looking at her that Raye had picked it up.

"Have you seen her?"

"Eva?"

"Who else?" Raye smiled the way she always did, as if she were on the verge of teasing him but with an understanding that belonged just to her.

"Yesterday, as a matter of fact. Roscoe had a stroke. I went to see him at the hospital, and Eva was there." He stated this simply, with little explanation, even though he knew there was more to it than that. Much more. He also knew that Raye probably knew it too.

"Is Roscoe okay?"

"He'll be fine. Eva left me a message last night."

"How about Eva?"

"She was shaken up about it."

"And?" Raye's eyes demanded the truth, as usual.

"And what?"

"You know what."

"Nothing has really changed," he said.

"Do you mean that your feelings toward her haven't changed or that things between you haven't changed?"

"Both."

They sat for a few more moments sipping their champagne until Raye said finally, "I'm happy now, and there was a time once when I couldn't see how I could even live much less be happy without Donald, but I see that now. You will see that about Eva too, Hutch, just give it some time."

"I don't want to be happy without Eva, Raye." He saw both surprise and distress cross her face.

"What are you going to do, then?"

"I don't know."

There was anguish in his voice and Hutch wished that it hadn't been there because he could see that his feelings had affected Raye's mood. Her eyes were sad now too, reflecting the feelings that she saw in his.

"I'll be okay," he said quickly and forced himself to smile, but Raye's face didn't change and he could tell that she took his smile for what it was. She could read him now almost as well as Eva.

"What about us, Hutch?" Raye asked the question in such a quiet shy voice, he barely heard her. He had been dreading that question because he knew what she wanted to hear and he couldn't say it. The truth was all he could give her, and he told her that as gently as he could.

"I'm still in love with Eva."

"Don't you think it's a lost cause if things haven't changed?"

"I don't know."

"Is she still with that musician?"

Hutch dropped his head, suddenly ashamed and not sure why. "It doesn't matter anymore."

"You're lying to yourself, and you know it."

"Maybe I am," Hutch said, sulking. Raye shook her head at him as if he were a little boy who had disappointed her. She poured another glass of champagne for both of them. The mood in the room had changed, and Hutch didn't know what he could do about it, if anything.

"You didn't answer my question about us," Raye said.

"You didn't leave Donald for me, you left him for you. You're clear about that, aren't you?"

"If I wasn't before, I sure am now," Raye said with an edge to her voice. But then her eyes softened and she reached for his lips the way she had the first time she had kissed him, and he put down his wineglass, pulling her close to him, kissing her lips where they turned up into her smile, and then her chin and throat, quickly slipping off her jacket. He could feel her shifting her body into his, and he held her close for a moment, feeling her heart beating against his chest, and not sure if they would end things this time as they had before. But Raye decided for him, sitting up and pulling away.

"Our last time is going to stay our last time," she said. "I know I could love you, Hutch, and in so many ways I already do, but I'm not ready to share another man with other women."

Hutch sat up now too, and finished the last of his champagne. "I'm sorry. You deserve more than that and we both know it."

They sat again, silent and still, neither of them sure what else to say.

"I'm thinking about going away," Raye said after a while. "I've always loved Paris, and I'm thinking about going to live there for a while. Learn French. Get to know the city. Have you ever been there?"

"No."

"It sounds like such a cliché, but it really is the most amazing city in the world. Everywhere you look there is something beautiful to see, hear or eat." Hutch smiled at her enthusiasm and the way her eyes lit up again. "Why don't you come with me?" There was longing in her eyes that she tried to conceal, and he looked away. "Just for a week or two. When was the last time you had a vacation? Money won't be a problem. I've got more than enough for both of us, and we could—"

"No, Raye."

"You can't leave for a couple of days? You need to get away, Hutch, maybe then—"

He kissed her to stop her from saying anything else. "I can't go anywhere but here," he said as gently as he could. He saw the flash of sorrow in her eyes, and then she closed them, willing it away, and when she opened them again it was gone. She stood up and slipped her coat back on, and spoke to him without looking at him. "Then I'll see you when I see you, I guess."

He stood up now too, grabbed her hand and pulled her around to make her face him, not wanting things to end the way they seemed to be ending.

"Raye, I don't want you to leave like this," he said, even though he wasn't sure if there was any other way to end it. She smiled the familiar smile and then hugged him the way they'd embraced in the old days, not fully touching his body with hers, with hesitation and distance.

"I'll be here whenever you need me," he whispered into her ear.

"I know you will," Raye said with a sad little smile and left his apartment for good.

# Eva and Isaiah

**E**va had always loved April. The April sun timidly breaking through the chill of March always promised that summer was on its way. April marked new beginnings for her, hinted at new chances and new expectations. She always made her yearly resolutions in April rather than on New Year's Eve. There weren't many resolutions this year—just the promise to herself that she would continue to work and hone her skills as an artist. And on the first day of her favorite month, she was exactly where she wanted to be—sitting in her studio on top of a red flannel comforter with a large sketchpad on her lap.

Although Eva had set up her easel, she still enjoyed sketching, not sure yet when and if the things she drew would grow into anything else—or if they were meant to. But this studio, built so long ago for her by Hutch, had become her temple, an almost holy place for her to draw and think. Sunlight poured in through the sky-lights and bounced off the stark white walls, and the fragrant smell of the incense she occasionally burned lingered in the air. When she came into her studio, she entered a world that belonged only to her, in which she could regain her balance and recapture some lost, essential part of herself.

Although she didn't like to get up in the morning, Eva worked best then, so during the week she made herself get up two hours before she was due at the library. She'd sip her morning coffee in her studio and sketch studies for larger pieces. Sometimes she would simply sit under the skylight and take in the sky, thinking of things she would like to work on. She'd also begun to paint again, tentatively at first, working mostly in watercolor and occasionally in pastels. One morning she woke up with Aunt Delia's old house on her mind and she'd taken her dream image of it—the mystical quality that it had—and tried to recapture its mystery in her drawings.

There was something magical about the way her ideas came to her—in her dreams or from random thoughts or inspired by some color or shape she'd noticed. Walking in the park one afternoon after work, she'd been so enchanted by a branch that had fallen across her path—the way the shadow and sunlight played on its branches, the almost lyrical placement of its twigs—that she'd stooped and studied it for nearly fifteen minutes. She'd tried to draw it in her studio the next morning. Another time, she worked on one of the sketches she had made of her dead son. She would let her mind run loose when she drew him, and she imagined now how he would have looked ten years from today, as a teen-ager, and she let herself weep for a moment with grief. His face was different each time she drew him, reflecting in small, odd ways the features of all the men she loved.

Except for weekends, she worked nearly every morning, even on holidays. On the days that she was lucky enough to get off, she worked all day, from morning until late at night. This first day of April was such a day. Helena had attended a conference the week before, and Eva had covered for her, working overtime most of the week. She had some sick days coming so she'd taken off through the rest of the week. It felt like playing hooky.

She'd brought the portable phone upstairs from her bedroom, and when it rang she picked it up on the first ring.

"Ma? What are you doing home? I was going to leave you a message." Charley had replaced "Mother" with "Ma" in the last few months.

"I had some sick days coming. What's up?"

"Precious called last night and wanted to know if you could help her address the invitations over the weekend. She got a place last week, did she tell you?"

"No. Where are they going to have it?"

"They're getting married in her church, but Precious asked the owner of this old club she used to sing in if they could have the reception there, and he said she could. What do you think?" Charley sounded a little doubtful.

"It's not our decision," Eva said quickly. "If you see her, tell her I'll be by on Saturday morning. Okay?"

"Sure."

Things between her and Charley had gotten easier.

They had worked together with Precious when she brought Roscoe home and took turns helping her care for him. They coordinated their evening schedules so that they could stay with him and ease the burden on Precious. And it had paid off. Although Roscoe still wasn't able to walk without a walker, his mind was as sharp as ever. Except for an occasional glass of wine, he'd cut out liquor and cigars and was taking his medicine faithfully. Since he and Precious had settled on a June date for the wedding, Charley and Eva spoke to Precious at least once a week about her plans.

"Talk to you later?"

"Okay, Ma. I love you."

"I love you too." Haunted by the memory of nearly losing her grandfather, Charley told her she loved her whenever they parted company, and Eva was always happy to hear it. She wasn't sure how long this somewhat saccharine peace between them would last, but things had changed forever. Charley had even become charitable about her relationship with Isaiah. She had run into him once at the house when she'd dropped something off for Precious, and had been polite if not particularly friendly, which was the most Eva could ask for.

Eva placed the phone back down on the floor and picked up her sketchpad. She went through her sketches again and then glanced at her easel, deciding to go back to Aunt Delia's house. She picked up her brush and let her mind flow free, back to the days when she was a girl. The images of the old place surprised and overwhelmed her. It still amazed her how many things remained with her: Aunt Delia's voice, Grandma Alvia's hands; their coded talk of spells and hexes; the Spanish moss that hung like lace from the trees. Her brush captured the memories that floated through her mind. As she worked, her thoughts drifted from the past to the present and back again to the past. She thought about Hutch.

She had seen him three weeks ago, around the first week of March, shortly after they had brought her father home. Roscoe was still in a wheelchair then, and she and Precious—fast friends now—were rearranging the house to meet his new needs. She was in the kitchen making gumbo when Hutch knocked at the door. She'd put on a cup of tea, sat down at the table and they'd talked for a while, the conversation relaxed and easy. They stayed with comfortable topics at first: Steven and Dana, her father's prognosis, the workplace. He'd been pleased when she told him that she was drawing again and that the studio was getting some use. Neither of them mentioned the skylight. He told her about his reconciliation with Steven and asked about her relationship with Charley, and had been happy when she told him about their meeting in the hospital chapel. They chuckled about Charley's sudden epiphany and sipped their tea quietly, both lost in their own thoughts until Eva mentioned that Charley had told her what Hutch had shared New Year's Day. She thanked him for being so candid, and he told her he hadn't had a choice, and that conversation seemed to lead naturally to her question about Raye.

"Donald settled out of court with her," Hutch explained.

"Are you and Raye still together?" Eva was surprised how difficult it was to ask and how glad she was to hear his reply.

"She's living in France for a while. She left in the middle of February. I'm not sure when she's coming back."

"Paris! Well, I guess Raye must have gotten everything that she wanted. Lucky girl!"

"Almost everything," Hutch said sadly and left it at that. "Well, let me be on my way," he'd said as he picked up his coat. "Tell Roscoe I stopped by and to save me some of that gumbo you're making." They both laughed as he stepped out the door, but before he closed it he asked, "So, is Isaiah Lonesome still living in the house?" His blunt question caught her off guard.

"Yes," she'd said, because he was, and Hutch had made a hasty retreat before she'd been able to qualify her answer or add anything else.

And that was the truth. Isaiah Lonesome was still living at the house, but if Hutch had asked the question she had asked about him and Raye, she wasn't sure what she would have said. Isaiah still paid rent, lived in the guest room and had "kitchen privileges," such as they were, but both their lives were more complicated now, and in the last few months things had changed. He came home much later than he had in the beginning and she was up and out earlier—either to her studio or to work. Oddly enough, their friendship had developed into the kind of tenant-landlord relationship Eva had envisioned in the first place. Since they had never really discussed or defined *what* their relationship was, now that it was fading it was difficult to say what it wasn't. They had made love several times in the last few months but not with the frequency or passion they had had in the beginning.

On Valentine's Day he'd bought her a bottle of good

champagne (good for Isaiah, anyway) and a dozen red roses, and after the trauma of Roscoe's stroke and her time with him in the hospital, Isaiah's gifts and the comfort of his body were two pleasures she hadn't turned down. But in recent months his reputation as a musician had begun to grow and increasingly he accepted gigs in other cities. In mid-February, he'd played at clubs in Oakland and Boston, and there was talk of touring Europe in June. Sky Langston's quintet had quietly become his, and the new owners of the club had begun to feature him weekly. Isaiah Lonesome was coming into his own and building a name for himself. He'd proudly shown Eva a piece in the *Village Voice* in which the critic heralded him as a major new talent. He'd done recordings with several well-known musicians and been singled out in reviews in *Downbeat* and the *New York Times*. There was even talk of a recording contract.

Sometimes they would talk in the kitchen on Sundays before she headed up to her studio or he headed to the city to work. But Eva knew no more about the inner soul of him than she had when she'd met him. He showed her only what he wanted her to see, and his beautiful eyes revealed nothing. She had never met a man who could give so much physically and so little of his soul, and she knew that if she were with him for twenty years she could know no more of him than what she knew today. The sex was still good but that was all there was and probably would ever be.

She thought about Isaiah as she worked and of how much they had both changed since that hot Fourth of July. She wasn't the same woman, and maybe she had him to thank for it. Perhaps she had changed him as well. It was impossible to know how your presence in somebody's life would alter his or her view of reality. How many times had she read stories about lives being changed by mysterious strangers? Sometimes people called them angels. She laughed out loud when she thought about Isaiah Lonesome as somebody's angel. But maybe she'd been that in his life. At the very least, she'd given him a place to stay.

She heard the kitchen door slam downstairs as he came into the house. "Hey, Bama Cat, what's going on? Be that way, then, I don't care!" he muttered, chastising the cat for her usual snub. Soon he began to play his trumpet, gliding through scales and riffs as effortlessly as when she'd first heard him, yet his playing was stronger, more confident and mature. It still had the power to thrill her. He stopped playing, and Eva assumed that he'd probably opened the refrigerator for his usual glass of milk or can of Sprite. He began to play again, something sensual and lilting, which Eva hadn't heard before. Paintbrush in hand, she listened for a while and then, inspired by the music, began to work again, almost to his rhythm. After about twenty minutes, he stopped and she heard him coming upstairs, whistling the song he'd been playing. He paused at the landing to the third floor.

"Hey, Eva. You up there?"

"Yeah. Took the day off."

"Can I come up?"

"Sure."

He was wearing loose-fitting cargo pants and an expensive, new sweater. Midnight blue. He hadn't put on weight, but his body looked more muscular. Whenever she saw him nude these days, she wanted to sculpt him. He was making more money and his clothes were beginning to show it. In January, he'd offered to pay more rent than their original agreement, and after hesitating, she'd taken it. He came over to her easel and glanced over her shoulder.

"Hey, that's nice."

"Thanks."

"You're into more abstract stuff these days, huh?"

"Abstract to you anyway," she said, and he grinned.

"That's like my music."

"Thanks."

"You're really good, you know that now, right? When I see some of the stuff you do, especially the stuff of the kid, it really touches me, you know what I mean?"

Eva hadn't told Isaiah who the "kid" was and how drawing him had liberated her, but it was good to know that she had gotten her feelings through. "You know, you're kind of an inspiration yourself, Isaiah." She was teasing him, but not altogether. Suddenly bashful, Isaiah glanced away, and Eva smiled, amused that she had the power to make him blush.

"Can we talk for a while?" he asked.

"Sure."

He took off his shoes and stretched out full length on the comforter underneath the skylight. "I need to run something by you."

Eva studied his solemn look. "Looks serious. I'm worried. You're never serious." She put her brush down and stretched out beside him, and they both gazed up at the sun. "So you didn't use it today."

He looked puzzled. "Use what?"

"That expensive soap you've been showering with. You didn't think I noticed, did you?"

He averted his eyes and then glanced back at her with a guilty look. "You don't miss a trick do you, Mrs. Hutchinson?"

"Not anymore," Eva said with a slight smile. Isaiah wasn't Hutch and this didn't feel like betrayal, not the way the other had, but it still made her sad, disappointed. Disappointment mixed with a dose of reality. They stared at the sun shining through the skylight and not at each other.

"Time for you to move out?"

"Yeah."

Eva turned to face him, studying his profile. He still had the prettiest eyes she had ever seen, even from this angle. "When were you thinking about going?"

He shielded his face from the sun as if it had gotten brighter. "I feel like we're on the beach, stretched out like this, the sun pouring in on us."

"When, Isaiah?"

"I was thinking about next week. I want to pay you for April, and even May until you find somebody else to move in. I *want* to give it to you. I can afford it now."

"It was never really about the money, Isaiah. Maybe at first, but not later."

"I know."

Eva took a deep breath. "How long has this been going on?" she asked.

Isaiah, still avoiding her eyes, sat up and rested his hands on his knees. "You ever hear Sarah sing that? You know she grew up in Newark. I have her singing it uptempo on one CD and then real slow and bluesy on another. Real sophisticated, you know, real adult.

Da, da, da da da. How long has this been going on?"
He started to sing, and Eva, tossing him a dirty look,
started to stand up, but he grabbed her arm, just tight
enough to keep her from leaving, and she sat back
down beside him. "It kind of just happened," he said.
"Remember I told you about the club being bought and
everything, and about Sky letting me take over for him
on some days. Remember I told you about that?"

"So you're sleeping with the new club owner." Eva
studied his face skeptically.

"Well, it's a little more complicated than that, Eva.
We had a thing once before, me and this chick, before
you and me got into our thing, and she bought the club.
She co-owns it anyway with Sky, and she's always like
really been into my music and shit, you know, a real
fan, and—"

"Penny Pedersen!"

Isaiah looked at her in surprise. "How did you know
it was her?"

"I don't miss a trick."

He lay back down and put his hands over his eyes as
if he were shielding his face, and Eva stretched out
next to him, then leaned toward him, took his hands
away, making him look at her.

"Isaiah, listen to me. You're making a mistake.
Yeah, I agree, it's time you moved out of here, but I'm
older than you, and I know what I'm talking about.
Penny Pedersen just sees you as some exotic creature
she can screw for a couple of months and then move on
to something else."

Isaiah smiled his enchanting smile and shook his
face from her hands. "Well, isn't that the way you saw
me?" he asked. Startled by his words, Eva shifted away

from him, but Isaiah reached for her, pulled her closer and nibbled the edge of her ear. "What's wrong with exotic, Eva? Don't you like exotic? I'll take exotic."

Eva, still mad, sat up. "Do you really think that's what our relationship was about?"

Isaiah sat up now too, suddenly as serious as she was. "I don't know what our relationship was about. But I came out of it better than when I went into it, and that says something."

Eva smiled in spite of herself. "So did I," she said. "You have a lot of things going for you, Isaiah. Maybe it's time you hooked up with some nice, smart girl your own age in a relationship that will go somewhere and—"

Isaiah interrupted her. "Hey, I tried a nice, smart girl my own age. Remember Charley? You probably had it right, Eva, that first time you met me, and you told me in so many words that you didn't think I was 'appropriate' for your daughter. You were coming from some weird-ass-mama protector thing, but I wasn't what Charley needed. I'm not what *any* woman needs who wants something permanent and long-standing.

"I know who Penny is and the main thing she's interested in and maybe that's okay for a while. Because the only thing I really care about is my music, anyway, and Penny Pedersen can help me get where I want to go, and that's all that counts to me at this point in my life." Eva was shocked by his words even though she didn't show it.

He gave her a prim kiss on her cheek. "You always want me to be more than I am, Eva. Somebody with some deep feeling part to me that I don't want to reveal or some weird sensitive thing going on inside me that

I've never been able to talk about, but I am who I am. What you see is what you get. I play music, Eva. It is the only thing in my life I've ever been able to depend upon, so it is the only thing that counts. The only thing. Not women, not love, not money." He grinned. "Well, maybe money. But music is the main thing, and when you're a musician you sometimes have to step outside the ordinary things that ordinary people attach themselves to. Sometimes you have to live different. That's how it seems to me at this point in my life, anyway."

"And you think Penny Pedersen understands that about you?"

"At least I know she's into my music, and we can both get what we want from each other without anybody getting hurt in the process. I can handle her, and she can probably handle me."

"Sounds like a mutual use to me," Eva said, not disguising the disgust in her voice.

He stretched down beside her, his hands now at his side. "Isn't that what it's all about between two people at the end of the day anyway?"

Eva studied Isaiah for a long time, and finally, giving him the benefit of the doubt, she smiled at him. "I know you don't really believe that," she said.

He studied her face for a moment, kissed the dimple that Hutch liked to kiss, then traced with his lips from the edge of her ears to a spot just under her chin that never failed to turn her on.

"Stay with me a minute," he said.

"You know it always takes us more than a minute," Eva said. She was completely aroused now, and tried to stand up again, but Isaiah grabbed her hand and gently pulled her down on top of him. "One more time?"

he asked playfully as if he were begging. Eva, a half-smile settled on her lips, let him kiss that spot on her throat again and the other parts of her body that he always liked to touch.

They didn't have the urgency this time that they'd had before, the almost savage need to be part of each other. There was a lingering tenderness about the way they touched each other, every caress and kiss slow and deliberate. Yet Eva enjoyed touching him as much as she always did. She loved the way the hair on his chest and legs felt against her fingertips, the taste of his skin as she ran her tongue and lips up over his shoulders and neck. In the time they had been together they had developed a comfortable ease with each other and a sense of play and how to please each other. But every touch now was bittersweet.

When he had kissed her for the last time, Eva slowly became aware again of her surroundings. This was the first time that they had not made love in the guest room, which now would forever be charged with sexual undertones and nuances. She'd never be able to enter that room again without thinking of him. But this room was different. Hutch had built it for her, and she was swept with guilt for a moment, for making love to another man within a space that had been his. But perhaps making love to Isaiah here had made this room completely hers; maybe she had claimed this room for her own in a way that she never had before. A new place for new truths.

The softness of the down comforter cushioned her body, and the April sun warmed her. Opening his eyes, Isaiah ran the tip of his tongue within and around the spot on her neck and down between her breasts and around her nipples and then the length of her spine, and they made love again.

"I wrote a song for you," he said when they had finished. "I was playing it earlier, when I came in."

"What's it called?"

" 'Dimple.' "

" 'Dimple'?"

Isaiah, sitting up now, pulled on his briefs. "I was going to call it 'Eva,' but then I figured if you ever got back with your old man, and I put it on an album and it got famous and everything, he'd get pissed off every time he heard it. I don't want to create any hard feelings between you and him or anything. But I love your dimple, so I decided to name it after that, so you'll know I wrote it for you."

*So will Hutch,* Eva said to herself. "Well, that was thoughtful of you," she said and kissed him.

"Want to hear it?"

"Please."

"Let me get my horn." He went downstairs to get it and when he came back up, Eva sat in the sun and listened one last time as Isaiah played her song.

# Eva and Hutch

## SATURDAY, JUNE 13

The fact that it was the thirteenth of June, the anniversary of the day Hutch walked out, didn't strike Eva until she was halfway to the church, and then she told herself it didn't really matter one way or the other. This bright warm June day was a perfect day for a wedding, and it belonged to Roscoe and Precious. She wasn't about to let stray thoughts about the demise of her own marriage darken it. She got to the church early and took a seat between Charley and one of Precious's stepchildren. Precious was decked out in a navy silk suit trimmed with rhinestone buttons that matched her earrings. Her red hair, free for once of the usual turban, was swept into an elaborate French roll secured with rhinestone hairpins. Roscoe was as elegant as ever in a dark business suit and conservative silk tie. His only concession to the occasion—and to Precious, Eva assumed—was a pair of rhinestone cuff links that glittered from his sleeves.

The ceremony was short and sweet. Reverend Goodson, Precious's elderly minister who looked as if he'd be more comfortable conducting a funeral than a wedding, started things off with a prayer. That was followed by short declarations from Precious and Roscoe that they would honor and respect each other for as long as they were together. Roscoe read a favorite poem by Paul Laurence Dunbar and Precious sang a cappella a song she had written for the occasion. The minister pronounced them husband and wife, and that was that.

On her way out, Eva overheard several older church members complaining about the ceremony's brevity, but most of the guests were as pleased for Roscoe and Precious as the couple were for themselves. Eva couldn't remember when she had seen her father so happy. Although he still had to use a walker and leaned on Precious whenever he could, he had mostly recovered. His short-term memory would occasionally fail him, but he remembered the things he wanted to. She knew he would always remember every detail of this day.

Precious stood on the church stairs and tossed her bouquet, a bunch of miniature yellow roses, which was snatched from the air before it hit the ground by one of Roscoe's old girlfriends. Shortly after that, everyone piled into cars and made their way to the hall that Precious had rented for the lunch and reception.

Eva drove to the hall, which wasn't far away, and heard the band playing even before she got out of her car. It was music she'd grown up with, the kind Roscoe played on the old hi-fi when she'd been a girl and they'd moved up North. It was how he went back to his roots, this music, played loud with its throbbing bass, screaming brass horns and stride piano thumping out a rhythm that screamed good times. Eva bopped her head like a teenager as she walked into the hall, which in the late fifties had been a club called the Haywire. Precious had sung there during its heyday, and the owner had given her a good price for the afternoon.

The place was slightly run-down and had a musty smell, but the tiny sparkling lights strung around the room and the sun pouring in through the windows made the room seem bright and festive. The band, which was called the Glowing Embers, consisted of fifteen musicians she had known in the old days all around the same age as Precious. According to her, they had made a name for themselves during the late fifties and the sixties, and several of them had once played with James Brown and the Famous Flames. Eva half-expected them to show up in gold lamé vests and hair processed into pompadours, and she was relieved to find them in tuxedos.

There were about twenty oblong tables placed in various spots around the dance floor. A vase of miniature roses, champagne glasses, and a plastic ice bucket filled with a bottle of champagne sat on each table. Many of the guests had apparently skipped the ceremony and come straight to the party. There was no formal arrangement; people sat pretty much where they wanted to. At one end of the room was a long table weighed down by a three-tiered wedding cake and platters filled with turkey, ham, roast beef and fried chicken, along with huge bowls of potato salad, cole slaw and tossed green salad. At the other end was a bar, which was where Eva headed because the line was shorter.

As she stood in line, she searched for people she knew and spotted old family friends and several of Precious's stepchildren. One of them whispered to the others and they all turned and waved. Eva grinned and waved back. It would take her a while to get used to this new extended family after so long with just Roscoe, Steven, and Charley. Thinking of her daughter, she searched for her in the crowd and saw her coming in with Steven, Dana and—much to Eva's surprise—Bradley, her ex-fiancé. Spotting Eva at the same time, Charley came over to greet her.

"Don't get your hopes up, Ma," she warned as she approached. "We're still friends, and I don't know what will happen besides that, so don't be making wedding plans." For a moment Eva could see shades of the old Charley, which made her smile.

"Just tell him I said hello." If there was one thing she'd learned in the past year, it was that people's lives were their own to lead.

She thought about Isaiah, and a wistful smile settled for a moment on her lips. She'd been surprised by how often he had called her, at least three times this month. He'd invited her to the club to hear him play, but she hadn't gone. Isaiah Lonesome could easily become a habit it would be hard to break. It was time to gracefully let him go.

"Is Daddy here yet?" Charley freely talked about Hutch with Eva these days, but her voice was still anxious.

"I haven't seen him. Are you sure he's coming?"

"They invited him. I sent out the invitation myself." Charley glanced around the room and sighed. "He didn't come to the ceremony, and Granddad invited him to that too."

It was hard to say what Hutch would do or how he was feeling. She hadn't spoken to him since she'd seen him at her father's house in March. She wondered if he even remembered the significance of June 13. Things between them were still unsettled. She had a vague sense that sooner or later they would have to make a final decision about their relationship, but she had no idea what that decision would be, when it would be made or who would make it. Without complaint, Hutch continued to pay the mortgage and many of the other bills, but he had his own apartment and needs and Eva knew it wasn't fair to expect him to continue taking care of a house he wasn't living in. They would soon have to decide what came next.

But Eva still loved Hutch, and although she couldn't yet bring herself to call him and find out what was happening in his life, she was still hungry for information about him, and she was able to glean bits of information from casual conversations with Charley and Steven. In April, Charley mentioned that Hutch had taken a week's vacation, and Eva's spirits dipped until she found out from Steven that he'd gone fishing in the Bahamas and not to Paris to visit Raye. Steven alluded to a big project that would force him to relocate for the summer, and her breath caught in her throat until Charley added that at her urging Hutch had turned it down. The last week in May, Eleanor Hammersmith said she had seen him house shopping with a pretty young woman, and Eva was depressed until Precious mentioned that as a favor to her Hutch had checked out an old house that her daughter-in-law was thinking about buying.

"Where are you sitting?" Charley asked, taking Eva from her thoughts. Eva pointed to a table on the other side of the room. "You going to sit by yourself?" Charley looked concerned.

"Yeah, for a while," Eva said, and gave her a smile to reassure her. "I feel like being alone for a while. I'll come over after I get some food."

"I'll save you a place," Charley said and gave her a kiss.

Eva asked for a glass of Merlot, and sat down at her table. She had gotten to the point in her life when she enjoyed her own company, and the spot she'd chosen did afford a good view of the room. She spotted Roscoe talking with guests, grinning like the newlywed he was. She saw Precious flitting from table to table, chatting, hugging and kissing anybody who came into her path. She watched as Precious swooped down on Charley and Bradley, hugged them and then whispered something that made them both blush. Throwing back her head, she laughed uproariously, and Eva could almost hear her laughter even though she was on the other side of the room. She gazed at Charley and Bradley, who seemed to be engrossed in conversation, their heads bent together, their bodies touching. After a while they were joined by Steven and Dana, whose plates were piled high with food, and the four of them pulled their chairs together. Eva glanced again and found Roscoe. He was alone now, his lips curved in a contented smile as he searched for Precious. As if directed by some force, her eyes were drawn to the door just as Hutch walked in.

She was always struck by how handsome he was. He was dressed in one of his good suits, charcoal gray, double-breasted. He had always been a man who wore a suit well. Eva knew he was far more comfortable in casual clothes or even his work clothes than he was in a suit, but you couldn't tell that by looking at him. He was instinctively a good dresser, which was one thing he shared with her peacock of a father. He waved at Roscoe, who had obviously forgiven him and gave him a generous wave back. His gaze rested for a moment on Charley and Steven, and suddenly he looked up at her and a grin broke out on his face. He made his way across the room toward her, just as Precious grabbed her arm.

"I've been looking all over for you, Eva. What are you doing all the way over here by yourself?" Precious was wearing too much perfume as usual, and the fragrance preceded her squeeze by a second or two. "Honey, I've got somebody you have to meet." Precious gave her a knowing wink as she slid into the empty seat beside her. Along with their budding friendship had come Precious's concern about the state of Eva's love life. According to Roscoe, Precious had pledged to find a "suitable match" for Eva as soon as she could fully set her mind to it. Nobody took her seriously, but Eva knew that sooner or later she'd have to tell her father's wife, as Roscoe suggested with an amused smile, "to mind her own goddamn business." The look in Precious's eyes when she grabbed her arm made Eva realize their talk would be sooner rather than later.

"Precious, I don't think—" Eva started to protest, but Precious interrupted her.

"I know what you're going to say, but you're here, he's here and . . ." Precious turned to a man who had suddenly appeared at her side. "Eva, I'd like you to meet my stepson, Derrick Halsey."

"Ma'am." Derrick Halsey tipped his head like somebody in a second-rate western and leaned forward. Eva caught a strong whiff of bourbon and Obsession cologne.

"Nice to meet you," Eva said and was about to make her excuses when Precious popped from the chair in which she'd been sitting and Derrick slid into it as quickly as if it had been choreographed. Eva smiled politely because she couldn't think of anything else to do.

"My mama tells me we're in the same club," he said. "Recently separated from long-term spouse," he added when he noticed that she was puzzled. Eva gave an involuntary groan. "That sound coming out your mouth tells me you feel about your ex like I do." Eva looked straight ahead. "So why did you leave yours?" She didn't say anything. "Sorry, I got to get my social skills together. I didn't mean to pry." He was clearly embarrassed so Eva gave him a hesitant smile, deciding to give him the benefit of the doubt. Derrick grabbed her wineglass off the table. "Can I get you some more of whatever you're drinking?"

"No, that's okay, Derrick, I—"

He studied the glass for a moment, and then grinned as if he'd solved a puzzle. "Got one of those wine-coolers, don't you?" He gave her a condescending smile. "I'm a Dewar's man myself. Lightest thing I drink is Michelob, but my son says—that's him over there with them sunglasses on—these wine-cooler things come with a kick. What kind you drinking?"

"Red wine, but that's okay, I—"

"Then red it is," he said with a grin as he headed toward the bar.

Feeling helpless, Eva tried to think of kind but firm words to discourage him when he returned.

Then Hutch dropped into Derrick's empty seat. "So how are things going?"

Eva smiled. "Okay, how about you?"

"Okay. Are you having a good time?"

"My father and Precious are."

"Well, they should be. It's their wedding." It was clear he was just trying to make conversation, but Eva didn't care. She also knew she was grinning like a fool; she didn't care about that either. Suddenly the band broke into a thumping rendition of "Papa's Got a Brand New Bag."

"James Brown!" Hutch said in amazement. "Come on, Eva. We got to dance to that!" Before Eva could object, they were on the floor, shimmying and shaking with everybody else who had downed their drinks and shoved their plates aside.

Inspired by the dancing throng, the Glowing-Embers-turned-Famous-Flames quickly swung into "Make It Funky" without missing a beat. Next came "The Big Payback," "Think," "Sex Machine" and "Hot Pants" in quick succession. Throwing her head back and laughing like a girl, Eva couldn't remember the last time she'd danced so hard. She spotted Charley swinging her hips wildly and Bradley self-consciously doing a determined two-step to the beat. Steven and

Dana spun around, both laughing, and even Roscoe, supported by Precious, moved around the floor with grace and surprising agility. When the band slowed down into "Try Me" and "Please, Please, Please," Eva collapsed into Hutch's arms, exhausted. It had been a long time since she had been in his arms, and she stiffened for a moment, not sure if she wanted to be this close.

"It's just a dance, Eva," Hutch whispered as if reading her thoughts, and she let her body ease into his.

He had always been a good dancer, a man who knew how to lead without making a point of it, and Eva had always enjoyed dancing with him. She let herself enjoy it now, drifting to the strains of the old James Brown band and into the memories of her teenage years, when it hadn't been so much James Brown as the Delfonics, the Whispers and Harold Melvin and the Blue Notes. Still holding her hand, Hutch walked her back to the table. Derrick, holding her drink, gave him a territorial once-over.

"Derrick this is Hutch, my . . . my h-husband," Eva said, stammering out the last word of the sentence.

"Lucas Hutchinson." Hutch thrust out his hand.

"Derrick Halsey. Precious's stepson." Derrick took and shook it. His eyes left Eva as he surveyed the room, obviously looking for somewhere else to go. Eva picked up the drink he'd brought her, noticing that he'd gotten her a strawberry wine-cooler.

"Thank you so much, Derrick."

"I don't know where Mama got these bartenders. None of them had ever heard of a red-wine cooler. You get what you pay for, I guess. You all go on and enjoy yourselves, now," he said over his shoulder as he turned to leave. Eva sat down and Hutch sat beside her. He took the wine-cooler and poured it in the vase of roses, then uncorked the champagne and poured them each a glass.

"It's a powerful word, isn't it?" he said.

"What word is that?"

"Husband. The mere mention of it sends brothers bearing wine-coolers scurrying to the opposite side of the room."

"I guess that makes it good for something," Eva replied, and Hutch threw her a sideways glance, his eyes hurt.

"What will it take to make you forgive me?" he asked after a while. Eva studied his face as if trying to decide if he was serious but still didn't say anything. Hutch gulped his champagne. "Tell me, Eva. I can't stand not knowing anymore. What do I have to do?"

"Did you ever find that *joy* you were looking for?" Eva asked, a teasing note in her voice.

Hutch sighed, finished off his champagne in another gulp and said in a weary voice, "You know what they say about the journey itself being its destination? Truth of it is, Eva, I didn't know what joy was until I didn't have it anymore."

Eva didn't bother to hide the smile that crept across her lips. "Joy does tend to be in the eye of the beholder," she said. Neither of them spoke for a while.

"Just tell me what you want me to do." Hutch finally said. "Do you want me to get down on my knees and beg you? Is that what you want?" Eva regarded him with amusement. "Okay, I'll do it!" Hutch popped out of his chair, dropped down on one knee in front of her, and grabbed her hand. "Please. Please. Please. Please," he said, singing out the words of the old James Brown song that the Glowing Embers had played a few moments ago. A little girl with pink ribbons in her hair who had been watching them from the next table covered her mouth with her hand and began to giggle.

Eva bent toward him. "Get off your knees," she whispered glancing around the room.

"I don't care anymore! I have nothing to lose. Do you want me to prostrate myself on the floor in front of you? Is that what you want?"

"Hutch, get off your knees," Eva said again, and he stood up, dusted off his pants and dropped back down beside her. The band slipped into a moody rendition of "We've Only Just Begun."

"It's a year today," he said.

"I know."

"You know that I still love you, don't you?"

"I still love you, too." Eva said after a few moments. She was surprised how easily the words had come, as if they had been on the edge of her lips ready to tumble out before she could even think about saying them. "Why did you leave me like you did?" Her voice was frank, and her eyes stared straight into his.

"Looking for something, I guess."

"Do you know how much you hurt me?"

Hutch shifted his eyes from hers and stared at the band. Eva saw that his eyes were watering. "Yeah. I know. You've hurt me, too. The question is, can we both finally get over this?" he asked without looking at her.

"I think we already have," Eva said. He stole a glance at her now, and his eyes were as loving as she'd ever seen them.

"Will you dance with me?" he asked, and Eva stood up and let him take her in his arms, and when he held her this time she let her body ease into his, giving him permission to hold her close.

"Can I come home now?" he asked just as the song was ending.

"I'll have to think about it," Eva said and smiled.

She knew the answer to his question the moment she heard it. But Eva also knew how easy it was for a man, even a sweet one like Hutch, to take a good woman for granted, so she figured she'd let him wait a while before she told him. But not too long, she decided. Not too long at all.

So sunshine did *follow darkness as mushrooms do rain when Eva and Hutch lived the lessons they learned. They cherished their strengths, honored each other and shared those feelings that seem easier to forget. It did strike Eva as strange, though, how all the good things that followed seemed to happen on "six."*

*Six days after the wedding, Hutch came home to stay, and Charley married Bradley six months after that. Six years later Eva and Hutch held their first grandson, and six weeks past that renewed their first vows.*

*Steven stayed with Dana. Raye stayed in Paris. Donald stayed away. Isaiah stayed in touch. Roscoe and Precious danced until the end of their days.*

*And somewhere in heaven Aunt Delia smiled.*